A Quest of Kings

BOOK TWO

of

WHILL OF AGORA

Michael James Ploof

Agora
Volnoss
Hornhollow
Sidnell
The Twin Lakes
Orenden
Shierdon
Fendale
Fennamoore
Brindon
Bearadon
Belldon
Eldalon
The Old Road
Cavanar
Ky'Dren Mountains
Brenahime
Brinn
Breggard
Opalmist
Ky'Dren Pass
Orington
Devandes
Kell Torey
Dy'kore
Ry'Del
Tren
Sherna
Thendor
Fendora Island
Do'Adore
Senteal
Turell
Plains
Burning Mountain
Eldon Island
Hentaro
Locknar
Heldon
Harrow's
Horton
Ebony Mountains
Orensteel
Nordon Sea
Uthen-Arden
Orindale
Gulf of Arden
Cerushia
Drakkar
Isladon
Del'Oradon
Shoreshell
Del'Harred
Elladrindellia
Indello
Pearlton

OTHER BOOKS
by Michael James Ploof

LEGENDS OF AGORA SERIES

Whill of Agora

THE SOCK GNOME CHRONICLES

Billy Coatbutton and the Wheel of Destiny
Billy Coatbutton and the Ring of Sockchild

For updates on upcoming release dates and book news, like Whill of Agora on Facebook

This book is dedicated to my wife, Melanie. You are the driving force in my life, and without you, I would not be half the man I have become. You have taught me the value of hard work, the importance of responsibility, and the meaning of true love. You have given me two impossibly amazing children and have made our house a home.

Thank you.

PROLOGUE

Dearest Sister Teera:

I hope that my letter finds you and finds you well. It has been nearly six long months since the reclamation of the Ro'Sar Mountains and the rise of King Roakore, and though his people now thrive, the world has become dark, and war is now upon us. From the Ro'Sar Mountains poured an army of nearly a hundred thousand Draggard, and they have spread death and destruction throughout the kingdoms. I pray that the dark plague which is Eadon's Draggard army has not yet reached you in Sidnell.

Whill remains lost to us—a fact that holds captive my heart and burdens my days with worry. I have failed him, and for this, I cannot forgive myself. Would that I could wield power like the Elves and cause my will to be that of the world. But I am merely a man, and as such, I am often powerless against the magic of the Elves, to my great frustration.

Rhunis remains at my side, and together, we search for any sign of Whill within Uthen-Arden. It is my belief that Eadon holds him captive within the castle of Whill's late father. I know not whether he still lives, but I must believe that he does. If Whill is dead then we are truly doomed; he and he alone can rid Agora of the evil of Eadon—this I believe with all of my heart. He is a good man, as good as I have ever known. With your help, he has become a man of great strength and virtue, and I thank you wholeheartedly for all you have done.

Eadon has successfully separated the kingdoms of men, Elves, and Dwarves. Like a wedge, he has divided us from one another in his acquisition of Uthen-Arden and Shierdon. Though I have tried to bring them together—man, Dwarf, and Elf—they remain too busy fighting off the hordes within their own lands to come together as a unified army. Even if they could, who would they strike? The human armies of Uthen-Arden and Shierdon are not truly in league with Eadon; they know not for whom they serve. They believe, as they have been told by their kings, that Whill is the master of the Draggard and Dark Elves do not exist. Eadon has even led them to believe that the Elves of Elladrindellia are the enemy.

Eadon wants nothing more than full continental war; it is his very design. It frustrates me to no end to see clearly his plans unfolding, whilst I am not able to gain the ear of our allies. It seems that the best weapon against men is a well-told lie; we are ever the unwitting victims of such fables.

Please send the girls my love. I hope to see you all again one day soon. Until that day, you remain ever in my thoughts.

Your loving brother, Abram

CHAPTER ONE

Roakore's Door and Zerafin's Blade

Roakore focused his will on the stone. He channeled the energy of the nearby Dwarves and mentally raised the stone slab from its perch at the foot of the mountain. It had already been readied and fixed with great hinges and locks. Once put into place, it would serve as the new door to the Ebony Mountains.

"That is gonna look amazing!" Tarren howled and stomped on the ground as the stone began to be laid into place. A startled Roakore jumped and, for the smallest of moments, let go of the great stone. His face grimaced under the pressure, and a few of his men passed out with the sudden energy sap. The slab was set upon its hinges with a boom. The cranks of the huge wooden pulleys were turned, and the five-foot-long and one-foot-wide bolts were moved into position; they hung from massive chains and were guided by Dwarven hands. Each of the six bolts slid through the greased hinges and made a soft boom.

Roakore bent and almost fell as he released the door and the great weight was lifted from his mind. "By Ky-Dren's bloody, dragon-killin' ax, boy, can ye not be screamin' when me and me boys 'r' up to such work?" he snapped.

The look upon Tarren's face made Roakore feel bad for his words, and he shook his head. "Bah, 'n' ye better be getting tough. Ye saw the raisin' o' the main gate. Now be getting on to yer trainin' with Lunara; ye got a two-hour walk before ye."

Tarren straightened at Lunara's name. "Now that is gonna be even more amazin' than the raisin' of the doors, it is." said Tarren, beaming.

Roakore had noticed a few months back that Tarren had begun to pick up Dwarvish during his stay with the Dwarves. He couldn't help but smile at the lad. Tarren had lived and worked and trained as a Dwarf for the last six months, at his own insistence. Abram had granted the request, as he would be busy with the finding of Whil.

Training with the Dwarf children was hard on the small lad; he was small even for a human. But, to his credit, he was quick on his feet and a fast learner. Lunara healed his daily wounds and breaks and instructed him in combat. He had begun to show much improvement in all aspects of his training, returning to his quarters each night with fewer wounds needing to be healed.

"I'll escort the lad Tarren to the lady, me king. If it suites ye, that is," Haldagozz stated as he put a big hand on the boy's shoulder.

Roakore scowled a bit at that. "End I be wonderin' which o' ye be more happy for it, eh, yerself or the boy?" Roakore asked with a raised eyebrow.

Haldagozz howled as if he were putting back a few pints at the tavern o' the gods. "Bwahaha! The boy, I'm thinkin'. If he didn't have the lady, he'd be dead by now, I'm bettin'."

"Ey', en' yerself too, no?" asked Roakore. Even as the words slipped his lips, he knew he had gone too far.

Haldagozz took a step toward his king and looked him in the beard. "Ey', it be true; en' I allowed the healin' at yer own word, me king," a hurt-looking Haldagozz attested. "If I got feelin's fer her, it ain't none but respect and gratitude. I'd be in the halls o' the gods by now if it weren't for yer words, me king. But they let me stay en' fight another day, a great gift from the lady Lunara, a great gift from the gods."

Roakore found the gaze of the Dwarf. "I know, I know, was kiddin' is all. Go on, get the lad gone, 'r he'll be late."

Haldagozz and Tarren started off, but Roakore called out to them. "A gift it was indeed, friend, that I should have such a Dwarf at me side."

Roakore watched them go; they were the first to pass through the great doors. Roakore laughed to himself.

Hah, a human boy and a Dwarf be the first to pass through Roakore's door. Fittin', I be thinkin', the boy Tarren has become like a son to me, though I got enough o' me own, en' Haldagozz is sure to be one o' me best soldiers. Bah, soldier, with his atti- tude en' new strength, he should be a personal guard. I'll make it so soon as I see Nah'Zed. I'm thinking the promotion'l get him away from Lunara a bit; that'll be a good thing. He can joke all he wants, but I see his heart. Ey', the Dwarf's in love, or I'm a bearded dragon egg.

Roakore sighed and let his thoughts focus on the door. It loomed before him one hundred feet high, forty feet across, and ten feet thick. Every inch of the multicolored door had been polished to a perfect shine. It did not blend into the mountain; rather, it stood boldly before all onlookers as a strong testament to the Dwarves within the mountain. It seemed to say, "Here we are. We hide from no one, and we dare you to approach this door with ill intent..."

Nah'Zed broke Roakore from his reverie as she approached with her ever-present quills in hand. She was Roakore's royal brain. Every king needed a secre- tary, and Nah'Zed had been a gift from the king of the Elgar Mountains upon Roakore's taking of the throne. She was, indeed, the smartest Dwarf Roakore had ever met, in terms of math and memory, and she was none too bad looking either, as Roakore had thought more than once. She was a little skinny for his liking, but that could be cured with many days in bed and many feasts.

"Why do you laugh, sire?" Nah'Zed asked with a smile.

Roakore pushed the thought aside and coughed. "Nothin', nothin', just admirin' the door is all."

Nah'Zed instantly went to one of her many scrolls. "Yes, the door. Shortly a band of Elves, as ye know, will be here to gift Roakore's door, as it is to be named from this day forth. They should be here a'fore midday, sire."

"Yes, yes, I be knowin'. It's to be a great gift, it is, from me friend Zerafin. They say it'll take more than a week, it will, en' more than fifty Elves'll be helpen'." Roakore said with wide eyes as he continued to inspect the vast door.

"Yes, sire, about the Elves, their lodging has been arranged and—"

"Bah, I be knowin'. I told ye, don't be tellin' me everythin' that be happenin'. I got me own worries and lists. If what needs to be done is gettin' done, then ye be doin' yer job, en' I don't need to be knowin' yer doin' it, 'cause when you ain't, I'll be knowin', understand?"

Nah'Zed scribbled furiously on her scroll and nodded. "Yes, sire."

Roakore sighed. "And you don't need to be writin' down everythin' I... bah, never mind."

Zerafin looked upon his seemingly sleeping sister as she lay upon soft silk cushions next to the quiet river. Their mother knelt beside her, gently stroking her unresponsive daughter's forehead. Zerafin could hardly stand her gaze as she looked upon him from his sister's side. Though it was a loving gaze, he felt undeserving of such affection; he had failed.

He and his sister had faced Eadon, and Avriel had done what she felt was right in the moment to save Whill. She had tried to perform the dying curse. She had been successful in a sense; she had unleashed all of her power and utterly destroyed the ship while protecting those she meant to protect, and she had attacked Eadon with blinding power. But Eadon was not hurt, and he had even managed to capture Avriel's departing soul and cause her body to remain alive.

He is indeed powerful. What chance do we have against one such as he? thought Zerafin as he turned from his mother's gaze.

I know what you would say, sister: Whill is our chance. Whill shall defeat him, and we will once again be able to return to our homeland. But how? Whill is lost to us. For these last six months, there has been no word from our spies, not a whisper of his whereabouts. The enemy has him, and he is likely dead, and we are likely doomed to suffer the same fate as Drindellia, our homeland. Eadon and his horde will scorch this land and kill until nothing is left but ashes and smoke and the fires of evil.

But if Whill is dead, why does Avriel remain alive? Eadon has no use for her other than to bend Whill to his own will.

He could be saving her to force surrender, but, no, Eadon has no interest in surrender. He wishes only to defeat violently as he did in Drindellia. So the riddle remains—why is Avriel alive? The fact that the attacks have not yet begun in full and that Eadon has not presented himself to either the Dwarves or humans would suggest that Eadon has not yet succeeded. Surely he has not found the sword of Adimorda. Though neither have we.

I believe the prophecy. I have to; without it, there is no hope. If the prophecy is to come true, then Whill must be the one to find the sword, and thus, Eadon cannot find it without Whill alive. But Eadon cannot wield the sword—no Elf can—it was made so that no Elf could wield it.

This thought process had been played out by Zerafin for months and was being pondered by a great many wiser and older Elves than himself. Still, no one had come to a convincing conclusion. If Eadon's only threat was Whill in possession of the sword Adimorda, why would he not simply kill Whill? Many conclusions had been thought up. The most popular was that Whill was dead and Eadon kept Avriel's soul from departing and killing her body simply to confuse his enemy, and if that was indeed the case, it was working. Another theory was that Eadon wanted to use Whill to find the sword and somehow harness the great power within it. A new thought had come recently from his own mother—an idea so strange it would not leave Zerafin's mind.

"What if Eadon believes the prophecy as we do?" his mother had asked.

Zerafin had looked upon his mother in astonishment and wonder. She'd stood before him with her back to the setting sun, beautiful even in her age.

Zerafin's mother, the queen of Drindellia, widow to the fallen king of the Elves of the Sun, had let herself naturally age since the passing of her husband. To a human, she would look about seventy but with a straight back and strong muscle tone. She had declared that her beauty was for her husband only and it would no longer exist if he did not. But Zerafin still found her beautiful, because beneath her gray hair and lined skin, he saw her strength, her majesty, and her great power.

She had raised an eyebrow. "Well? Suppose that Eadon believes that Whill shall kill him, destroy him as the prophecy says. What if he believes it and also wishes it to happen?"

Zerafin had thought for a moment, and his brow had shown his confusion. "But why would Eadon want the prophecy to come to be?'

Why indeed? Zerafin asked himself, still staring at Avriel. *The answer to that question is the answer to the riddle. If Eadon seeks death, he could easily find it himself as so many Elves have done before him. It makes no sense.*

One thing was clear to Zerafin. If Avriel lived then there was a good chance that Whill did also. It was time for the vigil to end. If Avriel was to be saved, Whill had to be found and freed.

The elders had agreed that the top priority was the preparation for the final war and the finding of Whill. Zerafin had spent five months in isolation within the woods of Elladrindellia. He and his sister's mission had been to bring Whill back to Elladrindellia alive, so that he might begin his training in the ways of the Elves of the Sun and become what he was meant to be, their last hope. In his despair upon arriving with the broken Avriel, Zerafin had begged the elders to give him an army and send him against Eadon and the entire might of the Draggard and Dark Elves. They had denied his request.

Preparations for war had begun, such as had not been seen since the final battle of Drindellia. Elladrindellia was a vast land, home to more than twenty thousand Elves. All but a thousand were born there after the coming of the Elves across the great oceans. In those five hundred years, they had thrived. The once-barren land was now forested and rich and dense. The Elves thrived there as they always did, as they always would, due to their great relationship with the elements and nature.

For more than four hundred years, until the recent Draggard wars, the Elves had lived in peace, storing their collective energy, waiting. Now the time had come. Their power was rested, their energy saved. Next to nothing had been used to fight in the recent wars in which they were always aided by humans. Soon the Dark Elves would know the power of the sleeping Elves of the Sun. All knew that though Whill was the supposed savior, the Elves of Elladrindellia would give the Dark Elves a fight not easily won, if won at all. Some elders dismissed the prophecy of Whill altogether, thinking they could win without him. Others thought they were doomed as they had always been and believed it to be a curse of the ancients.

Of the more than twenty thousand Elladrindellia Elves, four thousand showed proficiency in the arts, and of those, more than three thousand were masters of at least one school of learning. The other fifteen thousand were no different than the average human, though with more advanced gifts and abilities. But they were the power behind the soldiers or Nanji, as they were called by the Elves. While the Nanji trained day in and day out, the others, the Enta, took one day out of three to pour their energy into the blades of the Nanji or the various stones and crystals used to harness such power. For more than four hundred years, the power had been accumulating to be used not only in the individual blades but also in one particular blade, Nifarez, the blade of Zerafin.

Given the task of finding Whill and bringing him back safely, the Elves had endowing Zerafin's blade with the power and strength of more than one thousand

Elves—each having given their energy for more than four hundred years. Zerafin's blade had been made more powerful than any yet known in Elladrindellia, a power truly unknown to anyone. The issue of the offering of power had been a great debate lasting more than a week. But Zerafin had proven himself time and again in the Draggard wars, and even when being tempted by the Dark Elves, he had proven righteous. Many had given their consent simply for the fact that he was the lost king's son and heir.

Zerafin looked upon his sister, his jaw clenching. He had come from the woods prepared for the task at hand. On this, the day before the offering of the blade and the beginning of his quest, he was ready; he was anxious, and what a curse it would be to stand against him in battle in the days and weeks ahead.

CHAPTER TWO

The Prisoner and the Assassin

Whill had not eaten in months; he had drunk only his own blood. His captors kept him alive with the same energy they used to torture him and revive him. How long he had been within the dungeons he did not know. His life beyond the dark, damp dungeon walls now seemed a fantasy. These times of rest, alone in his small cell, were torture far worse than that of any blade. The silence was maddening, the anticipation of the torture to come, unbearable. They would not come for him sometimes for days, and other times, they would give him only a few hours' reprieve. His anxiety outweighed his physical pain, which he had become accustomed to. The wounds would be healed before they killed him, but his mental pain was never healed.

The torture was not always to his body; indeed, physical pain was a reprieve from the mental torture. The vicious Dark Elves were masters of mental torture, bombarding Whill's mind with horrific scenes. Terrible illusions played out in his mind—images of himself killing innocent men, women, and children alike. In these twisted visions, Whill had seen himself commit the most heinous acts imaginable. But the most effective and painful torture was that of hope. Occasionally Eadon had created the illusion that Whill was with Avriel. Whill would awaken next to a stream within a forest of dancing light, and she would come to him. In her arms he found peace, love, and silence. For days the fantasy would play out, until finally, violently, the illusion would end.

Now, Whill hung from his shackles, which cut sharply into his flesh. The only things within his dark, dank cell were the echoed cries of fellow prisoners. He did not feel the shackles burning into his skin, nor did he hear the cries. In his mind, he was within the gardens of Kell-Torey, seated across from Avriel and Zerafin. He had blocked his mind from the world completely, living within his meditation. After so many months of torture and mental probing, he had finally snapped. He created massive mental walls, a fortress of willpower, which, to his torturer's surprise, was thus far impenetrable.

Remember, it is not the rock that you are moving or the water that you are controlling at your will. It is the Keye within the vessel; it is to the spirit of energy within all things that we connect. Avriel had spoken the words, and Whill had taken them in, but he did not register their meaning at the time. Now, in his defensive coma, he took in every word. She spoke to him from her heart stone, which he now wore beneath his skin and muscle, against his breastbone.

He remembered that her spirit had been taken by Eadon just before the great explosion that had destroyed his ship and killed his friends. That thought he could not bear, and he fled from it, returning his mind to the distant garden, to Avriel and the sun in her raven hair.

"How long has he been in this condition?" Eadon asked Velkarell.

The Dark Elf torturer turned his tattooed face from Whill to Eadon. "Nine days, lord. He has built a mental wall."

Eadon's thin eyebrows perked. "Really? This is sooner than I thought."

Velkarell walked toward Whill and punched him in the face. Whill's head flew back, and blood poured from his nose for a moment; otherwise, he did not respond. Instead, he laughed in his dream state. Velkarell presented his fist to Eadon. The Dark Elf's knuckles were sizzling as if acid had been applied to them. The melted flesh dissolved from his knuckles all the way to his wrist. Velkarell did not grimace from the pain; instead, he closed his eyes, and in seconds, the skin returned to normal.

"As you can see, the human has made pain pleasure, and his body has gone into a lethal, self-preserving mode."

Eadon smiled and took in a long breath. "How long did it take you to master the ways of self-molding?"

The Dark Elf torturer looked to Whill with slow-burning resentment in his eyes, and grudgingly, he answered, "Fifty years."

Eadon walked close to Whill and studied his face. "And Whill is but twenty years old. Already he can heal himself and others; already he can drain the energy of his victims, and already he is as advanced as a five-hundred-year-old Elf."

Velkarell looked uneasily toward his master. He did not want to doubt his master's plans or cunning, but he could not help but speak. "My lord, he should be killed. One such as he..." Velkarell lowered his eyes to the floor under Eadon's gaze. "Forgive my ignorance, but I do not understand why you would allow the one named in the prophecy to live."

Eadon looked upon his servant and smiled as he lifted the Dark Elf's chin with a finger. "There is much you do not understand, my worthy student. Why would I destroy my most brilliant creation?"

Eadon turned from a confused Velkarell and walked to Whill. He took Whill's chin in his hand and raised the battered man's head. Eadon mentally extended his consciousness at and into Whill's mind. "Wake up, boy!"

Whill's eyes opened wide, as if he had been splashed with cold water in the middle of a nap. He gasped for breath and looked around wildly. Finally his eyes rested on Eadon. Whill spit in his face. Eadon's face did not so much as twitch as he wiped the spit away. "You have mastered pain, Whill, and you no longer have fear. Many Dark Elves do not survive what you have these last months, or their minds do not. You have been cleansed; now your training can begin."

Eadon said no more to Whill as he turned and walked out of the cell and in passing whispered something to Velkrell. The Dark Elf torturer turned to Whill with a menacing glare, took a dagger from his belt, and cut Whill's chains, releasing him.

It was legend that the assassin could sneak up on the moon and kill it, without the sun ever noticing. He was cloaked in shadow; under the darkness he wore a tight leather-wrapped war suit. The thick leather strips were wound around his tall, thin build. The suit covered his body fully. His midnight-black hair and full beard covered his face. Within both tight black leather-bound boots he carried a six-inch Dwarven steel dagger, jeweled with black pearls. Four bands were wrapped around each leg, holding eight three-inch darts, sixty-four in all. His belt held various small pouches containing herbs, poison elixirs, poison powders, powdered dragons' breath, a cloth-covered grappling hook, twenty-seven feet of Elven silk rope, various smoke bombs and other small explosives, and many other tricks. Upon his belt from his left hip, he wore a two-foot short sword. Upon his right, he wore a two-and-a half-foot Elven killing sword; its name was Arelliune. In the small of his back a two-foot greatly curved Dwarven hook sword was holstered. Attached to each forearm was a hidden throwing-star holder that would produce a star in whichever hand was flexed a certain way.

Over his weapons and suit, he wore a black dragon-hide tight-stitched cloak that was ankle length with a long, wide hood, in which his face could never be seen. Many more weapons and the like were concealed within the endless hidden pockets of the cloak. A great many of his items had been enchanted by Elves, both Dark and Sun.

A chance encounter when he was fourteen years old had found him saving the life of a Sun Elf. He had been scouting for his father, a highwayman, outside of Kell-Torey when he stumbled upon a horrific battle scene. More than forty Draggard lay dead upon the road; only one remained alive. The lone Draggard loomed over a badly injured female Sun Elf, who was without weapon or the strength to use one. Her face was resigned to serenity; she had accepted the moment.

The boy had ran up on the Draggard as fast and quietly as a boy could, and he'd leapt at the beast with his mean, poison-tipped dagger arched back. He landed on the Draggard's back and grabbed a horn with his left hand as he jerked his entire body into the blow. The dagger thrust into the beast's eye up to the hilt. The Draggard reared violently and would have thrown off the boy had he not already leapt away. The beast staggered backward and then to the left and finally fell to its knees and heavily to its face.

The boy had quickly run over to the body and gave it three kicks; it was dead. He'd then turned to the Elf, who was weakly calling him with her hand. She pointed but could not speak; her throat was slashed and bleeding badly, her face ashen. He followed her finger to a pouch thirty yards away. The boy rushed to the pouch and brought it back to the Elf. Her eyes fluttered, and she wavered. Frantically, the boy untied the pouch and reached inside and took out the only thing within it, a purple four-inch crystal.

Getting no response or direction from the dying Elf, he had laid the crystal in her hand. Instantly, her hand clutched it, catching his hand in her iron grip. The crystal hummed like a thousand bird wings as a blinding blue light engulfed them for a few moments and then was gone. In that moment, healing energy poured from the crystal into the dying Elf and, through their contact, into the boy. She was fully healed of her wounds, and not only her strength but her vitality was returned, and her rings and necklace were recharged.

Energy had also coursed through the boy, and, having nothing to heal, rather than killing him, the healing energy had caused him to grow. Not only into a man did he grow but into a tall, lean, strong man.

He had stood in his ripped clothes staring down at his long, powerful hands. He'd looked to the Elf and laughed, and to his amazement, she'd laughed alike with a voice of such sweet music as he had never heard before. In that moment, he loved her and always would.

"I am called Krentz." The Elf said with a wide, beautiful smile.

The boy responded, "I am called Dirk." Not recognizing his voice, he coughed awkwardly. "Dirk Blackthorn."

In return for saving her life, the Elf had taken Dirk under her wing. They had disappeared east into the mountainous wild of Uthen-Arden, and there Dirk learned many things from the mysterious Elf maiden. Five years he spent with her, and then one day she had gone, as he knew she must.

Dirk laughed to himself at the memory, but quickly stopped and mentally chastised himself for the idiocy. He gave himself back to the night upon his rooftop perch. He watched from the shadows of the building's chimney, and he waited.

Soon he saw the mark, just on time, come out of the saloon. The bald man staggered, danced a small jig, and waved to the unseen pub patrons. He staggered down Pleasant Street just below the watching assassin. When Dirk saw his quarry begin to turn left down Crow Street, he instantly sprang into silent motion. Dirk ran the length of the rooftop with little-to-no sound; while he ran, he kept low and prepared his cloth-covered hook. Dirk twirled and leapt as he reached the end of the roof; the hook was thrown even as its destination was lost to sight.

Above the drunken man a shadow whispered into the night; the man staggered and looked up as the night slammed into him. He was wisked into the vicelike grip of death. He knew as soon as the cold, iron grip seized him with but one arm, that he was doomed. Through the back door of a closed shop they went, and the man was set upon the floor without a sound and gagged with a rag that had a strange, bitter taste of…

'Poison!" the drunken man's voice screamed into the rag, but it was too late. He became dizzy, and fear struck him until he smiled stupidly.

Dirk knew by the man's eyes that the drugged rag had done its work.

He reared on the drunken man, and his eyes took the giggles from the man.

"You are here to kill me, eh, eh? Aren't you now? Why yer a demon, you are!" The man said with a muffled voice, and he began to whimper and cry.

"Shut it, mate, or else I gotta take your tongue. I want answers from you. Now listen, and answer on thee life or lose it."

Dirk let out a breath and tensed. "Well then, nod if you understand."

The man nodded.

"Now answer me this, who is Whill of Agora? Eh?'

The drunken man looked puzzled.

Dirk removed the rag with a threatening glare.

"It's just a myth is all, just a rumor."

Dirk smirked. *Finally*, he thought. "I like myths. Tell me more."

"Well…" The drunk man sat up and slumped. "He is the one that kicked Rhunis's ass right here in Fendale. By the gods, he did. I was there; I seen it with me own eyes. Beat 'im, he did, 'n' rightfully so. He got his own weight in gold as reward. Well, he was said to be about the city for a few weeks or so, and then he ups and vanishes. Rumor came on the wind that he got pirated by Captian Cirrosa of all pirates. He and his pal there, Abram, be credited with the killin' o' Cirrosa— got rewards owed 'em by all the countries of Agora and that of the Dwarves to boot! Then comes word of some crazy Elf magic saving the life of some kid from here in Fendale; poor kid's parents was killed in a fire said to be set by Cirrosa and his men, and now the lord admits they knew about Cirrosa bein' in town and they didn't want to alarm the people…gut rotten dragon shit!"

Dirk's hand covered the drunken man's mouth with the speed of a viper. They both listened; Dirk's eyes warned the man of sudden death should he make a sound. A minute passed as Dirk listened through the enchanted jewels in his earlobes. He found the song of the night. He heard a nest of rats thirty yards away in the adjacent street. A newsletter rustled in the faint breeze, and dogs fought over food three blocks away. Laughter spilled out of countless taverns. The night did not listen back, and they were alone.

Dirk removed his hand. "Continue."

The drunken man gulped and whispered. "Well, also word come from Sherna of another strange Elven style healin' done by Whill to some dyin' infant; then he ups and leaves there. A few days later, the town was invaded by a fleet of over a hundred Draggard on their unholy winged masters. The battle of Sherna it is called. Already the songs are being sung of the victory. Why, Whill of Agora is the secret hero amongst the people, all the people, of every country."

The drunken man looked strangely at Dirk. "Why, you must know as much about the man, eh? Why the questions?"

Dirk answered as he always did. "What I know is *from* questions. You know the answers I seek. What else have you heard about the Elven legend?"

The drunken man lurched; he had hoped this question would not be asked, for to speak of it was death. But because of the drugged rag, he could not lie, and he grimaced and whined as he told the midnight-man what he had sworn a blood oath not to.

"It is said that this Whill of Agora is some kind of Elven savior." He winced and doubled over.

"And?" Dirk insisted.

The drunken man could not resist telling the truth. "There is said to be a sword, A...Ad...Adromida, the most powerful of all the Elven swords that have ever existed. This sword is said to hold the power of a thousand Elven lifetimes." The drunken man gulped.

"Why do you and your, associates, know so much about this Whill? Surely the sword story is just gibberish," Dirk pressed, feeling that perhaps this time he would get a good lead.

The drunken man whimpered and struggled against the urge to tell the truth—the words that would surely doom him to the brotherhood. Dirk punched him in the face, and the impact made the man's head jerk and his neck crack. Nothing was broken, but it was a reminder and a threat.

"We know that the story is true, because we know of the sword." The drunken man violently blurted out, hating himself for being weak. "We are the brotherhood of the Red Dragon; we keep the secret and prepare for the day, as we have for four hundred years."

Dirk smiled to himself and took in the sweet, sweet smell of knowledge and victory and power. In his world, there was only power or the lack thereof. His interest was the attainment of power of every kind, ultimate power. He, like all of them, knew that the Draggard wars might surely destroy all of Agora. These were rough times, and Dirk's fortune had tripled, because he was not only a survivor; he thrived in all conditions and prided himself in as much.

The Dark Elves were an invisible threat, but their power was felt. The Draggard wars had waged for decades, Dirk did not remember a time before the wars. But if a war was being waged, Dirk had to do what was best to survive, and that meant siding with the most likely victor. Dirk had met many an Elf, Dark and Sun, and he had sided with neither as of yet. He used their power but took nothing from either theology. He was a man unto himself, casting off with disdain all attitudes and beliefs, rules and regulations, traditions and agendas. He lived and worked for himself and his kin only— to be Dirk's friend was a rare, if not dangerous, honor.

He would side with and make partners of the victor of the outcome, but recently he had come across information that might lead him to be able to affect the outcome either way. He knew that if the sword existed and if he could find it, then he could sway the battle the way of his choosing; he would have ultimate power, if for a moment. But he must decide which way to sway it.

Dirk knew one thing and one thing only—if you could play any game, by anyone's rules, without qualms or protests, then you could win any game, which meant you could win the big game of life. And Dirk was very good at winning this game, so far.

"What do you know of the whereabouts of the sword Adromida?" Dirk asked.

The drunken man cowed, still under the spell of the drugged rag. "We do not know the whereabouts of the sword but that of the Red Dragon, the ancient keeper of the sword."

Dirk's eyes gleamed with the unseen moonlight. "Where is he?"

The drunken man bowed to the floor, thinking death would answer his words.

"I do not know. A few select brothers know half the story, and half of those know more and so on, but I ain't but a thirteenth-degree brother. Only the thirty-third-degree brothers know all, and there are but seven of them at a time."

He laughed at Dirk, not caring anymore, knowing his life was gone with the words he had been forced to speak. "You caught yourself a tadpole, sir; you need to be catching bigger fish if you are to fill your big appetite for trouble."

The man laughed manically after Dirk as he strode away, and Dirk could hear his laughter for three blocks, until the explosives set the building aflame in an instant.

The man had given information that would see him dead anyway, and Dirk needed to make a statement, a little introduction of himself to the Brotherhood of the Red Dragon. What better way than to kill a thirteenth-level brother? He would climb the levels one by one and get to the top, and then he would find the Red Dragon, and through it, obtain that which tilted the scales in the coming power struggle. He would side with the winner; better yet, the winner would side with him.

CHAPTER THREE
A People Divided

Abram burst through the balcony doors. Annoyed, he packed his pipe and lit it with an Elven fire stone. Rhunis came and stood next to him, more annoyed and just as fatigued by the last three days' politics. They had been round and round every topic and had gotten nowhere since the meeting had begun. In attendance were Abram and Rhunis; King Mathus of Elcalon; Arkthar, son of the fallen Fenious, and newly made king of Isladon, only twenty-two but tall and strong for his age; the Dwarf kings, Ky'Ell of the mountain kingdom Ky'Dren, which separated Eldalon from the rest of Agora, and King Du'Krell of the Elgar Mountains, the largest and richest Dwarf mountain kingdom—though all Dwarves conceded that Dy'Kore was and always would be *the* home of all Dwarves. Representing the Dwarves of the rebuilding kingdom of Ro'Sar or the Ebony Mountains was one of Roakore's sons, Wrendal. The Elves had no representative, although it was accepted that Abram would know their mind on most topics and decisions.

The Elves had not shared anything with the human kingdoms or the Dwarves, for fear that spies would know their mind. The Dark Elf Eadon had intercepted the fleet that had landed upon the shores of Isladon; he had laid in wait, and it had been disastrous. He and his Dragon-Hawk had laid waste to ten ships alone. There had been one or many spies during the last endeavor, so now the Elven policy was that they would not speak openly about the movements or plans of the Elven forces, but they would assist, with great force, any military action by either humans or Dwarves against Eadon and the Draggard

The mediator of the meeting was an elder from the small island nation of Eldon. He was a blind man of ninety-seven, but he had a mind sharper than a Dwarven axe. He was benign in all things, simply keeping order to the meeting and maintaining a ruling formed of pure logic. His name was Fracco.

In the last six months since the battle for the reclamation of the Ro'Sar Mountains, where Elves, humans, and Dwarves had fought together and won, there had been many battles. Though they had won the day, many thousands of Draggard had escaped, and they had plagued all the lands of Agora ever since.

Entire towns were destroyed, seemingly at random, in all the human kingdoms. The bounty for a single Draggard head was more than fifty pieces of silver, enough to feed most families for years. So far, ten thousand Draggard heads had been taken, but many remained.

The Draggard Wars had dragged on for decades, and there had been countless battles, mostly upon the eastern seas or the fortress island of Fendora. Fendora had been lost and reclaimed half a dozen times. Always the Draggard came in waves and from only the east, until the weeks before the fall of the Ro'Sar Kingdom twenty years before. Until the invasion of Ro'Sar, the Dwarves had nothing to do with the Draggard Wars unless they were protecting their allies' borders or their own.

All of that had changed since the taking of Ro'Sar twenty years ago. Now, with the help of Abram and Rhunis and the legacy of Whill of Agora, a hero to all peoples and many Dwarves and Elves alike, the three races were beginning to work together, albeit slowly.

The lines in the sand had been made and the enemy defined. Sides had been taken, oaths pledged. Humans and Elves and Dwarves had forgotten all their differences for the time being, be they land claims, gold and silver rates, trade disputes or the like. The kingdoms of Isladon, Eldalon, Ky'Dren, Ro'Sar, Helgar, and Elladrindellia had declared war on the Dark Elves, the Draggard, and the leaders, not the people, of Shierdon and the Uthen-Arden Empire.

The human kingdoms of Shierdon and Uthen-Arden had been plagued with massive civil war for the last six months, during which neither kingdom did anything to aid in the fight against the Draggard, and both were rumored to be secretly ruled by the Dark Elves. Though it was true that Eadon, through his generals and minions, had infiltrated and now controlled Shierdon and Uthen-Arden, it was not always easy to decipher the truth of the outside world if you lived in a sheltered community.

Many good people, whether a fisherman of Shierna, a blacksmith in the small town of Brinn, a barber in Del-Oradon or any one of the hundreds of thousands of citizens and patriots of the nation, sent their sons to fight the wars of the kings—regardless of the reason behind the war. Trust in the nation's rulers and tradition led most minds. Almost all of the soldiers of the kingdoms of Shierdon and Uther-Arden thought that they were fighting against the Draggard themselves. The Dark Elves had long ago learned how to rule humans simply, with no force at all, so easy were the humans to manipulate with plays and newspapers and song and dance.

Eadon had recruited the most esteemed men of all human sciences, giving them great wealth and power, and had learned all there was to learn of humans, for the last fifty years. Ainamaf, the king of Shierdon had been replaced by Travvikonis, Eadon's son and a general of three hundred years. Although he was young for a general, only five hundred and sixty, he had mastered four of the six schools of Orna Catorna, that of the

Ralliad or druid and all four disciplines of the Krundar/elemental, Gnenja/warrior, and Zionar or telepaths.

The Uthen-Arden king, Addakon, Whill's uncle, was being impersonated easily by Eadon. Both Eadon and Airamaf could change their appearance at will, though many Elves had achieved this feat in the past. But unlike the others, these Elves could not be detected for what they were, even with Elven mind sight.

Propaganda campaigns ran heavily in both kingdoms. Though many rumors of the truth lingered, they were dismissed mostly as the ranting of drunkards and crazies. Any talk or publication against the kingdom's leaders had recently been outlawed as treason, punishable by death.

False-flag attacks were run weekly by Eadon's Dark Elves. Draggard would attack a town with small armies of humans dressed as Eldalonian or Isladonian soldiers. In would sweep the valiant knights of Uthen-Arden or Shierdon, and every soldier and Draggard would be killed. Entire cities had been wiped out by Eadon and blamed on the Elves, Dwarves, and humans.

To live in Uthen-Arden or Shierdon since the battle of Ro'Sar, meant to live in a world of lies and false enemies. Yet most people of Uthen-Arden considered themselves above all other nations and secretly thought that Uthen-Arden should have taken over all of Agora long ago.

"I tire of these dragon-shit politics. The people have spoken; we must act," said Rhunis.

Abram blew smoke into the night wind and looked out over the city. "The people do not know the facts; most of them know less than lies. The people of Uthen-Arden think they are the ones fighting off the Draggard armies that *we* command."

"But we know the truth, and we must act on the people's behalf. The royalty of this continent are not being affected; it is the people," Rhunis growled.

Abram chuckled. "You are preaching to the choir, friend. But I will remind you that Whill's parents were royalty and were killed, as was Roakore's family, the recently slain Fenious, and also the Elven king. Yes, my friend, everyone has suffered in this war."

Rhunis let out a breath of frustration. "Sorry, friend, my blade craves action, not talk, and my feet wish for a road with a purpose, rather than my arse on a seat and mouths yappin'."

"I understand. Then let us end this foolery and start a damned offensive."

Abram tapped out his pipe and entered the great room.

The room settled, and the many diplomats resumed their slumped posture. Abram stood up and said, in a purposefully loud voice, "May I take center for a moment on behalf of every citizen within the realm of Agora?"

Fracco listened intently to the silence and nodded. "Abram of Uthen-Arden has the floor."

Abram put his knuckles to the table and leaned forward slowly, with his head down and breath loud. He raised his head, and sweat trickled into his graying beard, the heat of the uncharacteristically hot night showing on his face.

"Friends, our people are not thriving; they are threatened. And I speak also of those that believe us to be the enemy. We cannot let our own people or soldiers think that the people of Uthen-Arden are our enemies. We cannot allow the invasion of any country by any other country. We must act fast, but we must act in stealth. All-out war between countries will end in many needless deaths. It will cause bad blood for centuries after this is resolved—as it will be."

Fracco raised a hand, as he did often during these debates. "What is on many minds here is the thought that we cannot give ground to any army, whether Draggard or human, no matter the ignorance behind their actions."

"Indeed," agreed Abram. "We will not give ground, but we must not openly invade. If we are to attack the Dark Elves, it must be through stealth and stealth alone. Their numbers are not so great that they cannot be defeated, nor is their power. Instead of entire armies fighting this war, it should be small tactical units, each with a purpose and each purpose vital. We must infiltrate the enemy and strike at the heart of the Dark Elves. They will not respond to anything less."

Arkthar, the newly appointed king of Isladon stood. "And how do you propose this stealth operation be performed? Are humans to try and take on Dark Elves? We are like ants to them. Did it not take the efforts of thousands of humans, Elves, and Dwarves alike to defeat the mere half dozen at the battle to take back Isladon? How many are there? Does anyone know?"

Fracco again spoke, "Abram stated earlier that there were not as many as one would think. How many would that be, Abram? I feel the lad asks, though he spoke out of turn and without even a customary raised hand."

Abram nodded. "By the estimates of the Sun Elves, there could be anywhere from a thousands to hundreds of thousands. There is no way to know, unless one was to go to Drindellia and find out—if that is even where they are. And at the battle for Isladon, there were hundreds of thousands of Draggard. The fact of the matter is that Whill of Agora, the one who is said to defeat Eadon, must be found and freed!"

There was a rustling within the room as the topic of Whill was presented yet again.

The Dwarf king Ky'Ell stood, and his booming voice took all attention. "I be agree'n thet the lad must be found. I be believin', as Roakore be, thet this man's got a great part yet te be played. But, we still got te be wagein' our wars if we are te help Whill."

The Dwarf king Du'Krell of the Elgar Mountains stood and spoke his peace. "I gots me more than four hunr'd miles o'mountain te be worryin' 'bout. Not te mention we lost us more 'n' a thousand te the rebuildin' o' the Ebony Mountains. We be surrounded by the Uthen-Arden Empire, an we got Fendora Island not far from us, which me spies tell be crawlin' with Draggard 'n' Dark Elves 'n' all kinds o' evil nowadays."

Du'Krell sat with a nod and gruff, "Hmm." He then added, "We got enough te worry 'bout sealin' our borders, then worry 'bout the humans. But we'll give safe passage 'n' refuge to any." He coughed and added in a lower voice, "...and to the Elves."

Speaking a little louder, he finished, "And we'll be helpin' 'n any battle close te home, ye can bet."

Ky'Ell eyed his cousin with a raised eyebrow. "And the helpin' with Whill 'n' the forces needed to infiltrate the enemy as Abram be statin' we be needin'."

Du'Krell looked around at the table with shifty eyes and finally raised his chin. "The Elgar Mountain Dwarves can give no more than five hundred Dwarves te the stealthy army 'n' such."

Ky'Ell nodded to his cousin. "The Ky'Dren Dwarves pledge the same support te the peoples o' Agora en' the Elves alike, five hundred Dwarves te the stealthy army 'n' such."

Rhunis stood. The torchlight mixed with the twilight as the sun slowly rose and put the length of the meeting at more than thirteen hours. "So it is agreed, and it has been put to writing. Let us now move on our enemies and let the liberation of Agora begin."

Abram thought back on the meeting. It had taken place one week after the retaking of the Ebony Mountains and Isladon and had lasted for more than two weeks. A union had been made between the human kingdoms of Isladon and Eldalon, with the Elf nation of Elladrindellia and the three Dwarf kingdoms. Continental war had not plagued Agora for more than five hundred years. But now war was here, and Abram feared that a great many lives would be lost to misunderstanding.

Many of the people within the kingdoms of Uthen-Arden and Shierdon believed, because of the constant propaganda on the part of Eadon, that their only ally was each other. They were led to believe that the Elves of Elladrindellia were the masters of the Draggard and that the Dark Elves did not exist at all. They were told that the humans of Eldalon and Isladon were in league with the Elves to steal their land and take their country. Many good, patriotic men were ready to send their sons to war against a false enemy, whilst being led by the true enemy. Abram was more than a little frustrated with how easily humans were misled with catchy slogans and theater and song.

He waited at the bar of the inn for Rhunis, grumbling to himself about stupid people. Rhunis had gone out into the city of Del-Oradon, within the kingdom of Uthen-Arden. They had come here four months ago to discover the whereabouts of Whill. They discovered, through their spy network, that Whill was within the castle of Del-Oradon. The castle had once been the home of his family line; now it was his prison, and the Dark Elf Eadon was his captor. His crime—he was the one named in an ancient Elven prophecy.

Abram did not know why Eadon did not kill Whill during the battle for Isladon and the Ebony Mountains. But he feared the worst, that Eadon had taken Whill as an apprentice. That thought gave Abram the cold chills, and he shook slightly.

CHAPTER FOUR

Falling Down

Tarren hit the floor hard, and blood flew from his mouth. The Dwarf boy that had shield bashed him laughed, as did many of the Dwarves within Tarren's fighting circle. Tarren got up shakily and removed himself from the battle ring. Two Dwarf boys took the center and began to duel.

I am sick of being smacked around by these Dwarves. If I was their size and had their muscle, I could pound them all, Tarren thought as he wiped blood from his lip and watched the clumsy Dwarf boys go at it. They beat Tarren because they were bigger, but he was getting better. He did nothing but read and write and train in Dwarven combat. His preferred weapons were twin axes, hatchets really. They were light enough to wield and could be very deadly if wielded well. The problem was that Tarren did not wield them well. Though they were light by Dwarf standards, they were heavy enough to be hard to control. Tarren controlled them better than all other weapons. Recently he had been working with a staff, but he was not ready to do battle with it yet, or so Lunara said.

He had been training with the Dwarves for the last five months, and he had taken his share of beatings. If it had not been for the Elf Lunara's healing abilities, Tarren would be bedridden from his many breaks and cuts. He had broken both legs three times and both arms twice, along with some of his fingers and toes. Dwarves were simply tougher; they could take a punch five times as hard.

Roakore had not liked the idea from the very beginning, but he knew in his heart that the boy had to do what the boy had to do. Tarren insisted on continuing the training, no matter the pain. Roakore knew the reasoning behind Tarren's obsession. The lad had been kidnapped and basically killed by pirates, though he had been healed by Whill. His family had all been murdered by the same pirates when he was taken. Tarren had promised himself that he would never be helpless again, nor would those he could protect. Roakore understood the feelings; he had been fueled by them before.

The Dwarf boy Helzendar nudged Tarren. "You gonna keep taking thet dragon shite from them stupid Elgar Dwarves?"

"Ain't you one o' Roakore's kids?" Tarren asked curiously.

"Yeah, 'n' so?"

"You Dwarves 'r' supposed to treat each other like the same clan. He don't be wantin' no sides taken between the Elgar or Ky'Dren or Ebony Dwarves," Tarren told Helzendar matter-of-factly.

"I ain't sayin' that there be nothing wrong with the Elgar Dwarves. I'm just saying them ones thet are always after ye 'r' stupid. Ain't no matter they be Elgar," Helzendar said.

"Unity is the only way to victory and peace," stated Tarren as he watched the duel before him unfold and end with one rather fat Dwarf boy getting the better of his opponent with an ax slam to the gut. The fallen Dwarf boy tried in vain to get a breath. He slammed his small fists against his chest, but the wind had been knocked out of him. An adult trainer lifted the boy's belt, and the Dwarf sucked in a grateful breath.

"How many times I gotta tell ye to hit the ground breathin' out, 'n' be flexin' yer fat stomachs. Ye gots to listen, lads. Getting the wind knocked out o' ye can be a killer on the battlefield! Same as gettin' kicked in the ole family jewels, tis why ye better all be wearin' yer metal cups!"

The trainer kicked the fallen Dwarf boy in the crotch as he passed. The strike of metal on metal rang out as the trainer's steel boot struck the boy's cup. The trainer nodded his approval. "These lessons should be as natural as wiping yer arse fer Ky'Dren's sake."

The trainer pointed at Helzendar and at one of the Elgar Dwarves that was part of the group of five that always went hardest on Tarren. Helzendar grinned to Tarren and took his place in the center of the ring.

Helzendar wore thick leather armor like anyone else. But his weapon was not one seen often. For Helzendar was tall for a Dwarf boy, lean with longer arms and legs than most. He used his size advantage in his choice of weapon, the half-moon spear. His wooden practice spear was four feet long, with a curved half-moon wooden blade at one end. The half-moon itself reached out like outstretched arms more than a foot and a half wide. At the other end of the spear was a large, fist-sized stone wrapped in leather that wound up the shaft.

His opponent was Krekra of the Elgar clan, his weapon, a wooden shield and long ax. Twenty Dwarves cheered and stomped their feet as the opponents circled each other. Helzendar was the first to act as he started his spear spinning overhead, gaining momentum. Krekra swung with his wooden ax, and Helzendar stepped back. As Krekra spun around to control the momentum of the swing, Helzendar began an attack of his own.

Whoosh, went the half-moon end of the moon spear at Krekra's feet. Krekra jumped over the attack and held his ground. Whoosh, went the stone end of the spear at his head, and he ducked. Feet, head, feet, head, Helzendar attacked Krekra continuously high and low.

Krekra timed the attack and readied to slip through it when Helzendar again went for the feet, the head, the feet, and, finally, the feet again. Krekra, expecting a head attack, ducked. The half-moon whooshed in with a blur and took Krekra's feet out from under him. Helzendar twirled with the blow and came around and down with the stone end, smashing Krekra's shield in two pieces. The astonished Dwarf desperately swung his ax from on low but had no leverage on his back to give speed or power to the blow. The stone end of the spear knocked the ax from his hands as the moon end came down around his neck. A quick boot to the side of Krekra's face put him to sleep.

The other Dwarf children looked on astonished; no one moved. The entire fight had taken less than twenty seconds. Helzendar twirled the spear around in a dizzying blur of perfection before letting it come to rest on the back of his neck, with both arms draped over it. "Next."

The trainer began to stomp his ax handle on the stone, and the Dwarves took up the applause.

Zerafin stood before the council of elders, his mother seated at the center of the twenty-seven. The offering of power was held within the center forest city of Cerushia, which, much like other smaller dwellings of the Elves of the Sun, was made of earth and trees. In many ways it resembled a human city of wood and stone, and in many ways it was completely different. Where humans harvested earth and stone, the Elves encouraged growth. Rather than build, the Elves molded.

Thick, gnarled trees made up the outer walls. They grew like vines entwined with one another in a knotting band around the perimeter of the city. And unlike inanimate human stone or wooden walls, these could be manipulated to attack anyone perceived as a threat or be molded to fit the needs of the dwellers.

Within the city walls, the buildings and homes and temples grew together in the same manner. Rather than doors, the great vine trees would part as one passed through a threshold. Windows could be made with a word. Therefore, the tree vines that consisted of the city were ever shifting and changing. From the tree vines grew large leaves that thickly covered the massive web from which they came. The city was a mass of green-leaved walls and structures with thick knots of brown vines. Green, yellow, and red moss grew where needed to cushion the feet or body. Throughout the city, ponds and gardens abounded. Stone walkways led here or there, but they too were at the will of the Elves and could be manipulated as such. Most humans, upon setting sight on the forest city, wept.

At the center of the city, within the great open-roofed temple of Suunlafen, Zerafin awaited his quest.

Hundreds had migrated from every corner of Elladrindellia to witness the offering of power. They sat in silence within the circular temple that had been grown larger than usual, stretching upward to the sky in a half globe. At the center of the circle in a ring sat the council.

"It has been decided by the council of elders, who for no other reason exist, to enforce the will of the Elves of Elladrindellia. You are charged with this quest, should you choose to accept. Find and retrieve he named by Adimorda, Whill of Agora." His mother read loudly from a leaf scroll that she held in her hands.

"Retrieve the soul of Avriel that she may be returned to her people."

Zerafin looked to his mother; her eyes were watery but strong and brave. She was more than a thousand years old, but life had not hardened her. She, like many Elves, had realized that enlightenment was not a state of detachment and apathy. It was a realization that pain was a part of life to be weathered, to be felt. Her eyes watered with fear for Avriel's soul and worry for Zerafin's fate. But her eyes were brave with her belief. The decision had been made; the outcome was left to the fates. If her son failed and her daughter was lost, she would lead an army personally to Eadon's gates and die fighting; many knew her mind, and many would join her in the final battle.

Zerafin stood straight and strong. "I accept the task offered me! It will be achieved, or I will not return..." He paused and met many eyes. "...alive."

Devarda, the elder of the council, the oldest of all Elves living within Elladrindellia, stood. He looked for a long moment into the eyes of Zerafin. The ancient Elf was master of all schools of knowledge, with proficiency in the way of the Ralliad. So proficient was he that he could shift into the form of any living creature, within the boundaries of his relative mass.

Devarda did not appear as an animal. He appeared before his people that day as he always did, in his true form as an Elf within a cloak of thick, dark green leaves that grew from his being as naturally as did hair from a goat. He turned from his seat and descended the thick vine stairs to stand before Zerafin.

"To aid you in your journey, we have endowed your blade with a collection of energy rivaled with none but the blade of Adimorda," stated Devarda with a deep, booming voice. He reached down into the entangled floor, and from it, a hole opened. Devarda reached into the hole and pulled forth the blade Nifarez. Those Elves that were naive enough to look upon the sword with mind sight were blinded and screamed out in pain. Those that did not could sense the great power within the blade. All looked on in silent awe. Devarda regarded the blade not at all but quickly offered it to Zerafin with a small bow. His eyes never left Zerafin's, and Zerafin's eyes never left the blade.

Zerafin's hands tightened around the hilt of the blade that had been forged for him in Drindellia, the sword that he had wielded for centuries. He knew the blade as the blade knew him. The sword hummed quietly in his hands, and the power begged to course through his veins. Zerafin had a difficult moment dominating the urge to tap the energy. His face strained with sweat as he dominated himself and the blade.

Devarda took three steps back, and all in attendance looked on in anticipation of Zerafin's test of the blade. Zerafin raised his hand, and fierce tendrils of flame shot forth into the midday sky. They reached upward with blinding speed and parted the lowest clouds.

Zerafin lowered his hand and stared in awe at his blade. He had not felt a dissipation of energy. His mind screamed of power, victory, dominance, overwhelming joy, fear, and warning. He dominated his emotions and focused on the task at hand. Zerafin allowed himself to not exist. He was a vessel of the power of the Elves. He had been given a gift. And he would fulfill his duty.

"The council of humans and Dwarves within Kell-Torey has come to a decision," said Devarda as he looked to the crowd and the elders. "To spare as many lives as possible, small tactical units will be unleashed upon our enemy. The peoples of the kingdoms of Uthen-Arden and Shierdon are not our enemies. Let this be known to all. They have been caught up in Eadon's web of lies and deceit."

Devarda gave Zerafin another contemplative look over and nodded absently. He addressed the crowd once again. "This curse we have brought upon the humans and Dwarves of Agora. True it is that Eadon would have come to conquer Agora eventually, whether we had come here or not. But the blame falls upon us for not stopping Eadon in Drindellia. For that reason, we will give aid to our allies the humans and the Dwarves. We are bound by a common enemy, a common goal. Therefore, we will fight together. Within a week's time, many hundreds of humans and Dwarves will come here from their respective distant lands."

The crowd of Elves murmured to each other and spoke in hushed whispers. Devarda waited until it died down. "These small tactical units will consist of Elves, humans, and dwarves. They will be made up of no more than twelve and no less than three. Together, we will strike at the heart of our enemy through stealth and unity. Though they do not possess the great powers that we, the Elves, do, there is much to be learned from the mortal beings. Do not doubt the ferocity of those that live a short life, for they are as a cornered badger in battle. Together, we will fight the Elves of darkness and the Draggard, and together, we will finally see an end to this sorrow."

Zerafin looked upon his kin and promised himself that he would see an end to Eadon, an end to this war. As would his sister.

CHAPTER FIVE
The Dark Creator

Whill was taken from the dungeons and led to a room deep within the castle walls. He knew where he was. He was in the castle of his forefathers, Del-Oradon, built after the great war of Uthen and Arden.

Del-Oradon was also the name of the city in which the castle stood. It was the largest city within Uthen-Arden. More than three hundred thousand souls called the city of Del-Oradon home, as did Eadon and a great many of his Dark Elves. Whill was pushed into a room as his guide took up guard near the door.

"There is hot water, food, and clean clothes. My master bids you to enjoy the many comforts you have forgotten. When you are done, he wishes to see you."

Whill stumbled and fell to the floor as the door closed behind him. After a moment, he raised his head to look upon a grand guest room. The room was lavish in design; the wall decorations contained more wealth than did his childhood town of Sidnell. An enormous four-poster bed took up only a small space. Three huge wardrobes spanned one wall; a balcony was centered in the middle of the other. Silks and tapestries of distant lands and highest quality lazily littered the room. The drapes before the balcony danced teasingly upon the sweet summer night air. Upon the breeze came the smell of roasted meat.

Whill raised his head and drunkenly stumbled toward the smell. Drool fell freely from his mouth as hunger pangs dropped him to his knees. At the center of the room, upon a table set for one, but made for four, was a small feast.

A roasted chicken took up the centerpiece, its skin browned and juices flowing forth to a bed of lettuce and cherry tomatoes. Set around it, like an army of delicious flavors, was a host of wonderful foods. There was water, tea, juice, milk, wine, and beer. There were baked potatoes, cobs of grilled corn, roasted peppers, beans, and carrots in butter. He saw succulent shrimps peeled and ready on a plate with a white sauce, crab legs by the dozens, and lobster tails by the pound. A side of beef glistened with dark juices. For dessert, there were cakes, pies, pastries, and more. Whill drooled like a drunken madman and lurched onto the table, devouring every steaming piece of food he could get his hands on.

He gorged himself on a lot of everything, drinking it all down with milk and juice and beer. He had not eaten in months; he had forgotten what food was like. Upon sight of the meal, he had lost his senses, feeling a primal pang of hunger so ancient and strong it dropped him to his knees. Whill ate like he had not for so long. Then he suddenly bent at the waist in pain and vomited.

Over and over, he purged himself of the food. Though he had eaten no more than he may have, indeed far less, his stomach was not prepared for such treatment after being so long unused. Once he was finally through and the heaves subsided, Whill returned to the food, and again, his body would not allow it. This continued until Whill passed out and found sweet oblivion.

When he awoke, he dared not return to the food just yet his stomach painfully reminded him of his folly. Instead, he stripped off his clothes and stumbled weakly into a large bathing room. Though he knew not how, a deep tub of steaming water awaited him.

Naked, he gingerly lowered himself into the hot water. Instantly he fell into the routine of bathing, using soap that had been set within a dish. Whill bathed for so long that when he finally emerged, the sun had begun to rise, and his skin was pruned. He walked to a large mirror hanging upon a wall and smeared it with his palm until his reflection could be seen. But Whill saw no reflection. Instead, he saw the sunken eyes and face of a stranger.

High and sharp cheekbones stretched the skin around them, and the eyes disappeared into shadowed pits of insanity. His hair was thin, his face gaunt, and many of his teeth were missing. The man before him appeared as an old beggar might.

Though the Dark Elves had kept him alive with healing energy, they had not kept him whole. Without food or water, Whill's body had begun to die slowly, though the Elves would not allow it to die completly. So instead it lingered, like some half-dead wraith. Whill turned from the mirror in rage and pain and stumbled, mumbling, to the bed.

He suffered no dream, no nightmares. He had lived through so many at the hands of the Elves that none would enter his sleep now. Instead, they returned with waking. He ate what he could and drank what he could, and he slept. For countless hours and countless days, he ate, and he slept. Always was there fresh food, and always was there fresh bedding. Finally, after what felt like days, Whill reluctantly arose after sleeping, ate, and did not return to the void of sleep. He bathed and, once again, looked into the mirror. Some of himself had returned to his reflection—enough so that he recognized it again, though he was still frail and weak, having lost at least eighty pounds.

Slowly the clouds within his mind parted, and he remembered Addakon and the fight. He remembered the explosion upon the ship and the Dwarven mountain's eruption. He remembered Eadon and…Avriel.

Avriel?

Her soul had been trapped by Eadon within an orb of light, her body...

Whill's mind screamed as he remembered that he was a captive and she lost; his friends were all dead. He thought of Abram, who was like a father to him; Rhunis, the bravest knight he had ever met; and Zerafin, his first teacher in the art—all dead. He was a captive, and Avriel was left to linger at the whim of Eadon for one purpose, control.

Whill was overcome by rage and overturned the table and with a swiping blow, split one of the bedposts in two. Like a bull, he raged toward the door, which opened. A Dark Elf appeared in the doorway with an inquisitive look on his face; he was met with a foot to the chest that sent him flying five feet into the opposing wall. Upon impact, the Elf rebounded with lightning speed and slammed Whill in the chest with an opened palm. Whill was thrown back into the room to crash against the wall.

"When you are ready, our master wishes to speak with you," stated the Dark Elf as he slammed the door closed.

Whill had dented the wall with his head and surrendered to slumber.

Fresh food once again forced Whill awake. He stood painfully and sat himself before another feast. This time, he ate slowly, methodically. He could not succumb to his hunger, else he gorge himself. Instead, he imagined the act like sharpening a steel blade, slowly, purposefully. Within the wardrobe, he found clothes and sandals that fit. He strode to the door and knocked.

He was guided down many halls and up many stairs until, finally, they came to a room. The Elf pushed Whill into it and looked at him with an arched eyebrow. The look meant immediate pain if opposed.

Whill turned from his guide and saw Eadon. The Dark Elf lord did not sit upon a throne; he did not sit at all. Rather, he stood at the center of the room before a large stone table adorned with many gems and stones, rubies and crystals. The jewels glowed brightly, and power hummed within them.

Upon the stone was a dragon egg and, to Whill's horror, a pregnant Dwarf female. Images of the Draggard flashed in Whill's mind, half-Elf, and half-dragon damnations of Eadon's creation. Eadon meant to meld the unborn Dwarf fetus and dragon egg into a new monstrous damnation of nature.

Whill hurried forward to the stone table and was stopped by a wall of energy no less solid than that of stone. He could do nothing but watch in horror as Eadon stood between the egg and pregnant mother with raised hands. From Eadon's hands came great, blinding bolts of lightning that did not dissipate like that of natural lightning; instead, they remained constant.

From each hand a bolt reached and struck the egg and the mother's belly. Eadon brought his hands together as the precious stones glowed brighter than before and the humming intensified to match the crack and buzz of the lightning bolts. As Eadon's hands came together, there was a loud explosion of sound and blinding light for only an instant, and then there was silence, so deep and complete that Will thought himself deaf for a moment.

When Whill regained his sight, he noticed that the mother was no longer with child and no longer lived. The dragon egg had changed in appearance. The egg and fetus had been forged into one, and from the egg would spawn a Dwarf's nightmare, a Dwarf-dragon crossbreed.

"Beautiful, is it not? She will be the first queen of her kind," said Eadon.

Whill could only look upon Eadon with murder in his eyes. "Why do you keep me alive? What have you done with Avriel?"

Eadon gave Whill the look of a disapproving parent. "Please, Whill, do not answer a question with a question. How will we ever get anywhere?"

Whill clenched his jaw and looked upon the dragon egg once again. "It is a hideous example of the evil lengths you will go to in your insane attempt to play a god." spat Whill.

Eadon chuckled, and the chuckle grew into a hearty laugh. He looked to one of his guards that stood near the only other door. "This kid is good. He practically nailed it. But I must disagree on one point, my young friend. It is not hideous. It is life."

Whill shook his head. "Not natural life. It is an abomination of nature."

"Wrong!" Eadon yelled, his voice booming unnaturally loud within the room, rage contorting his face. "Nature is of this world! I am of this world, and I have created this beautiful life-form. Is it also not then natural? You see, if I created it and nature created me, nature created this being—just as nature created the Draggard," said Eadon as he strode around the table to stand close to Whill.

Whill unconsciously leaned away from the Dark Elf and took a step back. Eadon was no less impressive than Whill remembered. He radiated power in a way that the sun or the moon might, the way that a waterfall or mountain struck awe by their sheer presence. To look into Eadon's eyes was to know that you were truly at his mercy, an object of his will. Whill knew he could never better the ancient Dark Elf; it was impossible. Agora would burn, and all those that knew a good life here would know it no more. The people and the land would suffer the same fate as Drindellia. Eadon and his monstrous army would eventually sweep the globe and leave nothing but a dark, smoldering planet. The world would become nothing more than another silent star among the heavens.

Whill knew that there was something beyond life, for he had seen the reincarnated spirit of his mother and the ghost of his father. He knew that beyond this world there was another. He cared no more to remain within this one.

Whill felt a throbbing at his temples and knew instantly that Eadon had been reading his mind.

"Other worlds after life there may be, Whill. But not all pass on. A soul can be kept, and it can be taken."

It was then that Whill knew the greatest fear he would ever face. Death would be no escape; it would offer no haven. Even in death, Eadon would control him, would use him. Whill was trapped. Avriel was trapped. As far as Whill knew, her body was dead and her soul a captive, forever at the mercy and will of Eadon.

"Her body is not dead; she is very much alive. The many energy stones embedded in her flesh held enough energy to keep her body alive and breathing, as they were meant to," said Eadon. He paused with a smirk. "Or hadn't you seen the stones?"

Whill lunged forward and struck the energy wall hard. "You are a sick son of a b—"

"Hold your tongue!" Eadon interrupted. "No need to get personal."

"Personal!" screamed Whill. "You have stolen a soul; you have destroyed your own homeland, and you have filled the world with darkness. You are insane, and you must be stopped!"

Eadon smiled and tilted his head. "And you will be the one to stop me?" he asked.

'I will. For it was told by Adimorda," Whill professed.

'Indeed it was." Eadon smiled. "It was indeed."

CHAPTER SIX
The Brotherhood

Dirk Blackthorn looked out upon the city of Del-Oradon. From his modest room within his modest inn near the center of the city, he could see his quarry much better. He had found other Brothers of the Red Dragon, the secret society he had been pursuing for more than a year. They alone knew of the red dragon tasked with the keeping of the fabled blade of Adimorda. Dirk had learned from a dying man that they were the keepers of the secret of the blade, should anything happen to the red dragon Zhola. No Elf had been entrusted with the knowledge, as was the will of Zhola.

Dirk had gotten the attention of the brotherhood. He had killed many of their own. It was said that there was a bounty on his head of fifty thousand gold coins. This amused Dirk greatly. For it was the highest bounty he had been cursed with in his many years; this meant that he had pissed off the right people.

The Brotherhood of the Red Dragon was set to meet this night, midnight, at a mansion of one of their own. Dirk awaited the hour. He watched the scattered clouds flirt lazily with the half-moon. His mind drifted to the wood of old, the forests of his youth, to her.

Krentz.

She had been the most energetic and life-loving being that Dirk had ever met. She was like a child in many ways but in many others like a woman. She had been his first and his last lover, for they had reached heights together that he would never reach with another. Nor had he met a woman since that even sparked his interest. Everyone was either a target or an informant, useful to his cause or not.

Krentz had been born a Dark Elf. But her spirit disagreed with the savage, dark, and brutal ways of her people. She was not of her kind, but nor would she be taken in by the Elves of the Sun, for her intricate black-spell tattoos gave her away to any that looked upon her. When Dirk came upon her at that early age, she had been on the run from her people. She had been hunted; they wanted her dead, and she would have died had it not been for Dirk.

They spent years together, years avoiding the many search parties that still hunted for Krentz. Never in all the centuries had a Dark Elf ever strayed from the way of its people. Krentz had created a precedent that Eadon did not want followed. He had sent more than one hundred Draggard after her, but she and Dirk had killed them all. The last year they spent together, they had done so in peace, within the forests of Eldon Island.

She had awoken one night, shaking in a cold sweat in his arms below the stars. "You will die because of me," she had said in a petrified whisper. "If you stay with me you will die!" she had screamed. They had fought over the dream for more than a week. Krentz had only become more sure, more scared. Dirk had pleaded with her not to leave, saying that they could kill whoever dared try pursuing them. She would hear none of it. She knew of her abilities of future seeing. She knew it to be true. She believed that she could change it by leaving Dirk forever; as long as she was never near him again, he would never die.

She left him before the morning sun, and he had not seen her since.

Dirk shook his head in disgust and looked to the moon's nightly advance with sudden alarm. As if part of a sick curse, Dirk was only vulnerable during those times that he thought of Krentz. Always he was alert to his surroundings, aware of those around him—unless she slipped into his thoughts.

Darkness had come to the world; lights glowed within the brotherhood's secret meeting place. The time had come.

He slipped out of his room, taking with him all that he owned. He would not be returning to the inn. He hit the street and walked in a circle around to the back of the stone building that the brotherhood would be using. The mansion was set on its own lot, near the center of the city. It was home to a rich merchant, one of the Brothers of the Red Dragon. The top tier of the brotherhood consisted of seven men, each with the full knowledge of all secrets of the order. They were the true brotherhood.

Dirk came to the gate of the mansion and walked the street along its perimeter. Never looking directly at the building, he took every detail in peripherally. He followed the building for a block. He noted several guards upon the rooftop of the stone building, crouched in shadow behind gargoyles, and many more near the doors and walking the perimeter.

He could have simply snuck into the mansion, slipping past the guards like a whisper. But that was no fun, not when he could utilize the opportunity of immobilizing so many targets. He knew that if any alarm was given, the seven members of the brotherhood would go separate ways and escape through different routes. That was unacceptable. Dirk knew that he needed to take each sentry independently.

His first target was the nearest guard. The guard walked the perimeter of the gate lazily, looking off into space as he marched. Dirk sighed to himself. There was nothing worse than bad competition.

He scaled the fence and jumped to a nearby tree branch, gaining the attention of the guard. The man looked up quickly and gripped his spear, and his helmet fell over his eyes. Dirk swept his legs and caught the armor-clad man in one arm while jabbing him in the neck with a poisoned dart. He looked around; no one had seen. Dirk lowered the guard slowly onto the grass to sleep off the effects of the dart. He followed the shadows to the next guard in line.

Dirk threw a stone into the bushes near a tree, and the second guard perked up and hustled over to the sound. Just as he arrived at the bush, Dirk was there, jabbing him in the neck with a dart from behind. The guard snored softly and would for an hour. Dirk focused his will upon his ring of shadow, a black pearl set in a ring of steel. It was something he had traded for the life of a Dark Elf. He became like a shadow then. To any that may look upon him, he would seem like a trick of the night and make one question one's tiredness.

Like a phantom, he ascended the mansion's stone wall. With the help of many enchanted stones set within the heels of his boots, he leapt from stone perch to stone ledge, grabbing a handhold easily with his similarly enchanted gloves. To any that saw him, he was the shadow of a nearby tree.

One that did not see him was the guard closest to him as he reached the roof. Dirk crouched down as he landed upon the roof behind a gargoyle. The guard, sensing something, began to unsheathe his sword but was stopped by a powerful grip that crushed his hand

and a fist that smashed into his forehead. A dart to the leg left that man sleeping as well.

So it went with the rest of the guards of the brother-hood, until Dirk peered through a skylight window at the meeting of the brothers. The members sat at a circular table in a small room within the left wing of the mansion. Dirk noted that no guards stood within the room but seven waited outside of it.

He smashed through the window, hooking his grapple at the same time. He descended the rope quickly and landed upon the table at which the brothers sat. Thud, thud, and thud, the darts thumped into the chests of the startled brothers. They in turn looked to their chests at the protruding darts. Dirk had hit them all in less than two seconds, spinning as he went. They hadn't even had the time to stand in protest. Glass rained down upon the table moments after Dirk had landed. No guards entered the room at the ruckus, for no one outside had heard a sound. The brotherhood rarely met to discuss business, and when they did, it was in a soundproof room.

Dirk looked each of the order in the eye, daring them to retaliate. Both Dirk and the brothers knew they could not, even if they wanted to. The poison in the darts he had used paralyzed the victims, leaving them only with the ability to speak and move their eyes.

None of the brothers spoke. Dirk sat cross-legged upon the table and brushed glass from his shoulder.

He reached out and took one of the brothers' glasses of white wine, looked at it intently, smelled it, listened to it, and drained the glass. He whipped the glass over his shoulder to smash against the wall. The brothers watched, eyes wide, paralyzed. Dirk then proceeded to take from its box a fine Isladonian cigar. He brought it to his lips and lit it with a candle.

"It is hard to get an audience with you people. I was quite disappointed when you refused my offer for a meeting. Now look what I have had to resort to, to get your attention," said Dirk as he lifted his hands outward and looked around at the brothers. He puffed on the cigar over and over, getting a nice, fat cherry going at the end. The gray ash cooled and looked like fine fabric.

"The darts protruding from your chests have administered a drug that as you know has left you paralyzed. What you do not know, is that it will kill you in less than fifteen minutes," said Dirk as he watched the eyes of all seven men widen. None spoke.

He slowly retracted a dart from the band on his thigh. "This, however, will reverse the effects of that dart so that you may live. All I want to know is the location of the sword of Adimorda, and you shall all live fat, happy lives."

The brothers all eyed each other; they looked mostly to one man in particular. He was an old man, with a beard to his chest and eyes that shown with defiance.

Dirk got up and walked upon the table to that man and kicked him in the face, knocking him out. The others looked to him with wide eyes.

"Now that Mr. Backbone of the order is out of the way, let's say we make a deal—your lives for a little information."

"Never!" yelled one man.

Dirk kicked him in the face, and he slept as well.

"Over our dead bodies!" cried another. He slept also as did three more after him.

Dirk centered on the only remaining brother that hadn't spoken.

The man was small and pudgy. He had manicured hands and the best clothes of all the men. Many rings adorned his fingers, and a wine glass, a beer glass, and a pipe lay before him. Dirk knew that he had chosen well.

"So?" asked Dirk. "Will you tell me what I want to know and save your own arse and those of your brothers? Or are you truly righteous at heart?"

The man whimpered and shook with the effort to move against Dirk.

Dirk rolled his eyes and looked to the other sleeping brothers. "They will all be dead in five minutes, as will all your guards, as will you be, my plump friend—unless you tell me what I want to know."

The man cried and slobbered, spittle falling from his sweating chin. "They will know I have betrayed them. My life is forfeit if I speak anyway."

Dirk smiled. "That is where you are wrong, my friend. My next dart will not only remedy the one that afflicts you all, but it will also render your memory void. You will all wake puzzling over a broken window and sore heads. Not even you will remember your own betrayal. You save the lives of yourself and your brothers, and no one is the wiser."

The fat man whimpered and cried and finally broke, with a minute left till his death. Dirk did as he promised and gave every one of them the antidote.

He walked along the perimeter of the mansion with the knowledge that he had sought for years and smiled to himself. Beyond him, upon the grounds of the mansion, a guard came to and rubbed his neck.

Dirk walked into the night whistling a happy tune.

CHAPTER SEVEN

An Invitation to Execution

Rhunis met Abram at the bar within the inn they had been staying at for a week. He sat down wearily and ordered a beer. He nodded to the barkeep and looked around the room. None of the few patrons within gave them any mind. He handed Abram a small scroll.

"Finally!" Abram announced and hurriedly broke the seal and uncurled the paper.

It was a short message written in a code that only he and Zerafin knew; they had agreed upon it when Zerafin had left for Elladrindellia with his sister's body. Abram read the scroll and then quickly caught fire to it with a nearby candle.

"Hey!" protested the barkeep.

"Apologies," said Abram. He nodded to himself and pondered what he had read.

Rhunis looked at him dubiously. "So, what did it say for Kell-Torey's sake?"

Abram looked to him with a smile. "Zerafin will be leaving Elladrindellia shortly; he will meet us here in one week." said Abram.

Rhunis took a large pull from his beer mug and set it down gratefully. He wiped the foam from his mouth. "'Bout damned time and none too soon. I found this while coming back into the city." He handed Abram a paper. Abram took it and tilted his head back to read it.

It read.

Come one, come all
Your great King doth invite all that may attend
To the newly finished Coliseum of champions
The 27th of this month
For the grand opening celebration featuring
some of the greatest gladiators
to have ever bled in the arena
In honor of this great day of blood sport
and festivities
All in attendance shall witness the trial and
execution of the most hated criminal
in all the lands of Agora
Bringer of darkness
Master of the Draggard
Enemy to all free humans of Uthen-Arden
Whill of Agora

Abram's jaw dropped, and his face shone with a strange mix of emotions—joy at hearing that Whill was indeed alive, sadness in the realization of his friend's sentence, and finally he felt rage.

"The bastard intends to kill him in public, make an example out of him." said Abram.

"Indeed," Rhunis agreed. "It said what? The twenty-seventh of this month, that gives us a week."

Abram's breathing had increased, and his mind raced. "Zerafin will be here by then. I am sure of it."

Rhunis grimaced. "That gives us little time to be ready to infiltrate the coliseum and break Whill out of there."

Abram patted his old friend on the back. "We must be ready by then, and we will. Zerafin will have soldiers with him; I am sure. For Whill's sake, we must be ready."

Dirk walked through the streets of the city to his destination, the great library of Oshtock. He doubted he would find what he sought, but if the information was not there, it was nowhere in the city. He passed a town crier on his way and paid him no mind, until something in the boy's hand caught his eye. He turned to the boy and absently handed him a coin as he took the paper. Dirk could not believe his luck. There, in bold print, was news of the new coliseum; to his amazement, Whill of Agora's execution was the main event. Dirk read it again and pondered the situation.

Nah'Zed hurried to follow Roakore down the hall and into a side passage. Roakore had just come from two days spent with his twenty-seven wives and was in one of his moods. Through another tunnel he went with a slight limp and down a flight of stairs, with Nah'Zed following behind.

"Sir?" She puffed. "Sir? You are due to meet the boy Tarren shortly fer dinner, along with Haldagozz 'n' the Elf lady Lunara n—"

"I be knowin' whats it is I gotta be doin' ya dolt. I be headin' that way didn't, ya happen te notice?" roared Roakore as he spun around on Nah'Zed, causing her to bump into him as she followed.

Nah'Zed hit the solid Roakore and dropped her quill and parchment and many papers. She looked to them and then up to the scowling Roakore, and her nostrils flared with anger. "I know ye be knowin' where ye be goin', but it seems ye ain't knowin' what ya be wearing to where ye be goin'! Ye got on yer bed clothes!" said Nah'Zed with frustration and slight embarrassment

"Me, king."

Roakore scowled at her and looked down at his bed clothes. He burst into a great belly laugh that was picked up by his royal brain. "Bahaha! Thought it was a wee bit breezy in this here tunnel." said Roakore as he tied tighter his bed robe.

Tarren and Lunara awaited Helzendar at the entrance to their living quarters. They slept but a minute's walk from Roakore, though Tarren did not see him daily. Indeed, weeks would go by without Tarren seeing the great Dwarf king, but he did not mind. He was so engaged in his study of the Dwarf language, history, customs, and battle techniques that he had not a minute to spare to loneliness.

He lived with Lunara, and from her, he had learned a great many things. She alone could have kept his mind busy with learning. But she understood that to live alongside Dwarves was a great chance for the boy, a great chance for her for that matter. She did not distract the lad from his teachings; there would be time for other lessons.

Tarren had an insatiable appetite for knowledge that Lunara respected. For a human child, his energy and enthusiasm was great enough to better that of many an Elf she had known. He learned all lessons taught to him, the first time. There was no need for repetition for the boy. The harsh and awkward language of the Dwarves came easily to Tarren, and he sometimes insisted on speaking it for days. Lunara had to admit that his pronunciation was perfect, without accent, while hers was not. The Dwarf talk was too rough and sharp for her Elven tongue.

Every time that Tarren came back from training, Lunara inwardly winced at his wounds. Many times the boy had needed to be carried back to his dwelling, once with two broken legs. The Dwarf boys were rough, and Tarren was an eleven-year-old human. The trainers treated him no differently; he was given no favor, as had been his wish. Lunara had treated his wounds as he received them, and always he left the next morning, chin bravely lifted.

Recently, he had come home with less and less wounds. Upon receiving them, be it a broken nose, a bruised rib, or a bent finger, he would insist on not being healed for hours at a time. During these times, Lunara watched him closely and worried while Tarren lay upon his bed, silently fighting the pain. He would not be healed until he had mastered the agony of his injuries.

Lunara was quite fond of Tarren, as he was her.

Helzendar finally showed, and Tarren greeted him with a punch to the arm, which got him a small shove and laugh from Helzendar.

"'Bout time!" said Tarren as they followed Lunara to Roakore's dining hall.

"Bah!" exclaimed the Dwarf boy.

"Me dad'll be late te this one, I be thinkin'. He been with his women folk fer two days now; we be lucky if he be showin' up at all," said Helzendar with a laugh.

Helzendar was one of Roakore's sons. He was tall for a Dwarf boy, even at age thirteen. He had a long, unruly head of dark red-and-brown hair that gave him the look of a wild and crazed Dwarf, but his eyes were kind and brown. He had not yet grown a beard; this meant that he was still a boy.

Helzendar had not seen his father often in his lifetime, but he understood the reason. He was but one of many sons of one of many wives. Roakore gave them all equal amounts of time and direction, at least he tried to. His father was a very important Dwarf, and Helzendar was proud to be the king's son.

Helzendar had been born within the mountain kingdom of Ky'Dren, years before the retaking of the mountain home of his forefathers. He had grown up with the Ky'Dren Dwarves as the grandson of the fallen king of the Ebony Mountains. His grandfather had failed at protecting his mountain kingdom; he had fallen to the Draggard seven years before Helzendar's birth. Helzendar had to live with the failings of his line, as did his brothers and his father. Though no Dwarf ever said anything aloud of the shame of clan Ro'Sar, he had seen the looks and heard the snickers.

Because of this, he could relate to the young human boy Tarren, being so far from home with truly no home to return to. He had watched the boy progress over the past six months in training, and he was confident that the boy would grow into a great warrior of men. Also, Tarren was Whill of Agora's boy, and if Whill was good enough for his dad, then Tarren was good enough for him.

They reached the dining hall and found the table set for five. Haldagozz was already seated to the right of the king's chair. He raised a glass and cheered as the three walked in. His cheer echoed throughout the great hall and was met with many smiles.

Just then Roakore burst through the door abruptly and slowed upon entering; trying to make it look as though he had not rushed. "Ey, then, ye all made it on time. Good, I be starving."

Helzendar eyed Tarren and Lunara with a smirk. "Looks like he got away from the wives intact—no matter that his coat be buttoned wrong."

They all looked and chuckled under their breath, or tried to.

Roakore had heard his son and looked down at his coat; a button was left at the top with no hole to go through. Without acknowledging that he had heard the joke, he ripped open his coat, sending buttons flying, and fanned himself. "It hot in here, or be it just me?"

Lunara could not contain herself and fell into a fit of laughter; Tarren and Helzendar followed. Roakore waited with a grim face as they walked to greet him and one annoying button spun noisily upon the table. He raised his chin and looked down on his son, wiping the grin from his son's face. They stared at each other for many moments until; finally, Roakore extended his arms and greeted Helzendar with a great bear hug that brought the boy's feet from the stone floor.

"A joker, just like your mother, eh?" laughed Roakore as he set the boy down.

Helzendar beamed. "Father, me king."

" N' what's this?" Roakore scowled at Tarren. "Ye be in league with Tarren, no doubt. A troublemaker if I ever be seein' one," said Roakore as he scooped Tarren up in a bear hug also.

"Me lady." Roakore nodded at Lunara.

Lunara nodded back. "Good King."

"Lads." Haldagozz nodded. "Lady Lunara."

"Haldagozz."

They all settled down to eat, and Roakore clapped his hands. Among Dwarves, dinner was served first, conversation followed. In through the side door opposite the one Tarren and the other two had come in came many Dwarf maidens with many trays of food. To Tarren's surprise, the trays carried not only the usual venison, pork, and beef, but also many varieties of ocean fish— the same as he had known his whole life in the coastal city of Kell-Torey. There was also crab, shrimp, and lobster, with drawn butter to boot.

"How did you…?" said Tarren speachless.

"Bah, it ain't no matter how. It being yer birthday, lad, I figured I'd give ye a bit o' home fer yer gift."

Tarren beamed at the king with shimmering eyes and dipped one of the shrimp in a red sauce and brought it to his mouth. Roakore held his breath in anticipation. Tarren chewed for a long while and finally swallowed; all eyes were on him. "Mmnn, mmnn!" he exclaimed with a jerk of his head and grabbed another. "Perfect, Roakore, it's perfect."

Roakore let out a breath and smiled from ear to ear. "'N' it better be, what, with all the trouble o' havin' it delivered fresh from hundreds o' miles away, 'n' havin' me chefs tryin' to perfect the recipes."

"They did great!" announced Tarren behind a mouthful of shrimp.

They all tried the shrimp and many of the other plates set before them. Then they eagerly filled their plates and began to dine.

They ate in silence for a bit and then fell into conversation. Roakore inquired about Helzendar and Tarren's training. Many stories of the mock battles were told. Lunara informed Roakore that Tarren needed less healing every day. Tarren blushed at the telling. Helzendar told his father that he had won the last four tournaments. Roakore nodded his head and smiled with pride between bites of a chicken leg.

Roakore lifted his foaming mug and cleared his throat. Before he could speak, the door burst open as an exhausted Dwarf in soiled clothes stumbled through the doors and fell hard. Everyone had jumped when the door burst open, and all had grabbed the nearest weapon, be it hatchet or a fork. Two guards came in cursing, one with his hand pressed firmly to his bleeding eye, the other with an exaggerated limp. They moved to grab the rogue Dwarf when Roakore noticed that the half-dead intruder carried a thick parchment.

Roakore raised his hand to stay the guards, and they froze. He leaned down and saw that the Dwarf had passed out. He took the parchment from the sleeper. Those at the table looked on expectantly as he read the paper to himself. He finished and passed the parchment to Tarren with a shaking hand.

He looked deadly serious, his eyes vacant. "Me human reading ain't what me talkin' be, boy; let me hear it clear from you in Dwarvish."

Tarren looked to the parchment with wonder as he took it from the Dwarf king. He cocked his head to read it.

"Come one, come all. Your great king doth invite all that may attend to the newly finished coliseum of champions the twenty-seventh of this month for the grand opening celebration, featuring some of the greatest gladiators to have ever bled in the arena. In honor of this great day of blood sport and festivities, all in attendance shall witness the trial and execution of the most hated criminal in all the lands of Agora. Bringer of darkness, master of the Draggard, enemy to all free humans of Uthen-Arden, Whill of..."

Tarren gulped and looked to Roakore with wide eyes. "Whill of Agora."

Tarren lowered the paper to the table, his appetite gone.

Lunara and Haldagozz looked to each other, thinking the same thing.

Roakore slammed the table with his heavy fist; the crack of his knuckles on the wood resounded throughout the hall.

"He lives! Ha-ha!"

CHAPTER EIGHT

Powerful and Powerless

Zerafin bathed in the river for hours. Finally, the first day's light crested the water, sending it aflame with color. The sun reminded him of the power he had been gifted with. Such power as had not been given in many centuries, now his. With such power, he could live without fear of foe for thousands of years. None could match the power he possessed but Eadon and the wielder of the sword of Adimorda. He'd known that these thoughts would come to him; they always did with the knowledge and possession of such energy and power. He had been told he would be tempted.

Zerafin was aware of the side of him that would seek to dominate and create a world of his liking. He was also aware of the side of him that wished for no power at all but simply a peaceful life. As his two sides bickered and Zerafin listened, he became aware of an approaching friend.

He walked from the river to the bank and stood in the long grass, looking to the forest. He did not bother covering himself; neither the weather nor the company called for it.

"Azzeal? I was wondering when you would be joining the hunt."

For a moment there was no sound but the breeze, then came a rustling in the woods. From the tree line leapt a large wolf. It was brown, for the moment, with streaks of almost black. But once its paws touched the long grass, it became dark green with strips of dark brown. Its head came to Zerafin's elbow; its body was massive. The great wolf looked to Zerafin, sat on its hind end, and began to scratch itself behind the ear with a hind paw.

Instantly Zerafin raised his head and let out a howl. The sound rose into the sky and suddenly cracked. The howl turned into that of a wolf, as did the body of Zerafin. The wolf Azzeal came out of his leisurely scratch and became alert, cocking its head in interest. Zerafin growled and pounced. Azzeal jumped back. The two great wolves circled each other.

The wolf Azzeal growled and swatted its paw at the air. As the claws sliced the air, they released an energy attack. The wolf Zerafin swatted the long grass, causing it to fly into the path of the energy attack and into the vision of Azzeal. As the grass was sliced in two, Zerafin bounded to the side and let out a great bark. Energy rushed from his mouth in the form of a sonic distortion that tore up the ground before him. Rather than counter the attack, Azzeal bored into the earth as his body took on the form of a large vine.

The vine spread across the grass and up a nearby tree. The roots took to the ground and surfaced behind Zerafin, grabbing hold of his hind legs. Zerafin growled. His wolf cry grew strangled and became that of an eagle.

He beat his great wings and took to the sky; his talons dug into the roots that bound his legs. The plant's vines attacked from the forest and entwined themselves to the great eagle's wings. Zerafin realized his doom and returned to Elf form. He raised his vine-entangled arms and dropped to the ground, his arms tucking his head in. From behind him, the water rose up to pummel the plant form of Azzeal. The vines receded, and the spinning form of Azzeal the Elf emerged and outstretched his arms in the direction of the water. Dirt flew up in a ten-foot wall and met the water with equal force. As the two elements became mud, their wielders returned once again to wolf form and leaped at each other under the rain of their own conjuring.

Zerafin was the first to draw blood as they came together and his jaws met the neck of Azzeal. But it had been a feint. As Zerafin's sharp teeth barely penetrated the neck of his opponent, Azzeal's jaw crushed his own throat. Out of panic, Zerafin called upon the power within his heart stone and thrust his forepaws into Azzeal's chest. The energy within the blow blasted the wolf back end over end into the forest.

Zerafin fell to his hands and knees as he returned to Elven form. He eyed his sword, which leaned against a boulder five feet away. The river water lapped at his bare ankles as his eyes went from the sword to the woods. There was a rustling in the woods, and Zerafin utilized his mind sight. Within the swirl of the forest-life pattern, he found Azzeal. As if waiting to be seen, the Elf took the form of a small green dragon, his maw opening with a great inhale. Zerafin let go of his mind sight and called up the water behind him. Great waves rose up and surrounded Zerafin as huge flames leapt forth from the forest, followed by the roar of a dragon. Steam hissed into existence as water met flame and surrounded Zerafin in mist.

"A dragon, no doubt, I take it your studies with the lost beasts have paid off!"

The dragon Azzeal leapt from the woods, his huge claws deepening the ground. He took two bounding steps and leapt into the air as he extended his wings in flight. Zerafin laughed and ducked as the tail nearly smacked his face.

"A dragon, no doubt!"

Azzeal, in dragon form, glided far out across the river and finally turned back. As he returned to Zerafin, he changed into Elven form and fell to the ground, landing before Zerafin in a crouch on one knee. He grinned and rose. Azzeal was a master at the art of the Ralliad, called druids by the humans. He could change into any animal form and that of plants and trees. He had not been seen in more than twenty years as he had been studying the form of the dragon.

He nodded to Zerafin, his gaze moving to the blade Nifarez. "You have been gifted a great power. The time has come then?"

Zerafin regarded the blade thoughtfully and nodded. "Indeed. The time has come for the sleeping Elves of the Sun to awaken. The reckoning draws near."

Azzeal growled deep in his throat with a smile. His feline eyes glowed. "A brother tree tells me that you go to free the one called Whill and the soul of your sister. You plan to storm the castle of Del-Oradon, aided by humans and Dwarves. A horde of Draggard and Dark Elves and Eadon, himself, await you." Azzeal laughed. "And you want me to come accompany you on your mad journey?"

Zerafin nodded, waiting for the laughter to end. Finally, Azzeal stopped, holding his side. "Well then, old friend…when do we leave?"

"Again!" Eadon bellowed as he watched Whill and the man exchange blows. This was Whill's tenth opponent, and he did not have much left for the fight. He had no sword or gems with which to tap into additional power. And Avriel's heart stone had been emptied long ago from the torture. He fought as a man now, and though he could more than hold his own, he had been fighting for an hour, nonstop. The dryness in his mouth was only quenched by blood. Sweat blurred his vision, and dozens of bruises and scratches and cuts, even teeth marks, covered his body.

The fighters used no weapons, but the fighting was brutal and to the death. Each fighter came at Whill with a different discipline of combat; each one was skilled at his own style. But Whill had learned all the many styles of hand-to-hand fighting many years ago with Abram, and he had practiced extensively in each.

The fighting was to the death, or so the many opponents thought, but none could kill Whill, and Whill would kill none of them. Instead, he incapacitated each fighter; expending much more energy than he would have had to if he had killed them. But this was some twisted game of Eadon's, and Whill was not going to give Eadon the satisfaction of seeing him kill the men.

A fist came at his face, which he blocked with a downward windmill of the arm; it was quickly followed by a boot meant for the gut. Whill spun away from the attack and suddenly came back in at his opponent, blocking the man's anticipated follow-up jab while simultane-ously twisting the arm that had dealt the blow. Whill had the man by the wrist and was still moving through his spin as he brought the arm up, ignored a blow to his ribs, and slammed his elbow into the man's armpit while holding the arm at an unnatural angle.

There was an audible pop as Whill dislocated the man's shoulder. Before the man could grimace in pain, Whill reversed his motion and backhanded the fighter and swept his legs out from under him. Again, he reversed his motion as his opponent fell and brought his fist slamming into the man's belly, directly below the breastbone. The impact of the fall and the blow to the chest rendered the man breathless. Whill stumbled with fatigue and fell to the floor upon his knees.

"Get…Up! You rotten maggot meat sack!" screamed Velkarell as he gave the warrior a kick with each word. "Fight or die."

The man finally caught his breath and sat up, cough-ing blood. After a minute, the defeated warrior stood on shaky legs and faced Whill, who still kneeled on the floor, one arm perched upon his knee, breathing deeply still.

"This man has bested me, if I attack him, I will die," the warrior explained between breaths. "Since I will die, I would rather die well, by the hand of the puppet master, not the puppet."

The man raised to his full height and squared off on Eadon and puffed his chest with pride. "If it is my fate to die here then face me like a man, Elf! Fight me like a man, if you even know what that means! We are sick of your dragon-shyte faces and your evil eyes looking upon our land like a fair maiden of youth you would like to bend over the blackberry bush!"

Screaming, he ran forward, fists rose in righteous defiance, revolution and murder in his eyes.

Whill watched as the warrior charged Eadon, and then the Dark Elf lord raised but a hand, and the man was no more than pieces of a man, his form was like that of sand. For three seconds, the pieces held the form of the man, but slowly they separated, and the warrior fell to the floor, with not a thud, but the splash of liquid.

Eadon cracked the knuckles on each hand slowly and then had a good stretch, the bones in his back popping. This, to Whill, seemed not a weird show of bluster, like schoolboys that were always afraid and picked on other kids, but rather a real force of habit, a tic. Whill had noticed a few in his time with the lunatic.

Whill could not understand what fueled this mad Elf's mind. What insane amounts of power and nightmarish ghouls would Eadon wield, create, and let loose on this world? What could be done against such a foe? How, in his lifetime, could Whill defeat one such as Eadon, when the Elf had practiced his art, all arts, for a thousand human lifetimes? Whill began to feel sick as his eyes found the pool of unrecognizable liquid that had been the warrior.

He threw up.

Velkarell laughed. "You are weak, you. You have no stomach for victory?

"No," said Whill from the floor. "I am still human!"

Velkarell laughed louder still. "You are human, and humans are weak."

Whill got to his feet and stood facing the Elf. "We may be weak, but we are fierce! We have killed dragons, Draggard, and even your kind, with no more power than that of our bodies and souls."

Whill spat in the Elf torturer's face and went on. "You are a disease! Bringers of hate-filled rain, creators of doom, deceivers of the soil from which you emerged, you are bringers of death and pain and destruction!"

Whill eyed the grinning Dark Elf with pity. His tone took on that which one would use with a child. "But you have no real power, do you? You have no power to create, only power to destroy. You hate the world for mirroring your vile, soulless selves, and you fear any afterlife for which you may have to answer for your evil. You fear death more than any human. You do not live; you run, and you hide behind power."

Whill's face was but an inch from Velkarell's as he spoke softly to the no-longer-grinning Dark Elf. "Your death will see you begging for mercy like a coward. You will never know the dignity and honor of this man that has just fallen."

Velkarell boiled with anger; his eyes were alight with a distant fire. His rage was a tangible thing as it filled the air between them and physically pushed Whill back a pace.

"Your rage is impotent toward what awaits you," Whill said. "And I promise, I will show you what waits."

"Shut up!" screamed the Elf. A sonic boom emanated from the Elf and blew past Whill without touching him. The blast did, however; tear a hole in the stone wall in a perfect shadowlike outline of Whill. Eadon burst into laughter and clapped his hands. Velkarell grabbed Whill by the throat and lifted him into the air, only to find his arms turning black, as if the pure darkness of the void ran through his veins. Velkarell screamed as his arm turned to dust and Whill fell to his feet. Upon landing, Whill punched the Elf so hard that the blow demolished the protective wards around the Elf's face and broke his jaw.

Velkarell fell back against a wall, quickly putting his face in his hand as blue tendrils of healing energy consumed his head, and a roar of agony and pain echoed throughout the room.

Whill slumped to the floor, exhausted after using so much of his energy smashing through the Elf's defenses. He did not care; he had caused the Dark Elf to lose face before his master, which was enough to justify so stupid a move.

Eadon clapped even louder. "What have I taught you, Velkarell? Nothing? That my newest pupil can get through your defenses so easily without training or even a second studying the arts…"

Eadon's voice became truly enraged. "Have I taught you nothing?"

Velkarell's face emerged from his hand, the same as it had been but for the look upon it. It was a look that Whill didn't think the Elf had worn in many, many years—humility. Velkarell let out a pent-up breath of impotent rage and turned his head in shame. "You have bestowed upon him greater gifts than you have any before him. This you have never done, master. It is unnatural that he can do what he can without training or discipline."

"Unnatural! Coming from the likes of you?" laughed Whill.

"He is what he was meant to be, as are we all," said Eadon.

Two female Dark Elves strode into the room as if they had been beckoned, and darkness followed. They gracefully shifted into the room in unison, their black flowing dresses identical. They were the same in appearance; twins, Whill presumed, though who knew? Some, Whill knew, could change their appearance with a thought. Even worse, some could even hide their true self from mind sight. Whill had seen Travvikonis and Eadon both do it.

Since Addakon's death, Eadon had paraded around the castle and city as the human king. As far as anyone knew, Addakon still ruled the country of Uthen-Arden. Though it was rumored that Addakon had died at the hands of Whill and that Eadon, the Dark Elf, stood in the king's place, no one believed such outlandish stories, and those that told them were ridiculed as conspiracy thinkers.

The twin Dark Elves bowed to their lord, and together, they gave Velkarell a look of disgust and, in turn, gave Whill a look of lust.

Neither one spoke. Instead, they looked to Eadon and waited.

"Take our young friend here down to the arena; he is to be given a regimen of men of his choosing."

Whill looked to Eadon as the twins each gently took an arm and began to lead him out of the room. He did not resist—he couldn't have anyway—they were like stone statues.

CHAPTER NINE

The Shadow of the Arena

Dirk stared at the giant coliseum, lost in thought. From his place near the window of the tavern, he had a clear view of the giant arena. Whill was to be executed there within the week. The new coliseum was rumored to be able to hold more than twenty-five thousand, and he did not doubt that every seat would be taken. Whill of Agora was the rumored savior of many people and a crazed terrorist to others. His execution would bring the largest crowd in history to the arena. With Whill's death would go Dirk's chance to acquire the greatest Elven power source ever created, and that simply would not do.

He had to think of a way to free Whill, but how? The man of legend was being kept within the castle and would probably only be escorted out of it when time came for his execution. If so, Dirk doubted that he could

free Whill from such a lair, even with his extensive abilities. It was a tempting feat, but Dirk had not survived
this long in his field by being stupid. And trying to free
a man from a Dark Elf stronghold was, indeed, stupid.

Dirk wondered if he should simply forgo his interest in
the blade and keep on as he always had. He had amassed
a fortune in his years as a hired assassin and could retire
today, living like a king in any city of his choosing, if it
so pleased him. But a life of leisure, getting fat and wasting away the years, did not appeal to him. Wealth meant
nothing if it did not bring power, and power was Dirk's
ultimate goal. He sought enough power to again find
Krentz and rid the world of any foe that might bring
about her vision of his death in her presence.

*With the sword I could do it. With the sword, the world
would eat from my hand, and none would dare stand against
me. With the sword, I could once again be with my fair Krentz.*

Dirk jumped as the waitress asked him again if he
cared for another drink. He swore under his breath
that the Elf maiden would indeed be the death of him
and mentally chastised himself for the hundredth time
for losing awareness of his surroundings at her thought.

"Yes, another pint of wine," he answered.

Dirk breathed slowly, shunning the thought of Krentz
from his mind and closing his eyes. He listened to the
room around him, calling upon one of the gems within
his earlobe to help him hear every sound within the
room.

"It ain't got nothing to do with skill. It got everything to do with study and hard-earned callous," a blacksmith argued to his colleague.

Dirk extended his senses outward.

"Best fiddler in all the lands he is. Saw him last week, I did, over at the old burnt beard," said another man across the room.

Dirk traveled through the room with his hearing, taking in all the conversations at once, slowly falling into a trance of awareness. It was then that he came to a whispered conversation at the far end of the room.

"I tell ya what, if the king thinks that he is going to be able to rid himself of Whill of Agora that easily, then he's got another thing coming," stated a man with a gruff voice.

"Oh yeah?" countered a weasel-voiced man. "The way I see it, if this Whill was so powerful, he wouldn't have gotten himself caught in the first place."

"Beh, you know nothing, Gerld! I heard what he can do just as well as you did. He healed a baby in Sherna and single-handedly killed a hunr'd Draggard. He and his buddy there, what's his name, Abram, done killed Cirrosa and his whole crew," the gruff-voiced man retorted.

"Yeah, yeah, and he pisses wine and farts opium smoke. You been listenin' to too many drunkards and crazies, Mik. This boy didn't do none of that."

"Then why is he to be executed? Eh? If the man is of myth and legend, then what be the point in the big show, huh? Use your damned head, Gerld! He is a real threat to the crown; else they wouldn't bother with the big show."

"He ain't no threat to the crown; he be their prisoner. And for good reason. I hear that he be in league with the Draggard and Dark Elves himself."

Mik scoffed at that statement, and Dirk heard him take a long swig from his glass. "All I know is that my brother-in-law got himself a gig with arena security, and he says that this execution ain't gonna be no cut-and-dry affair. They are gonna give Whill a group of men, and a battle is gonna play out in that arena, and I, for one, am going to be there for it."

Dirk opened his eyes and looked to the arena.

Another man piped in from another table. "I'll wager ten silver that Whill, the traitor of men, cries like a babe when the time comes. Serves him right, siding with the Dark Elves and stinkin' Eldalon."

Mik rose to his feet and pointed a finger at the eavesdropper. "Listen here, you sheep-minded follower. Where was your great king when the Draggard invaded the Ebony Mountains, eh? Where was your great king when his twin brother was murdered for the crown? Holdin' the bloody blade, I say!"

The man that had interrupted rose to his feet so fast his chair skidded across the floor. "Listen here, you conspiracy freak. Words like that against the king be punishable by hangin'."

Mik took a step toward the man. "Case in point, sir! Any king that outlaws any kind of speech be a corrupt scoundrel and no king of mine."

Dirk left the tavern as the fight broke out and ducked his head as the royal guard went running past him. Scenes such as that was commonplace in the last few months as the city and, indeed, the entire country teetered upon the brink of civil war. Though the propaganda machines worked tirelessly to spread lies against Whill, there were still those men and women alike that could tell lies when they heard them and saw the world for what it was. It was the masses, though, that had the vote on what was real and what was not, and, unfortunately, the masses were not always right.

Dirk headed in the direction of one of his informants. He would have to find out the whereabouts of Whill and quick, if he was to free Whill from his doom before the week was out.

He reached the rendezvous and found his informant waiting for him. He took a quick survey of the nearby street and surrounding buildings. He sensed no eyes upon him. The informant nodded when he saw him and walked over to Dirk.

"So what do you have of use for me, Nick?"

"Well, hello to you too, Dirk," Nick responded with a fake pout.

Dirk did not respond. He had decided that he did not like the skinny, twitchy man very much after all.

"Straight to the point it is then, eh?" Nick asked with a twitch.

"My money is straight to the point, is it not, Nick? Quit wasting my time."

"Alright, alright, there ain't no more common courtesy anymore, there ain't. So I been askin' around and got me eyes looking this way and that."

Dirk rolled his eyes and took a slow, deep breath.

Nick wisely got to the point. "What I hear is that this Whill character has been holed up in the castle, down in the dungeon, for more than six months. He'll be training with the rest of the prisoners by day. And by night he is to be brought back to the castle."

"How good is your information?" Dirk asked.

"Why, as good as it ever is."

Dirk conceded the point with a nod and handed Nick a small sack of coins and turned and walked away.

"Alright then, be seeing you around!" Nick called after him.

Dirk took a roundabout route back to his lodging. His mind worked out all that he had learned. It would be almost as hard to spring Whill from the stadium as it would be to get him out of the castle. The stadium would be heavily guarded with humans and Dark Elves alike. It would take a small army to break Whill free from such a place. If he was left there during the night, it would be easier, but he was being transferred out of the arena at night.

Dirk turned down an alley and pondered the situation. Ahead he noticed three would-be ruffians taking notice of him. Their bodies stiffened as he neared, and he saw two of them lower their hands to their pockets. He toyed with the idea of letting them attack, just to clear his head with a little combat, but dismissed the idea. Instead, as he reached them, he swept his cloak to one side of his body, showing the many weapons stored there along his person.

The young men looked to the many weapons and to Dirk's face. They backed out of his way as he slowly shook his head, indicating that it would be the last bad choice they would ever make. The only thing to be seen under the shadow of his enchanted hood was two moonlit eyes gleaming.

He walked on. No matter what he thought of, the idea seemed like nothing less than suicide. It then occurred to him that as he had seen the flyer about Whill, so too would Whill's friends. Dirk had heard enough to know that Whill moved in some powerful circles. It was rumored that he had such friends as Elves and even the Dwarf king of the Ro'Sar Mountains. Whill was the grandson of King Mathus of Eldalon. Dirk knew also of the prophecy and would wager his wealth that they would be coming for Whill before his time was up. He did not need to free Whill from his bonds; he simply had to be in the right place when Whill's friends did. He had to get himself arrested.

His decision made, he journeyed to one of his pre-determined hiding places within the city. Into the city's sewer system he slipped, without being seen by any but the rats. A short walk into the grime-covered tunnels brought him to his destination. He removed a series of bricks from the wall to uncover his hiding place.

He then stripped himself of everything he wore, weapons and armor alike, until all that remained were his underclothes. He stopped and thought again for another way but found none. Once again committed to his choice, he shrugged off the empty feeling of being without his many weapons and trinkets and armor and reapplied the bricks.

Confident that his possessions were safe, he returned once again to the street. He had gotten rid of his weapons and the like, but one thing remained that he could not be rid of. Krentz had given it to him during their time together. It was a single gem embedded into his chest. He could not call upon the energy within it at will, but it would respond to any injury he might attain. He could only hope that it would go unnoticed by the Dark Elves, for he had no way to be rid of it.

He walked until he found his mark. There were two of them, actually, walking toward him down a fairly busy bit of street. To attack a guard of the city was punishable by death these days, and the extreme punishment made it that much more surprising an act. Dirk came in low and fast and took the first guard by surprise, sweeping his legs and landing a blow to his unarmored face before the man knew what was happening. Dirk jumped and spun on the next guard, who was busy wondering what had happened to his partner. The kick connected with the man's armored chest and sent him back many paces.

The guard on the ground tried to pull his sword from the ground but fumbled. Dirk landed another blow to his face with his bare foot, and blood sprayed. Dirk spun back as the other guard's sword slashed through the air and missed his face by inches. The infuriated guard slashed again and again, and Dirk twirled out of reach.

"This is how the mighty Del-Oradon Guard fights an unarmed man?" Dirk yelled, getting the attention of all nearby.

The street fell into a hush as all eyes turned to Dirk and the guards. Taverns and shops alike emptied. People peered through windows and began to fill the street.

"I have done nothing, yet these scoundrels attack me—I, who am unarmed and of no threat. Down with the guard! Down with the king!"

The guard upon the ground got to his feet as the other circled around Dirk, trying to put his brother at arms at Dirk's back.

Dirk saw the ploy and went with it, crafting one of his own. "Down with the gut-rotten king! Down with the guards—his pawns against the people of this nation!" Dirk howled with all his might.

Many in the crowd began to cheer in approval; many disappeared, wanting nothing to do with the rebellious spirit at hand. The two guards rushed Dirk at the same time, from each direction, as he had anticipated. He jumped high into the air and performed a backflip over and out of the reach of the soldier behind him. The two men crashed together with a loud retort of armor upon armor, and Dirk, upon landing, booted the nearest in the rear, causing them both to fall into a mess of flailing arms and armor.

"Down with the king and his clowns!"

Two more soldiers emerged and hollered at the crowd to be gone. Dirk grabbed tomatoes from the nearest cart and began to pelt them both. Furious, the men charged. Dirk charged also and came up under the sword of one so quickly that the man blinked in astonishment when Dirk smashed him in the face with a tomato. Dirk quickly spun out of reach and ran back to the vegetables. Again, he began to pelt the men as they chased him round and round the marketplace. Now a huge crowd of hundreds filled the street and watched the fiasco. A dozen more guards came pounding down the street and parted the crowd.

"Down with the clown guard! Down with the false king of Uthen-Arden! Long live Whill of Agora! Long live Whill of Agora!" Dirk continued to holler as the guards fanned out and flanked him. He now had the attention of hundreds of people and was safe. Though a few guards may have tried to kill him then and there, a captain of the guard was now present. He would not allow an unarmed madman to be killed in broad daylight with hundreds of witnesses, or so Dirk hoped. He prepared himself mentally for the beating that would follow and charged the line of guards. He barreled into one, knocking him over, before he was grabbed by half a dozen and driven to the ground.

Abram and Rhunis stared at the model of the arena they had hastily constructed. They had spent hours trying to devise a plan of attack and had come up with little. Abram packed his pipe and lit it as he walked to the window of their room within the inn. Outside, the crowd had dissipated, and the raving man that had caused the ruckus had been taken away.

"There were many cheers for the man who spoke of Whill," Abram noted as he looked to the distant arena. It towered over all other buildings and could be seen from nearly all points within the city.

"Indeed," Rhunis agreed.

"What if we…No, never mind, that will never work."

Rhunis slammed his fist down upon the table in frustration. "We need an army of a thousand men to directly attempt such a feat."

"We do not have a thousand men," said Abram as he watched his smoke ring float lazily toward the window only to be obliterated in the breeze. "What we have is the element of surprise."

Rhunis scoffed. "Surely Eadon will be expecting and will be prepared for a rescue attempt. This entire thing may be a trap. Making Whill's execution public, announcing it to the world…he is practically inviting us into his clutches."

Abram nodded in agreement. "Indeed, but what are we to do? Foil Eadon by not trying to free Whill? He is to be killed. We must intervene."

"Why has Eadon not yet killed Whill then? Why wait six months before executing him? There is nothing Eadon could hope to learn from Whill through torture. He is baiting us, my friend."

"I have not waited in the dark to hear word of Whill to sit idly by now that I have found him. I will free him from the Dark Elves, or I will die trying!"

"Old friend, I do not doubt your resolve. Among men, you are one of the greatest warriors I have ever known, but against the Dark Elves, what power do you have?"

Abram rapped his pipe on the windowsill and pocketed it, pondering the question. "The only power I have is that of faith. I believe in the prophecy; therefore, I believe that Whill will not die in the arena. I believe he will be freed to fulfill his destiny."

"Then let us not run in haste into the arms of the Dark Elves. Let us await the counsel of Zerafin."

Abram looked again to the arena. He knew Rhunis's words to be true; he understood that haste in the matter would be folly. If the execution was indeed a trap, then there was to be no surprise attack. He would do Whill no service by being captured or killed. But what if Eadon was through with Whill; what if he had not been able to break him? Abram had to believe that Whill would make it out, and he intended on being the one to help him.

CHAPTER TEN
The Silverhawk Rider of Ro'Sar

Roakore inspected his ax in the torchlight; the blade had known its share of nicks and scrapes over the years. Satisfied with the edge, he put his collection of sharpening stones in their leather case and stowed them away within his traveling pack.

Nah'Zed watched her king with a scowl the whole while. Roakore ignored the glare. His mind was made up: he was king after all, and the decision was his alone. Whill was set to be executed in less than five days, and Roakore had pondered the situation for two days too many. He would not be moved in his resolve now that his mind had been made up.

Finally, after so long watching Roakore pack and sharpen his blade while ignoring her, Nah'Zed could take it no longer. "You been king for less than a year, sire;

yer place be here! We're still rebuildin' for Ky'Dren's sake."

"Hold yer tongue! We been through this! Me mind's made up."

"Yer people need ya here, sire!"

Roakore turned on Nah'Zed with a scowl, but his anger quickly died as he saw the tears that streamed down her cheeks. Roakore let out a sigh. "Aye, and me friend be needin' me too. I can't be two places at once. Whill be in the worst kind o' trouble, and I be able to help him."

"But ye said yerself, sire, the Elf—"

"Zerafin," Roakore corrected her.

"Zerafin and Abram and the rest o' them will be sure to attempt a rescue; ye said it so yerself."

"Aye," Roakore agreed. "And I'll be there to help"

Nah'Zed bowed her head in defeat.

Roakore lifted her chin with his hand and brought her eyes to his. "Whill would do the same fer me. And I would do it for any o' me friends. Fret not; it been quiet along the mountainsides since the reclamation. I be leavin' the clan in the able hands o' me son. Besides, Whill be an important part o' this fight. Helpin' free him be the best thing I could be doin' for the clan, for all the clans."

Nah'Zed wiped her eyes with the back of her hand. "You be puttin' too much stake in this Whill."

"You were not there; ye didn't see the dark scourge that emptied from me mountains and spread across the lands. An that be but a fraction o' their numbers. The Draggard be ravishin' all the land as we speak, and the war ain't even truly begun. If the Dark Elves ain't stopped, all the land will burn and the mountains will crumble. Whill o' Agora be named in an ancient prophecy to be the one to put a stop to the Dark Elves, an' I, for one, be believing it."

Nah'Zed squared her shoulders and looked her king in the eye. She took up his traveling pack and nodded. "Then be swift, me king, and may yer ax be true. For every day you be away be a day o' sorrow for the Ro'Sar Mountains."

Roakore made his way up the great, winding stair. It had been recently added to the city and led to a high chamber near the peak of Mount Havrokk. He had made the journey almost daily in the last six months, and now he was glad he had.

As he crested the top of the stair, he heard the telltale squawk of Silverwind. She stood rigid with anticipation behind her cloak of camouflage that made her blend in flawlessly with the surrounding rock wall; if Roakore had not known what to look for, he may not have noticed the great bird. Upon seeing Roakore, Silverwind gave a great squawk and changed back to her natural color of bright silver.

Roakore greeted the massive bird with a big smile and a handful of hawk's bane. Silverwind tentatively took the treat from her master's hand and crooned with joy as she ate and the king petted her head.

Roakore nodded to the human nearby. Horris had been a Silverhawk trainer of the Shierdon Kingdom. When word came down through the black-market contacts that a certain wealthy Dwarf was offering a fortune for a Silverhawk chick, he had jumped at the opportunity. He had brought Silverwind to Roakore and received his fortune; he also stayed on to help the king train the bird, for a hefty fee of course.

"She ain't full grown yet, but I would bet she will hold your weight...I think. I loaded a pouch of hawk's bane, and the new saddle should be more to your liking, king."

Roakore petted the bird's lowered beak as it savored its bane; he pulled on a saddle strap and simply grunted.

Horris presented Roakore with a cloak of black feathers, those of Silverwind. "Now for the true test, sire; now for the 'test o' Silverwind,' as you would say. If you put on the cloak and it remains black, it is not to be. If it turns silver, well, then you know...then, my friend, you can fly."

Roakore eyed the cloak with trepidation. He was not a Dwarf that often, or ever, knew defeat, since that dreaded day so long ago. He had resolved to never again fail in something that he had set his heart and soul on. He dreaded putting on the cloak to find it black.

Roakore reluctantly took the cloak with his right hand; then he found his resolve, and he listened to his gut. Silverwind was not going to bond with any other than the most confident of persons. She would not allow any but the utmost courageous and bold a rider.

The great hawk eyed Roakore and the cloak intently, her racial memory reminding her of what such a moment meant. Her eyes went wide, and she took a step back, ruffling her feathers and spreading her wings in warning. Roakore hesitated as he took the cloak in both hands and faced her. She let out a great squawk and backed up a step from the king, pounding him with the wind of her wings. Then she hissed.

"I be needin' ya to help right many wrongs, great hawk." Roakore stepped closer. "I be needin' yer help in rescuing me friend."

Silverwind squawked angrily but held her ground. With her head low, her feathers bulged to increase her size and intimidation factor.

Roakore put on the cloak swiftly with an outstretching of his arms. Silverwind turned in a half circle and smashed him in the side and shoulder with a gut-rocking blow. Roakore flew into the nearby wall, hard enough to make him see a few stars.

He got to his feet in an instant, clearing his head with sheer willpower as his father had taught him. "Let the mind be dizzy and confused; let yer soul take over."

Roakore faced the great bird in his black cloak of failure. He squared his feet and bellowed, "Silverwind,

I named ye! I am to be your rider! Together I promise great adventure and glory!"

The bird cocked her head and took a step toward the Dwarf king, his entire body no larger than her neck. She leaned her head to the right as if to groom herself, and then she shyly batted her eyelids and crooned. Roakore burst out in a smile and reached for her.

Horris had no time to warn Roakore as the bird's great beak came up and caught him between the legs and lifted him so high that his head smacked against the stone ceiling fifteen feet above. He fell like a rock.

Roakore groaned and heeded his father's advice and got to his feet, though to his dismay, he found that his feet would not hold him. He reached up and felt his bloody head. A knot had already begun to form. Roakore let out a deafening roar, and the hawk perched, ready to attack, and waited.

"She is testing you good, king. This is a time of trials. Fail here and you may die."

Roakore grimaced at the trainer. "What the bloody hell am I supposed to do now?"

Horris backed to the safety of the room entrance, directly adjacent to the twenty-foot-wide archway leading to the night sky behind the hawk. "I cannot help you in this. This is your 'trial by feathers' as they call it. You and you alone can tame this bird or be killed by it."

Roakore thought about another plea, but he quickly dismissed the idea. *What gesture would I respect? Hhmm. That which I already respect, of course!*

Roakore walked bravely toward the bird until his face was but a foot away from hers. He then smiled. The bird tilted its head slightly to the right, a telltale sign. But Roakore did not wait for the resulting action; rather, he put all of his weight and strength into an uppercut blow to the bird's beak that caused its head to snap back suddenly and clip the ceiling.

The great bird shook its head and reared until it hit the stone wall behind it. Roakore squared his legs and made fists that caused his knuckles to pop. "I be yer rider, bird!"

Good," whispered Horris as he slunk behind the archway to the stair, one eye only peering at the battle. "Now, she will truly try to kill you."

Roakore could hardly ask what Horris had said, and the bird was charging. He was deafened by an ear-piercing shriek that literally made his ears bleed. The great bird came at him, meaning to squash him with her weight. But Roakore proved the quicker as he slid sideways and out of range. He rebounded off the wall to the right of the bird and came in hard at her side with two flying boots. The blow sent the hawk lurching to the side to almost fall from the open archway to the night beyond.

Roakore climbed upon her back as she lurched and spread her wings to catch herself from the fall. Even as

Roakore climbed the base of her neck, she regained her footing and instantly rolled upon her back. Roakore was crunched with over one thousand pounds of bird. Fearing that his bones would be crushed to dust under the great weight, he instinctively called upon the stone around him.

Silverwind was slammed sideways off of Roakore by a slab of stone that suddenly protruded from the wall. Another slab caught the bird on the other side, and two came from both above and below to trap the bird in a viselike grip. Silverwind thrashed and kicked until finally Roakore rose and, facing the bird, ordered, "Be still!"

Silverwind froze; its eyes wide.

"Now is the time! Make the connection, just as we have learned. Hurry, lest the moment pass you by! You have her attention and respect!"

Roakore grabbed the trapped bird's head with his strong hands and pressed his head to that of Silverwind's. Their eyes met, and instantly, the connection was made, and the cloak of black feathers began to glow bright silver. Roakore released Silverwind from the stone trap but held her head steady.

"Yer mine, bird, and yer name be Silverwind. As I be yer rider, we'll make history, we will; that I be promisin'."

Horris clapped and smacked Roakore on the back. Silverwind was on him in a heartbeat, knocking him to the ground and letting out an ear-piercing cry. She held him there with one massive claw that covered his entire body and looked, with a tilted head, to Roakore.

"Bwahaha! She means business now, don't she, Horris? She be waitin' fer me to give the go-ahead to take yer head off! Well done, lad, well done!"

Horris could hardly find the breath to answer. "Thank you, sir."

"Let him go, Silverwind; save your beak for one more deserving."

Just then Tarren came huffing up the stairs, calling the king's name. "Roakore, Roakore, wait!"

He was followed by Lunara and Haldagozz and Roakore's son Helzendar. Tarren's eyes went from the nine-foot-tall Silverhawk to Roakore's cloak of silver feathers.

"By Ky'Dren's beard, Father, ye got yerself a Silverhawk?" asked Helzendar.

"Oh man, are the Shierdonians gonna be mad ye got one of their birds," said Tarren and whistled.

"Bah, let 'em be whatever they want. They don't own the creatures; the creatures be ownin' themselves. And if they be that upset, let 'em come try an take her from me!"

Tarren stared in wonder at the magnificent wings of the bird as she looked longingly to the mouth of the chamber and the night sky beyond. Roakore also noticed the bird's look and began loading his bags.

"You are going to try and free Whill, aren't you?" asked Tarren.

"I be doin' just that, laddie."

"C—"

"And before you ask, the answer be no!" Roakore interrupted.

"But—"

"This ain't no game, son. There ain't no place for a child on this quest. I be goin' into enemy territory here."

Roakore watched as Tarren's head sank. He understood the boy's want to go, to be part of the adventure. But the truth of the matter was that he was a child, and battle was no place for him.

"Besides, ye got the trials comin' up, don't ye?"

Tarren did not answer; he simply sulked.

"Well?!" demanded Roakore.

"Yes, I got the trials coming."

"Well then, finishin' the trials is what you'll be doin'. Till then, you be in Lunara and Haldagozz's care. When we free Whill, he can decide where yer place will be, fair enough?"

"Yes, sir."

Roakore finished loading his packs on the saddle and strapped his ax to his back. With the help of Horris, he climbed into the saddle of the bent bird. He carefully strapped himself in and checked the straps with a tug. Satisfied, he faced his son.

"Ye be keepin' an eye on Tarren here also, lad; he be the ward o' me friend."

"Yes, Father, me king."

Roakore saddled up, pulled the reigns left, and turned the great Silverhawk to face the ledge.

"Father? What's it like eh? Bein able to fly an such."?"

Roakore turned to his son and shrugged. "I aint knowin, son, but I'm 'bout to find out. Hopefully it don't feel like fallin' to me death."

Helzendar stared, openmouthed.

"Wait," urged Lunara as she ran forward. "The Silverhawk has no armor or protection from enemy arrows."

"She can't hold the weight o' me and armor, lady; besides, it would interfere with her camouflage."

"I know, good king. Would you allow me to add some protection to your mount?" Roakore eyed the Sun Elf healer. He had seen her work before and knew her skill. Haldagozz himself had been brought back from the brink of death, and, indeed, he had been made stronger, his bones thicker. Roakore welcomed any defense offered.

"Aye, do what ye will then."

Lunara nodded her thanks and began to chant softly to herself as she waved her hands slowly from one end of the great bird to the other. Small sparks, like static electricity, popped and hissed near and around the Silverhawk, each beginning to grow and strike out to one another. The great hawk stirred, but Roakore hushed her. He could feel the energy like a tickle up his spine as it engulfed him and his mount. With a deep breath, Lunara finished.

"The ward will protect her from enemy arrows and much more. But it will take from her energy if the blow is too much. Be careful, Roakore. Do not fly into danger thinking she is invincible. Do not test the ward or dive foolhardily into danger because of it."

Roakore looked taken aback. "Me? Dive into danger?"

Haldagozz let out a great belly laugh at that, which was taken up by Roakore also. Without further words, he kicked the chest of the great bird, and it jumped to comply. Three great strides took them to the ledge and beyond. The group ran to the ledge to watch the first flight of Roakore.

Silverwind tucked her wings and dropped like a stone as Roakore held on for his life. In the moonlight, he could make out the many mountains that made up his kingdom. Though the wind took it, he could not have caught his breath at the sight of the great peaks, and the tears that found his eyes were not only from the incredible wind.

Silverwind fell for a few hundred feet before opening her wings and catching the night current. The force of the maneuver made Roakore want to puke, but he choked down his gorge. Freezing tears fogged his sight, and he remembered the glass goggles upon his head.

He frantically put them on and tucked his head to catch his breath. Finally, he pulled the cloth over his face that Horris had said would help him breathe.

Now able to see and breathe, Roakore took in the mountains around him and was awed. As Silverwind banked hard left around a peak, Roakore let out a great howl that was met by the delighted screech of Silverwind.

CHAPTER ELEVEN

What Say You Dirk Blackthorn?

Dirk was taken to a holding cell of the city guard. He was charged with several counts of attacking a guard and disturbing the peace. The disturbing-the-peace charge was worth a night in the cell; the attack charge was much more serious. He waited for the inevitable for only two hours and was brought before a judge, whom sentenced him to death. As he had anticipated, he was offered a chance to redeem himself before the king in the gladiator arena, and he took it.

Now he and many others sparred within the arena training room, a vast space beneath the seats of the arena, large enough to hold two hundred men. There were many there like him, sentenced to death for some crime against the kingdom. Dirk loathed having to keep company and share quarters with such scum; rapists, thieves, and the like. But he did so anyway. He watched, and he learned, and he fought like a champion. Already he had broken the nose and jaw of a man and the arm of another. This got him a beating from the guard, but it was worth it—for he had caught the attention of the legendary Whill of Agora.

Whill had come the day before to watch the many condemned men; it was rumored that he was to pick a team that would fight alongside him within the arena in a few days' time. Dirk wondered what all the fuss was about. Indeed, the Whill he had seen did not look like someone that songs were sung about or stories told. He was a too-thin man with sunken eyes and a distant stare. He looked like death had already taken him.

Nonetheless, Dirk fought hard when he knew Whill was watching. Whill had left on that first day without choosing anyone, but Dirk was sure that he had caught Whill's attention.

There were many other warriors within the group of over two hundred prisoners. He recognized half-dozen plainsmen of the north, whom were incredible with a spear and sling. A few men he even knew from the streets, cutthroats and killers each. There were also defectors, soldiers that had refused an order or had simply abandoned their post.

One warrior in particular had caught Dirk's atten-tion, and he was sure she would catch the attention of Whill also. She was a barbarian from the northern island of Volnoss. He had not caught her name yet and knew only that she had been arrested for killing two guards in some skirmish on the northern border of Arden. Dirk had seen her take on seven men in hand-to-hand combat without breaking a sweat. She was well over seven feet tall, and while not quite muscled like a man, she was heavily muscled all the same. She wore white bear furs from her northern region, but in this climate, they consisted of only trousers cut off at the knees and a top that covered her large bust but not without revealing much of it.

Most men that attacked her, though she was huge, still felt strange about attacking a woman, and a beautiful woman at that. He watched many a man fall for her smile and a toss of her long blond hair, only to be taken out by her masterful fists. He would not be so stupid.

Though Dirk was without his weapons, there were many readily available. He had chosen for the training a wide variety of them. Having practiced extensively with an Elf, he enjoyed a bit of an advantage over most. He had chosen for these fights, however, double swords. He did not assume that he would be fighting anything as thick-skinned as the Draggard here, and he could take any man with his twin blades.

The following day Whill came once again to the training center and watched while his human guards stood watch. Many men tried hard to gain the attention of Whill, as it was believed that those that were not chosen would fight against him and those he did choose would fight with the legend. One man, whom had yet to be beaten, turned to Whill after defeating yet another fellow trainee and threw his blade to the ground.

"Well then! Mr. Whill of friggin lore! Let's see what all the fuss is about then. Why should we be fightin' hard to win your approval if you ain't yet even shown us your own skill? Who says we be wantin' to even be part of your death club? Eh?"

Just then the king of Uthen-Arden stepped out from the stair leading to the arena. None but Whill and the hidden Dark Elves knew that it was truly Eadon, wearing the king's image. The man shut his mouth, but the king had heard his words.

"It is true, is it not?" said the king. "All we have yet heard of you, Whill of Agora, are songs and rumors. Why should any believe you are but the feeble man we see before us? What have you done that is not but a fable? If you are indeed the savior of legend, why is it that you cannot even save yourself?"

The man that had spoken before straightened and smirked. Whill looked to the king with nothing but disdain. "I will not play your games."

The king arched an eyebrow. "Is that so?"

He turned to the prisoners and gestured to them all. "Who would fight for a man that does not take up the blade when called out?"

He looked back to Whill. "Who would stand by your side voluntarily, when you are obviously nothing but a coward hiding behind legend? Hmm? Who would stand behind Whill of Agora?"

"I would!" The words left Dirk's mouth before he had willed them. This was a perfect time to get Whill's attention. Dirk stepped forward and faced the man who had challenged Whill.

Whill's head jerked as he seemed to see Dirk for the first time.

"Excellent," said the king. "A fight to the death then! Guards, give them blades with an edge! Let us see how well a follower fairs against one less inclined to delusion."

Dirk smirked at the proclamation and indicated that he preferred the twin blades. The loudmouth man took up a giant broadsword. They both looked to the king to begin.

"Might we add a prize, aside from life? For your loyalty, I will grant you freedom," he said to the loudmouth.

He addressed Dirk and seemed to ponder something. "For you…a place at the side of Whill during his execution. So that you may at least die for what you believe. Now, fight!"

The loudmouth was on Dirk in a flash, the giant broadsword whooshing through the air in a huge arc that would cleave the head off a bull. Dirk twirled out of the way, but the man only used the momentum of the great sword to spin with the attack and came in with another. Dirk knew the man's mind and came in after the first swipe had passed and before the man could bring the blade around, slamming both hilts into his face with a crossed-sword blow that sent him flying.

The man fell like a stone but quickly recovered. He regained his feet and wiped the blood from his nose and mouth. He spat blood and again charged Dirk. An overhead blow was deflected high and to the side. As the man ran by, Dirk caught his foot with his own and sent the man once again sprawling in the dirt.

Dirk looked to the king. "Are you sure you would not like to change your wager? I could kill this man with but my hands."

The king cocked his head at this. "Indeed? Then, by all means, drop your blades."

Everyone looked to Dirk. The training had stopped, and even the guards watched on in fascination. Dirk dropped his swords and faced the man with his arms slack at his sides.

The loudmouth smirked and came in with an over-head blow, which Dirk dodged. Another blow came in from the right, another from the left, and both were dodged. Dirk brought up his fists and began to dance a fighter's dance.

"I give you this one chance, loudmouth. Accept defeat, and I will not kill you. Attack me again, and I will rip out your throat."

The man responded with an unintelligible growl. He screamed in frustration and came in with an impaling blow. Everyone thought that the blow would land, when, at the last moment, Dirk twirled to the left and came across with a nose-shattering backhand to the man's face. The loudmouth staggered and turned, but before he could even think of a counter, Dirk was on his back, literally, hammering elbows into the man's neck. Dirk crossed his legs over the man's body and caused him to fall to the dirt, with Dirk on his back.

Loudmouth's blade had fallen under him along with both hands, essentially pinning them. Dirk grabbed a handful of hair and, with his other hand, reached for the man's throat. He then made good on his promise. Dirk stood from the dying man as his breath gurgled.

Whill watched the dying man and slowly brought his eyes up to meet Dirk's. Dirk could not begin to read the look on Whill's face. Whill looked again to the dying man and then to the king. "His reward will be honored?"

The king could only raise his chin in defeat and nod. Whill walked on to survey the other fighters without so much as a glance back at Dirk.

After Whill strode away, the king pointed at Dirk. "Bring him!"

The Elves left the coast and thick forests of Elladrindellia and came out into the sparse plains of Uthen-Arden.

The night was faintly illuminated by a moon mostly hidden by cloud. But to an Elf, it mattered not. Rain had ravished the plains for over two weeks, and the fresh smell of life was intoxicating to Zerafin.

The horses would have fallen dead had their riders not been Elves with the ability to transfer energy to them and keep them running comfortably. But the horses still needed food and drink, lest they be uncomfortably driven. The long grass growing near a small stream offered such a chance for pause.

The Elves reared their steeds and dismounted, letting the animals graze as they may. They would pause for a half an hour and be on the road once more. Stealth was not needed as they could hide themselves from any human eyes easily enough. Zerafin would lead his Elves near to the gates of the city where they would break up into groups and begin the infiltration of Eadon's castle. Many understood this to be quite possibly a suicide mission, but none cared, and all had volunteered.

Zerafin had welcomed the help, but he was the only one of the group that had vowed not to return unless he freed Whill and the soul of his sister, Avriel. Zerafin was sure that the execution of Whill was a trap, for without Whill, Eadon's hopes to find the blade would be in vain. The greatest question on Zerafin's mind was, had Eadon already acquired the blade?

Dirk was brought high up into a castle tower. It was, he assumed, the king's own dwelling. Upon entering the room, Dirk was pushed forward, and the guards closed the door with a slam. The king strode from the shadows of the vast room and spoke but a word, and every candle within burst into light. The king shimmered and distorted, and before Dirk stood an imposing Dark Elf.

Dirk's senses screamed for him to run, that he should not be here. He had judged horribly in his plan. Dirk knew that before him stood the legendary Eadon, the very Dark Elf that had sent so many assassins after his dear Krentz.

"I see that there is no point in playing games with you…What did you say your name was?"

"I didn't."

Eadon chuckled. "Very well."

Dirk felt a strange presence within his mind, a stabbing blade of ice that numbed his resistance instantly and caused his mind to cry only surrender.

"Dirk it is then," said Eadon as the blades of ice receded, and Dirk let out a groan and grimace, instantly furious for the trespass on his mind, but also equally afraid of the implications.

"Yes, even now you are contemplating the fact that I can steal from your mind anything I wish. So rather than go through the painful process of tearing my answers from your simple mind, how about you simply answer me truthfully?"

Dirk looked to the window, gauging the distance between it, himself, and Eadon. The Dark Elf followed his eyes. "Go ahead; give it a try. It should be good for a laugh at the least."

"What is it you want to know?" growled Dirk angrly.

Eadon moved to a cabinet and opened one of the glass doors. He withdrew a bottle of dark liquid and proceeded to pour two glasses. He held a glass up to the candlelight and moved it slowly, causing the liquid to swirl gently. He strode to Dirk.

"Eldenberry wine from the vineyards of Drindellia," said Eadon. He brought his nose to the glass and took in a deep inhale. A subtle moan escaped him.

"This one is six hundred years old. I froze it in time, so to speak; I can almost remember the year when I smell it."

He handed Dirk a glass. Dirk eyed the Dark Elf and smelled the wine; he lifted it to his lips and emptied the glass. The wine was delicious, but he hardly noticed. Eadon took a sip from his glass and marveled. "The pleasures in life never cease."

When Dirk did not reply, Eadon added, "Nor does the pain."

Still Dirk remained silent. Eadon returned his and Dirk's glasses to the cabinet bar. "You will not beg for your life, will you? You will not grovel or plead. You will die defiantly. There is nothing I can do to you that you are not prepared for—of course, I think that I could think of something. But when you are more than five thousand years old, torture loses its appeal. I would much rather come to a conclusion that we can both agree upon civilly. I would rather not take your mind; I would rather it was given freely. If you work with me, for me, I will keep your beloved Krentz alive."

Dirk flinched at the mention of Krentz; he did not bother trying to hide his emotion. Nothing could be kept from Eadon it seemed.

"Did you not know that she had been captured? It is true, my Dark Elves found her not three months ago. She is my prisoner."

The Dark Elf turned and looked out of the window. "If you please me through your actions, then I will let you both live, and I will let you be free, forever untouched by anything of my creation, untouched by the Dark Elves. You will be given a pass for all of eternity."

Eadon turned and walked slowly toward Dirk. "What say you, Dirk Blackthorn?"

Dirk set his jaw proudly, thinking of spitting in the Dark Elf's face. If it was his own fate on the line, he would have done so already, but the life of Krentz was on the line. With effort, he swallowed his anger and rage. "I will do what you ask, for the life of Krentz."

Eadon only smiled.

CHAPTER TWELVE

Fire Off Yonder a Ways

Roakore traveled into ever-warmer skies long into the morning and afternoon. He had passed the border into Uthen-Arden long before the sun had come up. He had traveled many miles, but he was becoming weary of the hours of tense inactivity upon the great Silverhawk. His legs were sore and his back stiff, and he could sense as much from Silverwind.

A smoke caught his eye to the south, and he began to steer his hawk in that direction. She let out a low hiss and attempted to veer back on course.

"Bha, bird, I be wantin' to know what be over there. See, something's ablaze, and it ain't no campfire," said Roakore as he pulled on the reigns.

Silverwind reared her head, nearly throwing Roakore from his saddle. If not for the strap across his lap, he would have fallen to his death.

"Listen here, bird, you'll be doin' as I be sayin'!"

Silverwind let out a squawk and began a gut-turning dive toward the ground. Roakore became weightless, and his complaint was swallowed as they dropped like a stone. Silverwind leveled out no more than ten feet from the ground. Roakore was bathed in pollen as her wings passed over a field of dandelions. He barely had time to scrape the flowers from his tongue when Silverwind turned sideways, causing him to be battered by a series of branches.

"That's it! Let me off you, ye blasted, crazy bird."

Silverwind immediately obeyed and landed. Roakore huffed and puffed incoherently as he fumbled with the strap that held him. As soon as the latch sounded, Silverwind took to the air once again, leaving Roakore to hold on to the saddle for dear life. Silverwind caught air and leveled out but quickly dive-bombed straight for a small pond. Roakore was left holding on only by the saddle straps, legs flailing. Silverwind abruptly turned in a full circle as she leveled out above the water. Roakore let go and fell with a splash into the pool.

The great weight of Roakore's ax sunk him straight to the bottom. It was not a very deep pond, maybe ten feet, but it was deep enough for a Dwarf to drown. Roakore frantically kicked off the bottom and almost broke the surface before the weight of his ax dragged him down again. Finally, after another attempt, he loosened the strap that held his ax to his back and swam with his last breath to the surface. He broke out into the afternoon air with a gasp.

He finally made his way to the shore and fell upon his belly, gasping for air. A soft, cherubic chuckle fluttered over the water and fell upon Roakore's ears. He turned his head with a jerk; his eyes darted to the tall grass upon the opposite bank. Roakore looked for his Silverhawk. He saw nothing of the beast but heard its telltale cry in the distance.

"Good riddance then beast." He swore to the heavens.

Again the chuckle echoed over the water. Roakore looked again to the grass but saw nothing. It sounded like the laugh of a child, but Roakore could not tell whether it was Dwarf, human or Elf. Whichever it was, it was a little girl.

Just then Silverwind landed upon the edge of the pond between himself and the sound. She looked upon Roakore for a moment with her one-eyed gaze then ignored him to drink from the pond.

"Bah! Who needs ye, bird? I'll get to Del-Oradon on account o' me own feet!" yelled Roakore across the pond.

Again the chuckle sounded and caused Silverwind to coo. Roakore looked to the grass and, upon picking himself up, began to walk toward the noise. With his first step came an end to the laughter. Roakore cocked his head and listened to the wind for a moment. He heard nothing but the faint breeze upon the tall grass and reeds. And then the wind changed, and upon it rode the telltale stench of the Draggard. It was unmistakable, a mixture of death and dragon dung.

Roakore crouched low and retrieved two of his hatchets. He looked to the pond, thinking of his ax. He was about to summon it when the girl's laughter was replaced by her blood-curdling scream.

Roakore bolted around the pond in the direction of the terrified child; his strong legs pumped him along at the pace of a swiftly galloping stallion. Silverwind took flight as Roakore's stone bird left his hands and whirled to life, zipping straight ahead of him and high into the tall grass. The grass was mowed down by the weapon, cut down at four feet. The stones finally stopped as they hit the chest of a Draggard.

The scales upon the beast's chest audibly shattered as the creature was thrown back into the grass dead. Roakore then saw five more Draggard and a terrified, dirty little curly haired human girl of no more than three. Roakore's blood boiled and rage filled his every fiber at the thought of these beasts touching the child. Roakore may have been tougher than Elven steel and more powerful than two bulls, but he had a soft spot in his heart for children, a tenderness and love equal in strength to that of his greatest rage.

Roakore lifted a hand as he ran, and the wet sand upon the lapping bank of the pond rose like a snake with no tail and struck out at the Draggard's faces. The sand traveled with such speed and force that the closest Draggard, who had not had time to raise an arm or turn its head, took the full assault in the eyes. The millions of minute stones that made up the sand buried themselves in its eyes and packed into its skull until it exploded. Time seemed to slow for Roakore during battle, as did his opponents, and he went into a fighting trance.

As the remaining four Draggard covered themselves from the onslaught of the lethal sand serpent that constantly battered their heads, Roakore let loose his twin hatchets. Even as he leapt into the air and over the girl, his weapons twirled through the air with great force, embedding themselves into the heads of two of the beasts. Roakore landed on crouched feet not three feet from the remaining two Draggard as the sand stopped and fell to the grass.

He hacked at the monster to the left of him with both blades aimed at the knee and hip. With a crunch, they contacted and the beast reared. Instinctively, its tail whipped around and shot at Roakore's chest, but he had already backed out of reach and engaged the Draggard to his right.

Roakore fought the beast unarmed, his hatchets still buried in the other screaming Draggard's leg. The beast lunged forward with its tail to stab Roakore in the chest, but before it could, the furious Dwarf caught it and cracked it like a whip, causing the beast to spin where it stood. With the Draggard's back to him, Roakore growled and ran up the scales of the monster and onto its back. It thrashed and reached behind it with its long claws but could not reach Roakore. Growling louder now, Roakore held on to the thickest spike upon the scaled beast's back with his left hand and punched it in the side of the head with his right.

Roakore's knuckles were huge and knotted like wood due to his spending three generations of men punching hard stone as part of his daily personal training. That was exactly why he trained as he did—you never knew when you may have to smash the skull of a Draggard with your bare hands—and the training had paid off. After the third blow, the Draggard's skull cracked, and it lost its feet.

Roakore fell with the beast and rolled, remembering the other monster. He rolled out of the way not a second too soon as the Draggard jumped five feet into the air with one leg. Its eyes were enraged with pain and hate, claws reaching to fillet skin. Before Roakore could make the beast regret its courage, the huge claws of Silverwind buried themselves in the monster's shoulders. Silverwind crushed the Draggard with her great weight and decapitated it with one peck of its sharp beak.

"That was me kill, ye traitor!" Roakore roared.

Silverwind gave out a defiant squawk, but the girl did not giggle. She stood at the water's edge, whimpering wide-eyed at Roakore. Roakore held his arms out non-threateningly and tried to calm the child as he walked forward. To his surprise, she ran to him and buried her face in his strong shoulders and soft Silverhawk cloak. Just then, he felt a jabbing on his armor.

He twirled with the child and raised a fist, swiftly bringing it around at his attacker. His fist stopped a hair from a small boy's face.

"Let my sister go!" The boy hollered in Roakore's face.

Roakore's expression went from one of rage to a wide smile. "Ye got a lot o' heart, eh, boy? I could crush ye like a bug, 'n' still ye attack."

The boy put up his fists defiantly. "My father could crush you, Dwarf!"

"Does that be so?" asked Roakore.

"It be!" answered a man's deep voice from behind him. He turned to see the speaker and met a large fist to the face. The girl was snatched from his grasp with the other hand as Roakore slammed onto the ground, hard enough to take his breath had he not known how to take a fall. He quickly got to his feet and shook his head then felt his chin.

"Heh, you got one hell o' a punch, human. Almost as hard as me grandma o' three hunr'd years, reminds me the slap I got for tryin' to sneak a biscuit at before dinner."

The man put down his daughter and squared off with Roakore. The two males stared each other in the eye, waiting for one to strike.

"Loo da."

The men both stiffened at the noise, neither breaking the gaze.

The little girl tugged on her father's pants and pointed. "Loo da! You be goo."

The man put a hand upon his daughter's shoulder and gently put her behind himself; she did not struggle but only said louder, "Loo da. He may ugly sleep."

The man dared break eye contact with Roakore for a quick glance at the dead Draggard. "Does she speak the truth?" he asked.

"Do they look like they be sleepin'?" retorted Roakore.

The man looked again. "They are dead."

"Well then, she be tellin' the truth."

He looked to his son. "Did this Dwarf kill these Draggard?"

"I do not know, Father. I found her a moment before you did."

Roakore lifted his arms and walked over to the water and crouched to wash the blood from his hands. "Who in the hells ye be thinkin' killed them beasts? Eh? Ye thinkin the tot done killed em with cuteness? Did ye not notice the hatchets buried in them two's heads?"

The tall man looked from Roakore to the Draggard; he kicked the nearest beast. The man was tall, nearly twice the height of Roakore. He was a giant among men, as wide at the shoulders as Roakore was tall. His massive muscles tensed and bulged beneath the fabric of his shirt with every move. Roakore guessed he could best a half a dozen men single-handedly. He hadn't been lying when he said the man hit like his grandmother—she was a strong Dwarf.

The man walked forward to Roakore and extended a hand in a human greeting."Name's Tarragon. This here is my son, Nathaniel, and my littlest, Freesia."

They shook hands, and Roakore extended his to the pond, palm out. Nothing happened for a moment as Roakore chanted under his breath, but then his ax emerged and flew from the water into his outstretched hand.

"Me name's Roakore, king o' the Ro'Sar Mountains."

Tarragon didn't bat an eye. "I know enough of the Dwarven folk to know none would claim to be such if it were not true. What brings you to these parts, good king, so far from your newly reclaimed mountain?

The fact that Tarragon knew of the recent Dwarven victory made his pride swell, as it did his chest. "I be on me way to help a friend and noticed the fire off yonder a ways and came to have a look-see." answered Roakore.

"Ah, yes, you saw it from the sky." Tarragon eyed the now-grazing Silverhawk. "I did not know that Dwarves rode Silverhawks from the northern kingdom."

"They don't," suggested Roakore. "I do."

"Can I ride it, Dad? asked Nathaniel with excitement. He was no older than Tarren.

"Be still, Nathaniel."

"Yes, sir." answered the boy without pouting.

Roakore looked again to the black smoke that was now receding. "Was it these damned dragon half-breeds what caused the fire?"

"Aye, they came again last night, set fire to two buildings in town, and took twelve souls into the blackness of night, three children and two women among them. They will be back again with the coming of night."

Roakore pondered the situation; the more he thought about it, the more incensed he became. But he could not take the time to help these people—he was on a mission and had but a few days to get to Del-Oradon, not to mention find a way to free Whill.

"How many people ye say ye got in yer town?"

"Nearly two hundred souls. The town is called Elderwood."

"Elderwood, eh? Never heard o' it."

"I don't imagine you would have. Might I ask, good Dwarf…You are a king of Dwarves; you must have a cunning knowledge of military formations and attack strategies. Could a poor farmer offer anything in return for a few words of advice on how best to kill these beasts?"

Roakore thought for a moment, and his stomach answered for him with a grumble. "A warm meal and I can offer some advice, but I got to be movin' afore midday. Me an' me bird got many miles to cover before nightfall."

At her mention, Silverwind squawked and took flight, flying far and out of sight.

"Well, me and me feet got a lot o' miles ahead of us anyway."

Tarragon shook Roakore's hand vigorously. "Warm food it is, and I thank you for saving my little girl. I owe you a life."

Roakore nodded with a grunt. Inside, he was warmed by the thought of what he had done and the luck of being dropped in the pond. *Maybe that bird be smarter than me be thinkin'.*

Roakore retreived his two hatchets, cleaned them in the pond, and headed southwest with Tarragon and his two children. Silverwind was nowhere to be seen. The big man looked also to the sky. "That bird of yours. It is a Shierdon Silverhawk, is it not?"

"Aye," grunted Roakore.

"A gift from the king?"

"Nay. Had it smuggled in, I did. Hawks' bane plants also, got me a garden o' it on the side o' me mountain."

The big man laughed. "It is one of Shierdon's highest crimes to steal a bird or transport the plant out of the country."

"Bah." Roakore spat. "They got them a Dark Elf posin' as their king. The way I see it, they got other things to worry about."

"A Dark Elf upon the throne? I do not mean to be rude, good Dwarf, but that is the most ridiculous thing I have ever heard."

Roakore squared off with Tarragon, and they both stopped. "You be callin' *me* a liar? I be knowin' more about the workin's o' the world than a farmer from Uthen-Arden!"

"Lumberjack."

"Whatever!" Roakore went on. "I be the direct descendant o' Ky'Dren. I be king o' the reclaimed mountain o' Ro'Sar. I seen me people slaughtered by thousands o' Draggard. I seen a dragon killed by a loan Dwarf. I seen Elves do things that you would never believe in a thousand years. You be livin' here in your world, but I be livin' in *the* world. There be a war wagin' between the Dark Elves and thier crossbred killers and the rest o' us. Or ain't ya noticed the Draggard scourge roamin' the land, killin' for sport? Word has it that one-fourth o' your human towns and villages have been destroyed by the beasts o' the Dark Elves. And the same number in Isladon."

Tarragon looked gravely in Roakore's eyes. "It is worse than even the rumors then?"

Roakore nodded. "It be a nightmare, and no one wantin' to be wakin' up to it."

CHAPTER THIRTEEN

Thank Me in the Morning

Whill lay upon his bed, not trying to sleep; he had given that up days before. It seemed that the last few weeks of his torture had been enough sleep for him. He had gone into a shell; he had gone deep into the cocoon of his inner mind. He became not Whill but simply…it. He no longer had an identity in that place, nothing that could tie him to Whill's life and nothing that could hurt him. He felt not physical pain or emotional anguish. He was simply a being…being.

What little light came through the window from the moon or the courtyard below played on the ceiling of his room, though he did not see it. He saw the explosion of his ship, the death of his friends. The only one alive was Tarren, and where was he now? How was he being treated?

Where was Roakore? He had forgotten about Roakore. Had he reclaimed his mountain? Had he died in the battle? Whill had heard no news from the outside world. Being a captive of the Dark Elves meant being a captive from the entire world, from reality. His years journeying with Abram seemed like a fantasy, a long, drawn-out dream. His life with Teera in Sidnell, his childhood home, seemed like a dream within a dream. The final battle with Addakon was the only clear memory he had.

He had faced his uncle, his father's killer. He had been out skilled and facing certain death. But he had faced his uncle nonetheless, and he had won. His father's spirit had fought through him and had defeated his murderous twin brother. The soul mates had become one. Repented and forgiven for their own sins, they had moved on. Whill's mother's spirit had moved on; the world had moved on without Whill, and so Whill had moved on.

He no longer cared. He was due to be executed, and he did not care. For how could he be Whill of Agora, the one spoken of in prophecy, the son of a king, the wielder of an ancient blade? How could he be Whill of Agora if he was here, tortured for six months without rest? Disfigured and healed, mortally wounded and healed. The horrors he had faced he could no longer recall, for he had wiped them from his mind as soon as they happened.

He existed now simply from that place which he had found. There was no pain, no struggle, only existence. His friends were dead; he had no people. He had nothing to lose, except Avriel, whom was already lost to him.

Avriel was the anchor that grounded Whill. She was the only thing keeping the boy that had been alive inside the man that he had become—Avriel, his first and only love. She was like nothing he had ever seen. A maiden cast out by a dream.

He pictured her hair cast by the wind, stroking her neck, her long, smooth, straight, strong neck, and her proud jaw and long ears, black hair tucked behind the left. Her head tilted slightly while she spoke. She spoke not with her throat but with her mouth. Every word extenuated by her mouth. She had lips made of sunrise and morning dew, eyes piercing and bright yet vulnerable and fierce.

Whill was grounded when he thought of Avriel, the only thing left worth caring about on this entire miserable rock. Avriel his love, the lover that never was, his Avriel, the only thing keeping his spirit tethered to life.

Far away in the castle Eadon turned from his focus on Whill's despair and addressed the waiting guard. "Bring me the barbarian warrior."

Shortly after, she was brought to his chambers, and the door was closed. Eadon smiled as he took in the sight of her. She was the largest human woman he had ever seen, in all regards. She stood waiting, her fire-filled eyes never leaving his. Eadon offered her a glass of wine, and she did not move.

"My beautiful warrior of the north, may I, as the Elven ambassador of my kind, welcome you to my newly acquired human kingdom? Your prowess has not gone unnoticed. And I wish to recruit you to the winning side of this battle in which we find ourselves…You are from the northern island of ice, Volnoss, are you not?"

The barbarian woman nodded. She did not speak. Instead, she stood, arms crossed, left hip protruding. Eadon took this all in with a grin. "Do you wish to work with me, or do you wish to fight to the death in the arena for your crimes? Which, I am sure, are ludicrous accusations."

The barbarian woman scoffed. "If they are ludicrous, then drop the charges, oh great one. Great shadow from the east, manipulator of minds, oh great puppet master. Which title do you prefer, your worship?"

"I see that we may disagree on some things," said Eadon as he swirled his wine and put it down.

From a box on the desk he retrieved a silver foot-long smoking pipe. The tip of his finger he used to light the intoxicating herb that burned and sent forth smoke into the room, finding the barbarian woman's nose. It did not have any mind-altering powers; what it did carry was nostalgia. For what Eadon smoked only grew upon the shores of Volnoss.

She knew then that this creature would not be defeated with the hand or the blade. And there was no hope in defeating his mind. She knew that any mental attack she would put forth would be feeble, like a mosquito attacking a man. So she listened.

"I offer you this, good lady of the north. My Draggard and Dark Elves have been ordered to infiltrate and to expedite the cooperation of all locals of Agora, including your home of Volnoss. My armies will land upon your beaches and march into your towns. No doubt, your people will act with great pride and stand firm in their beliefs whilst fighting to the bitter end, and bitter it shall be if you let it happen."

He walked slowly closer to her as he spoke. "My lady of the north, you could act as the ambassador of Volnoss. Extend the olive branch to the Dark Elves, which will inevitably conquer this entire land. You can bridge the gap between our people. With your cooperation will come the safety and the prosperity of Volnoss. No longer will you sit in the cold darkness, expelled from Agora since the barbarian wars. No longer will you hear how your people were thrown out; no longer will you be put down, left to lick the boots and hide from the shorter, weaker Agorans. Your people can thrive and be prosperous, or you can simply be left to your iceberg; it is your choice."

Eadon again walked to the barbarian woman and offered her the wine. He noted that she did not tense at his nearness, a feat that few beings could claim. She took the wine. He went on.

"And for your cooperation, I will give you the former human kingdom of Sheirdon, so that you and your people may once again walk upon your homeland and smell the sweet scent of freedom. The choice is yours, my lady. Will you follow me? Will you extend your hand? Will you take hold of your people's future? Or will you leave them to a fate of extermination and death? What will it be, Aurora Snowfell?"

Aurora eyed Eadon up and down, getting a measure of the Dark Elf. "Face me in a spar, no unnatural powers; we will see what I decide then."

Eadon laughed. "Are there any unnatural powers? Is it not simply power?"

Aurora Snowfell did not laugh, nor did she smile. "Do you agree, or are you wasting my time?"

A hungry growl escaped Eadon's throat as he unbuckled his sword with a smirk. He said nothing. Aurora rolled her large shoulders and began to bounce back and forth on her feet; she bent slightly at the waist. Eadon stepped forward and smiled at the result of her voluptuous frame bouncing from side to side. Aurora pounced on the distraction.

She struck out fast and hard with her large, knuckled fist and caught Eadon square on the chin. He was thrown back into his wine cabinet, completely shattering the wood and glass. He landed on his feet and shook his head. "Indeed, I have made a good choice in you."

Aurora roared and charged the Dark Elf. Eadon stood his ground. The seasoned barbarian came in not like a bull, as one might expect, but rather with a graceful leg sweep, which forced Eadon to jump over it. Knowing this would be his only defense, she quickly brought the other leg up and over, aiming at Eadon's chest. But the highly nimble and far more seasoned Dark Elf knew her mind, and in his leap, he caught her leg with both hands and flipped over it. Aurora quickly reversed that leg, only to have Eadon catch it with the back of his knees. He dropped his whole weight onto it and once again flipped, bringing her with him.

She landed awkwardly with twisted legs. Before she knew what was happening, Eadon had climbed her prone body and mounted her chest. He pinned her arms with his legs and proceeded to drop two elbows to her face, and she heard her nose crack. In an instant, Eadon was off of her, offering her his hand.

Aurora wiped her mouth with her hand. She reveled in the blood. Few males had ever made her bleed, and most of those that had, had either become her lover or had died by her hand. To a woman of the north such as her, powerful and strong, her men needed to be stronger still, lest she birth weaklings into the clan. To find one stronger than she was not a common event.

She grabbed the offered hand and kicked Eadon in the face while pulling him down. His head snapped back with a sickening sound. In an instant, she was upon him. Before his head could recoil, she grabbed his collar and pulled him into her punch. Her fist, as large as his head, slammed into his gut. When his head finally snapped forward, it was met with a flying elbow. Eadon's jaw cracked. When, inevitably, his hands came up to grab her hand from his collar, she grabbed the hand at the wrist and twisted it in a full circle. Bone cracked, and tendons snapped.

Aurora had Eadon on the tips of his toes, holding him by the broken arm. Her huge boot of whale skin came up and met his groin, lifting him from his feet. Aurora used the momentum of the kick, along with the leverage of the arm hold, to bring Eadon up over her head and to slam him to the ground on the other side. She leaned forward and offered her hand to the defeated Dark Elf lord. Eadon laughed, an eerie, gurgling laugh due to his ribs puncturing his lungs.

He ignored the offered hand and stood. He arched his back and groaned in ecstasy as his ribs snapped back into place and his lungs healed. He reached for his broken arm and snapped that back into place. His broken jaw healed, and his cuts closed.

"I said no unnatural powers, and you agreed."

Eadon lifted a hand to his chin and cracked his neck to the side. He rolled his shoulders. "Indeed, I did, and indeed, I have used no unnatural powers. My ability to heal is part of who I am. I am a Dark Elf. I have reached enlightenment, and I have mastered every school of Orna Catorna. Indeed, I have invented several others. My ability to heal is as natural as your size and strength, as is my ability to do this."

Eadon extended his hands toward Aurora, and she was thrown back against the wall. He pulled one hand toward himself, and she was forced through the air to land at his feet.

"That, my lady, is one of my gifts. Shall I show you another? There are many other schools of knowledge I could show you. For instance, this one in particular took me fifty-five years to master."

He lifted his hands, and the stone floor came alive. Serpents of stone coiled out of the floor and wound around Aurora's limbs, standing her up to face Eadon.

"This is one of my favorites, though it took me better than ten thousand moons to master."

A spark came to life within Eadon's palm and grew quickly into a ball of blue flame. Eadon smashed the ball on the floor and, with his hands, guided the hungry, licking flames, away from the tapestries and books to bite into Aurora's legs. She screamed in anguish and shook in her stone shackles. She focused all of the pain into her strong arms and into her muscled legs. Aurora squeezed with all her might and power, using the pain to energize every fiber of her warrior being. The stone that held her shattered, and she brought a boot up to Eadon's face.

"And this!" Eadon yelled. "Is one of my own creations!"

Eadon simply gritted his teeth and intensely looked into Aurora's eyes. Instantly, her body fell to the floor as her very soul was ripped from her body, hovering where she had stood. Aurora Snowfell had never known such panic, such horror, such absolute terror. She saw him through her human eyes as her body hit the floor, but she also saw him through her spirit eyes. To her soul, he appeared in his true form, a magnificent black flame of colossal energy. The very sight of him was more than she could take, and her spirit yearned for the door to the next world, anything to be away from this demon of children's nightmares.

Eadon opened his mouth, and from it came a writhing black tendril of energy. It found the mouth of Aurora's spirit body and forced its way down her throat. She gasped and was back inside her body. The pain was gone; the fire was out. Silence filled the room, only disturbed by the drinking of wine by Eadon.

She stood on shaky legs. She could feel the thing that Eadon had made enter her being. It hummed inside her core, emanating a power that she found herself afraid of.

"What I have given you will give you three times the strength of any attack upon you. No opponent will be able to stand before you. As long as you carry out my will, you will retain this gift."

Aurora clenched her fist, feeling the great power surging through her. With great effort, she ignored the pulsing within her.

"You have the fealty of the barbarians of Volnoss. We will be your northern hand, now and forever…Under the conditions you outlined earlier."

Eadon smiled at his newest captain's moxy.

"Of course."

CHAPTER FOURTEEN
A Helping Hand

Abram stared at the small scroll, not seeing it. His mind was elsewhere. He had received a message via falcon from Zerafin that the Elves would meet him two days hence. From there, Abram would join with Zerafin in the infiltration of the castle. Abram had been laying out a plan with Rhunis. The scarred knight was this minute gathering supplies for what Abram had planned.

Abram had learned that Whill's execution would consist of a large-scale gladiator battle within the arena. He would be given a small force, and eventually they would be slaughtered by overwhelming numbers. The fight would drag out for a while, Abram knew, if Whill was in his usual form.

The most important part of the plan included freeing the dragon Zhola, if he was still alive. The releasing of the dragon along with the chaos that Abram had planned was sure to give them a window of opportunity, no matter how small. If they were successful, they would be traveling to Elladrindellia with Whill and the soul of Avriel soon.

The plan will work, thought Abram.

He puffed on his pipe and spoke aloud to himself. "It has to."

Roakore emptied his mug of wheat beer and burped loudly.

"Thank you," said Anellen.

The Dwarf gave the wife of Tarragon a smile and nod, pleased that she was aware that to burp was to compliment the cook. Much excitement had begun to buzz around the small village when word that a Dwarf king was here to help repel the Draggard. Many had known loss at the hand of the Draggard, and all were scared of the night to come. The day had been spent fortifying homes and sharpening blades. But all knew that tonight would not be any different than last night. The Draggard would come, and they would all be dragged into the night one by one; their screams would echo through the forest for hours. That was the mind of many before word of Roakore had come.

Tarragon had brought Roakore home to eat before beginning plans for the defense of the town. He ate his fill also, for he knew that he would need it soon.

The Dwarf king dropped the last chicken leg onto his plate and burped again. He washed it down by finishing another mug of wheat beer. He lit his pipe and stood. "Alright then, let's see what ye got fer warriors."

Tarragon led Roakore out of his house, and outside waited the entire town, men, women and children. Roakore looked over the townspeople. They looked like they had been through hell. They had gotten little to no sleep, having fought or stood guard all night. The little ones had been kept awake by terror, the women kept awake by worry, and the men kept awake by the rage that they were impotent to defend their families. All had been kept awake by the nightlong screams of those taken into the darkness by the demonic horde. Many, mostly family members, could not bear the screams of their loved ones and charged into the darkness to help. Their screams had eventually added to the chorus. A few men had to be tied down, lest they charge to their deaths trying to help. Jarred was one such man.

At six foot four and nearing three hundred pounds, it had taken five men to subdue him when his wife and son had been snatched from their houses and taken into the night of screams. He remained tied to a chair, hands and feet bound. He had lost his mind it seemed. His eyes were bloodshot and wide; his jaw tensed as he constantly ground his teeth. Tears had cleaned a line down his dirty cheeks, only adding to his insane look.

Roakore came to him and stopped. "Why is this man bound so? He be a traitor?"

Jarred's nostrils flared at the question, and he looked to Roakore with murder in his eyes. "The beasts took my wife and son. These cowards tied me up so that I would not run into the night; they stopped me from helping my family, the sons of bastards!"

"You would have died with them," replied a man from the crowd.

"That was my choice!" screamed Jarred. "My choice, and you took it away! You took it as you take it now."

"We need you here tonight, to fight; you are no use dead, not to us or your family," another man from the crowd retorted.

Jarred snarled, barely maintaining control. "I will fight! As soon as I am free of my bonds those of you that stopped me will die!"

Roakore listened to the exchange, and he turned to Tarragon. "This be true? Was this man stopped from helpin' his family?"

Tarragon nodded. "Aye, and his life was saved. He would have joined the others in death had he charged into a darkened night full of Draggard."

Roakore looked like he had been slapped. "It is his right to do what he wants! His right to charge into death if he be so choosin'. What cowards would rob a man of his vengeance? His honor? His right?"

Tarragon did not reply; he simply bowed his head. From the crowd stepped a man in his early sixties. He wore a bandage upon his left forearm and walked with a crutch. When he spoke, his deep, powerful voice made one forget his apparent frailness.

"What cowards, you ask? I am his father. Twas I who ordered him bound. Was my blood they took last night also, my grandson and daughter-in-law. I want to see them pay as does my son. But to run off like a fool into the night is not the way to help or avenge my family. I alone take responsibility; I alone should be blamed for saving my only son's life."

Roakore thought of his own father. How he had robbed him of his own glorious death defending his mountain. Roakore had been ordered to retreat, something unheard of to the Dwarves. But Roakore had obeyed, and twenty years later, he took back his father's mountain. He pondered the situation.

"Cut him loose."

The crowd murmured. Tarragon raised his head. Jarred's father did nothing.

"We cannot!" yelled a man from the crowd. He had been one of the men to restrain Jarred. "He will go on a rampage and charge into the woods."

"No, he will not," said Roakore as he looked to Jarred and walked closer to the man. "He will prepare to fight alongside meself and his townfolk tonight."

Roakore's eyes met Jarred's and matched their murderous sheen. "We will prepare for the beasts, set our traps, and lay in wait." Roakore continued to walk closer.

"We will kill every last one of the hell-spawned demon-bred dragon beasts! And we will find what survivors remain."

"What survivors?" insisted Jarred, tormented by hope.

"The Draggard will begin where they left off night last. The setting of the sun will bring the screams of the taken. It is their way of torment. Some will have survived the night."

"There is a chance they are alive?" begged Jarred.

Roakore nodded. "A chance, mind ye. I don't be claimin' yer family be alive, some will. Wanna find out for yerself?"

Jarred ground his jaw and nodded.

"Let him loose or I leave! I will not fight for a people that would deny a man his glory," Roakore spat.

Tarragon looked to the crowd. Their silence was their consensus. He produced a knife and cut the man free. Jarred sprang from his bonds and shoved Tarragon to the side. He stormed past Roakore and reached for his father's throat with madness in his eyes. He began to choke the man. His father dropped to his knees and did not bother to resist. He labored to speak.

"You lost your son...he was taken...what if he had tried...to give himself...to them? My son..."

Jarred's face contorted into that of a beast in anguish. A grief-stricken wail escaped him as he released his father and fell to his knees. He hunched over and sobbed as waves of sorrow washed over him. His head rested upon the chest of his father, and the man held him like one would a child.

Roakore turned away from the scene and bade everyone do the same. "Come, leave the grieving to grieve. You got three hours, get what sleep you can, say what prayers you will. In three hours, we prepare for battle!"

Roakore used the three hours to survey the town's layout. With a population of no more than two hundred, it was not a large town. But the folks here spent hard hours working the land, and all had lived through harsh winters. They had weapons of mostly wood, pitchforks and shovels and hoes. But there were also axes and a few swords.

Roakore looked to the church and nodded to himself. He had found his wedge. He looked to the sky and whistled. He waited, but there was no sign of the hawk. He screamed to the heavens this time. "Silverwind, ye damn-stubborn, good-for-nothing bird, I be needin' yer help. They be needin' yer help. This be the end, lest ye help me here and now fight fer these folks. I won't be flyin' no coward! Ye hear? SILVERWIND!"

There was an ear-piercing squawk as the bird flew from behind the church and landed so near to Roakore that they bumped chests. The bird cocked its head as if taking a measure of the Dwarf king.

"That's me girl," roared Roakore as he mounted the great bird, and together they flew high into the sky to survey the enemy. Higher and higher they went, and Silverwind suddenly turned as blue as the sky. Satisfied that they were invisible to the eye, Roakore steered Silverwind in ever-widening circles until they spotted the Draggard camp.

The beasts had settled to wait at the rocky foot of a small hill. More than fifty of them there were fighting for position upon the rocks. Roakore spat down on them as they sunned themselves like dragons. He could barely make out a few fair-skinned people huddled at the center of the mass. Roakore took a few mental notes, gauged the distance to the town, and flew back.

When he landed, he found the three hours up and the townsmen and women ready and gathering supplies.

"What is the plan?" asked Jarred when Roakore landed.

"We be needin' a few things." said Roakore as he thought and absently stroked the Silverhawk's neck. "That church there. Is there a back door?"

The priest stepped forward, bandaged and weary as any. "No, good king, there is not."

Roakore pointed at the priest and four others. "Go make one, three men wide and one high. And able to close quickly and secure from the outside. Go!"

The men disappeared. "Blacksmith!" yelled Roakore.

"'Ere!" said a grizzled man with an ever-dirtied apron and arms like a tree trunk. Upon his shoulder rested a well-used hammer.

Roakore looked the man over with approval.

"What be yer name?"

"I be Hanhollad."

"Hanhollad, I will be needin' every fire pit ye got glowin' red, and every piece o' metal ye got, weapons and scrap."

"Yes, sir."

The blacksmith and his three apprentices hurried off.

"Does that church have a basement?" Roakore asked the crowd.

He nodded as someone answered in the affirmative. "Good. I need every bit o' oil ye got down there. And plenty o' rags and scrap wood. Fill the basement till one can't be walking down there."

A group ran off to comply. Roakore then handpicked fifty of the burliest men and women. "You all stay back with me. Gimme a large paper and quill."

The paper was brought, and Roakore laid out his plan. Tarragon listened, and the local scribe took notes. The plan would be recited until the moment came. Tarragon looked to Roakore when the plan was laid out. "But, good king, won't that put you in mortal danger?"

Roakore scoffed. "Don't be worryin' bout me. Everyone do their part, and we may just see morning."

Everyone went off to do their part. Roakore and his select fifty met the blacksmith hard at work. The fires raged, and sweat glistened from the working man's skin. "As you asked, sir."

There was a culmination of dull axes, swords, and spears in a pile. Roakore smiled. "If you would, I would like to test your hammer and anvil."

The blacksmith handed over his hammer and watched, curious as the rest.

Roakore picked a dull ax at random and fed it to the fire. He took it out and began pounding away with that familiar rhythm. Into each strike, he added his will and intention, molding the metal with his mind until it was as strong and sharp as any. He cooled it in a bucket of water and handed it to a dumbfounded man. He repeated the process for hours, turning every weapon and scrap piece of metal into a lethal killing tool. Lastly, he took two swords from the pile, looked Jarred over once and nodded to himself.

The two blades he heated to glowing red and hammered them together with hammer and mind power until they merged to make one massive, five-foot-long sword. He cooled it and handed it to Jarred.

Jarred accepted the perfectly balanced blade with both hands. A tear found his eye and a smile his face. Roakore smiled also. "You'll be needin' that where I'm bringin' ya."

Night began to fall. Roakore took reports from the many different groups. Torches had been laid out from the steps of the church, widening as they descended away from the place of worship to the town beyond. The women that would not be fighting huddled with the children before the church. The windows of the building had been boarded shut, and the backdoor was ready. The oil and cloth lay in wait beneath the floor. The plan was clear, and all knew their role.

Roakore gathered from his pack a few small dragons' breathe bombs and a lantern. He loaded everything on his mount and eyed the townsmen one last time. They locked tired, weary, and scared, but ready to fight to the death. Roakore was proud.

"When ye see me again, ye will be fighting for your lives. You know the cues; ye know yer jobs. May Ky'Dren lock over ye."

"Thank you, good Dwarf king of the mountain Ro Sar," said a woman among the crowd.

Roakore nodded and mounted Silverwind. "Thank me in the morning."

Jarred was grasped by Silverwind by the shoulders, and together, they flew into the darkening sky and disappeared in a haze of color to match the setting sun. The screams began then, and Roakore could hear the curses of Jarred below him. He steered Silverwind low and in the direction of the taunting Draggard horde, not five hundred steps from the town. The beasts marched on the town once again, with the screaming hostages at the center of the pack.

Roakore flew in a path that would bring them directly over the horde. "Give 'em hell, man!" hollored Roakore as Silverwind let loose the hanging Jarred and his five-foot-long sword.

Jarred fell screaming and landed near the outer ring of his townsfolk. "Everybody down!" he warned as the great sword came around in a full arch. Draggard scales cracked, and blood flew.

Just then Roakore lit and dropped the four dragons' breath bombs directly into the Draggard horde nearest the town. They screamed as many were engulfed in flames. Jarred swung the heavy sword with all his might, clearing a path through the fire and bidding everyone to hurry and run for town. The six survivors ran for their lives. Roakore watched as one was taken up by Jarred. Even in the flames Roakore knew that the boy was Jarred's son, and he also saw that the mother had fallen. Jarred's anguished scream and deadly sword work crushed all beasts before him.

Jarred and the survivors made for town as Roakore jumped from his mount, and together, they stopped any Draggard from following. The surprise attack lasted long enough for Roakore to claim five heads and to give Jarred and his people time to reach town. As the Draggard became wise and began to dangerously press, Roakore mounted the bird once again, and they veered off toward the town.

The furious Draggard followed. Teeth gnashing and growls raging, they pursued the pair closely into the town square.

"C'mon, ye stupid beasts," laughed Roakore as he dismounted near the church and ran to the door.

The children screamed as he motioned for them to go into the church. The Draggard charged harder at the sight of their prey. Roakore let out a sharp whistle, and from the darkness came the townspeople, charging into the monstrous Draggard. The beasts were stopped in their tracks before the church steps as the townspeople barreled into them from all sides. Roakore dropped from his mount and engaged the nearest monster. As he buried his ax deep into the Draggard's chest he wondered if the trap within the church would be needed. The two dozen townspeople were tearing into the beasts with a ferocity only known by those that have recently lost loved ones, many with nothing left to lose.

Roakore blocked a Draggard tail meant for his head. His huge ax came sweeping back in a blur of motion and took the attacking beast's arm off. The creature reared in pain, but Roakore advanced mercilessly. He hacked and chopped until the Draggard moved no more.

Next to him, a man fell dead with a spear through his neck. Jarred avenged the man's death with the deadly long sword, which cut through the beast's scales and crushed its head.

Though the men and women fought bravely, their numbers were thinning quickly. Roakore gave another whistle, and Silverwind answered with an ear-piercing squawk. The great Silverhawk dove into the fray and lifted a Draggard from the battle. She flew high and dropped the hissing monster onto its kin. Again she dove but this time landed next to Roakore, crushing an unlucky Draggard under her great weight. Roakore bid the townspeople retreat to the church as he and Silverwind squared off with the remaining group of at least twenty Draggard. Jarred remained behind with them as his townfolk scrambled up the church steps.

"Go on, Jarred, get with yer people!" yelled Roakore and sent his stone bird whirling into the advancing horde.

Jarred brought the heavy long sword down hard into the shoulder of a Draggard, severing its arm. He laughed wickedly in the face of the beast. "And miss this? Not for the world!"

Roakore's laugh echoed Jarred's. Silverwind took a spear hit to the neck, and sparks emanated from the impact. It seemed that Lunara's enchantment was working well. And it was good that it did. A half-a-dozen Draggard had rounded on the bird and were taking turns landing vicious blows. Silverwind took a Draggard's head in her beak and crushed it with apparent ease. She put the deadly beak to work on another, snapping its spear like a twig and gutting it with a lunging attack and a razor-sharp claw. The other Draggard did not relent, and Roakore screamed with rage as his beloved mount was attacked from all sides.

"Fly, ye crazy bird, fly!" screamed Roakore as he engaged another. Down came a spear; up blocked his great ax. The beast spun and followed up with a sweeping tail and, simultaneously, the butt end of the spear.

Roakore hopped the tail but not high; instead, he jumped quickly and came down with both boots on it. He hewed the tail in two with his ax, though it meant taking a hit from the spear handle. But being prepared as he was for such a move, he was not hurt by the spear. He raised an arm and caught the handle in his armpit and spun with the blow. The beast howled in pain as blood spurted from its tail. Roakore took up the spear and deftly threw it past the injured beast to strike another in the neck—one that had meant to stab Jarred in the back.

Jarred turned and laughed. The blood of his foes covered the madman; his own blood flowed freely from many wounds. Tears shed for his lost wife sliced through the blood, leaving strange markings on his cheeks. His wild, bloodshot eyes scanned the line of enemies, searching for his next opponent.

The signal sounded, meaning that everyone was out of the church. Roakore and Jarred retreated into it, and a dozen Draggard followed. Roakore's stone bird followed the beasts and took the last in line in the head.

When all of the Draggard were inside the church, the men outside slammed the doors shut and swiftly drove nails home, sealing it.

Jarred looked to the hissing Draggard and then to Roakore. "You sure this is gonna work?" he asked.

Roakore looked perplexed. "Of course it's gonna work! It be me plan after all!"

CHAPTER FIFTEEN
Our Consequences

Abram turned down a dingy side alley; refuse and garbage littered the path. Rhunis followed a few paces back, his senses honed in on his surroundings. He watched the rooftops but saw nothing but the waning moon and her phantom gray lovers, the remnants of a cold fall rain recently passed. Darkness lived here, not only the shadows that fled from the street torchlight but the kind found in the hearts of men.

Their quarry was dragons' breath, the liquid extract found within the glands of mature dragons. It was gotten at great cost, as many men died in the venture of obtaining it. Word had it that the man they were set to meet had large quantities at his disposal. This, of course, was ridiculous as no one but dragons had dragons' breath at their disposal.

A thought had occurred to Abram when he heard of the supplier from not one or two but three separate sources. If anyone was to have endless quantities of dragons' breath, they would have to either be a dragon or be really, really good friends with one or the person, or Elf, had captured one. The hunch felt right. If Eadon had kept Zhola alive, he could be milking the dragon daily of its fire-feeding venom. After all, a continent-wide war cost money, and if one were to have an endless supply of dragons' breath, one would be rich. And Eadon would have no qualms about supplying every scumbag, ruffian, and pirate that had the gold to pay for it. It was called liquid gold after all, and from Zhola, Eadon would make it flow. This also meant that Eadon had a hell of a lot of explosives at hand to arm his human armies with.

Abram came to the door marked with nothing but a chicken bone nailed to the top; he knocked out the code and waited. Rhunis stood at his back, scanning the world of shadow surrounding them. The door opened slowly, moaning from lack of use. No one was to be seen within the doorway. Abram called to the darkness.

"Well then, anyone home?"

No one replied. Abram turned and nodded to Rhunis to follow suit. They walked five paces when a voice came from the doorway. "What be your quarry?"

Abram turned and approached the door. A dark form stood within the threshold.

"We are here for dragons' breath."

"Shhh, damn you, not so loud." said the figure with a hiss.

Abram chuckled. "What is the big secret? This is a smelly back alley littered with rats and scat. You think the authorities give a dragon's arse what goes on here? As long as they get their cut, there is no need for worry, eh?"

The figure's hood moved as if the doorman were looking over Abram. "You are a strange one you are."

Again, Abram chuckled. "Said the creepy, dark shape from the darkened doorway."

Rhunis laughed at that as did the creepy, dark shape from the doorway, which made him even creepier. His laugh was not the "ghost song in the forest creepy," but rather, the man was a "smells women's hair secretly and shudders" creepy. This made Rhunis laugh all the more. He pushed past with torch in hand and faced the smaller, shorter, far less broad creep.

"We knocked out the code; we have the jewels. Shall we pass or shall we kick your...door down? We have business with your man."

The hooded figure suddenly exploded into action, grabbing Rhunis's throat, sweeping a leg, and slamming him into the wall while at the same time producing a dagger that stopped roughly behind the veteran knight's earlobe.

"It is not wise to threaten the guard of my master. One may find himself very dead at the end of such an exchange."

Rhunis smiled at the hooded figure and looked down at the man's neck. Rhunis's own dagger was pressed hard against the cloaked neck. A small disturbance rippled around the point of his blade, the power of a Dark Elf's energy armor. Rhunis smiled wider. "One might, if he was not wise enough to use his cowardly armor against a foe more skilled than he. Yes, one might end up very dead at the end of such an exchange."

The hooded Dark Elf pressed harder with his dagger, breaking skin. His nostrils flared at the insult. Rhunis let his smile go cold. "Face it, Elfie, if you challenged me without all the fancy flare, fire casting, and trickery, man to man, you would lose, and I am old."

The Dark Elf sneered. "Stupid human, I have powers you cannot understand. Old you say? I am nearly five hundred in years. I bedded your grandmother's grandmother." He laughed. "Do not talk to me of power and age."

He moved to the far wall and opened yet another door. "Go!"

Abram and Rhunis went. Upon passing the Dark Elf, Rhunis stopped. "I didn't get your name."

The scowling Elf narrowed his eyes. "Dyr I am called."

Rhunis tried to hold it in but failed, and he smirked at the Dark Elf. "Next time you should say that there will be Dyr consequences."

Dyr cocked his head to the side, not understanding. "Now you know the name of your killer, human!"

Rhunis chuckled again, which he knew infuriated the Elf. "If you kill me, at least you will be remembered for something." He turned and followed Abram down a winding staircase.

As the door above closed, Abram turned but kept walking. "Why?" He chuckled. "Why would you tempt death so?"

Ehunis thought for a moment. "Does it matter? I have tempted death all my life. I guess death doesn't like me."

Abram shook his head. "One day you will tempt death, and he will answer, my friend."

Ehunis hummed his agreement. "Won't we all."

They came upon the end of the stair, and before them stood another door. Abram sighed and kicked the code into this one. A small peephole opened, and an eye looked them over. From behind the door came the order. "Put your weapons on the table behind you."

"No," answered Abram.

The guard hesitated. "You are required to leave your weapons behind, or you may not enter."

"No," repeated Abram lazily. "We are here for business; we are not assassins. We pose no threat to Dark Elves as powerful as yourself, and we will remain armed if it pleases your master. We have great wealth and a need for services, which we have been told your master can provide. Our only terms are that we remain armed. I would not hand over the blade of my grandfather for any price."

There was silence, and for long minutes there came no reply, and then they heard, "Enter as you will."

Abram and Rhunis entered the room; their eyes took in the layout out of habit. One sweeping glance told Abram that there were seven guards. There were two at the door, one in each corner of the square room, and one behind the figure seated at a large wooden table. A door stood a few feet behind the seated figure. That another guard or guards waited behind that door, Abram did not doubt.

The familiar sound of a strong hand gripping a sword hilt was Rhunis's way of telling Abram that a weapon was trained on them. Abram saw it then, a hole cut into the mouth of a cannon within a painting of a pirate ship.

Abram walked the length of the large room in seven strides and addressed the seated figure. "We have come here to do business with businessmen, not paranoid amateurs. Kindly have your man behind the painting take the crosshairs of his crossbow off of us."

"No." The figure answered just as Abram had. "You have insisted on remaining armed, as have I."

Abram nodded. "I would hate to inconvenience you with my spilt blood should the weapon misfire."

The figure's hood fell back, revealing the tattooed and pierced face of a Dark Elf. "I assure you, if it misfires, I shall not let it touch you."

The Dark Elf smirked. "I promise."

As his last word was issued, there was a click and the whine of an arrow whizzing across the room. As fast as a striking snake, Abram's dagger was before his face. The arrow would have been deflected had it not been stopped a hair's width from the blade by a swirling phantom hand.

From the seated Dark Elf's neck, the swirling tattoo had leapt out and taken the form of a fist. The hand turned to mist, and the arrow fell. The room stopped breathing, and everyone waited. No hands went to weapons, but everyone's thoughts did. Abram was the first to move. He sheathed his dagger and squared on the Dark Elf. "Business then?"

CHAPTER SIXTEEN

Oakenheart

Tarren had watched in awe as Lunara planted an oak seed by moonlight. She had added water and sang to the heavens until sunrise. He had dozed for a moment when the first rays of the sun shone forth over the horizon, and the first beam fell upon the spot in which Lunara had planted her nocturnal seed.

Tarren staggered back as the seed within the earth sprouted forth and grew into an oak tree of full maturity before his eyes. Tarren had backed nearly twenty feet, but Lunara had stayed. As the sun rose and the tree grew, she straddled a branch that grew below her. She rode the branch almost fifteen feet, and when it had stopped, it looked as though she sat upon a horse, so thick was the branch and so large the tree. Lunara had stroked the tree and whispered to it. The tree groaned, and its leaves sang like the waves of the great oceans. Lunara kissed the tree and jumped from her branch.

No sooner had she landed than the branch broke loose, clean from the tree, and landed at her feet.

With Tarren's help, Lunara had carried the large branch to the base of the tree. The day was spent talking with the tree, or so Lunara had said. To Tarren, this magical business seemed very strange. Not to say that he did not believe in magic, he, like any other eleven-year-old boy, did believe. But where he had imagined quickly casted spells and rituals, he found elaborate ones.

Night came and once again, the moon found its place in the heavens. Lunara presented Tarren with a Dwarven hatchet.

"Cut from the branch a piece as long as yourself."

Tarren took the small hatchet. He looked from the hatchet to the thick branch and guessed it would take him the better part of the night to complete the task. Lunara waited, and he did not complain. Instead, he began the tedious task of chopping at the wood with the small hatchet.

The wood was thick and strong, and Tarren quickly realized that it would take him longer than he had first anticipated, by far. He realized also that the hatchet was dull. He stopped and looked to Lunara once more, sweat having already begun to bead his forehead. She waited with a raised eyebrow. He did not complain.

Tarren steadily chopped at the branch long into the night, pausing only shortly to stretch his tired muscles and take a swig from his water flask. Lunara sat and talked with the tree as Tarren labored through the night and into the morning. It was not until the sun took to the midday sky that Tarren finally cut the branch in half. He collapsed where he stood and panted for long minutes. He drank from his flask eagerly and gingerly poured water over his blistered hands in turn. A hiss escaped him as the water stung his bloodied hands.

Tarren joined Lunara near the small fire and presented his hands. She looked at him with pity. "I am sorry, Tarren. But the oak says that if you are to receive his blessing in this, you must not be given help."

Tarren gave the tree a look. Without breaking eye contact with the tree, he tore two pieces of cloth from his shirt and wrapped his hands. He drank and ate of his rations and soon fell asleep under the bows of the great oak.

Tarren woke during the night to find Lunara dancing around the cut tree branch, singing beautifully to the moon. He cringed as he flexed his blistered hands and got to his feet once more. He was sore everywhere, and blood had soaked through his bandages. He paid it no mind and took up the dull hatchet once again and began working on the end of the branch.

Hour after excruciating hour, Tarren hacked at the tree branch. Lunara watched in silence, but giggled now and again as she spoke with the tree. Tarren did not ask what was said; he did not care. He would show the tree that he was not weak, and he would finish the task.

Long into the morning he worked, and the closer he got to cutting through the branch, the more excited and energized he became. Seeing the end near with only an inch left, he hacked and chopped with all his might until, finally, his hatchet cut through the last of the branch and struck earth beneath. Tarren dropped the hatchet and shouted to the heavens in triumph. He then passed out and slept with a smile.

He awoke to a world once again bathed in moon-light. To his dismay, he found that his once-blistered hands were now raw and throbbing. He accepted a drink from Lunara and looked to the branch he had shaped. Lunara smiled widely as she watched him. "You have done well, young human. The oak is pleased with your inner fire."

Tarren looked to the tree and nodded, not knowing how to respond to a compliment from a tree. He laughed to himself. "If Pa could see me now."

Lunara then walked from the fire, and from her pack, she took a thick, sharp blade.

"Oh, but you get to use a sharp blade," Tarren accused with an incredulous laugh.

Lunara smiled and nodded. "Indeed, I made the tree to grow, did I not? That was my test."

She said no more and went to work carving out large chunks of the thick branch. Tarren changed his bandages and ate, and, seeing that she would be a long time as well, he slept. The afternoon came, and Tarren awoke to find Lunara still at work on the branch. But she had made good progress. The once-thick branch was now as thin as his wrists.

Tarren went to her and offered her a drink. She took it gratefully and drank her fill. The rest she dumped over her head and sighed with pleasure. She wiped her brow and went back to work, whittling the wood.

Tarren guessed that she would be done well after nightfall and decided to make a feast of their rations. First, he changed his bandages with much discomfort. The raw blisters had dried and begun to scab. Tarren cursed himself that he had used the wrong kind of cloth and had not applied any salve. But he had been stubborn and not used his head. He hissed and kicked a rock as he peeled one badly stuck bandage from his palm. From his pack he retrieved his healing kit and found the balm.

After bandaging himself with fresh cloth, he built up the fire to get some decent coals ready. Had they not been thousands of feet up upon the side of a mostly barren mountain, Tarren would have hunted something better than salted meat. But he made do with what they had, and by the time nightfall came and Lunara finally stood from her work, Tarren had prepared a small celebration feast of roasted boar and potatoes with carrots.

Tarren quickly forgot the food as Lunara turned from the branch and the boy saw the finished work. What had once been a huge oak branch had been turned into a beautifully carved and rune-covered staff. Four feet long and perfectly straight, the sides of it were as smooth as an egg, where the raised runes did not cover it.

Mesmerized, Tarren walked, with a hand outstretched, to the amazing creation before him. Lunara stopped him with a kind hand to his arm. "Let it sit. You had a wonderful idea with the food. Let us eat, and heal, and we will continue."

Tarren did not argue, and with Lunara, he sat and ate. He tasted not his food and stared at the magnificent staff and imagined himself wielding it. Lunara finished her third helping of food and took a long pull from her water flask. Tarren burped and patted his belly, which elicited an exhausted laugh from Lunara. Together, they shared a long, silly laugh that could only occur with exhaustion, and Tarren realized that Lunara had not used any of powers on herself during the work.

Lunara took Tarren's hands in hers and finally healed the blisters. He sighed as the throbbing pain subsided and his palms were made smooth again.

"Your sacrifice has been made. I am sorry I could not heal you sooner.

"That's alright," said Tarren as he eyed the staff eagerly. "Now what?"

Lunara smiled at his eagerness. "Now I have much more work to do. But first I rest. We shall continue tomorrow."

Tarren gave a frustrated sigh and quickly caught himself from complaining. Lunara settled into her bedroll near the fire and sighed, content. She turned upon her side and rested her hand upon her jaw, regarding Tarren.

"What is it like, growing up as a human boy? You are the only one I have ever met. Are all boys like you?"

Tarren blushed as he threw two more pieces of wood on the fire and settled into his own bedroll. He mimicked Lunara's pose and scrunched up his nose. "Being a boy is…I don't know…like being a boy, I guess. It is all I have ever been; it is all I know."

Lunara shook her head. "You don't know if it is all that you have been. But what I meant was what is your life like?"

Tarren thought for a moment. "Well, my father had an inn, family run since the days of my great-grandfather. I worked there and did quite well for myself tending guests' horses and bags and such. My sister worked the tavern, my nana the rooms. I was schooled in the basics at the Estar School of Learning for four years."

"What did you learn?" Lunara interrupted.

"Well, we were taught to read, write, and to do numbers, the history of the lands, and basics in the language of the Dwarves. It is quite fun speech, really, very to the point."

Lunara turned upon her back and gazed at the stars between partings in the clouds. "I find the language rough and hard to make sounds. It is like spitting all the time."

Tarren giggled and then laughed, and his laughter echoed off of the mountainside, creating a chorus of childish glee. Lunara smiled widely and chuckled. Tarren strove to speak through his fits and finally spat out, "I know, right? Roakore never speaks softly. I can't imagine him putting a babe to sleep."

Tarren scrunched up his face and scowled, doing his best Roakore impression. "Sleep, li'll baby. Don't ye be crying; there be Draggard need be dyin'. Now shut yer eyes, eh!"

Lunara broke out into hysterical laughter as Tarren finished his song. His impression of Roakore was spot on, down to the last inflection. It was Tarren's best voice mimic; albeit, he was a boy without the booming voice of the Dwarf king.

They chuckled for a long while and finally settled to gaze upon the sky. Lunara bade him continue. "What else did you learn?"

"Well, those things come first. After that, you continue on at other schools, if your family so deems it and if your funds make you able."

"Funds?" Lunara asked.

"You know, money. If you aren't a prodigy or rich, you aren't going to go to the best schools."

Lunara was dumbfounded. "You mean that only the privileged or geniuses have access to your greatest knowledge?"

Tarren thought about that. "I guess so. Why? Any Elf can learn anywhere, without paying?"

"We do not use money; we had never learned of it until coming here."

Tarren scowled, trying to comprehend a world with no money. "Then what do you do for work? How do you...I don't know...how do you pay for things?"

"Well, back home in Elladrindellia, we trade what we can't make for things we can. We do favors and call upon favors as well. We help each other at times without want for favor, for in that way, one gains more favors unasked. Do you understand?"

Tarren did, and he smiled. "It sounds wonderful."

Lunara hummed. "It is."

No more was said that night as they both fell fast asleep beneath the great oak. They slept until the sun's rays broke over the nearby mountaintops and bathed them in warmth that chased away the night's chill. Breakfast was had, and camp was cleaned up in short order. Lunara settled next to the carved staff and from her bag began to extract many different-colored jewels.

"Come, Tarren. Before I add the stones, we need to bind the staff to you." From her belt she withdrew her dagger. "This will hurt a bit," she told Tarren and took his hand. With the blade, she cut a long gash in his palm. She retrieved the staff and held it before Tarren. "Squeeze your hand over the staff."

Tarren complied, and blood dripped from his fist onto the runes of the staff. Not a drop spilled from the wood but rather was absorbed by the runes and carved leaf-and-vine pattern that adorned the staff from end to end. The runes and carvings glowed for a moment as the blood filled the crevasses and disappeared into the wood altogether. Lunara set the staff upon her lap and healed Tarren's cut with a whisper and an outstretched hand.

"Gather the hatchet please," the Elf asked, and Tarren complied.

From the top of the hatchet, Lunara removed a small red ruby and set it within the center of the staff. The wood molded itself around the jewel and held it firmly.

"The ruby atop the hatchet I enchanted to collect a bit of the kinetic energy of each of your many swings. It gathered much of the energy and stored it within. This gem holds the energy of your will also and will, from this day forth, store a bit of the kinetic energy that is produced by its movement."

Lunara produced another gem from her bag, a diamond. This too she fastened to the staff in the same manner. "This diamond my grandmother enchanted to gather energy from the sun."

Again she reached into her bag, and Tarren watched keenly, fascinated and growing more excited by the moment. This time she withdrew a round onyx orb the size of an apple and carefully placed it atop one end of the staff. The wood became fluid at Lunara's command and reached out from the tip of the staff to form a wooden talon and grasp the orb tightly. The onyx orb glowed red at its center and became dark once more.

"The orb will gather the energy of the moon."

From the bag Lunara gathered seven gems and set them among the swirling runes. Before she could tell him, Tarren asked excitedly, "What do those do?"

"These have been enchanted with protection spells. They will make your parries and your blocks stronger. It will also protect your body, within reason."

Finally she extracted one last item from her bag, a long, straight blade of Dwarven steel. Tarren watched with awe as she sang to the staff, and it opened at its center. Within the staff she inserted the blade, and the wood molded closed around it. Lunara took the staff in her hands and raised it to the heavens.

She closed her eyes and chanted loud and fast. The runes upon the staff glowed brightly in the waning light as the sun set below the mountain peaks. The wind picked up as the light died and sent Lunara's hair dancing wildly. Thick, dark clouds overtook the heavens and swirled above as Lunara continued her frantic chanting. Thunder boomed and lightning cut through the heavens, and Lunara held the staff high. Her chanting reached a crescendo, and more roaring thunder joined in the chorus. With a great exclamation, Lunara slammed the staff to the ground, and a blinding bolt of lightning tore through the sky and hit the onyx orb upon the top of the staff. The lightning hissed and crackled as it was absorbed by the staff. Lunara's hair stood on end as the lightning buzzed and crackled.

In the blink of an eye, it was over. The thunder and lightning receded, and the clouds began to disperse. The silence that followed in the wake of the tumult was unsettling. Lunara turned to Tarren and offered him the staff. Wide-eyed, he took it.

"This staff I bestow upon you, young Tarren. Name it as you will."

Tarren grasped the staff in wonder. He looked from it to the great oak from whence it had been given.

"I name you…Oakenheart."

Lunara nodded. "Oakenheart will grow in power and strength as you grow in power and strength. It has been forged of your will and the power of nature."

CHAPTER SEVENTEEN
Burning Love

Whill watched as Dirk Blackthorn disarmed and defeated yet another opponent. Dozens of men had fallen to his blades, yet not one of them had landed a single blow. Dirk was possibly one of the best fighters he had ever seen in action. Not only was he apparently knowledgeable of all forms of fighting and how to defend against them, but he also possessed the raw talent necessary to be such a devastating foe. He was quick as a cat but, at the same time, strong for his size. He could wield all weapons well, but with a thin blade and a dagger, he was lethal.

Whill had decided that he would take Dirk as one of his fighters, along with ten other men and the large barbarian woman. They would be his army; they would be his warriors. *The crowd will get a show.*

If he was to die, then he would do so in a blaze of glory that no one present would soon forget. He would kill all that came before him, Draggard, Dark Elf, man;

it did not matter. He would leave a legend so great that not even Eadon would be able to silence it. He would show these puppets exactly what revolution looked like.

He asked a guard to line up the potential fighters and walked down the line. As he passed Dirk, the man gave him a smirk. Whill stopped before him. "I hear you were arrested in the square for inciting a riot in my name."

Dirk nodded. "This is true."

"Why?" asked Whill.

"Because of what you stand for."

Whill let out a small laugh. "What do I stand for?"

"Revolution!" Dirk quickly answered. He eyed the guard and moved closer so that only Whill could hear. "We have a common enemy, Dark Elves."

Whill nodded. "I will take this man."

He continued down the line and chose the rest of his fighters, including Aurora Snowfell. The remaining fighters were escorted out of the practice area, and Whill was left with his twelve warriors.

"You have all been sentenced to death. Yet you fight with passion and purpose. This is why you have been chosen. Though we will be outnumbered by tides of opponents, I expect that you will fight bitterly to the end. We are all doomed to die, but I would rather die with honor. Together, we will show the people of Uthen-Arden the meaning of honor."

He walked the line back and forth as he spoke, measuring each man. "Will you fight with me?"

"Yes!" came the answer.

"Will you bleed with me?"

"Yes!" They answered louder this time.

"Will you die with me?"

"Yes!"

Whill stopped in his pacing and outstretched his arms. "Then let us prepare to die."

Roakore and Jarred made their way slowly backward to stand side by side near the alter of the church. The dozen Draggard advanced slowly, some down the aisle on their feet; others crawled over the pews like lizards. Roakore gave the signal, and the dragons' breath was ignited in the basement, and all hell broke loose.

There was a great explosion that rocked the very frame of the building. The floor in the middle of the church exploded into a huge fireball. Roakore pulled down Jarred, and they shielded their heads from the huge slivers of wood that were thrown through the air at high velocity. Three of the Draggard were blown to pieces, and another was engulfed in flames and fell into the inferno.

The others were riddled with wooden daggers. Two fell from their wounds, but the remaining six furiously charged Roakore and Jarred. This group of beasts had seen many battles and had fought together often. They did not barrel in foolishly but rather spread out in a circle, spears held high, tails curved and ready to strike above their heads like a scorpion. They looked demonic in the firelight. Their green-and-dark-black scales shone like polished glass. Their eyes were the color of the fire around them, and their teeth and claws reflected like daggers.

Roakore and Jarred stood back to back as the jabs from the Draggard spears and tails forced them back. Jarred lunged forward and stabbed, but three blades met his. Time was running short. The fire from the basement was claiming an ever-larger area of the floor, and already the roof was on fire. Beams groaned, and rows of benches fell into the inferno.

The six surrounding beasts pressed Roakore and Jarred with spears and tails alike. Seeing their doom coming in the form of those gleaming spears, Roakore acted on instinct, mentally grasping the metal of the spears and forcing them to the floor. Still the tails came; he felt Jarred's body at his back suddenly tense and shift. Before Jarred could give the warning, Roakore ducked as the man screamed, "Down!"

The great sword came around in a loud whoosh. Many Draggard tails were cut in half. One was deflected from its path by the sword, while another found its mark, sinking deep into Jarred's leg. The bone snapped, and Jarred crumbled to the floor. Roakore, in a rage, called upon the stone tips of the spears once again and pulled them from the floor and sent each back to their owners. The six Draggard stumbled back as they were impaled by the spears. One fell, screaming, into the ever-widening pit. Jarred cursed the beasts from the floor and hacked at the nearest Draggard's ankle. The great sword cut deep into the monster's shin, causing it to fall next to the screaming man.

Roakore brought his ax to bear and took the opportunity before him. He smashed the face of the nearest Draggard with his huge ax, spun, and kicked the Dark Elf creation into the fires below the church. He swung again and took a beast in the side; he pulled his ax back quickly, opening the creature.

Jarred grabbed the Draggard in a headlock and wrapped a leg around the beast. He squeezed with all his might. The Draggard tail ripped from his leg and backed to strike like a scorpion tail. It hovered for only a moment before striking, but before it could hit home, Roakore hewed it in half as he twirled away from his latest victim.

Jarred squeezed harder still, the face of his beloved wife burning in his mind brighter than the rising flames. Steam emanated from his tears of pain and anguish, and rage pumped rivers of blood through his knotted muscles. The Draggard desperately raked Jarred's face as it struggled against the madman. The claws cut deep into Jarred's flesh, but he felt nothing. With a loud snap, the Draggard's neck was broken; its body jerked and became limp. Jarred lay upon the floor, blood drenched and spent. His leg bled profusely, and he had lost an eye. His head swam in the heat, the air becoming thick and black. Jarred choked and laughed to himself, watching Roakore chop the head off the last Draggard as the roof caved in and the building collapsed, and he and Roakore fell into the raging inferno below.

Dirk was taken below the castle to the dungeons. The damp, dark prison was not unlike dozens he had seen before; the only difference here was the guards, Dark Elves. He followed Eadon down a corridor that smelled of damp earth, sweat, blood, and death. The screams of the tortured echoed off the walls in a dizzying plethora of wails, sobs, and shrieks. Here the Dark Elves tested their art and the endurance of mankind.

Dirk had been in many similar dungeons, or jails, but none carried with them the dread found within these walls. He was not a man that scared easily, but here, deep within the underground chambers of Del-Oradon castle, Dirk knew fear.

Eadon led him to a doorway with two guards and stepped aside. "Please, do go in."

Dirk eyed the steel door with dread. He did not fear what lay in wait for himself within the torture chamber. He feared finding her. Dirk took a deep breath and turned the handle. The door swung smoothly. Faint light entered the darkened chamber and bathed the naked form of a tattooed Dark Elf woman. She hung limp and unconscious from glowing red chains that bound her bleeding wrists.

Krentz.

He fell to his knees inside the threshold and sobbed.

The door behind him closed to the sound of Eadon's quiet laughter. Krentz stirred in the blackened room.

"What? Who is it?" she demanded. "Who is there?" Her voice was losing its power and beginning to quiver.

"Who?" she mewled and began to sob. "No. No! No! No, not you, not you...Dirk."

He stood from where he had fallen, and as if on cue, two torches upon the wall blazed forth with light—the work of Eadon no doubt.

Krentz squinted against the stinging brightness. Her eyes focused on her lover. She recognized Dirk, and her face relaxed. A smile crept across her mouth. Quickly, it subsided and was replaced by a scowl and then a look of hatred.

"No!" she screamed and thrashed against her chains. "No more. Show me no more of his face! No more!"

Dirk's heart broke once again as he watched his beloved convulsing and thrashing in delirium. He went to her, arms extended. Krentz screamed and kicked him hard. With his strong hands, he grabbed her legs and pushed himself between them. Her body relaxed at his touch. He brought his hands to her face and held it firmly. She whimpered a feeble protest. Dirk's lips found hers, and her protests stopped. The kiss lasted for a time unknown.

When finally they parted, their eyes met. Tears of joy streaked both of their faces. They remained in each other's arms, her bare, tattooed legs around his hips. His arms coiled around her body, one hand upon the small of her back, the other holding her neck. His fingers found her hair; he pulled, taking her breath away. She shuddered, as if crying, but smiled. They both laughed at the memory of it. She had always been so sensitive to his touch. Again they kissed; this time it was less urgent, their familiar kiss and their rhythm. They smiled between kisses and laughed. Dirk brought her close in his embrace, his head resting upon her chest, her cheek resting upon his hair. She breathed him in and shuddered, and again, they laughed.

There they stayed, not speaking. Dirk's strong legs held her up, giving her relief from chains that had kept her on her toes. Krentz slept deeply for the first time since she had been captured. She slept, and Dirk listened to her laboring heart.

Krentz dreamed of times gone, memories shared. She dreamed of those many years spent living in the wild and on the island of Eldon and of herself and Dirk sparring, singing, dancing, and making love beneath the stars. They had sat in the grass, sometimes talking for days. They had watched as the sun was born, and they watched his death. They had sung to the moon as she searched nightly for her lover and rejoiced with her as she and the sun were one, if for but a moment. That day, day had become night, and Krentz and Dirk had mirrored the sun and moon's embrace.

She awoke with a smile and kissed his forehead. "Why have you come here? I fled from you to save your life. You died in my dream, and you died because of me."

She blinked and a tear fell. "I cannot live knowing that you will die because of me."

"You would rather I live without you, that which *is* my death? I have been dead since you left. I have felt more alive these last moments than I will in fifty lifetimes spent without you. Leave fate to the unknown, my dear Krentz. We only have control until we don't, and then we sleep. I choose you, and I will not be robbed of my choice, not even by you, my love."

Krentz wiped a tear from his face with her cheek and softly kissed the spot. Slowly, she dotted kisses from his cheek to his lips. He bit her lip softly, and she tensed, and her breath quickened as if she had plunged into cold water. Point made, Dirk kissed her softly.

"Very well," she said when, finally, they parted lips. "I will ignore the vision. But if you die as you did, I shall follow you into the dark. That I promise."

"Then I shall simply never die," Dirk replied with a grin

CHAPTER EIGHTEEN

Dragons' breath

Aurora's body barely stretched out upon the floor of her small cell. She counted out her two hundredth push-up with an easy breath. The energy that the Dark Elf had forced into her body coursed through her veins and muscles. She had been pushing her body hard for three hours, yet she did not tire, did not hunger for food, and did not need water. Her body hummed with the exertion. She counted out number 250 and kept going swiftly. Her mind raced as she thought of the possibilities of her newfound power.

Not only could she free her people from their frozen island exile, but now she could challenge the chief of the northern barbarians, Icethorn. She would defeat the chief easily, and she would lead her people to glory. Finally, they would take back their homeland of northern Agora, and finally, they would know retribution.

She would once again restore honor to her family's name; honor that had been tarnished forever by the arrogant chief. Years before, Aurora's father had challenged the chieftain upon the fields of Orthax. Her father had bested the chief and stood over him, prepared to deal the final blow. Icethorn's gray dragon had swept in and scooped up Aurora's father in its wicked claws, flown high into the sky, and dropped him.

Time had stopped for eternity as Aurora watched her father fall through the air, his voice booming a curse upon the chieftain. The force of the impact threw up a plume of snow that reached upward to the heavens. Aurora had been the one to close his eyes. She had sworn revenge upon the chief that day, and soon would be her chance to exact that revenge.

She would defeat the chief and claim the Dragon Staff of Eztule. With it, and the help of the Dark Elf Eadon, she would lead her people home. She needed only to fulfill her duty as Eadon's general, and her first appointed task was to kill Whill's mentor, Abram. Aurora knew nothing of this man; she knew only that she must succeed in her task, for the sake of her people.

Zhola reminded himself not to fight against the barbed chains that held his wings tightly against his bruised and battered body. He reminded himself that to accept the pain was the only way to live with it, to defeat it. He had become accustomed to the constant pain over the last six months since Eadon had taken him and Whill captive.

Eadon had tried to invade his mind and find the whereabouts of the legendary sword Adimorda but to no avail. Zhola had known great pain before, but Eadon had indeed expanded the ancient dragon's definition of the word. Eadon had bombarded him with mental assaults on numerous occasions, but Zhola refused to crack. Though Eadon was indeed ancient, and also the most powerful Elf alive, Zhola too was ancient and powerful.

The great red dragon fought off every attack successfully by locking away the knowledge of the sword deep within the recesses of his mind. Zhola himself knew not the location of the blade, only clues with which to find it.. He could free the information if he chose, but not until he chose. Dragons' minds worked much differently than any man, or Elf, or Dwarf, for that matter.

Eadon had attempted to force his way in. He had tried to bombard Zhola with illusions and hallucinations, but all attempts had failed. Zhola would not give the clues to the whereabouts of the sword, ever. He was happy to die first rather than see Eadon attain the blade. Eadon's frustration had been great, his retribution, horrifying. But Zhola would not crack. His mental fortitude was the result of his great age and many centuries of practice.

So there he sat, chained to the floor and thick stone walls. He had also been hamstrung, the wounds left to fester. He had dealt with the pain easily enough, but once the maggots began to fester in his open wounds, he became quite irritated. He would have filled the room with fire and cauterized the wounds had he anything left within his fire glands, but he was milked daily of his dragons' breath.

The tubes had been stabbed through his neck, into his glands, and the precious liquid was siphoned out constantly. It collected in the corner of the large cell, near the door. Its constant dripping into the gallon jug was another part of his torture. He was chained to stone every four feet or so with wicked, barbed chains, enhanced of course, by the twisted Dark Elves' charms. Usually, the barbed chains would rest upon his thick scales harmlessly, but these glowed red hot at the barbs and were only stopped from burning deeper by the chains.

Zhola had blocked out the pain and the dripping of the dragons' breath and the feeling of the writhing maggots within his flesh. He now rested within his inner world. A dragon's mind was much different than other creatures. They tended to be solitary creatures, even hibernating for decades. Because their minds were much calmer, they were content to simply be.

Zhola stretched his consciousness out into the ether and searched for Whill. He had been able to reach him before; rather, he had sensed Whill faintly. For Eadon had many spells surrounding the boy, to keep him from prying minds.

The Elves would come soon. Zhola knew it was but a matter of time. Why they had tarried so long, Zhola could not guess. He was eager to be done with this business of the sword.

Zhola huffed smoke through his nose as he wondered why he cared at all. *Let them kill each other and leave us alone,* he thought. But they would not leave the dragons alone. Eadon would tear across the entire world, spreading death and destruction like wildfire, should he get his way. Zhola sighed as he was reminded by his sense of duty that it was the responsibility of all beings to fight and try to defeat any that were an enemy to life.

Zhola believed the prophecy; he always had. He did not, however, believe in Whill at the moment.

"Business then?" Abram said as he took the seat opposite the Dark Elf.

The Dark Elf nodded approvingly. "You are quick for a human, quick indeed."

The Dark Elf eyed Abram thoughtfully and raised an eyebrow. "Perhaps you have had...enhancements to your person, possibly help from an Elf?"

Abram scoffed at that. "Or perhaps I am good at what I do."

"Perhaps," the Elf mimicked.

Abram laid a weighted sack upon the table; he opened the drawstring and dumped a fortune in jewels onto it. A thousand torches reflected off of the jewels, casting a multicolored spectrum of light upon the Dark Elf's face. The studded piercings in his eyebrows rose.

"This should be sufficient payment for one gallon of dragons' breath." stated Abram.

The Elf eyed the collection. "What did you say your name was?"

"I didn't," stated Abram dryly.

"I like to know the names of those I do business with."

"As do I," Abram retorted. "In human society, it is considered polite for a host to introduce himself first... and it is also considered rude to attack a guest."

The Dark Elf sneered. "When I attack you, you will know it!"

Rhunis laughed from his place beside the seated Abram. "That was clever. Did you make that up yourself?"

The Dark Elf did not find humor in the jest. Abram guarded his mind as he felt the Dark Elf extending his mind out toward Abram's. He had feared this would happen upon discovering that they dealt with Dark Elves. He had been shocked to find that the guard at the first door was a Dark Elf, and he had instantly known their danger. How they were going to get out of this place unrecognized, he did not know. He simply hoped that these Elves did not know of him.

The Dark Elf laughed, and Abram knew he had failed. The Elf had read his every thought. "Of course we know who you are; your faces have been projected to us by our great master, Abram of Arden."

He looked then to Rhunis. "And the great dragon slayer, the scarred-knight Rhunis." The Elf eyed the scar that covered half of Rhunis's face. "You know, we have ways to mend that."

"I like it just the way it is, Elf. I did not almost die for it to have it replaced."

The Elf ignored him. "How rude of me indeed to not introduce myself to such esteemed guests as you. I am Sarrazon."

Rhunis and Abram nodded their heads in greeting. "We have a saying, 'well met.' But it is not warranted at this juncture," said Abram.

Sarrazon laughed at that. "You are in good spirits for one that has just handed himself over to the enemy, one that will soon be in the hands of the great Eadon."

Abram was not listening; he had closed his eyes and shut out the room. His mind screamed a name, in the hopes that the Elf had indeed reached the city and, by slim chance, was near. Sarrazon heard it and leapt to his feet. Abram hardly noticed as he continued to mentally scream the name and project with all his mental might. *Zerafin!*

Sarrazon extended a hand, and a shock wave of energy hit Abram and Rhunis so hard that they were thrown back to slam into the wall. Abram's concentration was broken. Sarrazon strode toward then, blade drawn. In his other hand, a ball of lightning swirled and crackled.

Zerafin was a few miles from the city when he heard the faint calling of his name upon the wind. He tapped into a ring upon a finger and focused on the sound. *Zerafin!*

The mental cry of Abram jolted him in his saddle. He reared his horse and focused on the location of Abram. Once he had found it, he dismounted and addressed the others. "Into your groups, your missions are known; I go now to aid an ally. I will meet my group shortly."

With that, he unsheathed his sword and tapped into its great energy. He raised it to the sky and mentally projected the blade into the air; it went, and his body followed.

Zerafin flew high and fast toward the city. Like a comet he was, as he flew over it, honed in on Abram's location, and crashed through the roof of the building from which the cry had come. Zerafin tucked his body and twirled through the wreckage. Creating a force field of protective energy around him, he landed on his feet, smashing the table at which Abram had just sat. Before he had entered the room, he had used his mind sight to determine the numbers he faced. Ten he counted. Abram and Rhunis's auras he recognized at once; the other eight were Dark Elves.

Zerafin landed and, at once, cast wards of protection over the two humans. Simultaneously, he let out a blast from his right hand; the shock wave threw the eight Elves back a step. The Elves recovered quickly and attacked as one with their blades and spells. The eight blades came at Zerafin, along with a myriad of spells. With but a thought, he brought a cylindrical wall of stone up from the floor and around himself and coated it with a spell to deflect all attacks back toward the sender. As soon as the energy attacks of the Dark Elves hit the energy barrier, Zerafin made the stone shield explode. It blasted out in a shower of projectiles of all sizes and a cloud of dust. As the Dark Elves moved to defend, he sprang forth with unnatural speed and decapitated the closest, simultaneously incinerating the head with white-hot flame, which shot forth from a ring upon his left hand.

The Dark Elf closest to the pyre scrambled to think of a defense and was forever quieted as Zerafin caused the stone below the Elf to throw him forward, and he met Zerafin's blade, Nifarez. The sword cut through all defenses and was pulled upward, splitting the Elf in two from the chest up. Zerafin then hit the defenseless Dark Elf guard with a blast that blew its body into a million pieces.

Zerafin had gauged the power of all in the room by then and had determined the guards to be of lesser power than he, greatly. Though one of them, their leader presumably, seemed a powerful foe. Even without mind sight, one could see a lack of fear within that Dark Elf's eyes. With the great power within his blade Zerafin easily defeated the remaining dark elves, all but the leader. Sarrazon knew his foe to be beyond him and smartly ran for his life as Zerafin battled the others.

CHAPTER NINETEEN
The White Dragon

Eadon eyed Whill from across the room. Night had fallen on the city, and the world was silent. Through one window the moonlit rain clouds seemed not to move, as if a curse had been laid upon the kingdom. This chamber Whill knew well, for it was the very same in which his father's spirit had avenged his life.

A multitude of torches burned upon the walls, as did dozens of candles scattered here and there. The many sources of light and shadow cast themselves as a cloak upon Eadon's face. A dead man lay at the Dark Elf's feet the pool of blood creating a scarlet canvas for the dancing light of the candles.

Whill returned Eadon's stare. "I will not fall for your tricks, old one. This and every other victim's death is on your hands. I will not be coaxed by you," he said as he turned to spy on the unmoving clouds.

"I can see that," answered Eadon as he wiped the blood from his dagger and sheathed it. "Would you die then? Rather than learn how to live? Have you not learned to fight, to defend yourself? Have you not taken the innocent lives of the slave men?"

Eadon waved a hand, and the corpse caught flame. The flame burned white hot until only ashes remained. Whill hated that nothing was sacred with this Dark Elf, and nothing was secret. His memories, thoughts, and emotions could be seen as easily by Eadon as Whill's own face.

"You are projecting, Whill," Eadon sneered.

Whill turned to look upon the hated Elf. "Why play these games if you know my mind? Why not make me a puppet?"

"Puppets I have, young friend. Students are a much more rare acquisition; a worthy student, of strength and power and wanting, is rare indeed," Eadon explained. "You will take the lives of men and Draggard, but not use their life force?" he asked.

"It is not a practice of the Elves of the Sun," answered Whill.

"Ah. But you are not an Elf. You are not bound to their ridiculous laws. Why do you limit yourself? Simply to cling to some misguided doctrine?"

Eadon strode toward Whill and offered him a glass. Whill took it. They eyed each other as they drank. Whill was not worried about it being poisoned. What would be the point? He returned to looking out the window.

"You are set to die soon, yet you do not care?" said Eadon as he replenished his glass.

Whill answered without taking his eyes off of the city, the kingdom of his forebearers. "No."

"But what of Avriel? You would leave her in her current state? You would not attempt to save her?"

Whill did not answer.

"You would give up without a fight?" coaxed Eadon.

"I have fought!" hollered Whill. He mentally chastised himself for letting Eadon get under his skin. "I have fought, and I have lost. I will not be tempted to your side. I face my death in peace; I do not fear death as you do."

Eadon's nostrils flared, and his eyes flashed for a quick moment, and the look was gone. "You cannot be convinced, I see. Perhaps there is another way. Come, I have something you must see."

Whill watched as Eadon walked to the chamber door but did not follow. Eadon gave Whill a look that dared him to disobey, and finally, Whill followed.

Eadon led Whill through the castle corridors and halls. They came to a large iron vault door. The door, like the one within the vaults of the Ebony Mountains, held something profound for Whill. He could feel it. Whill knew, also, that Eadon's last game piece was Avriel's soul. He stared at the door and shook his head slowly.

Eadon cocked his head and smiled, as if proud of Whill's deduction of that which lay beyond the door. Whill shook his head more vigorously and took slow steps back.

"No. I will not play your gods damned games any longer!" He faced Eadon and charged at him. He stopped and screamed in Eadon's face, their noses nearly touching, "I will not be a part of your twisted games any longer!"

The white dragon awoke from its slumber. It spread its wings and growled, bending low, stretching. Instantly, the beast's senses alerted it to prey. It turned and eyed the nervous goat chained to the wall ten feet away.

The dragon was hungry, and it was glad for the meal, though the meal lacked the thrill of the hunt. It longed for the open skies and long-stretching forests full of prey. Never had the dragon flown, nor had it hunted in the forest or upon the fields, only within the realm of dreams.

The dragon sighed, a puff of smoke emanating from its snout, and pounced upon the goat. It took its time, eating one leg at a time and enjoying the satisfying crunch of the bones under the pressure of its strong teeth.

It stopped in its feeding when it heard a ruckus outside of its cell. The dragon growled low in its throat when it recognized the voice of its hated maker. The dragon wanted nothing more than to feel the Dark Elf's bones between its teeth. Eadon had created it, but he had also imprisoned the beast. Though it had only hatched a week ago, it had been forced to grow to full size in that short time, through Eadon's dark magic.

Though the dragon had never left the cell in its short life, it knew a great many things due to racial memory. Dragons were unique in that they were born with a vast amount of knowledge, passed down through the millennia.

The dragon knew a great many things, and it recognized Eadon as a hunter of its kind and the creator of the Draggard. It had tried to kill Eadon as soon as it had attained the ability to breathe fire. But Eadon had easily avoided the flames and had made the dragon pay dearly for its attack.

There was another with the Dark Elf outside the massive door that kept it locked within its cell, perhaps a minion of Eadon's. The dragon readied its fire glands and watched the door.

Spittle riddled Eadon's face as Whill screamed, and his was a face of distilled rage. Eadon moved to backhand Whill, a blow that would have broken the young man's jaw had it not been blocked. Whill brought his hand up as quickly as a cat's paw and blocked the blow and grabbed Eadon's wrist. The two shared a stare for many moments, neither moving. Eadon's face was a picture of calm, while Whill's was one of hatred and grim determination without a hint of fear.

Something within Whill's mind snapped. He had never wanted to hurt someone as badly as he did at this moment. He saw only red as the many possibilities of what lay beyond the door flashed through his mind. The rage drove him beyond reason, shores away from sanity. His mind dove into the deepest caverns of his psyche, the shadowed corners of his darkest side. He returned to that place within his mind where he had kept all of the pain and memories of his torture. There they had been kept locked up by Whill's subconscious, as to not haunt him until he went mad. In his moment of murderous rage, Whill threw open the gates holding that side of his scarred mind at bay. Power surged through his body; he felt a change within, a shift.

Whill extended his hand and screamed with murderous rage, and from his hand shot foggy black tendrils of dark energy. They slammed into Eadon's extended palm as he blocked the blow. Steadily, they pulsed, and steadily, Eadon absorbed Whill's attack.

"You cannot begin to harm me, Whill. Your every attack will be absorbed by me and added to my power," said Eadon with a sneer.

Whill screamed and pressed the attack harder. He could feel his energy quickly fading, though he cared not. He ended the energy attack. His frustration and rage at being so helpless against Eadon surged within him, and he dealt Eadon a double-fisted blow to his midsection. Eadon was unaffected, but Whill was thrown back many feet, his attack having been turned against him.

Whill dragged himself up from the floor. His rage gone, his anger sated, he did all he could do—he laughed. His laughter echoed off of the walls and through the hallways, a laugh of pure mirth. Whill continued to laugh as he slowly walked toward Eadon. The Dark Elf simply smirked at him, amused. Whill's laughter became maniacal. He tried to speak, but he could not. He pointed at Eadon as he laughed.

"You..." he said between chuckles. "You are a coward." Whill finished with a great fit of laughter. Whill had reached Eadon and stood before him. He lifted his arms and went in circles and spoke as though to a crowd.

"I give you, Eadon, the coward."

Eadon's amusement disappeared. Whill went on.

"The king of lies, the murderer of his homeland, the creator of monsters with which he might hide behind. The Dark Elf of legend, the coward, Eadon of Drindellia!" laughed Whill.

He turned on Eadon and spat in his face. The spittle did not hit Eadon, however, and instead dripped down the invisible energy shield just an inch from the Elf lord's face. Whill laughed all the harder.

"Behold, all ye, the great and powerful Eadon. His power is so great that he will not be spat on, nor shat on. None shall harm the great coward, but he will harm all."

Whill's laughter was cut short as Eadon took him by the throat and lifted him off of the stone floor. Whill spoke without breath. "None...will...mourn... you."

Eadon threw him at a far wall, hard enough to crack the stone and a few ribs. Whill sucked in the precious air and got to his feet slowly. He opened his hands and clenched air as blue tendrils of healing energy quickly wove their way beneath his shirt, mending his ribs. He staggered, the healing taxing him. Bravely, he stood to his full height. "You are a coward, Eadon. That you cannot change, not with all the power in this world. You will die alone, and no tears shall fall, unless they be those wrought by pity. Like a crazed dog frothing at the mouth, you need to be put down."

"You will..." Eadon began.

"I am speaking, coward!" Whill hollered and took steps toward the Elf. "Why not simply end it now and let me put you out of your misery? Because should you let me live, I will teach you the meaning of hell."

"Enough from you!" Eadon barked and shot forth from his left hand a ball of pulsing red energy. Whill extended a hand in defense, and the spell turned and slammed into Eadon's invisible energy shield. Sparks and fire flew forth from the Dark Elf, none touching him. He looked on, wide-eyed.

Whill staggered again, the magic taxing him greatly. He laughed once again and slurred like a drunkard. "Looks like I learned a new trick, eh, coward? For that shall be your name hence...forth." said Whill as he slumped down against the stone wall.

Eadon only smiled in wonder. "The prophecy has made you powerful indeed."

Whill chuckled to himself. This time his mirth was genuine and not brought on by lunacy. He had sent back the attack of Eadon, a defense Eadon had just used on him. The first spark of hope Whill had known lit deep within him, washing warmth throughout his body. Hope regenerated his spirit. He, it seemed, had the ability to mimic any spell used upon him. It had not occurred to him until he had sent back Eadon's attack. Now it made perfect sense. He had been healed as an infant; therefore, he had the ability to heal Tarren. He had been attacked by the Dark Elf with some kind of pain attack, and he had known numerous such spells during his time of torture. If Whill could mimic those spells, he could mimic all.

As if Eadon had been reading his mind, Eadon raised an eyebrow. "Perhaps you can. But that is a far cry from being able to cast quick enough to be effective."

Quickly and violently, Eadon unleashed a barrage of multicolored energy assaults upon Whill that he could not begin to counter. Eadon had his turn at laughter as Whill was engulfed in a fireball and slammed into the wall. Eadon walked over to the charred and twitching Whill. He kicked him in the face, his boot taking an amount of skin with it. He allowed Whill's breathe to become very shallow before healing him.

Eadon walked to the door and turned with a flourish. He eyed the tattered Whill. "Enough of these games, perhaps another time."

He opened the great doors with ease and let them fall inward. A great wall of fire burst at his back harmlessly as he chuckled. A great white dragon roared behind him. Whill's eyes went wide, and he prayed he did not look upon...

"I give you the maiden of Elladrindellia, the beautiful Avriel," said Eadon to Whill's horror. Avriel reared as far as she could against the chains and breathed forth fire yet again.

Whill cried in disbelief. Eadon laughed as the wall of fire dissipated against his raised hand. He hit Avriel's dragon body with steady, pulsing dark energy that had her roaring and writhing in pain.

"Stop!" screamed Whill as he ran toward Avriel, but he was stopped easily by Eadon's strong arm. He was raised into the air by his shirt. With the other hand, Eadon continued to torture the dragon. He screamed into Whill's face above the roar of the tortured Avriel.

"Your fealty, boy, or there will be no end to her pain!"

"Leave her alone!"

"Your fealty, Whill of Agora!"

Whill's mind raced, and he stopped in his thrashing. "How do I know it is her?"

Eadon released them both. Whill never took his eyes off of the white dragon. She curled up and breathed heavily, her murderous blue eyes watching Eadon's every move.

"Oh, it is her alright, though I have made her forget who she is. Or rather, her soul has not yet been awakened within her new body. That, I was waiting for you to witness firsthand."

Whill could only watch, horrified, as Eadon chanted low to himself and directed a hand at the dragon. A spot within her center glowed brightly and then subsided. The dragon stood and regarded the two with newfound interest. Her large blue orbs settled upon Whill, and recognition was within them. She then turned to Eadon and reared back in horror. She roared and suddenly stopped at hearing her own voice, that of a dragon. She looked down at herself as if puzzled. Extending a huge wing, she looked upon herself. She looked again to Whill and tried to speak. Rather than words, the sound was a chorus of strange growls and guttural noises. Then Whill heard the voice of Avriel faintly within his mind. He spoke to her as her voice floated up out of darkness and into his mind.

Avriel!

Whill?

Avriel!

Whill walked forward daringly into the cell and came within feet of her. She came forward also, until her chains would not allow it. Her head was half the size of Whill's body, her eyes as large as his head.

Whill? What has happened? I had died, and...what has he done? Why am I within this body? How?

Whill could only extend a hand and touch her face. She turned on Eadon. *This is your dark magic!* Her mind screamed, and her mouth roared.

Eadon laughed. "I should think you more grateful for my saving your life when you so unwisely tried to end it. Your soul needed a proper...host. Be glad it was not a Draggard queen, princess."

Neither Avriel nor Whill contested that fact; instead, they looked to each other's eyes. Eadon watched the two with a grin. Avriel broke the gaze and bade Whill with her mind. *Look upon me with mind sight.*

Whill did as she had requested. It took a moment, as he had not practiced it in some time. But once his mind sight was achieved, he gasped as he laid his awareness upon the spirit before him. Avriel's soul looked like nothing he had ever seen. It shone from the projected corporal form of the Elf maiden with a brilliance that could have blinded his eyes. Her three forms, that of the iridescent dragon, Elf maiden, and soul, moved in unison and spoke as such. Whill focused upon Avriel as he knew her.

"I see you," was all that he could utter.

A teardrop fell from the dragon's eye; the soul pulsed brightly, and the phantom image of Avriel kissed Whill's lips. It was the kiss they had never shared. *Come back, Whill,* came her voice in his head.

He did so, and before him, once again, was the beautiful white dragon. A part of him was restored then, a part that had died when she had died, when they had all died. Avriel was not lost to him after all, and never again would she be.

"She can never be restored to her body; none know the secrets to the art—none but me. I alone can restore Avriel to her true form." Eadon bravely strode into the cell, within Avriel's reach.

"Give me your fealty, and she shall be restored. Together, we can bring peace to this land. Bring me the sword of Adimorda; pledge your fealty to me, and you shall live to be a king."

Before Whill could answer, Avriel's mind screamed, and her mouth roared in defiance. From her mouth spewed forth liquid fire. It hit Eadon in the chest, driving him back through the door into the hallway beyond. Avriel relentlessly continued to douse the doorway and hall with her liquid fire. She suddenly stopped and began to choke and cough, like a dog that has eaten grass. Whill shielded his face from the flames with his arm and leapt behind a scaled leg.

So great was the heat that the stone began to melt and, like lava, drip to the floor below. The hallway was an inferno. Avriel quickly ran out of fire breath and breathed heavily from the exertion; smoke bellowed from her nose.

They both watched the doorway, but Eadon did not retaliate. It was quiet. Very abruptly, the temperature in the room changed from a melting inferno to below freezing. As Whill stood, there was less than a second's warning to wonder what was happening. He and Avriel and the entire room were covered in thick sheets of ice. Whill was frozen still, though he was not frozen throughout. Avriel too was covered in a beautiful shroud of ice. They remained that way for some time, trapped within their ice tombs, unable to breathe.

They watched from behind the ice mold as Eadon strode into the room, lifted each hand slowly, and then shoved his palms out before him. From his hands blasted a shock wave of energy out into the small, enclosed room. The blast shattered the ice that held the two and traveled on to utterly destroy the wall behind them.

They were thrown from the room as Eadon's blast only grew in intensity. Over the ledge they flew as rubble and debris bit into both skin and scale. Avriel was caught by her chains and dangled by her hind legs, her wings outstretching as she attempted to right herself. Whill barely had time to grab onto one of her clawed feet as he fell past. He swung up on it and caught a good hold with both hands. He looked down at the sloping roofs and the five-story drop to the courtyard.

Whill heard, but did not see, Eadon at the ledge; as he slashed his sword down and cut Avriel's chains. Avriel instantly brought up Whill into her grasp and turned. Extending her wings, she kicked off from the tower and began to glide. She was unbalanced and a fledgling, but she glided.

She attempted to fly out of the courtyard, but her tail was entangled in chains, and she needed to land. But what was the point in that—she would only be beaten and reprimanded by Eadon. No, this was her chance to rescue them both. If only she could clear the wall, and the one beyond, and fly free across the green forests to the forest city of Cerushia.

Avriel felt the tension as Eadon caused the chains that dangled from her ankles to wrap themselves around her legs and wings and squeeze. She curled Whill up tight and rolled across a rooftop, only to be pitched off to fall a hundred feet to the courtyard below.

If she had been falling straight, she would have come out worse, but as it was, the pitch of the roof caused her chained form to roll for many feet before crashing into a supply wagon.

"Do you pledge your fealty to me?!" Eadon bellowed from the tower as he leapt off, extended his arms, and turned into a man-sized crow. The crow circled the bloodied and tangled pair and soon swept down almost to the ground. The legs of an Elf touched down, and Eadon returned to his Elf form.

The driver of the supply wagon trembled at what he had seen and could not withstand Eadon's glare; he simply withered down to a dust pile. Eadon spread his hands, and the chains that held Avriel exploded from her. She gently opened her wings to reveal an unhurt Whill. He stood in the shadow of the wing and walked out onto the wreckage. He turned his back on Eadon and looked into the white dragon's eyes. She looked at him but did not see him; her mind saw only what her soul felt, a presence, faint, ever-so faint, but familiar. Whill then felt it too; together, their minds spoke, *Zerafin*.

They had been projecting, intensely, and Eadon overheard their minds' words.

"Yes, do you feel him?" he asked. Then he bellowed. "Zerafin! Oh, great warrior of the dying Elves! Come and face me, so that you and your sister shall die together!"

Eadon grinned and turned on Whill and Avriel. From his hands flew gnashing, twisting, biting, and hissing snakes of living lightning. They bit into Avriel's scales and jolted her stiffly upon her side. She let out a roar of tortured pain that Whill had never heard from a creature.

Eadon smiled all the more and sent an excruciating pulse of the lightning at the white dragon.

CHAPTER TWENTY

Convergeance of Power

Two miles away, Zerafin cocked his head to the sound. Even Abram and Rhunis stopped in their loading of the bottles of dragons' breath and listened to the unnaturally loud voice of Eadon as he made his challenge. Indeed, every soul within the city proper heard the words. Abram knew the look on his Elf friend's face, though it was usually seen upon a certain gruff Dwarf. He searched for the words and said, "Zerafin, should you do this?"

Abram saw Zerafin's answer in his burning eyes and felt an energy surge course through the Elf. It bit at his hand and made it numb. Even through the pain, he held contact with the Elf. "Do not do this; we must stick to the plan," he begged.

Zerafin gently removed Abram's hand and shot up and out of the hole in the ceiling.

Whill watched helplessly as Eadon shocked Avriel. But then into the night shot a white flame. It stopped and shone brightly before shooting straight at them. Zerafin's blade was like a comet as it slammed into Eadon's protective energy shield. To Whill's astonishment, there was a clang of swords as Eadon found it necessary to block. Zerafin charged forth, unleashing a devastating array of attacks, feints, and counterattacks that had Eadon backing away. Finally, the Dark Elf shot forth a blinding array of dark energy at Zerafin, which Zerafin countered with a parry of the blade and an outstretched hand to the sky. Zerafin parted the clouds above as his power shot forth and rained down pure light from the heavens.

Clouds parted and the heavens thundered as Zerafin brought the whole of the power of the sun down upon his dark opponent. All in the courtyard were temporarily blinded by the beam of light. Eadon screamed in anguish as the sun burned through his many wards and his fine armor, biting his flesh. Zerafin then unleashed a shock wave that moved the very earth. It hit the Dark Elf and sent him crashing through the base of a tower.

He turned to his sister. "Fly now!"

Avriel, the white dragon, did not move from her spot. Instead, she roared in defiance. She would not leave without him.

Zerafin growled and swore under his breath and sent a fireball into the rubble.

Dozens of Uthen-Arden soldiers came running into the courtyard, swords drawn. Whill noticed also that three Dark Elves had come to see what the disturbance was, or rather, they were beckoned by Eadon.

Eadon strode out of the flames unharmed and eyed Zerafin with a grin. He turned to his Dark Elves. "Take Whill to his chambers. I will deal with the siblings."

The words barely left his lips before Zerafin slammed his sword into the ground. The shock wave spread out and knocked the standing human soldiers from their feet. As he retracted his sword, the ground began to bulge and ripple. From the ground rose an earth elemental, made of dirt and stone. Once erect, it stood more than one hundred feet.

"Protect the human and the dragon!" Zerafin bade the elemental and, in a flash, engaged Eadon.

Their swords met with a thunderous explosion as they battled. The human guards did not know what to think. Many scattered for safety at the appearance of the earth elemental. Those brave enough to attempt to attack it were quickly destroyed. Volleys of spells bombarded the creature as the Dark Elves moved to gather up Whill. The elemental put itself between Whill and Avriel and the Dark Elves as the many spells slammed into it, sending huge chunks of earth falling from its wounds. The elemental roared and swatted at the incoming spells. With a huge earthen foot, it kicked aside a Dark Elf that got too close; the blow sent it flying into the castle wall with a thud.

Zerafin and Eadon exchanged blows, each more powerful than the next as they tested the extent of each other's powerful weapons. Whill watched on helplessly and turned to Avriel. "We must fly while we can. Come now, lest your brother's rescue be in vain."

Avriel snorted smoke from her nose and reluctantly turned from Zerafin and Eadon's battle. She lowered a shoulder, and Whill scrambled up onto her neck. She leapt off the ground but was hit by a fireball from one of the Dark Elves battling the elemental. The gigantic elemental slammed its foot down on the distracted Dark Elf, burying it deeply. Avriel landed hard and roared with pain.

The elemental then took a swipe at Eadon as he leapt up and over Zerafin. The being's hand hit the Dark Elf but simply disintegrated on impact. Eadon landed and slashed at Zerafin's back, his sword moving in a blur. The blade hit Zerafin's energy shield and disintegrated it in a shower of sparks. Blood flew as Zerafin was cut across the back. Blue tendrils of healing energy were already surrounding the wound as Zerafin fell back and turned. From his left hand, he let loose a shock wave of energy that blasted Eadon and sent the Dark Elf flying.

The elemental roared and stomped upon yet another Dark Elf. The Elf was buried deeply but was not killed. His energy shield took the brunt of the blow, and the ground below the earth elemental shook and erupted as the Dark Elf blasted up through the earth, shooting through the foot and leg of the elemental and out of its knee. Earth and stone fell away, and the elemental fell, having had its leg destroyed. It hit with a resounding boom atop many of the stunned Uthen-Arden soldiers.

The Dark Elves ignored the downed elemental as the dirt gathered once again to reform the destroyed leg. Avriel put Whill behind herself and turned to the Dark Elves and bathed them in her white-hot dragon breath. The flames shot forth and were deflected harmlessly.

Whill was tired of being helpless, and with all his will and strength of mind, he outstretched his hand and summoned to him one of the blades of the fallen human soldiers.

"Avriel. Remember how you lent Zerafin's blade your power upon the ship Celestra?"

"Yes," she hummed.

Whill held his sword high as the dragon, Avriel, bathed it in fire. The flames shot forth in a thin line and were utterly consumed, heat and licking flame alike, by Whill's sword.

Whill smiled widely as he felt the distilled power of the dragons' breath hum within the blade, beckoning to be released. He ran three short steps and jumped up and leaped higher still from Avriel's dragon knee. Twenty feet he soared, and he came down with a howl and cocked sword upon the lead Dark Elf. Before he landed, Whill looked upon the Elf's tattooed face; it was that of his torturer, Velkarell. Rather than being filled with fear upon seeing one that had hurt him so, Whill was enraged. And when he fell upon the Dark Elf of his nightmares, Whill put into that blow all of the anger, fear, pain, and sorrow that Velkarell had caused.

Whill's leap was watched by all within the courtyard. Time froze, and all that existed was the wild-eyed, crazy man flying through the air. All watched as his blade turned white hot and flames leapt forth hungrily.

There was a blinding flash as Whill descended upon the Dark Elf torturer with a scream of defiance, and the courtyard was bathed in shadow. The Dark Elf put up his blade to block and expended huge amounts of stored power upon his shield, yet Whill's blade cut through all defenses. The sword cut through the Dark Elf's chin, chest, gut, and groin, leaving the injured Elf to simply gawk in astonishment and horror. Whill landed upon a foot and one knee and instantly drove his blade into the Dark Elf's neck and out his skull. The blade then erupted in white-hot flame that engulfed Velkarell but did not touch Whill.

The Dark Elf fell in a pile of ash; only his inner gems remained. These Whill picked up and took up within his fist. His back arched and his body jolted as he took from the gems all of the stored power within them. His sword glowed with the addition of energy, and Whill turned to the next Dark Elf with a grin.

Whill engaged another Dark Elf as Zerafin screamed to his sister and bade her once more. "Fly now!"

This time she did, knowing that there would be no victory here. She flew swiftly, and she flew high as below her, her brother's powerful sword met Eadon's.

Whill smiled to himself as he watched Avriel fly away and over the walls of the courtyard. He engaged the Dark Elf before him, his borrowed sword aflame once more. This Dark Elf, however, did not count on a parry to save him. He had seen Whill's power, and he knew to be wary. The Dark Elf raised a hand, and Whill was lifted off the ground. He put up a shield with his mind, and that shield hummed with the energy of the blade. But the seasoned and practiced Dark Elf dove into it and unwove the energy shield in an instant. From Whill's grasp, he took the flaming sword, and the flames went out as he absorbed the energy within. Whill screamed in defiance as the Elf grinned in victory.

Zerafin could not at the moment lend Whill any energy as he used the majority of his blade's energy to battle Eadon. They both had expended massive amounts of power in the fight, and Zerafin knew that Eadon was angered to be depleted so. But he also knew, as did Eadon, that Zerafin would lose this contest.

Zerafin felt his sister's energy and grinned to himself. He heard in his mind a language he had not used since she had been a child. Eadon shot at him a great amount of energy in the form of black tendrils, which surely would have broken through his defenses. Rather than take the blow, Zerafin morphed himself into the earth. Taking the form of his native land's most beloved plant, the Evervine, he dug deep.

Eadon followed suit and dove into the earth as a plant, one and the same. Like so many fighting worms, they engaged each other's roots. Eadon entangled them below the surface. Zerafin then emerged as a flowering vine and changed to his Elven form. He caused the ground to turn to stone as he leapt high and landed upon the back of his diving, dragon sister. He sent a blast at the Dark Elf that had beaten Whill, sending him flying, and Avriel grabbed hold of Whill with a claw.

As Eadon angrily broke through the stone and turned to his Elf form, he spotted the escaping dragon. He reached out and with his mind yanked Whill from Avriel's claw. Whill fell through the air and hit the ground hard. Eadon roared with rage and shot forth a spell at Avriel and Zerafin.

Zerafin knew what was coming; he expected Eadon, in his anger, to send a death spell at his back as he flew away and had ready a counterspell that would inflict Eadon as it would himself. He had no choice. If Eadon wanted to expend the energy to cut through his highly blessed and powerful sword, he would have to unleash a huge amount himself. And Eadon would never guess that rather than raise a massive shield, Zerafin would turn the blow against him, killing them both.

Eadon hollered with rage, and the inevitable spell ripped through the night and hit Zerafin in the back.

Zerafin took the hit, and with everything he had, he sent back the spell. Eadon was likewise hit in the chest, his spell having, after all, been molded as to cut through all defenses. As soon as the spell hit, Eadon knew his folly. For even as Zerafin bent in agony against the spell, so too did Eadon. His mind raced as he bent in pain and watched his hand shrivel into uselessness. He laughed to himself at Zerafin's cleverness as he sent healing energy through his body.

Zerafin, too, watched as his hands curled up into useless husks as his sister flew high and far. Yet he smiled to himself—for he knew that Eadon had likewise been afflicted.

Eadon reeled in tortured agony as his body rotted, and simultaneously, he stopped it through great amount of healing. The Dark Elf that had held Whill released him and forgot him altogether as he gawked at the injured Eadon.

Like a wolf that dreams of one day killing the pack leader and taking the mantle, he walked closer to his bent lord. This was the first time that he had seen his master afflicted so. He licked his lips and brought up his sword to strike down his master. His blade was stopped by another Dark Elf, one more loyal to Eadon.

"You have killed yourself," said the Dark Elf as Eadon turned and, with his blade, cut in two his attacker. Eadon caught the traitorous Dark Elf by the face as his lower body fell in a bloody heap. Eadon stroked the dying

Dark Elf's face and kissed him. And from his mouth, Eadon took all the power within him. That power he used to fight his affliction, which he would not relent in the use of, for he knew that without help, Zerafin would run out of energy to counter it with. Zerafin would soon die from the crippling spell, and Eadon did not mind making it slow.

"Lord!" said the Dark Elf. "Should I send for them to be killed or taken?"

Eadon laughed as he looked to Whill, defenseless and lying where he had fallen after the Dark Elf had released him.

"Neither, Zerafin will be dead soon, and the dragon cannot be helped. No, let the Elves of the Sun see my power, and let them cower."

Avriel flew her brother to a field many miles from the city, a place where the only eyes were that of the trees; even these Avriel looked at with suspicion. Zerafin fell to the earth and curled in a ball; the sickness with which he had been afflicted was killing him.

Avriel belched fire into the sky at her impotence to help. She could not yet in this form perform Orna Catorna. She watched helplessly as her brother lay dying.

"Call our brethren!" she begged. But Zerafin already had.

Within minutes, five Elves of the Sun had arrived, and they tended to the dying Zerafin, whom was now unconscious and withering. After a half hour of effort, Azzeal came to the worried dragon Avriel and gave her the news.

"The poison spell will not abate or be cured. Eadon suffers as well but does not end it. We are expending massive amounts of personal energy to keep the cancerous spell from killing your brother. At this rate, we cannot commence to keep Zerafin alive and help Whill this day."

The Sun Elf bowed his head to his dragon princess. "What will it be?" he asked.

Avriel cursed her dragon tears and roared in frustration. She quickly got a hold of herself and addressed the gathering Elves. "Azzeal and I shall remain behind to aid Whill. The rest of you will expend all efforts to keep my brother alive until he reaches Elladrindellia, where you are released. Let it be known that my brother freed me in his efforts, and my fate since is my own to determine, and the outcome of such shall not fall upon his shoulders."

The Elves all bowed at their princess and then turned to swiftly take the dying Zerafin home. Avriel turned her back on her brother and focused upon the city.

It was the day of Whill's execution.

CHAPTER TWENTY-ONE
Refugees

Jarred fell into the flames with a smile upon his face. He chuckled to himself as Roakore fell with the Draggard, hacking at it still.

So this is how I die, thought Jarred.

He closed his eyes and thought of his wife as the flames licked his flesh in hungry, burning anticipation of their meal. But rather than being engulfed in flame, Jarred slammed into cold stone instead.

Confused, he felt to his sides, and his hands felt cold stone. Roakore was chanting urgently in the dark. He had caused the stone of the church's foundation to rise up from the ground, entombing him and Jarred. Within the stone refuge, the heat did not reach, and Roakore caused it to grow high and above the roof of the burning building, like a chimney. Through this shaft, fresh air could be drawn.

Jarred laughed as Roakore fell to the stone floor. Faint moonlight found its way down the chimney and shone on the smiling and blood-soaked grin of the powerful king of Dwarves.

The fires died down after many hours, and the townspeople began to dig through the smoking rubble, searching for the fearless Dwarf king and their man. Soon they came to the strange stone cylinder with its far-stretching chimney. They marveled at the sight and were shaken from their reverie only by the pickax of Jarred's father.

"Come now, lads; help an old man."

Just as the men were about to lend a hand, a muffled voice came from within the stone. "Put down yer bloody tools, ye fools. I'll not have me work be tampered with. Back away!"

They all complied, and watched as four lines of separation appeared in the stone and the slab was forced forward to fall with a boom. Out walked the bloodied and battered pair into the smoldering morning light, Roakore aiding the limping Jarred. Cheers went up into the sky—the only happy proclamation the town had known since the first Draggard attack.

Silverwind landed among the rubble and literally pounced upon Roakore. With a coo, she rubbed the side of her head against Roakore's face. The Dwarf only chuckled and said, "Atta girl, fret not. Be takin' more than a handful o' beasties to silence me."

The bodies of the Draggard made a great, stinking pyre that afternoon. All but the heads were burned;

those, numbering some thirty, were set on pikes in a circle around the town, as warning.

Roakore's and Jarred's injuries were tended to, the king only having a few scratches and one good gash upon his leathery skin. The Dwarf counted his new stitches merrily as he took another pull from a rum bottle. "Six hundred en' fifty!" He belched loudly and laughed at the astonished medicine man who'd sewn him. "Nearin' a thousand I be, haha!"

Jarred's injuries were much more severe. He had lost an eye, and one side of his face donned four deep Draggard claw gashes. He had a broken leg and had a great number of other cuts, yet he breathed, even smiled. Roakore held the rum bottle to Jarred's parched lips and didn't soon set it right. He then quickly poured the bottle over the drinking man's face. The stitches bubbled, and the man sputtered, hissed, and cursed.

"Bah. Quit yer belly achin'. Yer alive, ain't ye? And this'll see to it ye don't get no infection."

Jarred moved to punch Roakore, and instead, his strong hand was caught by one stronger. Roakore laughed and into that hand, gave the bottle of rum. "Finish it; you'll be needin' the tranquilizer."

Afternoon came as did a hearty meal. The people took what was left of their stores and cooked a feast. A majority of the food was prepped for the road. With winter coming and their town in ruin, their livestock and crops demolished, they had need to leave and find refuge within the closest town or city that would have them.

Roakore dined with the townsfolk and knew their minds as he eyed the supply train forming for their sojourn. He finished his soup and, with a burp, stood. "Good people!" his voice boomed throughout the ruined town. All turned their heads to regard the king.

"If ye would, I be proposin' that ye seek out the eastern door o' me mountain. Take with ye me words put to paper and mine insignia, and ye shall be welcomed into me home with open arms. I bid ye stay with me people until the spring, whence ye shall return to your town and build it yet again, more grand then before. Trade between yours and mine shall profit us both for long years to come"

The townspeople were left speechless. Jarred's father stepped forward and, on the people's behalf, thanked him and accepted. Roakore only laughed and took another helping of stew.

Night came shortly. At the center of town had been made camp; some two hundred townspeople slept in a circle. Pikes had been set up and trenches dug. A watch of thirty men stood guard over the sleepers. Tomorrow, they would head out before the sun. To the Ebony Mountains they would travel. More than a five-day journey it would be for the slow-moving train. Despite the need for the stored energy, few slept—out of fear of a return of the past week's nightmares come to life.

Indeed, none would again feel safe until they reached the mountain fortress.

Roakore peered upon the star of the kings through faint cloud cover and was reminded of his friends. He wondered, as he often did, about Whill. He had been much saddened by the news that Avriel had been lost, in spirit if not body. He wondered if Zerafin and Abram and Rhunis were planning to intervene to stop the execution. Roakore bet that they would. And what a surprise it would be when they rescued Whill from the arena.

They will get a show, thought Roakore as he fell into a much-needed heavy sleep.

Before the rising of the sun, the townspeople were up and ready for their trek to the Ro'Sar Mountains. The morning was cool and the grass damp with dew. They had many injured among them—a fact that would slow their progress considerably. Roakore took note of this and went to Jarred's wagon. He found the man stubbornly at the front of the wagon; his son sat next to him. Though he ran a high fever and his eye now donned a blood-soaked patch, he sat at the ready, reigns in hand.

"Aye, when ye get yerself to me halls, ask for the lady Lunara. If ye can get there alive, you'll be glad fer her help. An' rightly so, you look like hell."

Jarred laughed weakly. "And you? Where does the road lead the great Roakore?"

"I be off to help a friend. And I be late."

Jarred leaned close and with a sparkle in his eye, asked, "Is it this Whill of Agora that rides on song and whisper? Then the tales are true? You are his friend?"

Roakore nodded. "Aye, he be me friend, and he be all they say o' him. And any friend o' mine ain't needen' to be sayin' his name in whisper."

Jarred nodded apologetically. Roakore turned and walked away then stopped. "I'll share me tale over some ale, when I return."

Jarred watched him leave. "I look forward to the day. Thank you, Roakore of the Ro'Sar Mountains!"

Roakore walked to the waiting Silverwind and there passed Tarragon. The man's face lit up, and Roakore squared on him.

"Get yer people to me halls right quick. Travel through the night, and sleep the afternoon an' so forth, till ye be safe. The moon be full, and night be as good as day. Stay out of the woods, and make haste. These lands be crawlin' with evil of all sorts these days."

Tarragon took his hand and shook it vigorously. "Thank you, Roakore, your kindness to my people will not soon be forgot."

"Aye." Roakore nodded.

The townspeople stopped to watch as the mighty Dwarf king of the west mounted his magnificent silver steed. He raised his great ax into the air as Silverwind opened her wings. They turned from silver to the green of the grass, as did Roakore's feathered armor.

"May yer legs bring ye swiftly to me doors."

With that, Silverwind leapt high and took to the air with powerful strokes of her wings. Her wings turned to sky blue, and together, they disappeared, making haste toward Del-Oradon. It was, Roakore realized, the day of Whll's execution.

CHAPTER TWENTY-TWO
Excecution Day

Dirk paced back and forth within his cell. He had not slept; he could not. He had sworn fealty to Eadon, and he had received many gifts for his allegiance. His gear and leather armor had been brought to him. How Eadon knew about it and found it, he did not know, nor did he care. Eadon had enchanted his leather armor with wards of protection. To his blades, Eadon had added power and strength.

Power coursed through Dirk's veins and muscles. He smiled in anticipation of the coming battle; he was eager to use his newfound power. He would complete the mission he had been tasked with, and Krentz would be free of Eadon. Dirk focused on his mission—to kill the friend of Whill of Agora, the old warrior Abram.

Roakore and Silverwind glided upon a strong air current that spirited them along quickly toward their destination. Roakore gauged that they were less than thirty miles from the city. He looked to the morning sun and guessed that he would be late. For the sun would reach midday shortly, less than fifteen minutes. He coaxed Silverwind with a light kick of his legs upon her flank. The great Silverhawk gave a cry and dove down and out of the current they had been riding. Roakore held on tightly and ducked his head as they dove and gained speed fast. Silverwind leveled out, and Roakore gave a whoop as the hawk's wings caught another current.

Abram and Rhunis blended in with the shuffling crowd as best they could. Ahead of them, within the coliseum, trumpets blared. The crowd of thousands could be heard, already cheering and stomping their feet. Abram and Rhunis did not know what had happened after Zerafin had so quickly flown to his sister's rescue. They had not seen or heard from any other Elf, but they continued on with their plan. Tucked in the inner pockets of their long coats, each man carried two apple-sized dragons' breath bombs.

The crowd filed into the coliseum, and Abram and Rhunis made it through the archway and to the stairs without incident. The city guard was prevalent within the coliseum, but Abram saw no Dark Elves—none in Dark Elf form anyway. He did not doubt that many of Eadon's Dark Elves watched from hidden places. Abram and Rhunis made their way up one level and found seats at the very edge of the sandy fighting arena. It was only a ten-foot drop to the sand below.

They settled in their seats and waited, as did the rowdy and restless crowd, for Whill of Agora to take the arena. Upon the sand, two gladiators fought to the death. But this battle held the attention of none of the rowdy crowd. They booed the fighters and hollered for Whill to be brought out. Abram looked from under the hood of his cloak to the adorned booth in which the king would sit. Eadon was not yet there, but he eyed a few hooded guards there—Dark Elves, no doubt.

One of the gladiators below was defeated gruesomely by his opponent. The crowd cheered and howled with bloodlust. Abram looked on with disgust.

"Eadon has made these people into savages these last two decades. What remains of the good people whom Whill's father once served?" he asked Rhunis.

"This is the nature of humans. We are quick to learn and easily molded. The problem is not the people but the hearts of their teachers."

"Indeed," Abram concurred.

The body of the dead gladiator was dragged from the arena, and the gates stayed open. The crowds hushed as all noticed Eadon, distguised as King Addakon, entering the booth. Abram looked on the disguised Eadon and scowled, noticing something strange about the false king's gait.

"Do you see that?" he asked Rhunis.

"Indeed, he seems to suffer. Could it be a ruse?"

Abram shook his head. "Possibly, or Zerafin gave him a hell of a fight."

Eadon, as Addakon, walked to the front of the booth and raised his hands to hush the crowd. Everyone quieted in anticipation.

"Good people of Uthen-Arden, friends, brothers, sisters. We are here today to witness the execution of the most hated criminal the lands have ever seen. He is the bringer of the Draggard, the destroyer of homes, the killer of children," Eadon's voice boomed unnaturally loud throughout the coliseum. The crowd responded with a mix of emotion. Some cheered the false king while others booed. Scuffles and fighting broke out within the seated crowd of over twenty-five thousand.

"The people are divided about Whill," noted Abram.

Rhunis nodded. "You too quickly judge the hearts of men."

Eadon looked out over the crowd. "Many among you have fallen prey to the legend of lies. His armies of Draggard ravish the land as you whisper false deeds done by a false savior. His poison fills your hearts and breeds doubt and contempt for the crown. That you would believe this madman's intentions over that of your king is deplorable," said Eadon with malice in his voice.

"Bring him out!" Eadon ordered, and the crowd went crazy. Boos and cheers resounded throughout the vast ocean of spectators. The gates were lifted, and Whill entered the arena with his fighters. They were armed and armored. Abram's spirit soared at the sight of his friend, and a tear found his eye. He hardly recognized him. Whill's hair was long and wild. His eyes were sunken, and he had lost a substantial amount of weight. He was but a shell of the man Abram knew.

Rhunis noticed this also. "What horrors has he faced these last six months?"

Whill and his fighters were given their armor and weapons. To Whill's surprise, he was given the sword of his father and the armor he had worn those many months ago. Many of the fighters brandished swords and crude armor; some wielded spears, others axes. The barbarian woman held a huge circular shield, nearly four feet wide and as tall. In her other hand, she swung a five-and-a-half-foot-long sword. The blade must have been very heavy, but the strong barbarian twirled and jabbed with it as though it weighed no more than a stick.

Whill noticed Dirk and his elaborate weapons and was awed. The man had set before him more weapons than any man could possibly carry, knives, swords, darts, throwing stars, iron knuckles, small bombs, daggers— he seemed to have enough weapons for a small army. Whill watched him closely as he effectively hid his small armory easily beneath his large, black hooded coat. Whill made a mental note to keep an eye on this man that seemed full of surprises.

From their holding cell, the prisoners could hear Eadon's speech. Knowing their introduction was forthcoming, Whill addressed his fighters.

"Your shackles have been taken, and your weapons have been returned. You stand now as you once did, strong, brave, and proud. Let not the false King of Uthen-Arden see you fall easily; let not the people forget the meaning of honor. This day, upon these sands, you fight as free men. This day, you fight for all free men. Fight for your people, your love, your children. Let us spark a fire of rebellion so bright as to blind all that would stand before it!"

The men gave out a primal cry and cheered. A smile crept onto Dirk's face as he saw the effect that Whill's words had on the men and the barbarian woman. Aurora Snowfell took a dagger from its sheath upon her leg and cut her forearm. With both hands, she smeared the blood onto her face, neck, arms, shoulders, and chest. She bandaged the gash and took up her weapons. All eyes had fallen to her, and now each man stared in awe.

Aurora lifted her head and grinned. The maniacal grin upon her bloodied face set cold the men's hearts as they beheld the fearless and beautiful barbarian warrior. She let out an animalistic, growling scream that caused many of the men to jump. They laughed and screamed with her. Whill turned to the gate as he heard their introduction.

The group burst from their holding cell and charged out onto the sand, screaming with raised swords. Many of their voices died as they saw, for the first time, the thousands of ravenous spectators. They took to the center of the sand and looked around in awe at the massive crowd.

Eadon sneered at Whill from his place on high. He opened his arms and addressed the crowd once more. Though he still suffered the rotting disease that he and Zerafin shared, no one would know from his strong voice that he felt any pain.

"Good people of Uthen-Arden, I give you the false hero and savior, Whill of Agora."

The crowd hushed as they looked upon the man of legend for the first time. Whill walked a few steps from his fellows and turned to look upon the entire crowd.

"Whill of Agora, in league with—"

"I would speak! We have heard enough of your poisonous tongue!" Whill interrupted. The crowd gasped.

Whill pointed a steady finger at Eadon. "This man is not your king. Your king died by my hand six months ago." The crowd hung on his every word, silent and astonished by his audacity.

"It is true that I am the son of King Aramonis and Queen Celestra. It is true that I am the rightful King of Uthen-Arden." Whill let the words set in and saw shock on the faces of many.

"I defeated my uncle, Addakon, for his crimes against my father, for his crimes against you, the people. Too long have you been fooled by this..." Whill pointed once again at Eadon. "...this charlatan! The Elf that stands before you now is not Addakon, but Eadon, the Dark Elf of legend, the true creator of the Draggard. This Dark Elf is the enemy of us all!"

The crowd broke into a chorus of boos and murmurs. Many cheers also erupted from those that believed in the legend of Whill.

Eadon clapped his hands, and eventually everyone quieted once again and looked to him. "Yes, indeed, I am actually a Dark Elf in disguise, and you are the heir to the throne, which I have stolen." The crowd looked on, their faces in disbelief and awe. Then Eadon erupted in laughter, and most of the crowd followed suit.

"Enough fables from this man. Open the gates, and let the execution begin."

CHAPTER TWENTY-THREE

Fighting For Freedom

Whill cast one last smirking scowl at Eadon and turned with his men to face whatever was coming at them through the gates. At first, nothing emerged, but then the ground began to vibrate, and the screams of many men echoed forth from the tunnel. Suddenly, men began to pour from the tunnel. Whill quickly realized that these were many of the fighters that Whill had not chosen, more than a hundred of them. They fanned out onto the sands and got into formation, twenty men abreast and five deep. Once in formation, they gave out a cry and charged. Whill turned to his fighters and saw fear on none of their faces. He gave a challenging cry of his own and charged.

To his right, Aurora sprinted past him, her shield leading the way. Whill pushed harder and tried to keep up with the barbarian. To his left, he watched as

Dirk passed him and leapt high into the air. The dark-cloaked assassin tucked his legs up in front of him and threw four darts in quick succession from the straps on his thighs. The darts shot through the air and hit four of the charging gladiators in the face, felling them all. Aurora gave a fierce battle cry and slammed her massive shield into the charging men. The force of the blow sent men flying, and as the shield went out wide and to the left with the blow, from her right came her huge broadsword to take the lives of any near.

Whill dodged spears and parried swords as he, too, engaged the front line. Everyone kept a wide breadth from Aurora and her swinging sword and bashing shield. The other nine men joined in the melee as the two groups of gladiators engaged in battle. With his first kill, Whill sapped the energy of his victim, strengthening his sword. He felt the familiar hum of the energy within the blade of his father. He did the same with the second and third, and with each kill, he gained more power. He had been a victim for six long months, always at the mercy of Elves that could render his body paralyzed with a glance. All of the anger, rage, and hopelessness he felt during his time in captivity burned hot within him.

Dirk went into his familiar routine with his short sword and dagger. He took on multiple opponents easily as the power that Eadon had bestowed upon him hummed within his many trinkets. His enchanted boots allowed him to move with inhuman speed, and his gloves helped his arms to move with a blur. Men fell before Dirk before they even knew they had been engaged by the man.

Aurora smashed aside an attacker with her shield and quickly punched out with it as another came at her from the front. The shield caught the man in the face, and he moved no more. She took up her blade in her shield hand and grabbed the fallen man by the ankle. With a heave, she sent his limp body flying into a group of opposing gladiators. Men looked on in awe of the beautiful warrior.

"What's wrong, boys? Never met a woman that hit back?"

A man came at her from the right with an overhead chop of his sword. Aurora stepped into the attack and let the sword glide away as it was deflected by her shield. The man spun with the momentum of the block, as did Aurora. But the tall barbarian had more than a foot of a reach advantage and used it to stun her opponent with a sword to the chest as his own blade found nothing but air.

Dirk landed in the middle of four men, and with a quick jab of his dagger between the closest man's ribs, he laid him low. A quick spin and slash opened another's jugular. He donkey kicked behind him, sending an advancing gladiator flying to the ground. Out came his short sword as he danced with death, always moving, always knowing the next move. Then a deep and power-ful growl sounded, and many men parted to find less lethal opponents, leaving the path open for a giant of a man.

Aurora hewed a shield in two and felt the crunch of bone beneath. A man came flying at her wildly and was met with a shield slam to the face. If Aurora had learned anything from the tribe's battle master, it was that there was always a coward eyeing your back. She turned, and, indeed, the coward came with a trident meant for her. With a powerful strike, she knocked the weapon from his hands and booted him in the face. His neck snapped, and he fell limp. Then a growl sounded far to the left, a growl that Aurora knew all too well as the challenge of a traitorous fellow tribesman known as Beartooth. He had engaged Blackthorn with his mas-sive five-foot-wide ax. Dirk was smart enough to keep his distance and dance away from the blow.

Dirk sidestepped a blow that would have hewn a thick tree and shot a rapid succession of poison darts at the giant's neck. With surprising speed, the man brought up a leather-bound forearm, blocking the missiles. Dirk learned what he had hoped of the man's speed. He assumed the giant was akin to Aurora, and the quick block proved it true. Dirk had noted Aurora's speed and her incredible reach advantage that many dead men had underestimated. The reach of the barbarian before him was even greater. Where Aurora stood well over seven feet, this bearded, wild man stood over nine. He wore furs of the north and had no armor but wrapped leather about his arms and legs. His ax was nearly as wide as Dirk was tall, and though it must have weighed nearly a hundred pounds, the giant of a man could recall the ax, midswing, with ease. Dirk circled the behemoth and threw a dart here and there, each one blocked by the shield-like ax. Dirk had not hit the man, but he had stopped him from swinging—the man having to use the ax against the darts. Dirk carefully calculated his next move, if he made the slightest mistake, he would fall victim to the massive ax.

"This one is mine!" yelled Aurora from behind Dirk.

The assassin nodded curtly. "By all means, ladies first." Dirk turned and ran into the main body of the battle. He had no doubt he could kill the giant on his own terms. But an opponent that could knock out a bull with a punch was not someone he wished to fight... fairly.

Abram watched as Whill began his familiar battle dance. A smile found the old man's face as he watched his pupil of so many years fight like a man of legend. Whill and his fighters were clearly the better, but they faced more than a hundred. Whill smartly kept his men together in a fighting circle, so as not to be separated by the enemy, though the barbarian woman and the dark-cloaked killer fought their battles their own way.

The barbarian woman was clenched in combat with one that looked to be of her people. The dark one ran around the outside of the attacking force, engaging and maiming his opponents while he ran. He slashed at the backs of thighs and ankles, hamstringing and dropping dozens. Others at the center of the group fell unconscious as Dirk leapt and sent a barrage of poison darts into them.

Abram nodded to Rhunis. "It is time."

None in the frantically screaming crowd noticed them as they bathed in the rivers of bloodlust. Abram and Rhunis left the arena and went into the hallways below. The noise of the crowd down below was ear shattering, but the two did not need to share words. They had planned their mission for weeks and had infiltrated the coliseum disguised as workers. They took roundabout routes through the many halls and tunnels and passageways below the coliseum, until they came to the spot. Rhunis kept watch as Abram lifted two thick boards and crawled into the inner walls. Rhunis followed and put the boards back behind him. Abram looked up to what he knew to be the floor of the royal booth. The two quickly went to work, fastening the dragons' breath bombs to the main beams of the overhanging booth.

Eadon's senses perked, and he looked to the floor. With his mind sight, he saw the two humans below.

He turned back to Whill's impressive display upon the sands and smiled to himself.

"We have flushed out our prey," he said behind a grimace of pain.

To his right, the Dark Elf Arkrel nodded as he looked to the floor. "The boy's mentor?"

"Indeed, but more importantly, two of the most respected leaders of men," Eadon stated with a satisfied smirk.

"Should I kill them now, sir?"

Eadon rolled his eyes, annoyed by his subject's idiocy and lack of vision. "No, you idiot," he hissed as the rotting curse ate his flesh, only to be repaired. "They must die before Whill's eyes, and they will. The mentor, Abram, is taken care of." Eadon gestured to the floor. "When those two ignite their bombs and attempt their pathetic rescue, you are to enter the arena and kill the scarred knight."

Aurora staggered back as the huge ax grazed her shield. She twirled with the blow but got a huge boot to the chest. As she fell back through the air and onto the sand, Beartooth brought his ax up and over in a mighty blow. Aurora had no time to roll to the side, and though she knew to never take a hit to the shield straight on, she had no time to tilt it. The massive ax came down with crushing power, knocking the wind out of Aurora. The shield held under the blow but dented enough for Aurora to feel a shooting pain in her forearm.

She kicked up and knocked the ax from Beartooth's grip. The barbarian let out that same nerve-racking growl and grabbed the shield with both hands and flung it, hitting one of the other gladiators in the head. Aurora stabbed out with her sword. Beartooth shifted to the side and caught it between his fur-hide-and-leather-covered forearm. With a twist of his body, he sent the sword flying from Aurora's hands. He reached down and took her by the hair and pulled. Aurora grabbed at his hands as she was forced to stand. With his free hand, he backhanded her in the face. Aurora was spun around on her feet but held by her hair. Beartooth meant to slap her again, but Aurora caught his hand with hers and twisted it back violently, causing him to have to let go of her hair. When he did, she kneed him in the crotch. He recovered quickly, however, and punched her in the face. The two circled each other, waiting. Both had a taste of the other's strength, but Aurora had not shown Beartooth what power still remained untapped within her.

He came at her with a whooshing roundhouse, which she ducked, and when the predictable upper-cut followed, she knocked the blow aside with one arm and landed a vicious elbow to the barbarian's throat. Beartooth clenched his crushed throat, and Aurora swept his legs. The shocked warrior landed like a tree, and Aurora was on him like a cat. With her knees, she pinned his arms, and with her fists, she pounded his face. A scream welled up inside her and grew louder and louder still as she punched the beast of a man repeatedly.

Aurora looked down at the unrecognizable mess that had been her enemy's head. She looked to her bloodied hands and smiled, and then she laughed. She remembered her trainer's words and turned quickly to find the coward at her back. There stood a man in a crouch, sword in hand, suddenly frozen in place. Aurora stood to full height and smeared the blood of her enemy upon her face. The man shifted on his feet, trying to find the courage to attack. When she picked up her sword, the man finally lost his nerve and turned to run but was stabbed in the heart by Dirk. He was dead before he hit the ground.

"Are you going to fight or flirt?" he asked Aurora with a smirk.

"Is there a difference between the two?" she replied with an arched eyebrow.

Avrel flew toward the castle on a quick current with Azzeal upon her back. She had still to get used to her dragon form, but she flew steady and strong. When she thought of her Elf body a pang of sadness and fear gripped her heart. Her thoughts threatened to spiral her into madness if she thought about it for too long. But her dragon mind quickly quenched the fires of madness and calmed her. Her soul occupied the dragon body and mind, just as it had her Elven form. She was still Avriel, but not in body. Her dragon brain brought with it all of the characteristics and intricacies of the dragon, and she found that her thoughts moved in very different ways. Each thought had a broader scope and depth, and though thinking seemed slower, each thought was more precise and clear.

Avriel flew so high that people on the streets looked like ants, but she could still hear the thunderous crowd in the arena below. Avriel thought of Whill and inwardly smiled to herself. She pictured him upon the sands, smiting all that stood before him, and she growled with pleasure. With a quick mental warning to Azzeal, she banked left and began her descent on the castle. Avriel set her eyes upon the tower that she knew held the red dragon Zhola. The feeling was akin to what she had felt when she reached out with her senses and felt the presence of other life-forms while she was an Elf. But this was different in that she did not have to try to feel him, she simply did. When she had mentioned this to Azzeal, he had simply nodded as if it were common dragonlore.

Avriel gained speed and felt Azzeal shift atop her back. She dove quickly and leveled out near the tower. She flew as close as she dared, and Azzeal leapt from her back. She looked back to see him fly through the air and suddenly change into a knot of reaching roots. He hit the wall and clung easily to the stone. His roots crept down and, like so many searching fingers, found the small window. Avriel flew high and fast to the clouds, where she would await the freeing of the great red one.

Whill killed the final gladiator and shuddered as the life energy coursed through his father's blade and hummed within his very being. He had felled dozens, and with each kill, he had gained more power. The crowd cheered and whistled, and thousands of feet stomped the seats. Whill looked around at the piles of dead and then to the only survivors of his group. Dirk wiped blood from his dagger while Aurora stood proudly in the sunlight like a barbarian goddess of war. The others of his group had fallen.

Whill looked to the sky, wondering if Avriel and the Elves would come to their aid. Surely Zerafin had brought an army with him. Surely someone would come. The gates opened once again, and the crowd waited in eager anticipation. Whill walked near to Dirk and Aurora.

"Stand firm, friends, allies descend upon us even now. I am for leaving this hellhole."

"What's the hurry?" asked Aurora.

They all laughed and turned to face whatever nightmare was coming through the gates. To the crowd's utter shock and horror, four spear-wielding Draggard entered the ring, and behind them came hulking beasts, the likes of which none had ever seen. Whill knew them to be Eadon's latest abomination, the Dwargon. They resembled Dwarves with their thick, stocky build and massive muscles, but that was where the resemblance ended. They were more than nine feet tall, and rather than skin, they had thick scales like a dragon and faces from a nightmare. Small, spiked horns covered their heads; beady black eyes regarded the world with malice, and mouths too big for their faces drooled in anticipation of blood. Four of them, carrying huge clubs, came stomping onto the sand behind the Draggard as screams and squeals of horror erupted from the crowd. The Draggard crept dangerously near to the edge of the stands, hissing and snapping at the crowd.

The cry of a hawk split the air, and all looked to the sky but saw nothing. Then came the battle cry of a Dwarf as Roakore suddenly came into view, as if out of thin air. He wore a magnificent coat of Silverhawk feathers and shone in the sunlight like a statue of silver. Ax in hand, he landed upon the sands between the humans and Eadon's beasts.

"A friend?" asked Dirk.

Whill could only smile widely, with teary eyes, and nod his head. Roakore looked to him and gave a trium-

phant, "Hahaa! Can't be lettin' you have all the fu—"
Roakore's words were lost in his throat as he turned to
face the Draggard and his eyes beheld the Dwargon.
He knew instantly what they were, and his blood boiled.
The idea of a dragon-Dwarf hybrid shattered the Dwarf
king's sensibilities. To think that a Dwarf woman had
been...Roakore could not bear the thought. He let only
righteous indignation fill his mind, and he charged the
abominations, tears of rage spilling onto his beard.

The crowd erupted as Roakore slammed aside a Draggard with the side of his ax and charged a Dwargon. The
Dwargon swung low at the fast-approaching Dwarf. But
the blow missed as Roakore dropped and slid under the
beast. He brought his ax up as he slid between its legs
and sank the blade deep into its groin. No sooner had the
monster crouched in pain when Roakore gracefully stood
from his slide behind it and buried his ax in its lower back.

Whill, Dirk, and Aurora charged the Draggard as
Roakore felled the Dwargon. Much of the crowd had
frantically begun to exit when the monsters had been
let into the arena; those that remained cheered and
hollered, loving the show. Whill called upon the power
within his father's blade, and with his left hand extended,
he shot a blast of energy at the closest Draggard. The
blast hit the creature in the chest and slammed it into
the stone wall twenty feet away.

Dirk threw a smoke bomb between himself and a
charging Draggard. He leapt high into the air and over

his suddenly blinded foe. The gems in his earlobes allowed him to hear the quiet whoosh of the Draggard's approaching tail. Dirk twisted and spun away from the spiked weapon and landed. With his short sword, he chopped the tail off at the base, and when the creature turned, it got a poison dark in each eye. Dirk turned away from the thrashing and twitching monster to face another.

Aurora shield slammed a Draggard to the side and ducked the massive club of a Dwargon. Whill came in from the side, and with a powerful swoop of his thin blade, he cut open the side of Aurora's foe. She finished off the screaming beast with a blow from her heavy broadsword that cracked open its head.

An explosion ripped through the arena, and suddenly, the booth in which Eadon and his minions sat went up in flames. The crowd went berserk, and people started to frantically fight to get out of the aisles and to the exits. In the pandemonium, hundreds of fights broke out as people trampled each other to get away from the flames that were fast consuming the stands near to the inferno that was now the royal booth. More Draggard and Dwargon filed into the arena as the booth came crashing down, spewing burning wood and banners everywhere. Whill tried to find the Dark Elf in the commotion, but Eadon was nowhere to be seen.

Two men came rushing out of a different gate, men that Whill recognized. With a growl of frustration, he cut down a Draggard that blocked his view from the two. Whill's eyes widened as he saw more clearly the two men fast approaching. Together, they took on an attacking Draggard and continued on into the fray. Whill's heart leapt and his spirit soared as he watched the two ghosts come nearer.

"Whill!" one of them screamed.

"Abram? Rhunis?" answered Whill with a joy he dared not indulge in lest this be some kind of trap. Perhaps this was one of Eadon's tricks; perhaps one of them was Eadon himself. Whill tried to deny what he saw, but he could not convince himself. He recognized their fighting styles and their mannerisms and knew them to be his lost friends thought dead.

Whill fought to get close to them, but dozens of Draggard and Dwargon had poured into the arena. The heat of the flames was becoming intense as the arena blazed and threatened to crumble. People screamed and cried as the flames took many of them; hundreds fell onto the sands and were attacked by the beasts within the arena. The exits were packed with frantic men and women trying to escape the death trap that the great arena had become. Many of the Draggard had leapt up into the stands and were killing spectators at will.

Aurora brought up her shield to the swing of one of the Dwargon's massive clubs. The blocked blow sent her flying back many feet, but she deftly rolled when she landed and came to her feet quickly. The Dwargon advanced and came down with a blow meant to crush her. She hamstrung the beast and spun around behind it to stab it in the side. It let out a howl and brought its club around. Aurora fell flat on her back to avoid the club and watched as Dirk soared over her and, landing upon the hulk's shoulders, stabbed it quickly in each eye. Dirk leapt from the dying Dwargon, sending a barrage of poison darts at another one's face. Aurora got to her feet again and hewed the head off a Draggard, grabbed its tail, and heaved it into its kin. From behind her, she heard a gurgled screech. She turned to find a spear tip inches from her body, held in the dying hands of a Draggard that had been impaled through the neck by a spear. Aurora knew the man holding the spear from Eadon's mental projection of him; he was the man that she was tasked to kill—Abram.

"There is always one coming from behind, lady," he said with a wink and entered the fray once more.

Aurora looked to the dead Draggard that would have surely skewered her—dead now because Abram had saved her. She grabbed the spear and aimed it at Abram's back. Her hand trembled, and her face twisted with a grimace. Abram engaged another beast; he would soon be out of range. She had to kill him; it was the only way to save her people. A part of her mind screamed to do it, and another argued the opposite.

She heard her trainer's words. "There is always a coward coming at your back."

Aurora was now the coward at someone else's back. The man had saved her life, but his death would secure a future for her people. She did not have the luxury of horror. She threw the spear with a scream of rage. The spear flew true and found its mark.

Whill fought his way past Roakore as he hacked at a dead Dwargon. Blood and colorful curses flew from the Dwarf king's mouth. A Draggard lunged at Whill with a spear, which he easily deflected. The glowing sword of his father sliced through the beast's belly, leaving a mess of entrails to fall upon the sand. Whill reached Abram as he battled a Draggard, and together, they took it down.

"Whill," said Abram with a smile as a Draggard spear hit him in the back and protruded from his chest. He staggered forward and was caught by Whill as blood poured from his mouth.

"No!" Whill screamed as he caught his oldest friend and lowered him to sit upon the sand.

"Gut-rotten' dragon scum born sons o' demons!" screamed Roakore as he saw what had happened to Abram. He ran to Whill and Abram and, together with Rhunis, kept enemies clear. With a grimace, Whill pulled the spear from Abram's back. Blood spurted from the old man's chest in gushes. Abram's eyes rolled, and his face became ashen. Blue tendrils of healing flowed from Whill's hands and engulfed his friend in light.

Aurora watched as Whill held his friend. To her utter amazement, she saw blue serpentine tendrils snaking their way from Whill's hand and into his friend's wound. She had to stop the healing, but the knight and fierce Dwarf had their backs. She thought that she could take the knight and the Dwarf, but seeing the Elf magic performed by Whill, she assumed the legends to be true. Aurora found her resolve and charged across the sand toward Whill and Abram.

A giant shadow fell over the fighters, and the roar of a dragon ripped through the air, deafening them all. Aurora skidded to a halt as a mammoth red dragon, the likes of which she had never seen, landed near Whill and his friends and began to bathe the attacking Draggard in flames. A half-naked Elf, wearing what looked to be leaves, leapt from the top of the red dragon and, to Aurora's astonishment, changed into a wolf the size of a horse. More flames erupted behind the red dragon as a smaller white dragon landed near Whill. Aurora cursed her luck and stabbed a burning Dwargon in the chest.

As the dragons began to belch flame, the Dark Elf Arkrel landed upon the sands and found his target. Rhunis stood back to back with Roakore as the two guarded

Whill and Abram. The Draggard and Dwargon were routed by the dragon flames. Arkrel stopped, strung his bow, took aim, and fired. The red arrow streaked through the smoke and flame and hit Rhunis in the chest. The wolf Azzeal leapt from the red dragon and bore down on the Dark Elf assassin with a growl.

Roakore's eyes went wide as he regarded the two dragons that had entered the fray. Bloodlust and thoughts of glory intoxicated him as he lifted his ax to strike the closer of the two, the smaller white dragon.

"Roakore, no, she is Avriel!" Whill screamed at his friend.

Roakore stopped short of his strike as the white dragon turned its head and their eyes met. The Dwarf king did not lower his ax, yet he did not strike. There was no anger on the dragon's face, and it did not attack Roakore.

It is I, good Dwarf. The red and I are not your enemy. Avriel's voice came to Roakore's mind. Astonished, he lowered his ax.

"Can ye believe yer eyes, Rhunis?" he asked, turning to his friend as a red streaking arrow ripped through Rhunis's chest and out his back, leaving a hole the size of a fist. Rhunis was dead before he hit the sand.

Roakore screamed in rage and looked in the direction the arrow had come. Near the edge of the burning arena, he saw the Dark Elf and the wolf that attacked him. Roakore threw his stone bird into the air and charged as the flying weapon began to spin until it blurred.

Whill saw Rhunis fall, and laying down the partially healed Abram, he ran to Rhunis's side. Whill muttered to himself, "No, no, no, no, no," as he turned the scarred knight onto his back. Whill looked upon the friend that he had faced in a similar arena in Eldalon, and there was no light in the old knight's eyes. Whill looked to Avriel hopefully, but the dragon only lowered her head.

He died instantly. He is lost to us. Let us be gone from this place. Tears streaked down Whill's ash-covered face as he looked to his fallen friend and then to the burning arena. With a determined glare, he lifted Abram and put him over his shoulder. Dirk approached Whill and regarded the dragons with apprehension.

"Are we to be left here to die?" he asked Whill with a glance at Aurora.

Whill looked at the two in turn and then to Zhola. "These two are allies; will you carry them?"

The dragon puffed smoke from his nose and nodded with a growl. Dirk and Aurora climbed onto Zhola's back, and each found a place between his long, thick spikes. Whill called upon the strength of his father's blade and climbed onto Avriel, carrying Abram. He seated his old friend before him and tried to hold him as best he could.

The two dragons fueled the fires of the arena with their flapping wings as they leapt and began to fly out.

Below them, upon the sands in the ring of fire that the arena had become, Whill saw Roakore and the Elf Azzeal battling a Dark Elf.

"Roakore!" he hollored as Avriel took to the sky and cleared the top of the blazing arena.

Roakore slammed into the energy shield of the Dark Elf as it fought to loosen itself from the roots that Azzeal has caused to tangle him. With his blade, the Dark Elf Arkrel slashed the roots that snaked their way around him. Arkrel's studies had not yet begun in the art of the Ral iad; therefore, he could not change his form and free himself from the roots. He became increasingly annoyed with the Dwarf's bombardment of his energy shield and frantically deflected the blasts that emanated from Azzeal. With a great surge of energy, the Dark Elf ignited the air surrounding him, and the roots disintegrated in flame. A red blast of energy snaked its way through the air and was met by a green blast from Azzeal. The two Elves braced themselves as their powers collided.

Azzeal proved the more powerful as he sent a wave of energy through his energy attack that blasted through the Dark Elf's attack and his shields. Arkrel was thrown back onto the sand, and fear gripped his cold heart when he realized that his energy stores had been drained in the fight. Roakore kicked the Elf in the side and turned to Azzeal.

"He killed me friend, Elf; he be mine!"

Azzeal looked at the Dwarf curiously and cocked his head to the side. "Be done with it then; his master has taken to the air."

Arkrel shot to his feet with a snarl and slashed his blade to fend off Roakore. Then he ran for the nearest gate.

"No, ye don't, ye coward!" yelled Roakore as his stone bird streaked through the air and took the retreating Dark Elf behind the knees. Roakore was on him in a heartbeat and knocked away the Dark Elf's feeble slash of his sword. Roakore kicked the prone Elf in the face and buried his ax in Arkrel's head.

With a squawk, Silverwind landed, and Roakore hurried to her and mounted. Azzeal extended a hand and incinerated the body of the dead Elf. He then took three running steps and leapt into the air and changed into a great eagle. Roakore muttered to himself about Elves and their damn magic as Silverwind took to the sky.

Whill held on tight as Avriel followed Zhola over the city and west to the city gates. Glancing behind him, he caught sight of Eadon on his Dragon-Hawk, bearing down on them. Fireballs shot from the Elf and blew up in the sky near the dragons. Avriel veered left sudderly as a spell exploded a few feet from her. Whill and Abram were thrown from where they sat. Whill grabbed a firm hold of one of Avriel's spikes and caught Abram's wrist before he fell to the city streets below.

"I got you!" Whill hollered over the wind and exploding spells.

Behind them, Whill saw Eadon, now less than fifty feet from them. Their eyes met, and Eadon grinned wickedly. From his right hand, Eadon shot a small black orb of energy. Whill helplessly watched as the orb hit Abram in the back and dissipated. Whill held Abram's wrist tightly and watched his friend with wide eyes as the landscape below changed and green grass replaced the city streets.

Abram let out a weary groan of pain and regarded Whill with a small smile. "Promise that you will finish this Whill. Prom—" Abram's words ended in a wheeze as his body stiffened and became like stone.

Whill screamed in horror as he watched his friend's skin begin to flake off like ash until, finally, his body fell apart and was scattered in the wind. Ash fell through the hand that had gripped Abram's wrist, and the hand became a fist. Whill looked to his fist in tormented anguish and screamed into the wind.

CHAPTER TWENTY-FOUR
Only Human

Tarren played with his food with no appetite. Lunara watched him as she finished her stew. The boy absently touched a hand gingerly to his newest bruise. He would not allow it to be healed. The black eye did not bother her as much as the two broken fingers with which he touched his eye.

"I wish you would let me heal those. What are you trying to prove?"

Tarren looked up from his food as if he had been disturbed from deep thought.

"Huh?" He looked to his fingers. "I am trying to prove that I remember that I am only human and I will not always have a guardian Elf to watch over me." He went back to playing with his food with his fork.

Lunara sat up in her chair. "Who said you won't always have me?"

Tarren's looked up at her, and wisdom and pain beyond his years shone behind them. "Everyone leaves!

I know you are young for an Elf, but you better get used to the idea. Everyone leaves—whether they want to or not."

Lunara did not know what to say to that. She simply listened, knowing that Tarren had more on his chest. Indeed, she could see with her mind sight the knotted flow of energy near the boy's heart.

"Whill was taken; Abram and Rhunis left." He stabbed a potato within his stew bowl. "Avriel is lost to us." Tarren looked to Lunara with tears welling within his eyes. "Roakore left, and my parents left...so quit trying to make me be liking you, 'cause one day, you will leave too."

He stormed out of the room and shoved past Haldagozz as he was about to knock. Tarren said nothing as he stormed off.

"They be waitin' for ya in the trainin' room!" the Dwarf hollered after him. Haldagozz shook his head and walked into the room and addressed Lunara with a smile.

"Lady." He nodded.

Lunara gave her friend a smile, but her attention wandered after Tarren. Haldagozz shrugged awkwardly upon noticing the Elf maiden's distress. "Bah. The boy, he'll be alright, and right so, he be a tough little bugger."

Lunara smiled at Haldagozz all the more. "Indeed, he is tough, but being tough without knowing how to be gentle makes one rough."

Haldagozz laughed. "You got a way with words, you do. But wordsmithin' ain't good for none but lyin'."

Lunara was aghast. "Have your people no poetry? No songs? How could you say such a thing?"

Haldagozz stuttered over his words. "S-sorry, miss, I meant no insult to ye. Was just talkin' without thinkin' much is all..." He lifted his hands in surrender. "Bah! I ain't one fer pretty talk and have no need fer it."

"I noticed," said Lunara with all seriousness.

Holdagozz mimicked her scowl until finally she laughed, not being able to keep a straight face.

Tarren met up with Helzendar outside the training chamber that would house the tournament. The son of Roakore could hardly hold his excitement for the upcoming games. Tarren, however, was not so keen on the idea.

Helzendar saw the look on Tarren's face. "Bah, cheer up. You'll do fine, don't doubt."

Tarren looked at him skeptically. "Easy for you to say. You are matched with your kin in strength. Try fighting someone bigger and far stronger than yourself."

"Got nothin' to do with it. Dwarves have killed dragons far bigger and stronger, don't be forgettin', an' humans have too. I guess this be your dragon."

Tarren smiled at the analogy. "I guess."

Helzendar patted Tarren on the back, almost knocking him over. "C'mon, just focus on your strengths. You be faster than most you will face."

They walked to the competition area where more than a thousand Dwarves had gathered. The Ro'Sar Games were an annual competition in which the youngest of Dwarves fought for status and manhood. One could not be considered a man among Dwarf society lest he had been victorious in the games. Each participant had to be at least thirteen years old to compete, and so Tarren had lied about his age; being only eleven, he had to. Lunara had seen through this lie but had not told anyone. Tarren was grateful for her discretion, and now he felt bad for his words. He had not meant them; he had just been very nervous and, though he would not admit it, scared of the coming games. But he was determined to prove himself to the Dwarves and to himself. He was impatient with his age and inexperience and inability to aid Whill and the forces of good in the coming war. He wanted so badly to help that he had signed up for the games in haste, knowing that he was in way over his head.

None of that mattered now as he and Helzendar made their way into the large chamber. They were recognized by their trainers and directed to the chambers below the arena, where they would arm up and await their turn. As was custom, teams had been formed. The most proficient of the young Dwarf warriors had been selected as captains, and each of them had chosen four kin. All except in the case of one captain, Helzendar, who had shocked everyone, even Tarren, by choosing the skinny human boy for his team. Helzendar insisted it had nothing to do with their friendship and that he saw the warrior within Tarren.

"You survived being killed by pirates; you traveled with me father and his great company before the reclamation. You are the adopted son o' Whill o' Agora. You be meant for great things, Tarren o' Fendale, and I be keen on seein' 'em be done." Helzendar had explained.

Tarren followed Helzendar into the arms chamber as they made their way to their team's room. The other three members of their team were armed, armored, and ready, some sitting, others pacing. One of them pumped out push-ups quickly in the corner. All cheered when their captain entered.

Tarren found his gear and his chest and weapon. He quickly went into the familiar ritual of gearing up for battle. This was the time in which Tarren could leave his troubled mind and go into a state of rhythm. Helzendar called it "the birth o' the warrior," the time when one forgot their namesake and became a warrior of the gods. During this ritual of putting on his thick leather padding and his heavy breastplate, shin and thigh guards, and arm and forearm gloves, he found his peace. Forgotten were fear, pain, cowardice, and self. In this time, he gave himself over to the will of the gods, praying that their will was his.

He pulled on his gloves and tucked his helmet under his left arm. With his right hand, he clasped the staff of his newest weapon. Crafted by Lunara, and covered in Elven runes, the staff filled Tarren with all of the courage he would ever need. She had spent days molding the staff upon the side of the mountain, and he had seen all of the work, energy, and magic that had gone into its creation.

He took a deep breath and nodded to Helzendar. He was ready.

CHAPTER TWENTY-FIVE
The Gates of Arkron

The two dragons, the Silverhawk, and their riders flew off to the west along with Azzeal. They looked behind them many times, but no one followed. Whill stared vacantly as they flew and barely made an attempt to hold on. Many times Avriel had to shift in her angle of flight to keep him balanced between her shoulders. She had tried to comfort Whill telepathically, but he withdrew from the contact and slipped deeper into his tormented mind. It wasn't until they had flown near the coast that Zhola guided them all down to where the tree line ended and gave way to the rocky coast.

There they put down, and the riders dismounted. Roakore immediately sprinted over to Whill and Avriel. "Where be Abram?"

Whill looked in his direction but gave no indication that he had heard Roakore.

"Aye, Whill! Snap out of it! Where in the bloody hell is he?"

Whill spoke, but his words cracked. "They were..."

Avriel lowered herself to her belly and shifted her body to the left. Whill crossed his right leg over her body and slid down her scales and plopped on his ass. He looked up at Roakore with watery, haunted eyes. Dark rings gave his sunken face a deathly pallor. "They were alive the whole time," Whill muttered.

Roakore took a deep, calming breath and knelt next to Whill. He took Whill's face in his hands. "What happened to him?"

"They were alive the whole time. They survived."

Roakore shook him and raised his voice. "Tell me what ye know!"

Whill made a mewling sound, and a strangled growl escaped his throat. He turned his head, but it was snapped back as Roakore forced Whill to look at him. The Dwarf slapped Whill in the face and screamed, "Where the bloody hell is Abram?"

Whill screamed back and pushed Roakore off of him. His rage and the power of his father's sword lent to his strength, and Roakore was thrown back twenty feet. He tumbled and finally stopped. Everyone looked on silently as Roakore got to his feet, dusted himself off, and walked back to Whill, who had gotten to his feet. Whill shook his head.

"Abram was injured. But I healed him. He would have died, but I saved him. We flew away, and I had him, my hands..." His voice trailed off as Whill stared down at his hands. When he looked upon Roakore once more, tears streamed down his soot-covered face.

"We were jolted by a spell, but I caught him. I had him by the wrist, but then Eadon...a black spell hit Abram. He smiled at me...And he blew away in the wind."

Whill eyed Roakore strangely and looked to Avriel with a confused look upon his face, and then he looked to Zhola and Dirk and Aurora. When he spotted the leaf-clad, Ralliad-master Elf Azzeal, he snapped.

"This isn't real!" he screamed and pointed at Roakore and the others. "You are not real!"

Roakore put up his hands, palms out, and walked to Whill.

"Stay back!" Whill hollered and backhanded his friend. Roakore was thrown back several feet and landed with a thud. "All of you! Stay back!" he screamed as he unsheathed his father's sword. He turned left and right and screamed at the air. "Where are you, Eadon, you son of a bitch? No more games! No more!"

Roakore slowly pushed up onto his hands and knees and got to his feet. "Ye crazy son o' rock moss, I be Roakore, for Ky'Dren's sake. You be knowin' it. We met on the side o' Ro'Sar Mountain. You and Abram and me, we killed many Draggard that day," he pleaded.

"Enough of your mind games. Get out of my head!" Whill screamed and charged Roakore, sword leading. Roakore braced himself, but Whill was intercepted by Azzeal. The Elf darted across the grass and produced a staff, seemingly from thin air. He steered Whill's blade up into the air and tripped him as he passed. Whill landed on his chest and slid. In a rage, Whill stood up and attacked Azzeal. His sword cut through the air with a thin whoosh again and again. Each blow was meant to kill, and each blow was deflected by Azzeal's staff.

Whill chopped at the Elf's side, but rather than block the blow, Azzeal changed into a tangle of roots that dropped to the ground under the attack and quickly disappeared beneath the dirt. Whill stabbed the ground, but his sword stuck. He pulled at it, but it would not move. Finally he growled like a bear and ripped the sword from the ground. With it came a tangle of roots and piles of falling earth. The roots sprang from the sword and wrapped themselves around Whill's face and body. They wrapped so tightly around him that Whill was powerless to move and fell like a tree.

Azzeal changed to his Elf form, squeezing Whill tightly with his legs. With one arm, he held both of Whill's at bay; with the other, he choked him. Whill screamed, and Azzeal squeezed until no sound came from him. Whill's sword glowed brightly, and from it, electric arks snaked out and encased the two in a ball of lightning.

Their hair stood on end, and Whill jolted in agony. He screamed through Azzeal's choke hold. "Let me die!"

Lightning shot out from the two and threatened to hit the others. They stepped back as Roakore yelled for Whill to stop.

Azzeal countered Whill's rage-filled energy attack with an orb of light that surrounded them both. The lightning was concentrated into one bolt, which arched up and was absorbed by the orb. Electrical charges cascaded down the curves of the orb and were grounded.

Azzeal grabbed Whill's sword and threw it outside the orb. The lightning ceased, and the orb withdrew. Whill had stopped struggling and just lay there, spent. Azzeal pushed himself off and stood, looking down at the broken man. "This is the savior of us all?" he asked Avriel with disgust.

"Best be watchin' your mouth, Elf! Me stone'll smash your rooted arse in a heartbeat!" Roakore warned.

Azzeal looked the Dwarf king over, unimpressed. "I have watched roots split stone for centuries, Dwarf."

Roakore walked over to Azzeal and scowled up at him. "I ain't needin' but a few minutes."

"Enough of this ridiculous banter!" Zhola yelled in all their heads as a roar and flame came from his mouth. Everyone stopped and looked to the great red dragon.

"Leave the boy and go! I grow weary of this, and I am hungry."

Roakore forgot Azzeal and turned on Zhola. "If ye think I'll be leavin' Whill with a bloody dragon, you be out o' your mind!"

Azzeal retrieved Whill's sword and looked to him. Whill still lay where he was, looking up at the clouds. The Elf turned his attention to Zhola. "You mean to bring him to the sword of Adimorda?"

Dirk perked up at the mention, and though he seemed to be absentmindedly flipping his dagger in the air, from behind his enchanted hood his eyes watched, and he listened keenly.

"I mean to be done with this business," answered Zhola."Be gone when I return," he said as he eyed them all, especially Roakore. He leapt high into the air and took to the sky. He flew out over the ocean. Avriel looked to Roakore. *Watch over Whill,* she bade him mentally and flew off after Zhola.

Whill had sat up and was watching the two dragons dive into the ocean like seabirds. They came out with fish between their massive teeth. Roakore approached Whill cautiously. He sat down next to his friend and looked on, worried. "I don't know what they did to you, lad, and can't imagine the horrors you seen. But you be amongst friends now; you be gone from that place."

Whill watched the dragons. He wore no expression. "They were alive, Roakore. They were alive the whole time, and I just rotted in that cell, helpless."

"Bah, what could you have done, Whill, against the likes o' Ead—"

"Exactly!" Whill interrupted. "What could I have done? What can I do now? So what if I find the sword—then what? What good will all that power be if I cannot wield it? I have barely learned to use magic; Eadon has had thousands of years! He has created dark spells no one has ever seen."

Roakore looked to the ground, wondering of the answer, but he had none. "I don't be knowin' such things, lad. All I know is I don't know nothin'. All I can do is have faith that Eadon can be defeated, and we may as well be the ones to be doin' it."

Whill shook his head, wearily. "I never wanted any of this. I don't want this responsibility. I do not want to be a king or a warrior; I have seen enough death already."

Roakore nodded in agreement. "None of us wanted it, Whill. But it has come to pass."

Just then Whill perked up, alert. "What of Tarren? What has become of the boy?"

"He lives; he be a guest in me mountain. Taken a keen interest in all things Dwarf, he has," Roakore said with a chuckle.

For the first time since Roakore had seen him again, Whill smiled.

"The reclamation was successful then? You freed your father's spirit?"

Roakore nodded, and his eyes watered a bit. "Aye, me father be free, and the mountain be ours again. But much has happened since you…left. Thousands of Drag-gard poured from me mountain and spread out across Agora. No one outside of a city is safe from the beasts."

Whill listened to the news without expression. They both looked out over the sea.

"What of your uncle, Addakon? What happened after you left with Eadon?"

Whill recounted the battle with Addakon. He told how his father's spirit had possessed his body and had killed his father's brother. He mentioned nothing of his torture.

Aurora and Dirk had joined them near the cliff; they had heard most of the conversation. Aurora greeted Whill with a nod, but she ignored Roakore. "I must thank you for getting me out of that place. You led us to victory bravely."

Whill nodded. "Now you may return to your people; good luck to you."

Aurora stayed where she was and searched for her words, her accent thick. "I have heard much of the leg-end of Whill of Agora. Even upon the frozen plains and forests of my home, Volnoss, your name is known."

Whill did not respond; he watched the hunting drag-ons. Aurora knelt down so that she blocked his view. "Let me remain at your side. I would fight alongside the man of legend—for we share common enemy."

Roakore got to his feet and looked up at Aurora with a scowl. "You be from Volnoss, eh? We be needin' no help from barbarian scum the likes o' yourself. Your kind were driven from Agora for a reason, you be knowin'. If not for the fact that you fought beside Whill in the arena, I would kill you meself."

Aurora made no move to respond to the threat. But anyone could see her temper flared at such harsh words against her people. "Was it not the Dwarves that first made war with the barbarians? You invaded our lands, burned our villages, and claimed our mountains as your own. And when you could not defeat us alone, you called upon Eldalon to do your dirty work."

Roakore moved to argue more but was stopped by Whill's hand to his forearm. Whill looked to Aurora. "What do you hope to gain from this?"

Without hesitation, she answered, "I would see an alliance between Volnoss and Uthen-Arden."

"Alliance?" he asked.

"Yes, you are the rightful king, are you not? My people will help. In return, I ask for an alliance."

Whill thought for a moment. "You have the authority to speak for your people?"

"I do," she lied. "Or I will. With word of you as an ally, I can sway the tribe's favor."

Roakore scoffed at that and grumbled inaudibly, but Whill ignored him. "You fought well in the arena. Your people will make great allies, no doubt. But I must warn you, my path is one of death. You would do well to leave now, before I lead you too to your death."

Aurora studied Whill for a long moment. "You speak as though you have given up. Do you not believe as the rest of us do?"

"Course he believes in his own self," Roakore interrupted. "He been through hell and back the last six months is all. Don't be worryin' 'bout this one."

Whill looked to his friend and was grateful for his words, though he did not agree. Abram was dead; Rhunis was dead. Avriel's soul was trapped within the body of a dragon, and for all he knew, Zerafin had died from his affliction. He didn't want anyone else to die for or because of him. Whill wished that they would all simply go away and leave him to his cursed fate. But he knew that they would not, least of all Roakore, who seemed misguidedly loyal to no end.

Dirk nodded to Roakore and addressed Whill. "I, too, would follow you on your quest to destroy Eadon."

"Course you would," Roakore chimed in with a disgusted glare. He turned to Whill. "What? We be in league now with dragons, barbarians, and assassins? I don't trust none of 'em!"

Whill smirked at his gruff friend. "You didn't trust me or Abram either."

Roakore stuttered over his reply, aghast.

Whill addressed Dirk once more. "You are obviously skilled. I watched you closely against the gladiators.

What does a blade for hire want with such a perilous quest as I have before me? We will all likely die in this endeavor."

Dirk nodded, conceding the point. "True, but if you are successful, I would have the favor of the king of Uthen-Arden, would I not? Besides, if you are not successful, there will be nothing but death and destruction at the hands of the tyrant Eadon. If I can aid in his destruction, I will."

The gravity of Dirk's words weighed on Whill's mind. He wanted to scream. He considered pitching himself over the ledge, but instead he sighed. "Then we have gained a valuable ally," he said and reached out and shook Dirk's hand. Dirk nodded, his face cast mostly in the shadow of his large hood. Through the enchanted hood, Dirk studied Whill. He determined that the man suspected nothing of his true mission.

Whill used the handshake to pull himself up. He looked from Dirk to Aurora and then to Roakore at his side, and finally to Azzeal. "What about you, Elf? Do you want to join the 'we are going to get our arses kicked club?'

Azzeal cocked his head to the side like a curious dog. "You find this funny, then? This is funny to you?"

"Actually, it is hilarious," Whill responded.

"You are a human brat that is too weak for this task," Azzeal spat.

"Indeed I am weak, and I am human!" Whill screamed as he pushed past Dirk and got closer to the Elf. "We are

weak. We are stupid. We are selfish, and we are slow."
He pointed his finger at Azzeal's chest. "Your people
brought this Dark Elf plaque to our lands, because your
entire nation was not strong enough to defeat Eadon!
And you bastards expect me to clean up your mess
because some old, dead Elf prophet said I would? You
hide behind a prophecy and spend your days talking
to trees, while my people die by your brother's hand.
You left me to wander the countryside, clueless, with
Abram, the only one man enough to attempt to help
me."

Whill's voice cracked at the memory of Abram and
their years of adventure, back before his world had
been turned upside down. He shook with rage and
tried to hold back the mounting pressure. He jabbed
Azzeal in the chest hard. "Let this be known to your
people, Elf! When I attain the sword, when I go to face
Eadon, I want the might of the entire gods damned
Elven empire at my back. You bastards are going to face
your fallen brother, or you are going to die trying. You
owe it to the humans; you owe it to the Dwarves, and
you owe it to me."

Whill saw movement peripherally and turned to find
Avriel had landed. With feline grace, she approached
them. "You have so much anger in your heart, so much
pain. I am sorry, Whill. Your words are true. We have
failed you, and we have failed you all.

"I am not angry with you, Avriel."

"I am an Elf, and, therefore, you are. You are a victim to your anger, a slave to your rage. It holds you back from your full potential. If you cannot let go, it will destroy you."

Whill could feel the rage still boiling within him, like an explosion contained within his core. It pulsed out in waves from his center and electrified his being. Through a clenched jaw, he spoke, "All I have left is anger."

"No, all that you still cling to is anger; you have forsaken all other emotions. You dare only feel rage, because you think that it is the only one that cannot be taken from you."

Whill looked down and to the side, shoulders sagging as tears spilled from his eyes.

"Love, hope, happiness. You do not dare feel these things."

Large tears welled in Avriel's dragon eyes, and she came closer until her snout lifted Whill's chin and their eyes met.

Remember love.

Her voice whispered in his mind, and he was once again within the meditation garden of Kell-Torey. The sun shone down upon Avriel in Elf form, sitting across from him, legs crossed. Her raven hair took on a bluish sheen in the light, and her smile warmed the darkest recesses of Whill's empty heart. Warmth that he had since forgotten spread over his body, and waves of contentment crashed over him. Whill reached out to touch her beautiful face, and her skin was hard and smooth.

Whill opened his eyes and looked into Avriel's dragon eyes. The living memory of the garden faded, but the feeling remained. Whill smiled at Avriel and laughed to himself.

Thank you.

She purred, and her deep humming caused the ground around him to vibrate.

Zhola landed and the ground shook. Spewing flame into the air, he mentally hollered. "Why do you remain idle?"

Whill walked to stand between Zhola and the group. "They are coming with us, all of them. Let us tarry no longer. If you mean to show me to the sword of Adi-morda, then let us be off."

Zhola clawed out the earth, sending piles of dirt and rock flying. "Fool boy, do not presume to command me! I have not lived thousands of years to listen to your childish prattle."

Zhola's roar echoed for miles as flames shot into the sky. The great red dragon bent until he was face to face with Whill. His nostrils flared, and smoke blew back Whill's hair.

"We go to the sword alone," Zhola growled.

"No, we go together, or I go not at all," Whill answered stubbornly.

Zhola growled and showed teeth that were as long and wide as Whill's legs. Whill showed his own and growled back.

"I should kill you myself and be done with this foolishness!" The ground rumbled with Zhola's deep voice.

"Then be done with it!" Whill screamed.

Zhola roared in Whill's face, and though no one could hear him, Whill screamed right back. The dragon looked around at the group. All brandished weapons and were ready to fight him; Avriel, too, was ready to pounce if need be. Roakore bounced on his toes, eager to carve a new cloak out of the dragon.

Zhola moved back from Whill and raised his head to his natural height. Looking down at Whill, he spoke, "Perhaps there is something to you after all, Whill of Agora; perhaps you are all a band of fools.

Everyone but Roakore relaxed their grip on their weapons. Whill nodded. "Perhaps."

Zhola turned his massive head to look to the sun; he then looked to the west. "Where we go, there is no game to be found. There are no plants to eat; there is no water to drink. Where we go, there is only silence and death. Hunt what you will, and bring what you can. We leave at nightfall.

"What is our destination" asked Whill

"Drakkar Island," said Zhola to them all.

"Drakkar Island!" roared Roakore. "That'll be the day that I follow a dragon to Drakkar Island!"

"If I wanted you dead, Dwarf, I would kill you now."

"You could try!"

Whill led his friend away from Zhola, and Roakore grumbled to himself the whole while. Before Whill could speak, Roakore started in. "Follow a dragon to Drakkar? Fight alongside a barbarian? Trust an assassin, who hides behind a hood like a trickster? And how ye be knowin' that white dragon be Avriel, aye?"

"The red dragon will lead us to the swo—"

"It'll be leadin' us to our death!"

Whill sighed, knowing that he would not convince his friend. He knew that for Roakore, to not attack the dragons took every ounce of his self-control. He did not trust them and never would.

"I cannot force you to do anything, King Roakore. You are my friend, and I know that you would come if I asked, but I cannot make that decision for you. You do what you want; I go to find the sword."

Whill turned from his friend and mounted Avriel. They set off together to hunt for what they could find.

Nearly two hours later, everyone had returned to where Zhola was sleeping with one eye open. The group had collected many roots and a variety of edible plants. Azzeal had changed to wolf form and hunted down a deer, which was quickly skinned and cut into pieces and then charred by Zhola's dragon breath.

Whill climbed atop Avriel's back once again, and Roakore mounted Silverwind as Aurora and Dirk mounted Zhola with apprehension. Azzeal, however, changed into a flaming phoenix.

Following Zhola, the group flew west. They flew on for hours and watched as below them the kingdom of Uthen-Arden was replaced by Isladon. As Whill surveyed the ground, he saw firsthand the destruction that had come to the land since his imprisonment. Though they flew high, Whill saw that many villages they passed over were empty. Many of the towns' buildings had been burned to the ground; others were only the skeletal remains of the main framework, black and charred like the fossils of a colossal beast long dead. Fields, that should by now have been harvested, stood bare or overrun by nature. More than once, Whill spotted huge packs of wolves scavenging through ruined towns, crows joining them in a feast of the dead.

The land was barren; an empty feeling permeated from it and instantly brought sorrow to bear upon the hearts of the onlookers.

Death spreads across the land in our absence, said Whill to Avriel's mind.

She growled deep in her throat, and the humming caused her entire body to vibrate under Whill. *It is indeed a dark time for man; it is a dark time for all the world it seems. It reminds me of...of home.*

They flew on into dusk and found more destroyed villages than standing ones. Those that remained had been fortified along their borders with makeshift wooden barricades and trenches.

Whill, what you said to Azzeal, about we Elves...

Whill began to make an apology but was cut off.

No, Whill, you were right. We brought this scourge upon you all; it has been and is our responsibility. We have put too much upon your shoulders. But you do not have to bear this burden alone; I shall see you victorious, or I shall see death.

Whill stroked her neck, glad to have her back with him. *I know you will.*

I am sorry about Rhunis and Abram, she said with much sorrow. Whill said nothing, but his throat tightened, and pain and sorrow poured through him once more at the thought of it. He was not yet ready to speak of it.

What has become of your brother? He asked.

He was cursed by Eadon with some sort of rotting disease. I know not of his fate. If I were in true form, I could scry him, but I have not been yet able to harness any of my abilities. When I left him, he was in great pain and nearing death. But there is much combined power among those I left him with. Hopefully they were able to carry him to Elladrindellia swiftly; there perhaps the elders will be able to break the curse.

Whill mentally comforted her as she had done for him at mention of Abram. It was not words to the mind in the form of a language; rather, Whill sent her a mental hug of sorts.

After you left, I saw Eadon struggling against affliction. Somehow Zerafin caused the curse to fire back on Eadon as well. Even in the arena, he seemed crippled by it, Whill told her.

Avriel purred at that. *Yes, if Eadon heals himself of the curse, I believe Zerafin will be free of it also. We can only hope that Zerafin can hold out long enough for Eadon to let it go.*

Whill smiled to himself, glad to know that Eadon was in great pain and that Zerafin had tricked the Dark Elf so. The fact that Eadon had been hurt was a great comfort indeed. Until then, it had seemed that the Dark Elf was impervious to all.

What is it like? Being a dragon?

Avriel thought for a moment and tried to suppress the terror of not being one with her true body. *It is strange. I have only just begun to study the ways of the school of Ralliad. Before this, I had only ever changed into wolf form. It is much different than that transmutation. In wolf form, I was still in true Elf form; this is different. My soul possesses this body fully. I find myself affected by its chemistry in ways quite different than my Elven body. It is said that dragons are born with the collective memories and knowledge of their ancestors. I have discovered this to be true. My dragon brain is linked to all those before me. I am aware of the history of my line, dating back eons. It is all quite overwhelming and confusing. Where my Elf memories faded with time, as one would expect after centuries of life, the dragon mind recalls every memory as if it were yesterday. I feel myself slipping more into the mind of the dragon. I can no longer feel the presence of my true form. I fear that my body has died, and I am forever trapped within this one.*

Whill remembered Eadon's words that he and he alone could return her to true form. He told Avriel this to her despair.

He is a master of manipulation and lies. It may be true, it may not; it is to be seen. I will not let it be my focus. There are bigger things at work here than my own fate. And I am guessing there are worse things to become than a dragon.

Hearing her words, he felt ashamed of his own selfishness. He and he alone could stop Eadon it seemed, and rather than focus on the task, he had allowed himself to wallow in self-pity. His own personal pain had become his entire reality. It all seemed so clear at that fleeting moment. He was possessed by pain.

The sun set and the group flew on into the night. When they became tired, Azzeal flew close and touched a wing to that of the dragons. When Azzeal touched Avriel's wing, Whill felt a warm surge of energy course through him. His aches and pains from riding dissipated, and his vigor returned.

Azzeal flew close to Roakore and Silverwind and bade the Dwarf to allow him to offer energy. *Good Dwarf, your mount tires from flying so long and hard. Allow me to restore her energy.*

"Do what you be doin' to help Silverwind, but stay outta me damned head, Elf!"

Very well, said Azzeal in Roakore's mind once more and touched the tip of his wing to Silverwind's. The Silverhawk let out a soft coo and a squawk.

Refreshed, the riders doubled their speed and caught a swift air current. The moon was their guide for the remainder of the night. They reached the coast of Isladon and left Agora behind. As the sun rose behind them, they were bathed in welcome warmth.

Whill watched the waters speed by below. His mind drifted to Abram, the man that had been as a father to him all his life. He had thought him dead for so long, only to be reunited and lose him once again. It occurred to him that this could all be fake, just another of Eadon's elaborate illusions. The Dark Elf had tortured him many times with such false realities. Whill had been convinced many times, only to be violently torn from his delusions. Whill wished that this was just an illusion; he wished that Abram were still alive. He did not know how he could possibly continue without Abram's wise guidance. But Whill knew that this reality was most likely real, for he had been lucid since being let out of the dungeon. Whill accepted the probability that this was, indeed, real, and his tears fell upon Avriel's scales and then mingled with the ocean waters below.

His rage should have been spent by now, but it would not abate. He heeded Avriel's words, but he was unable to feel anything but rage, anger, and sorrow. He knew he should have been happier to see Roakore alive and well and Avriel alike, though she was trapped within the body of a white dragon. But Whill would not allow himself to feel any happiness nor hope. Realizing this, he knew that Avriel was right. To him, hope and joy and happiness had become the tools of his torture. Eacon had seen to that. He knew that the Dark Elf had hoped to inflict him with such a mindset, and, indeed, Eacon had been successful. But this knowledge did nothing to alleviate Whill's fear. Too many times during his torture he had been shown illusions in which he was free, once again traveling the wide world with his friends. Too many times he had seen his friends die, one after another, during those dark sessions deep within the depths of the dank dungeon. Whill was left a husk of the optimistic boy he had once been. He was the same person now in name only.

Though he wanted to, he could not allow himself to feel too deeply for his living friends, for they, like Abram and Rhunis, would die before his eyes before this dark business was through.

They flew on into the afternoon as the sun crept at their backs. Below them the blue-green waters tediously wore on hour after hour. Unlike the ever-changing landscape of the countryside, the waters offered only the occasional school of fish just below the surface or a flock of seagulls. Behind them, Agora slowly slipped from view, like a dying behemoth sinking into water. They had spent many hours without land in sight in either direction when, finally, before them, land could be seen.

It was not until night had fallen over the world and the stars cast their heavenly light upon the waters, that they finally reached Drakkar Island. The legends Whill had heard saying that Drakkar was a dead island proved true. Not a tree nor plant nor single blade of grass grew upon its steaming land. Instead, it was covered with a strange gray-black rocklike substance. Drakkar's shores were sharp and jagged; the beaches of rock mingled and curved like a giant's hair. In the distance to the west loomed a single mountain without a peak.

Though Azzeal had given the mounts his offered energy, the dragons and Silverhawk were exhausted and sore from their long flight. The riders had not fared any better. The dragons landed, and the riders each dismounted stiffly. Roakore even fell to the ground with a groan and was not able to stand for some time. He sat upon the stony beach of the island, rubbing his legs and grumbling. Aurora, too, sat upon the stones next to a panting Avriel. Dirk had fared better than any of them as he had often gotten to his feet atop Zhola and sat on his heels to rest his legs.

"Gather your strength and eat what you will; we make for the volcano at first light," Zhola told them all.

The group rested but none slept. Many times the silence of the night was disturbed by the roar of a dragon. Some of the eerie cries came from far away, and others seemed much closer. Both Avriel and Zhola sat alert, staring at the volcano and sniffing at the air occasionally. Roakore never loosened his grip on his ax, nor did his eyes leave the sight of the volcano.

The first rays of morning broke through the sky, chasing away the stars. Zhola stood and stretched his muscle-laden hind legs one at a time as a dog might.

"The others of my kind will not be happy to see you all here. Follow my lead, or I cannot ensure your safety."

"I'll ensure me own safety dragon," Roakore mumbled.

"And if they attack?" asked Aurora.

"If they attack, then you will die. This is your last chance to turn back." No one moved. Zhola nodded and let out a puff of smoke. "So be it. You are all very brave, or stupid."

"Then let's get it over with," Whill told them all. To Zhola, he said, "It was smart to hide the sword within a volcano."

"The sword of Adimorda is not within the smoking mountain."

Roakore took up an offensive stance and squared on Zhola. "Then it is a trap! Told ye not to trust the blasted dragon!"

Zhola scowled at Roakore. "The sword is hidden in Drindellia."

Avriel and Azzeal perked up at the mention of their homeland, and Roakore looked confused.

"In Drindellia?" asked Whill.

"Yes, within the smoking mountain is an ancient doorway built by the Elves long ago and brought here by me."

Azzeal looked to the volcano with wonder. "The gates of Arkron…" The Elf snapped out of his reverie and saw that the humans and Dwarf were staring at him, waiting for him to elaborate.

"The gates of Arkron were built long ago by one of the same name. Arkron was a very talented Elf, but he was most skilled in creating new spells and using Orna Catorna in ways no one had ever imagined. His greatest achievement was the creation of his gates or portals. One could step into one of his gates and immediately come out of the other, whether it was a few feet or many miles away. This was many centuries ago, long before the fall of Drindellia. Many of our people wished the gates destroyed, deeming them too dangerous due to Arkron's methods. Somehow, he had discovered how to bend the very fabric of our reality, connecting the gates to one another in a seamless unity. Seven pairs of gates he built, and they were spread to the farthest reaches of our lands."

"An' ye're saying that we're gonna just go waltzin' into a portal when we ain't knowin' what is on the other side?" asked Roakore.

"It seems that Zhola knows what is on the other side," said Whill.

Zhola concurred with a low, humming growl. "As I have yet mentioned, death and destruction await us. When I last saw the smoldering ruins of Drindellia, there was not but death to be found there. The cities burned, and the land bled. I ferried the gate here to Drakkar Island by raft across the great ocean. Over calm waters and violent alike, I towed it for many months and finally reached my destination. Once I had buried the gate deep beneath the volcano, I sought out my kin and told them that I had found a home for them, a place free from humans, Elves, and the vicious Dwarves."

Roakore chuckled.

Ignoring him, Zhola went on. "So now Drakkar is home to dragons and feared by all, and it keeps the secret gate safe from those with ill intent."

"What happened to the other portals? Are they known?" asked Dirk, who until then had not spoken, only listened.

"No," answered Azzeal. "Three pairs were destroyed during the fall of Drindellia. One was brought with us on our sojourn to Agora. But many feared that its twin would be discovered and that Eadon would send his army through, so it was tossed overboard and lies on the bottom of the ocean. Three other pairs are unaccounted for; it seems we have discovered one of them. It was guessed that Eadon was in possession of them, but now it appears he may only have two of the seven."

"And you say that entire armies can travel through these portals?" asked Aurora.

Azzeal nodded. "Yes, and your thoughts have been our own. Eadon could use these portals to march an army of Draggard from Drindellia to Agora instantly."

"If he ain't already," stated Roakore as if coming to an epiphany. "We have always wondered how he did it. How so many Draggard could have kept on pourin' through our tunnels, though we slew thousands. It explains why no lookout ever gave warnin'."

Roakore began to shake, and his face became red with rage. "There was a bloody portal in me mountain!" His eyes went wide as he followed the thought down dark passages. "There could still be!" He began pacing in circles and wringing his hands together. To the ground, he spoke. "I been flyin' around in the company o' dragons and barbarians, and there well may be a gut-rotten bloody portal o' Eadon's in me mountain! Hand o' Ky'Dren slap a stupid Dwarf's arse!"

"You do not know that it remains," Whill tried to assure him.

"And I don't be knowin' that it aint!" Roakore yelled a bit too loudly.

In the distance, there could be heard a growing number of dragon sounds. Growls and shrieks and deep roars echoed across the island. "Now you have awakened my kin. Mount up, and remain close to me."

As Whill went to mount Avriel, Roakore stopped him with a strong hand on his arm. "What if the portal remains in me mountain?"

"When this business is through, I will return with you to look," Whill assured him.

CHAPTER TWENTY-SIX
The Scepter of Krowlen

Tarren began to follow Helzendar into the arena when a hand upon his shoulder stopped him. He turned to see Lunara smiling at him. "I am sorry you were upset earlier. Please take this to aid in your contest."

She handed him a simple golden ring. He began to shake his head in protest but was cut off. Lunara's tone became serious and took on a motherly note. "You are an eleven-year-old human boy fighting Dwarves seven times stronger and years older. This will even the odds."

"No," he said, shaking his head.

"You are a stubborn boy, Tarren of Fendale."

"Some things got to be done all by myself, Lunara. This is one of them. If I pass wearing your ring, I will wonder if it was because of the ring."

She closed her hand and withdrew her arm. "Dwarves have died during these tests."

Tarren nodded. "But no human has yet."

"*Yet,*" countered Lunara cryptically.

Tarren smiled up at Lunara, with such courage in his eyes that hers watered.

"Then at least accept my well wishes." She hugged him. "Bless you, Tarren. May you strike true and your enemies nigh."

"Hey!" protested Tarren, releasing the hug. "Did you just—"

"I did nothing but wish you luck," said Lunara straight-faced.

Tarren searched her eyes and finally shrugged. "Here goes nothin'."

He turned from her and made his way into the arena. The cavern was massive. Stalagmites and stalactites reached high and hung low. Into them had been carved seats, and from them hundreds of Dwarves would watch the spectacle below. Aisles of seats were also carved into the walls of the natural cave. The stone floor was slick with mist from a waterfall at the opposite end of the arena. A great fire burned behind the waterfall, and so the cavern was illuminated with dancing light. It shone upon the walls and was refracted by the mineral-rich stone in such a way that there was not shadow, only dancing, multicolored light. It filled the cavern and, at first, was disorienting to Tarren.

The crowd roared and stomped, and the racket echoed deafeningly in the cavern. It was like an ocean tide of voices, ebbing and flowing and crashing in crescendo with a life of its own. Tarren swooned and patted Helzendar's shoulder and steadied himself. "Good luck," he said, trying not to sound nervous, but he was sure his voice sounded like a squeak.

"Bah, luck be havin' nothin' to do with it," Helzendar boasted. Then his face changed, and Tarren saw the slightest look of concern. "Have no doubts, Tarren, you be faster than even meself. Keep your feet movin' and go for the eyes."

Tarren nodded to his best friend and looked to the center stalactite with the others as a loud voice boomed over the crowd. All speech stopped, and the high priest Bouldarr greeted them all.

"Good Dwarves o' Ro'Sar, whose king be Roakore son o' Ro'Din, nineth king o' the Ro'sar Mountains. This be the day o' the trials."

The crowd gave a cheer so loud that Tarren feared one of the mammoth slabs would come crashing down on their heads.

"These strong, young Dwarves stand as a testament to our revenge, our steadfast determination, and the victory o' our king."

Again there was pandemonium as the chant for Roakore was taken up. Tarren blocked out the noise and took the opportunity to scope out the arena on the level below him. The arena that would hold the trial was a maze that he guessed was nearly two hundred feet long and twice as wide. Stalactites protruded from the ceiling, threatening to crush those below should the world decide to twitch. They made Tarren feel his smallness.

Judges walked the tops of the maze walls. From their vantage point, they would be able to call out any Dwarf that was successfully hit by an opponent. The fighting was not to the death—though there were accidents. A competitor was called out when they received what would be a killing blow with metal weapons or were knocked out. For the trial wooden weapons, like those they trained with in practice, were used. Tarren gripped his staff, Oakenheart, tightly, his mind racing to memorize the maze.

The high priest Bouldarr again addressed the crowd; calling names from a long scroll, he divided the Dwarves into groups. Tarren was ecstatic to hear his name called along with Helzendar for the same team. The fifty fighters had been divided into ten teams of five, each with a captain. To no one's surprise, Tarren's team captain was Helzendar. Tarren knew it was not for his station but for his clear excellence in fighting and his leadership qualities that Helzendar was chosen. Tarren did not miss that many of the Dwarves, while not outright scoffing at the idea, nevertheless, were not happy having "the weakling human" on their team. But their apprehension had disappeared and been replaced with jubilation when they learned that they would have Helzendar at their side.

The Dwarves separated into their groups, and Dwarf boys, that had only just stood together as mates, began to eye the opposite teams, sizing up the competition. Vulgarities abounded, and taunts were yelled. Helzendar brought his group together in a huddle.

"This be it, boys. If the game be capture the flag, Tarren be our carrier, and ya'll best watch his arse like it were yer girl's arse. If the game be to get some object first, I want Tarren after it and us at his back."

One of the Dwarves rolled his eyes at the mention of Tarren again. "You got a problem with me orders, Cake?" Helzendar asked.

Cake's real name was Grimlock, but no one but his mother called him that. He was possibly the fattest and widest Dwarf Tarren had ever seen, child or adult. He was nicknamed Cake because he was rarely seen without it in hand. He had no beard yet and wore only a long tail atop his shaved head. His rosy cheeks bulged so much that it appeared his eyes were nearly closed. His nose hid behind his face, and his brow was ever furled. But when he smiled, he lit up like a baby, and it was hard not to smile too.

Cake looked to his captain and to the others in turn. He had just shown a sign of disloyalty, and he knew his folly. He stuttered to make right his mistake. "I...I...it's just that the human is so small. I ain't yet seen him win a fight." He looked to the other Dwarves on his team for support but found none. "C'mon, he's done broke more bones than most people know they got. He ain't no warrior."

Helzendar scowled at his teammate. "He keeps comin' back, don't he?"

Cake stuttered in the affirmative. Helzendar grabbed Cake's armor and jerked the fat Dwarf forward. "He fights bigger, stronger opponents, and he always bleeds. He suffers daily to achieve his goal, but he always comes back for more, don't he?"

Cake nodded, and Helzendar released him. "This human be the ward o' Whill o' Agora, you be knowin'. He already seen things that would make you shat your pants, and mark me words, one day he'll be a great leader o' men."

Helzendar let his voice rise all the while as he chastised Cake. He wanted to intimidate the other teams a bit, not to mention stand up for his friend. Cake bowed his head and blushed at the attention they had earned. Quickly, those near turned away as Bouldarr began to explain the game.

"Today's trial will be capture the flag."

The crowd murmured, and the nearby Dwarves whispered conspiratorially. Helzendar gave Tarren a wink.

"Also...I'll have me voice heard; settle down now," Bouldarr bade the crowd and put up a quieting hand. "Also, there will be a quest object."

The crowd sucked in a breath, and frantic talk broke out again amongst the competitors. Everyone began to crane their necks, trying to find the quest item. Before Bouldarr said it, Tarren saw it, and his eyes widened.

"Whichever team is left with their flag in possession at the end wins...or, whichever team reaches the scepter o' Krowlen first shall win instantly," Bouldarr declared and pointed high to the top of the glimmering waterfall. There, dangling from a rope near the mouth of stone that fed the falls, hung the Scepter of Krowlen, once possessed by the high priest Krowlen. The crowd ooked and aahed at the priceless relic.

Bouldarr let his hand drop and looked to the fighters.

"Those young warriors on the winning team will all pass their trials, and others also that prove themselves in battle. Teams to their starting points, and may the best Dwarves be winnin!"

The crowd roared, and the group was led to their maze entrance. There at the entrance stood a blue flag on a three-foot pole. Tarren looked to Helzendar with apprehension. The last thing he needed was a target on his back. The Dwarf ignored the look. Instead, he looked to Cake with a scowl. "You keep everyone away from Tarren, and your discrepancy be forgotten."

Cake frowned, confused.

Helzendar sighed. "You want to redeem yourself? Then protect Tarren like you would the last piece o' cake on Agora!"

Cake smiled this time, now understanding. In his eyes his thoughts played out, first a smile of realization, then grim determination, then a puzzled look as he looked to Tarren.

"But cap'n. I would eat the last piece o' cake."

Helzendar shook his head in frustration. "Don't be eatin' me flag runner, Cake, just protect him."

Helzendar pointed at one of the other Dwarves. This one was lean, even for a Dwarf, and had black curly hair that hung down to his gray eyes. He was alert and smiling, barely able to contain his excitement.

"Trett, you are gonna be our spy. You stay ahead o' the group as far as the next maze turn, unless otherwise ordered."

"I got this, boss," Trett exclaimed cockily.

"And you, Brezzerk," Helzendar addressed the last of the group. "You watch'r backs by a corner's length. If you see someone coming, give word, and we all stand together and fight in the same formation. Trett at lead, Cake behind him, Tarren and meself, and Brezzek in back, got it?"

"Yes, sir!" was said by all. They all took their places and readied their weapons.

Dwarves possessed strength up to seven times that of the average human; therefore, they did not often carry swords but rather huge axes and war hammers. Cake carried such a war hammer. Its handle was short and thick, and though metal weapons were not yet wielded by the training Dwarf boys, many of the weapons had steel-reinforced shafts, lest the great weight of the blade snap the handle in two. Such was Cake's hammer shaft; its head was a smooth-cornered block of wood as big as Tarren's torso. It was bound in leather at the head's center, with small rubies weaving around and down the handle. A blunted wooden spike, eight inches long, poked out of the top of the war hammer's head.

Trett carried twin single-headed axes, their shafts long and thin with wooden half-moon blades. Brezzerk was one of a few Dwarves that used a shield and sword. The blade was nearly eight inches wide, double-edged, and four feet long. The thickest point, down the center of the blade, was four inches. The sword was the same thickness throughout. It had not a point but a curved tip; it was meant for hacking, not stabbing, and, appropriately, it was named Hacker by Brezzerk. His shield was of identical weight as his sword, for maximum efficiency, and covered him from shoulder to shoulder, neck to kneecap.

"You thinkin' the other groups'll go for the scepter, captain?" asked Brezzerk.

Helzendar shrugged. "I don't know 'bout the other captains, but I intend to get it, and Tarren be the one to do it. He be faster than most and more nimble. I say we take and get to the stone face o' the waterfall's wall and guard while Tarren climbs it."

The Dwarves nodded in agreement, and Trett began moving into the maze. Only when he peered around the corner and waved them on did the group proceed. Tarren found it impractical to carry the staff and flag separately and took them up together in both hands as one.

They met no one as they journeyed through the maze, but the sounds of fighting and the roar of the crowd indicated that some of the groups had clashed. To their dismay, the Dwarves found that the maze led them farther away from the waterfall and hanging scepter. But Tarren assured them that all of the halls of the stone maze had gone far and wide from the start.

"You all must have seen the large opening in the center. I would guess that all of the ways lead there, as to force the groups to collide. It is there that we must be swift and cut across to the entrance to the waterfall," he informed them.

Soon they came to a crossroads in the maze, and there, at the four corners, were three prone Dwarves, lying where they had fallen and been called out by the judges. One such judge walked the maze walls to the group's right and watched the fallen Dwarves to be sure they did not communicate anything to those still in the fight.

Everyone looked to Tarren, and his mind went to work. He had glimpsed this section of maze earlier, but the memory was not clear enough for him to be sure.

"This way." He indicated the passage to their right and away from the falls. Before anyone could argue, he cut them off, "This be a maze. The other way toward the falls don't mean that is where they lead. This way."

Helzendar nodded when Trett looked to him for approval, and they headed down the right passage. After a short time, Trett raised a hand after jerking his head back around the corner. He made a fist, put up three fingers and began to back up.

"Were you seen?" asked Helzendar.

"Yes," answered Trett.

"Fall back, shoulder to shoulder."

A war charge was heard coming from ahead as three Dwarves turned the corner and charged. Trett, Cake, and Helzendar stood together, blocking the way completely. Cake's massive war hammer swept across and took one Dwarf in the shoulder. The blow slammed the attacker into the wall and left him unconscious. The other two slid to a stop and squared on the three. Helzendar and the others quickly overpowered the two, and their flag was taken.

Once again, the group got into formation and ventured through the maze. When again they came to a split in the maze, they went left. When Trett raised a fist they all stopped. Either Tarren's memory was right, or they had gotten lucky, for they had reached the center opening, and it was a killing field.

Nearly a dozen Dwarf boys lay where they had fallen, and judges waited at the top of the stone to witness the next battle.

"Them idiots atop the stone will give our location away," Tarren cursed.

Helzendar looked to one and nodded with a scowl; he adjusted his helmet and looked to be contemplating. "Or they are giving away another group's location."

"You want me to flush 'em out, boss?" asked Trett as he bounced anxiously.

Helzendar considered his eager lookout. "Good idea. Check the ways leading from the center, be swift and do not engage—"

"I ain't for running from the enemy—"

"You ain't runnin', ya idiot, you're scoutin'. If you ain't for listenin to orders, you can be relieved."

"I can listen, boss. I got this."

"Then go!"

Trett complied, and Helzendar took his place. He peeked around the corner and counted the disqualified Dwarfs. He knew many of them by name, and judging by the flags littering the ground, he guessed that three teams had fallen here. Counting his own team and the one they had beaten, the field had nearly been cut in half. Now only five other teams remained. Unless, of course, others had fallen that he was not aware of.

Tarren looked back and then forward again, listening. The crowd had become very quiet, and every far off face he could see seemed to be staring in their direction. Alarms went off in his head.

"It's an ambush," he murmured to himself. "It's an ambush!" he said louder. It was too late for warning. As he spoke, four Dwarf boys dropped down from the tops of the seven-foot-high stone walls. One came down with a huge ax; his entire body arched into the blow meant for Cake's back.

"Cake!" Tarren yelled.

Another leapt right at Tarren and would have landed on top of him had Helzendar not intercepted the flying Dwarf boy with his half-moon staff. He came up and under the Dwarf and caught him in the curved end of his staff. Using the Dwarf's momentum, Helzendar flung the boy over his shoulder with a heave. The screaming Dwarf boy flew into one of his fellows, and together, they landed with a thud. The fourth Dwarf landed between Tarren and Brezzerk, who was charging in fast. He slammed into the Dwarf with his shield as the boy landed.

"To the other side of the maze!" cried Helzendar, and he pushed Tarren to run for the opening before they were bottled in. Brezzerk stayed behind, battling the attacker as Tarren, Helzendar, and Cake charged forward blindly into the opening. Cake nearly bowled over Trett as he ran at them; four Dwarf boys chased after him. Trett quickly dropped to the ground and slid past Cake as the fat Dwarf boy slammed into the four charging opponents. Helzendar and Tarren leapt over the fallen Dwarves as Cake wrestled with them.

Trett came up out of his slide and leapt at Brezzerk's opponent. With his twin axes, he scored two hits, one to the Dwarf's helmet, the other to his back. The Dwarf was distracted long enough for Brezzerk to take advantage of the opening and smash his blade into the other Dwarf's chest. The blow sent him stumbling backward, and a judge called him out. They chased after Tarren and Helzendar into the opening.

Tarren looked quickly around the wide convergence of halls. It seemed as though more than two teams had grouped together to take out the others. Blocking every one of the exits were at least two Dwarves. Helzendar abruptly skidded to a halt, and Tarren bumped into him. Trett and Brezzerk came rushing to their side. Cake, however, had been called out along with those he fought.

There were no words spoken, only glances and nods from the enemy captains to each other. The air became thick with anticipation, and Tarren feared this was the end for his team. He gripped his staff and his team's flag tightly, his mind racing for a plan.

Then he saw, far off ahead of them, at the other end of the maze, a lone Dwarf climbed the stone wall next to the waterfall. One hundred feet above him hung the scepter that could end the trial.

"Someone is going for the scepter!" he yelled.

Those ahead of him did not see what the rest of them saw, but a few noticed that the crowd was split between looking at the small battlefield and the wall climber. Many began to cheer on the Dwarf as he expertly climbed the stone. He was nearly halfway already.

"After him!" ordered a captain to Tarren's right.

"Don't let them get there first!" cried another.

The captain of the Dwarf that had snuck off and now climbed the wall screamed, "Don't let anyone down that hall."

Fighting quickly broke out between all the teams as Dwarves rushed toward the halls that led to the falls, and others fought to block the way. Tarren and his team were all but forgotten, standing there at the center of the clearing.

"Them other Dwarves walked atop the walls and weren't disqualified. No one ever said we couldn't. Get to the falls! Get that scepter!" Helzendar frantically told Tarren.

"Gotta get me on them walls first."

Helzendar looked to the walls and nodded. "Follow me at a distance o' six bricks." And then he ran toward the heart of the fight, where more than a dozen Dwarves fought for control of the exit leading to the falls. Trett and Brezzerk were close behind.

The son of Roakore stopped ten feet from the far wall and turned and clasped his hands together low and crouched. Tarren knew Helzendar's mind and ran at his friend and stepped up onto the open hands of Helzendar, who then heaved Tarren up into the air.

Tarren was startled by his flight as he soared over the fighting Dwarf boys and came in fast toward the top of the wall. He had too much momentum to be able to make the landing without falling over the edge into the maze, so instead of trying to land, he sprang into a leap off the top of the wall. Skipping from on to the other, he barely cleared the gap and landed on the edge of the opposite wall and fought for balance.

He looked back upon the center of the maze and found the rest of his team fighting their way through to the center exit to the falls. He turned toward the falls and saw that the lone Dwarf was well past halfway.

Behind Tarren, two Dwarves climbed up onto the maze walls and started in his direction. Tarren wasted no time and began to run along the four-foot-wide walls toward the glimmering waterfall.

The two Dwarves followed in swift pursuit, deftly maneuvering atop the walls of the maze. When the maze turned, Tarren leapt and landed and ran on without missing a beat. He came to another turn and leapt over the gap. He dared a glance behind him and saw the Dwarf boys still in pursuit.

The crowd cheered for the Dwarf climbing the stone face as he neared the top and reached for the scepter. Tarren was distracted by the spectacle and had to quickly leap as the maze wall turned left. He cleared the gap but landed awkwardly, staggering all too quickly toward the ledge. He was forced to leap once again but did not have the momentum behind him to clear the gap. He slammed into the edge with his chest and clawed at the smooth stone for a grip. From his precarious location, Tarren watched as the Dwarf boy reached too far for the scepter. His fingers had come within inches of the prize when his hand slipped from the wall, and he fell screaming into the frothing water below. The crowd fell silent with a collective gasp.

Tarren watched after the fallen Dwarf, wide-eyed; only the sound of heavy boots coming quickly shook him from his shock. He heaved and clawed and finally climbed up onto the stone wall. One of the pursuing Dwarves leapt once, twice, and came down on Tarren with double axes. Tarren leapt backward and rolled as he landed and came up on his feet, ready to run. His opponent gave him no time to run, however; he came with spinning axes and a fierce snarl, slashing and chopping.

Tarren danced on his toes blindly as he attempted to evade the wooden axes. With his staff, he batted away the onslaught. He ducked an ax strike and slammed the staff into the back of the Dwarf's left knee. The boy gave a howl and bent to that knee, Tarren came in strong with the butt of his staff at the Dwarf's face, but his injury had only been a feint. The Dwarf came across with the back of an ax blade and hit Tarren in the head. Tarren had tried to dodge the blow but was still clipped in the forehead hard enough to send him spinning.

He spun from the blow and landed on his back. The Dwarf boy was on him in a flash. He leapt high into the air and came down with both blades arched in a deadly strike. Tarren rolled quickly over the ledge. He fell into the maze once more, and his breath blasted from his chest on impact. Luckily, he was prepared and did not lose his breath. It hurt, but Tarren forgot it quickly. He was glad that he had recently been trying to withstand the pain of his injuries as long as possible. He had learned not to fight the pain, not to bask in his agony and let it rule him.

He got to his feet and ran down the stone hall toward the waterfall. In front of him, the other Dwarf boy landed, blocking his way. Behind him, another jumped down from the wall. Tarren remembered his training and got over the overwhelming challenge. He went into his routine of spinning and dancing with the staff. Before the two could jump him, he attacked the one behind him. With a leap and twirl, he came in with a swiping blow to the Dwarf boy's head. The blow was deflected, and Tarren spun and struck again. Left, right, and left again came Tarrens blows; each was deflected, but his opponent was kept at bay. Tarren reached down and quickly scooped up what dirt he could from the floor and threw it in his opponent's face, and before he could recuperate, Tarren turned and charged the Dwarf that blocked the path behind him.

The Dwarf boy met Tarren's charge and swung a spiked ball overhead with one hand. He carried a thick, curved blade in the other. Tarren looked frantically to the stone floor and found a small crevice. He slammed the end of his staff into the crack and leapt high and vaulted over the Dwarf. The staff came out from under him as the boy collided with it. As Tarren landed and pulled the staff with him, the boy hit it with his chain. The chain of the spiked ball wrapped itself around the staff three times, and Tarren was jerked to a stop. His legs shot out ahead of him as he clung to the trapped staff.

The Dwarf boy grinned wickedly and yanked on the chain as hard as he could. Tarren held on as his head snapped back and he shot through the air and straight at the Dwarf. With momentum behind him, generated by the strong Dwarf boy, Tarren let go of the staff and shot out a strong elbow that hit with a crunch of the Dwarf's nose. They fell in a heap, and Tarren scrambled to stand. Blood poured from the Dwarf's nose, and Tarren was elated with pride, until the boy began to get up.

Tarren was yanked back from his inward gloating and quickly gathered up his staff. From out of nowhere came the twin-ax-wielding Dwarf. The axes came down fast and hard, but Tarren managed to deflect them with his staff. He could not block such strong attacks head on; instead he used momentum and his long staff to change the attack's direction. The Dwarf rained down his powerful strikes, any of which would have laid Tarren low. He frantically blocked and dodged the attacks, but he was steadily being pushed backward against the wall.

To his relief, Helzendar came to his aid, leaping from on high and knocking out the ax wielder with his half-moon staff. Helzendar turned on the other Dwarf and yelled to Tarren, "Quit screwing around and get to that scepter."

Tarren heeded his words and took off in the other direction. A short jaunt through the maze and Tarren came to the end. Before him was the raging waterfall, and high above hung the shining scepter. He set his staff through the strap on his back next to the flag, spit in his hands, and rubbed them together. Finding a grip, he began to ascend the slippery stone wall. He got no more than five feet high when suddenly he slipped. He'd missed a foothold, and the sudden shift in weight caused him to lose his grip on the wall. He slid down the stone, desperately trying to get a grip and lanced on his backside.

The watching Dwarves let out a gasp and then a chuckle as Tarren got to his feet and rubbed his bum. He scowled at the spectators and started again up the stone face. He moved slower, more methodically this time, making sure that he had three strong holds before he moved a limb. From the crowd came amazed proclamations such as, "Is that the wee human boy?" and, "It be Tarren," and the like.

A wooden hatchet slammed into the stone next to his face, sending flecks of stone flying. He dared a glance back and saw a Dwarf cocking back for another throw. Tarren tensed for the hit. If he was struck in the head or back with the hatchet, he would be called out, and he would possibly even be knocked from the wall. He looked down at the distance he had traveled; it was a long way down.

The second hatchet never came, and Tarren did not have to look down to see the reason, he could hear the sounds of battle below and knew that Helzendar or someone from his team had engaged the attacker. He was more than halfway up the stone face with the waterfall raging next to him when the crowd began to cheer and whistle. He looked down and saw that someone had gotten by Helzendar and was quickly, even recklessly, climbing after him. Tarren knew that panic and fear would find him falling to his death far below, so he pushed both of these feelings away and continued steadily up the rock face.

The boy was too far behind, and Tarren was now nearly level with the scepter. A few more careful handholds and he clung looking sideways at the hanging prize. Tarren knew that he could not reach the scepter with his hands; he had seen the Dwarf's fall after attempting that very thing. So instead he made sure he had a firm grip with his left hand and his feet and reached back for his staff. Using the staff, he carefully hooked the chain that held the scepter. Tarren's heart pounded as he unhooked the prize and breathlessly pulled it toward himself. He raised his staff carefully, and the scepter slid down the length of it. He grabbed hold of the scepter in the same hand that held the staff as the Dwarf that had been climbing toward him pulled his foot loose. Tarren was yanked from his precarious perch and fell with the water of the falls.

He fell nearly thirty feet and flailed his arms and legs and screamed. Below him, he could see the hole in the base of the stone face through which the waterfall poured. It was only a ten-foot half circle, but Tarren was falling far right of that, toward the hard stone below. He closed his eyes as he spun in the air and lost sight of the hard ground below. Through the anxious silence of the cavern echoed only the cry of Cake, "I got ye, little guy!"

Tarren hit Cake, and the impact slammed the fat Dwarf to the ground. Tarren blinked up at the waterfall as he realized that he was not dead. His heart hammered in his ears, and he felt as though he might explode. He began to laugh, and under him, Cake's soft groaning turned into coughing laughter. Helzendar ran over to them and joined in the mirth. Tarren raised the scepter into the air and laughed all the harder.

Cake and Tarren were helped to their feet by Helzendar, and together, the three held the scepter high in victory. The crowd erupted in cheers that echoed through the cavern. Tarren beamed and was overjoyed to have had his hard work pay off. He was now a young man by Dwarf standards, no longer a child.

CHAPTER TWENTY-SEVEN
Drakkar Island

Whill and his assorted entourage flew toward the volcano with the sun at their backs. Already they could see that many of the dragons had taken to the skies and now circled the volcano. There were too many dragons to count; some flew to and others fro. Others speckled the sides of the volcano, basking in its heat. They were a variety of colors, some white like Avriel, others red like Zhola. There were also dragons of gray, green, black, blue, and brown. Some were speckled, and others had spots, and a few had dark stripes, large and small. However, few were as large as the immense Zhola, who, due to his great age, was one of the largest dragons in existence, with a wingspan of over sixty feet.

Avriel flew close to him, and Roakore trailed not far behind upon Silverwind. Dragons had reached the group, growling and shooting flames so near to them that all could feel the great heat of the dragons' breath.

Zhola roared in response, and the dragons' breath subsided, though they remained close as he steered for the base of the volcano and descended.

They landed among dozens of dragons, and more came from above the ridge of the volcano. The dragons had been resting, basking in the great heat of the volcano's slopes, and they were not happy to be disturbed by the foreigners. An immense black dragon, nearly the size of Zhola, landed before them and gave a great roar, which silenced all. The great black dragon looked at them all in turn. His dark blue reptilian eyes were the size of a soldier's shield, and they bore into any they fell upon. When he spoke, the ground shook faintly with the humming—for he did not speak mentally but with his mouth—and though his large mouth and tongue were not made for words, he spoke Elvish well enough for Whill to understand.

"Zhola the Red, be you bewitched by Elven magic to bring to our home the likes of humans, Elves, and...a Dwarf?" His eyes flared with rage and shot menacingly to set upon Roakore.

Zhola stood taller and took a step forward. "Krashakk the Black, I have business within a chamber built by me when you were but a whelp—I, who brought my kin to the fire mountain. Stand aside!"

Krashakk scowled at Zhola as his kin landed among them by the hundreds. In came others from the hunt of the ocean to see what the trouble was upon their island. Some were as small as lions, and the whelps were many in number—for the year before had been a mating year, and many unions had been made. The whelps and many more adult dragons watched the test of dominance.

Though many of them were of the same mind as Krashakk, none interrupted. They would wait and see the outcome of the fight. Krashakk had become the alpha among the many dragons that called Drakkar home, though they ventured wide and far, one and all, often and sometimes for years and decades. He was the eldest of the blacks and from an Agoran line of dragons, an ancient line that had been driven from the Ebony Mountains, though he was not born until after the routing. His racial memory showed him clearly the images of the Dwarven foe and the standard which had flown upon their flags. This same standard, he had noticed upon Roakore's large belt. The black dragon stood taller still than Zhola—a direct challenge—and took two steps forward.

"I speak for all here in saying that you shall not pass, and the trespassers will be eaten!" he boomed.

"You speak for yourself and none other unless I hear their voices," roaored Zhola, and he shot flame into the sky above Krashakk's head. He opened his wings and loomed over Krashakk and then took three steps forward, until his scowling red eyes and horns were but two feet from the black.

"I speak for my line!" snarled the black. "This Dwarf you have brought to our home is of the line of those that drove the blacks from the Ebony Mountains. I will have revenge, even if it means feeling the wrath of the great Zhola!" he growled.

Zhola took a step back and looked to Roakore, with no love for the Dwarf. Indeed, he would have liked to kill Roakore himself. "Is this true, Dwarf? You are of the Ebony Mountains?"

Ignoring Zhola, Roakore snorted his snot and spit upon the side of his ax and then took three large steps forward. "I be the bloody king o' the Ebony Mountains, you bloody black demon, and I be willin' to finish the job me forbearers started!"

Zhola turned back to face the black dragon. "He is yours to do as you wish. I seek only the chamber below. Once we've passed through it, you will see no more of these creatures."

"Very well then." said Krashakk with a small bow as he forgot Zhola and turned on Roakore.

Whill sprang forward and stood before Roakore, arms out. "He is not to be harmed! We go through to the portal one and all or not at all."

"Lad, you don't be needin' speak for me. I got me own mouth! Now get outta me way while I send this black demon o' the dragon gods back to hell!"

Zhola had already begun to walk to the gate at the foot of the volcano, and the others were inclined to follow, even Avriel, who was glared at by many of the dragons young and old—for they sensed something about her was not right.

Whill could do nothing; he could not offer to fight alongside Roakore, as the Dwarf would have none of it. Neither could he stop the fight in the midst of so many dragons. He walked clear with the others and stopped to bear witness. Zhola roared after him, "To the gate and to the sword! No matter who wins the fight, you will want to be past the gate before the end. Already many of my kin stir."

Whill heeded the dragon's words and mounted Avriel and reluctantly headed toward the gate with the others. Roakore had begun to circle the black dragon and started his stone birds a whirling. He sent the weapon spinning off to the right, and taking three running steps, he leapt atop Silverwind. The bird beat her wings and leapt into the air.

Krashakk beat his glossy black wings and roared a laugh. "You are not wise to take to battle with a dragon within the skies, Dwarf king; there we are as sharks in wat—" Just then the whirling stone bird slammed into the back of the dragon's head as it passed by, quick as a hummingbird. The dragon roared and staggered with a flutter of wings. He shook his head, and with renewed vigor, he followed the hawk and Dwarf rider into the sky.

Roakore bade Silverwind to climb higher, and she did so with great fervor. Her long, piercing cry ripped through the air as those below watched the chase. The black dragon, with his powerful wings, slowly caught up to the hawk, and though he was in range, he did not let loose his fell breath of deadly flame. At this angle and speed, Krashakk would only eat his own flame, and Roakore had counted on this. He suddenly steered Silverwind to bank hard right and turn over into a fast dive. Krashakk's head snapped to the side as he followed his prey and banked swiftly also.

The hawk leveled out and quickly turned as the summoned stone bird whirled past—so close to Roakore's head that he heard well the whiz of his weapon. The stone bird kept on its course and slammed into the unsuspecting dragon's left eye, gouging it badly. The black dragon tumbled end over end and fell limply for many moments before once more catching the air. While Krashakk had tumbled, Roakore had turned and gained the advantage of height. He and Silverwind now flew directly over the dragon. Holding on to his ax with one hand and the reigns with the other, Roakore stood in his saddle and yelled against the wind to his trusted mount. "Now don't be lettin' me fall to me death, ya hear!"

With that, the crazed Dwarf king flung himself from his saddle and fell thirty feet through the air. He descended upon the surprised dragon with a yell and a wild look in his eyes. Ax first, he slammed into the black dragon. The ax cracked scale and sunk deep into Krashakk's left shoulder. At the same time, Roakore's body slammed into the dragon, and one of the black dragon's short, thin spikes drove into Roakore's thigh. Pinned to the dragon's back, Roakore ignored the pain and chopped at the beast mercilessly.

Dragon and Dwarf blood rained down upon the sides of the volcano as Krashakk desperately fell as much as flew to the ground below, where he might loosen the cursed Dwarf warrior. As the ground rushed up to meet them, Roakore lifted his leg from the pointed spike without as much as a groan of pain. With his other foot, he kicked off the dragon's back and yanked his ax free of its neck. As Krashakk landed violently upon the ground below, Roakore was grabbed by the talons of his mount. Silverwind dropped him shortly after and landed near him as Roakore guided his stone birds down upon the injured dragon. He had practiced daily with the weapon and could keep it aloft with only a steady thought at the back of his mind.

The stone bird whizzed by and took the dragon in the eye once more. Blood flew, and the dragon's head snapped. Through bloody teeth came liquid fire in gushes as the enraged and injured black dragon bathed Roakore and Silverwind in flame. Roakore quickly brought up a stone wall before him and frantically called up more stones, as those which he raised quickly turned molten and melted. Silverwind was hit by flames and liquid fire alike, but the enchantments of Lunara held back the attack. Krashakk charged the pair, and through the flame, his thick, barbed tail swept across and slammed them both to the side.

Roakore recovered quickly and pulled up another wall of stone. It rose up in his defense, but with it came molten lava from the many deep channels below the volcano. Roakore's eyes widened as a grin and a maniacal giggle overcame him. As the black dragon spewed his fire breath once more, Roakore dove to the left of his wall and mentally directed the stream of lava to slam into the body of the beast.

Krashakk howled in agony as the lava covered his side and right wing and burned through the thick scale and muscle beneath until bone could be seen. Roakore dropped his ax, and with two hands, he summoned a thick stream of lava from each side of himself. As Krashakk thrashed and roared in pain, the two streams of dripping molten rock were shoved down his throat and surged into his body. The dragon's roar turned to a gurgle as his body swelled in size and violently burst, sending bits of dragon and lava in every direction, and only charred meat and bones twitched beneath the cooling and graying lava.

Roakore grasped his great ax once more and held it high; he roared a challenge to all of the dragons. "C'mon then, who be the next demon to die by me hand?"

The challenge was met by dozens of thunderous roars and great plumes of fire as the outraged dragons began to stir. Whill and the others had reached the arched gate of the volcano. Whill turned and yelled back at his fearless friend. "Roakore!"

If Roakore heard him, he gave no indication. Sweat poured from his forehead and dripped down his beard as he mentally called upon the lava to burst from the ground around him. The dragons hissed and growled, roared and screamed. Dozens took to the skies and descended upon the mighty Dwarf king. Any that got too close felt the sting of spewing lava as Roakore guided his newfound molten weapon from one dragon to the other.

Whill watched helplessly from the gate as the dragons descended, and he turned to Zhola in desperation. "Help him!"

The red dragon was well within the mouth of the large gate, waiting patiently. He watched the distant battle and knew the Dwarf's doom. "I will not fight my own kind for the sake of a Dwarf! Let us make haste to the portal before the wrath of all of Drakkar is upon us."

Whill was about to ask Azzeal to help his friend when he saw Roakore mount Silverwind, and together, they disappeared from sight. Dragons' breath converged where he had been and bathed the ground in flame. Whill quickly called upon his mind sight and saw the two flying toward the gate. Whill gave a victorious cry and turned to run down the hall.

"Roakore follows! Hurry to the portal!"

None argued as dozens of angry dragons of all colors and sizes charged the gate. The group scrambled down the hall leading to the heart of the volcano. It was a natural cavern, big enough for Zhola by many yards. He led the group down the dark passage that became even darker as they turned left with the tunnel and then right and down a flight of stairs built for dragons.

There was no need for illumination down in those dark tunnels—for the fire of the pursuing dragons lit the chambers all too well. Whill mounted Avriel as the group came to the stairs, Azzeal turned into his bird form, and Roakore glided down upon Silverwind.

Dirk attempted to glide down with Zhola and jumped up upon his back. The assassin was met with a quick winged elbow that sent him flying.

"I have tolerated the two of you upon my back because you were spoken for by the chosen one, but we do not fly now, and you can use your own feet."

As Zhola leapt and glided down the stairwell, Aurora offered Dirk a hand up and shrugged. Together, they bounded down the steps in great leaps, though Aurora took them two at a time and Dirk one. Each step came up to Dirk's shoulder, and they were very slick due to the constant humidity within the volcano's guts.

At the bottom of the stair, the tunnel broke into two, one going left, the other right. Zhola went right, and the others followed him. Behind them, many dragons had already begun the descent from the top of the stair, and they were catching up quickly.

"Bah, we got 'em tunneled. Won't have to fight more than two at a time up there where the tunnel narrows a bit. I says we go through there and turn to make a stand. We could kill dozens!" The Dwarf plotted with wide eyes and battle lust. "The gods would sing me glory for all time."

Aurora ran alongside the Silverhawk and saw the look in the Dwarf king's eye; she had seen that look before and had worn it many times herself. It was the look of the hunter, and the Dwarf was the slayer of dragons. She still did not like his people, but she could not deny him respect.

"Good Dwarf…" She breathed through a steady and paced breathe "Is your bloodlust for the dragons so great that you would have us all die to kill but a few?"

Roakore looked down at the barbarian from on high; he wore an incredulous expression. "I never said nothing 'bout dyin', giant woman."

Zhola roared, causing the tunnel to quake beneath their feet. "When this is through we shall have words, Dwarf."

Roakore only laughed as they came into a large cavern thrice the size of the widest tunnel they had yet ventured. Opposite them stood the arched gates of Arkron. The stone gates stood more than fifty feet high and again as wide. They were not adorned with jewel nor sculpted pattern but were perfectly rounded and as smooth as glass. As the flames of the pursuing dragons brightened the room, the gate had begun to glow with an inner fire that captured the light of the flame and caused it to burst into millions of tiny, dancing lights.

The group crossed the room, and Zhola reached it first. He dug in his claws and stopped with a skid before the gate. Behind them, the first of many dragons barreled into the room and began to cross the hundred feet between them. Zhola spoke the name "Arkron," and the gate came to life. The cavern floor and walls vibrated slightly as a deep hum emanated from the gateway. There was a blinding flash of light, which turned many of their heads. When they could look again, they saw not the wall behind that gate as they once had but rather a rippling rift of pulsing blue light blurring the view of a cavern beyond.

"It works," said Azzeal breathlessly, and he smiled.

"Quickly!" roared Zhola as he turned and gave a piercing warning roar to his kin. The others wasted no time and dove for the portal.

CHAPTER TWENTY-EIGHT

Drindellia

Whill dove into the gateway as the dragons crashed into the chamber spewing flame and shaking stone. He felt a warmth run through his body, as if passing by a sunny window on a summer day, then the commotion of the room within the volcano disappeared and was replaced by silence. He came through the other side of the portal onto smooth stone surrounded by bright light.

They were in yet another stone room, this one much smaller than the other. Finally Zhola came crashing through the portal and roared, "Arkron!" and the portal closed as it had opened. Darkness covered the room. Azzeal murmured a word, and a crystal atop his staff began to glow brightly. Zhola did not take time to survey the tight room as did the others; instead, he walked forth and crashed his head through a stone wall opposite the portal. The others followed him into yet another cavern; this one was also a natural cave.

"This way," Zhola bade them and turned left when they came to two tunnels.

Soon the group came to the mouth of a cave. As they reached the exit, one by one, they walked through it and into night.

"Damn Elven magic! What is this? It be but after midday, yet the sun is gone. What devilry is this?" Roakore bellowed, looking up at the moon of all things.

Azzeal looked out over the tree line; they were high up on a large, stony hill. By the moonlight, tears could be seen in his feline eyes. He fell to all fours and grabbed handfuls of earth and smeared the dirt upon his face. "It is dark here because we are now far across the ocean to the east. We are in Drindellia. Once again I lay eyes upon my lost homeland."

The Elf's eyes glowed in the moonlight as his body convulsed and his skin rippled and grew fur in the blink of an eye. He transformed into wolf form and with front paws upon the ledge, he howled into the night. The sound went on for minutes and echoed across the land in a haunting chorus. Clouds that had partially hidden the moon now departed, and the world beyond the ledge was revealed in moonlight.

From their vantage point atop the lone hill they could see in all directions, and all around them was forest. Even in the faint light, Whill could tell that something was not quite right about it. The trees were black, twisted, and gnarled, and shadows lingered too long in the breeze. When Azzeal's howl had died down, the world around them returned to silence. A shudder ran down Whill's spine as he used his mind sight, and though he scanned over all that he could see, he saw no life force besides that of the sickened forest. This information he relayed to the other humans and Roakore.

Aurora's chest heaved as she took in the night air with her nose to the sky. "This is unlike any forest I have seen, and the wind carries the stench of death."

"The land has been poisoned by Eadon and his creations. They long ago purged this land of wholesome life," said Azzeal. "All that now remains is a tainted and blackened land, a plagued shadow of the beauty that it once was."

Whill heard a mournful humming from Avriel, and looking to her, he saw large tears quivering upon her dragon eyes. She bent her head in a bow, and the dragon tears fell to the stone below. In her shimmering orbs, Whill could see his silhouette and the moon. He did not know what to say to console her, so he said nothing and simply put a hand upon her scales.

"Alright, where is this sword then, dragon?" Roakore asked gruffly, hiding a small sniffle.

"I do not know," Zhola answered. Everyone turned to look at the giant red.

"What do you mean you don't know?" asked Whill.

Zhola looked to the southern horizon. "A half day's flight that way leads to the ancient Elven city of Vollorynn. Within the city is a great library, within the library a book, and within the book a clue."

"You hid the truth even from yourself so that you could never give it away against your will," said Dirk impressed.

"Correct, and that is the path. We leave at first light."

They made no fire, and all but Zhola and Azzeal retired to the cave. Whill sat away from the others near to Avriel, and he looked deep into the dark pools of her eyes. It was hard to think of her in there, trapped in a foreign body and so far from her true form. She was yet another one of Eadon's bargaining chips, as Abram had once told him she may be—Abram, his mentor, his father, his brother, and friend. Whill felt a vast emptiness in his heart. Though he had come to accept that Abram was dead during his torture, losing Abram hurt no less the second time.

The weight of Rhunis's death weighed upon his heart also. The old, scarred knight had been a good friend and ally. Whill thought back on the bar fight they had found themselves in and chuckled. Avriel hummed deep in her chest and turned her weary head from rest. "What is it?"

"Just remembering the bar fight in Kell-Torrey and the look on those thugs' faces when you healed Parpous Hellios's severed arm." He laughed.

Avriel's dragon laugh came out as a melodic hum and growl, vibrating Whill's entire body. "I don't recall it being much of a fight," she purred. "Roakore was throwing those men around like children."

Whill laughed harder still at the memory. It felt good to laugh, and he dove into the emotions that came with it. His laughter slowly turned into tears as memories of the times shared with Abram and Rhunis flowed through his mind. Avriel's voice came with a humming, soft and deep. "Rejoice in the memories of the fallen. Remember them always and smile. But do not let your own pain tarnish memories that should warm the heart. You must learn to control your emotions. You are a slave to your pain. You are no more free from Eadon's chains now than you were while in his clutches. You are addicted to your pain."

"I am not addicted to my pain! Do you even feel as we do? Elves have their ways, and we have ours…I have mine!" Whill lashed out.

"We feel pain as you do—though we understand that to allow it to consume us is to relive the pains of the past anew. Too often people take on the role of the victim and wallow in their torment for ages. If you truly want to heal your mind, you must let go."

Whill knew her words to be true; they resonated verity. Defeated, he pulled himself together and attempted to let go. He delved deep into the corners of his own mind, seeking out the path to the source of the pain, the rage. Following his thoughts and feelings backward through his mind, he came to early memories of his childhood. He had first felt the helpless rage as a young boy, left behind time after time by his father figure. He liked living with his aunt and was adored by his female cousins, but he longed to follow Abram into the wide world.

There, deep in his memories, were the roots of his pain and rage. Frustration at being too small to come along, pain at learning that Abram was not his father, and the simmering rage, carried for nearly two decades, because Abram would not tell him his lineage. Whill realized that a part of himself almost hated Abram for his secrets, for his strict training schedule, and for pushing Whill so hard. Deep within the roots of his primal pain, far beyond memory or reason, was a deep, dark spark of rage and sorrow and injustice: It was the memory of being cut from the bliss of his mother's womb by a blade and being forced into a cold and dangerous world.

Whill shuddered, and he released a breath as though he had been holding it forever. The revelation disappeared in an instant, like a candle blown out, leaving only a floating river of smoke to hint at the truth of the flame.

You must forgive him Whill. You must forgive yourself, and you must forgive the world.

Once again, Whill knew the truth of her words, and he tried to let go of his pain. He forgave all of the causes of it. He immediately felt a weight lifting from him, and he felt a peace he had not known since his years spent wandering the wilds of Agora with Abram. He let go. But the roots of his consciousness were no easier to dig up than those of a great oak. These roots were at the core of who he was; they were his ego's identity.

Dirk rested against the wall of the cavern and watched Whill and the dragon from behind his enchanted hood. To anyone looking at him, he appeared to be sleeping. With the jewels upon his earlobes, he listened to their conversation. It was apparent that Whill was an emotional wreck. Though it was an understandable reaction for a person that had lost friends, Dirk did not find it acceptable in a warrior of legend. The young man appeared weak to Dirk, and had he not seen Whill in battle, he would be inclined to write the legends off as rubbish. Whill had laughed one minute and cried the next—a fact that frustrated Dirk all the more. The idea that Whill could somehow defeat Eadon was laughable. Whill was dangerous without some ancient sword of power; Dirk could not imagine the destruction that would be wrought if Whill possessed such an outlet for his festering insanity. He felt no safer imagining Whill with the sword than he did Eadon, and he would do what it took to free Krentz.

He did not care for the world's problems—for while people lived there would always be struggle. Whether kings or emperors or Dark Elves from foreign shores, someone would always be there to enslave humans in their own stupidity. Dirk was not about to take on the mantle of being a hero to the blind masses. He held loyalty only to Krentz and to himself, and only for himself and her would he fight.

Dirk bathed himself in his resolve but could not think himself out of one realization. The world beyond the cavern's mouth was one of death and destruction; the wasted land had been reduced to the burning embers of Eadon's malice. Part of him knew that Drindellia's fate would become Agora's and that many would die. Yet another part of him argued that those same people would die eventually anyway, and maybe for the better—should their religions prove true. Who was he to attempt to interfere in a fight for people that would not fight for themselves?

A voice came into his mind so suddenly and clearly that he jumped, startled. *I see you seeing me, assassin. Your hood does not hide your eyes from me. Why do you study Whill so?*

Dirk quickly composed himself and directed his thought at the dragon as he had learned to mind speak with Krentz. His thought voice came calm and steady. *Why not use your mental abilities to glean the answer from my thoughts?* he asked and enjoyed the dragon's hesitance to answer.

He had deflected her question and boldly put her on her toes with his own. The dragon looked him in the eye, though his hood fell to his mouth. Dirk fought his dragon fear and stared back, still as stone. He felt her mind nudge his and fought the panic of his thoughts being intruded upon. Eadon had done it to him, and it had been the most unpleasant feeling the assassin had ever felt. But Dirk knew also that Avriel was an Elf of conviction and belief—she was of the type that took her people's laws as the gospel. She would not invade his mind.

He repressed a shudder as he stared into the dragon's eyes and fought for control of his mental imagery. If Avriel did read his thoughts and deciphered that he intended to steal the blade and betray them all, he would be eaten whole. Dirk chastised himself for thinking about that which he was trying not to think about; that was the problem with fighting mental projection. Avriel did not even have to invade Dirk's mind if she could get him to project his secrets at her. Dirk closed his eyes and let Avriel fly from his mind as he forgot all but Krentz. It was the thought of her tattooed and studded face in the moonlight that he used to ground his mind. He easily fell into thoughts of her and was no longer in danger of divulging his secrets to Avriel.

You love this woman, this Dark Elf you think of so?

Dirk was annoyed that she had seen his mental projection of Krentz, but it was better he projected that than his other secrets.

She is not what you think; she is not like her people, he responded.

The white dragon stared into his eyes, unblinking. *Are you like her people? You have many Elven trinkets about*

*you, both light and dark. Were they given as gifts? If so, then
you are the friend of my enemy; if they were stolen by you, then
you are indeed skilled.*

Dirk answered smoothly with his mind. *A little of both,
if you must know, Elf-dragon, but I am not the friend of your
enemy. My enemy is Eadon and his devilish creations.*

Avriel continued to stare into Dirk's hidden eyes. For
a long moment, she did not speak. Dirk went back to
thinking of nothing but Krentz, so much so that after
a few minutes, Avriel's sweet, Elven voice startled him,
and he nearly jumped.

*He is your enemy because of this Dark Elf woman you love
so? What has he done to her?* she asked.

Eadon holds her captive in his dungeons, he answered
softly.

Her voice changed, and Dirk knew that she had seen
a hole in his story. *Whill told me in conversation that you
had been arrested for fighting with guards and protesting the
king. You shouted the name Whill of Agora throughout the
streets. But it seems that you truly allowed yourself to be caught
so that you could what? Try to free your lover?*

Yes. Dirk answered truthfully as his mind drifted to
when he had seen her last, chained to the ceiling in
enchanted, stinging bonds, her energy sapped, and
her clothes shorn. They had lost themselves in a kiss of
reunion and promise, and they had held each other so
tightly that not a hurricane would have separated them.
He could still feel her firm body pressed against his,

her lithe legs wrapped tightly around his hips...Before he could think too far into the scenario and reveal his secret loyalty; Dirk snapped out of his enchantment and answered the accusation.

It is a little of both, Elf-dragon. I believe in Whill's cause, and I mean to free my Kr—I will see her free no matter the cost. It is to Whill that I look for help in my cause, because his cause is mine. I would see her freed as I would see Whill help us all to free ourselves from the bonds of oppression.

Avriel said nothing more that night and Dirk believed her to be convinced, for he had told her the truth. A part of him did believe that Whill was in the right and that his cause for freedom was just and noble. Dirk knew it to be true, but when it came to the life of his lover, his most true friend; he would choose her over the world. Besides that, he had no idea to what extent Eadon's powers went. He knew not if the Dark Elf could somehow scry him. If he diverted at all from his mission, Krentz would be killed, of that much Dirk was sure.

Now that Avriel's curiosity had been sated, he focused his mind on another potential threat to his mission, Aurora. He had seen her throw the Draggard spear that had fatally wounded Abram, and he had been intrigued by her since. What was her mission? Surely she had been recruited by Eadon also, though he had not mentioned it to Dirk. It occurred to Dirk that she might have the same quest and that she may not only be in the way but might also be his competition. If he wanted her out of the way, it would be easiest to simply kill her with a poison dart while she slept. But Dirk never did anything without gaining from it the maximum reward for his effort, and he could do much to gain the trust of the others if he revealed to them that it was she that was a spy.

Nearer to the entrance than anyone else, Aurora rested but dozed for only a few minutes at a time. The energy that coursed through her kept her steadily at maximum efficiency. Her muscles were hard as stone when relaxed, and her tendons were ready to spring into action. She lay there yearning for battle, hoping that they would find some reason to have to draw unholy blood. The land around her must have been teeming with dark creatures of every sort, she imagined. She waited anxiously for morning and their flight into the ruined city of the Elves.

She had failed Eadon when she failed to kill Whill's mentor, Abram. And she knew that her people were indeed doomed. Her only hope in salvaging the situation and turning it to her favor was to gain the favor of Whill and his Dwarf friend and the Elf-dragon. She would try to save one of their lives, perhaps, or kill enough of the enemy to gain their respect and garner their favor. The Dwarf and the Elf-dragon she had realized were Whill's good friends, and the strange leaf-clad Elf was known by the Elf-dragon. The only ones whom no one really knew were the shadowy killer, Dirk, and herself.

She did not trust the man for his dark attire and obviously devious ways, as he was like a black lynx stealing chicken eggs in the night. She wondered briefly if he was also a spy of Eadon's. If so, she would gain much respect by flushing him out publicly.

You tried to kill the man's friend, and now you will try to gain his friendship in return. If not for Whill and his friends and the escape upon a dragon, you would be dead or left to a life of fighting like a dog.

I would have escaped, she argued with herself.

Maybe, maybe not, but you did escape, thanks to Whill, the other part of her mind countered.

Whill healed the old man and cheated me of my prize!

You were the coward at someone's back; you have no honor, and you are a disgrace to the tribe, as your mother always said you were. You ran off to seek out help against the tribe's wishes, like a silly girl with romantic fantasies of a world that is not harsh and dark and always cold. You are a disgrace.

I did what needed to be done; with the favor of Eadon, I could have secured our people's future.

You know that is a lie. Eadon would have given you nothing; you were a pawn and nothing more. You would have been his slave all of your days.

But there is still Whill; there is still a chance. If he finds this sword and gains the power that it seems to possess, he may lead his followers to victory. I must join our people to his cause, lest they be slaughtered by Eadon's dark forces.

Her mind spun, and she argued with herself long into the night. About a half hour before dawn, she got up and stretched her legs. The orange-and-pink glow of the morning sun bathed a misty cloud cover in faint light. No stars could be seen as the heavens above began to pour rain. The thought of flying in it brought a smile to her troubled face.

Curled up next to the warmth of Avriel's dragon body, Whill slept well for many hours. And when the morning light finally shone beyond the mouth of the cave, he sprang to his feet alert, energized, and ready. He was anxious to take to the sky and seek out the mystery of the sword of Adimorda. He emerged out of the cave with the others and found Zhola and Azzeal standing upon the ledge, looking out over the sickly forest.

The sun had risen, but it was impossible to tell where it was beyond the thick gray cloud cover and sprinkle of rain that steadily fell. It could have been noon for all Whill could tell. An idea occurred to him, and he called upon his mind sight to gauge the location of the sun. Within seconds, the clouds vanished, and Whill sucked in a startled breath when he looked upon the morning sun that had risen recently.

Zhola turned from his perch, and the hum that came from him shook the stone. "We fly south to the lost city of the Elves," he growled.

"First we be eatin' breakfast," Roakore informed him as he stroked Silverwind's head while she ate from a feeding bag.

Whill mounted Avriel, and together, they jumped from the ledge and took to the sky flying south. Aurora and Dirk climbed atop Zhola, and he too leapt from the cliff.

"Come, Dwarf, you don't want to miss all the fun, do you?" laughed Azzeal as he leapt from the ledge and took his bird form. Roakore removed the feeding bag, which earned him a squawk of protest.

"Bah, don't you be worryin' Silverwind; there be more where that came from. Let's go now. You ain't gonna let a dragon show you up, are you?"

Silverwind squawked and ruffled her feathers, making her appear much larger. Roakore spit at the feathers that hit his face as he mounted his bird.

The group had flown south through the rain for an hour when the clouds crackled with thunder and lightning flashed brightly, illuminating the world of shadow below. There was no green to be seen within the forests, and the great trees were but husks of what they once were, and those that lived were twisted and spoiled. The cry of a large bird pierced the rain and the hearts of those that heard it; it was Azzeal's cry of despair in seeing his beloved homeland. Avriel answered it with a cry of her own and belched forth flame into the sky, turning the rain to mist and steam.

Whill beheld the extent of the plague upon the Elven lands and was forlorn to see no end to the dark forests or barren wastelands. To the north and west the forest continued on into the gray horizon. To the south was a foggy wasteland, and to the east was a dark lake that did not reflect the sky. Whill shivered.

The Dark Elves had drained the land long ago, taking from it all life force. Whill's mind flashed with images of a dark, plague-stricken Agora. Fear for his own homeland gripped his heart. Surely the disease of the land could not go on to the ends of its shores. Whill knew the land to be nearly three times the size of Agora from the maps that he had seen. It was impossible to imagine such a vast scale of destruction.

They flew on south over great ridges and valleys, dark forests and smoldering wastelands, and everywhere Whill felt watched by unseen eyes below. Finally, near noon, they could see a great city of stone ahead. Whill laid eyes upon the Elven city in ruin, the once-beautiful Vollorynn, and a lump found his throat. The city was a marvel even in its present state, so grand that Fendale and even Kell-Torey were dwarfed by comparison. Towers that must have once stood a thousand feet high were cracked and broken, strewn throughout the city like the corpses of gods. Statues of heroes unknown lay in ruin, and great craters littered the city. There had once been a great battle here, and many lives had been lost.

CHAPTER TWENTY-NINE
Clues in the Dark

Zhola flew in a circle near the center of the city. When he was satisfied that it was clear, he descended and, flapping his great wings, landed next to a caved-in building. The others landed as well and looked to the dragon.

"These are the remains of the great library of Vollorynn. It once contained the greatest wealth of history of the Elves and a great many other things. The words you will find here will capture your mind for hours and days. Do not tarry, and linger not whilst inside; find the book and return swiftly."

"You do not mean to come with us?" Whill asked.

"I am too large, stop being foolish, child. Go forth and seek out a tome bound in brown leather with not but one marking—that of a soaring red dragon set in gems. I have instructed Azzeal on its whereabouts during the flight; he will be your guide.

Whill looked around at the group and then to Azzeal. The Elf was not paying attention but rather looking upon the remains of the city longingly. He opened his mouth as if to cry out, but a voice heard in a dream echoed forth in song. Everyone froze as they were gripped by the words; the city itself seemed to listen. The wind fled from the Elf as his song carried to the gray heavens and the clouds stopped weeping. His was a song of blessing, remembrance, and promise. He sang of the green father, blue skies, starlight, and the Elven mother of light. Even the Dwarf was moved by the words, though he knew but a few. Dirk raised his head as would someone basking in summer sunlight, and his hood fell back to reveal his closed eyes and stoic face.

From the many dirt-filled cracks and crevices of the stone walkways, small green vines sprouted. A surge of energy rushed forth from Azzeal and through all near to him. Everywhere more sprouts protruded and weakly stretched upward to the glowing clouds. Azzeal's song ended, and he fell to the stone upon his knees and whispered to the nearest vine.

The spell broken, Roakore coughed gruffly and walked forward to the ledge of the cave-in. "I didn't come all this way to watch ye start a garden, Elf. We be findin' this damned dragon book or not?"

Azzeal looked up at Roakore with a strange grin and burst out laughing. "They grow once again; there is life once more." He walked swiftly to Whill and put a hand upon his shoulder. He faced Whill with all seriousness. "The land can be healed!"

Azzeal released Whill and arched his back in a great yell of triumph, hollering in Elvish, "The land can be healed!" The cry became that of a wolf as the Elf changed and sprang to the edge of the crumbled stone, nearly knocking Roakore over. The wolf turned back and looked to the others, his tail wagging. He leapt down into the labyrinth of the ancient library. Whill nodded to Avriel and followed along with Roakore, Dirk, and Aurora.

Zhola called after them, speaking to their minds. *We will guard this entrance. But beware; there are many things that have lived through the culling of life here in Drindellia—things made to thrive in waste and death.*

His words shook through the stone as the group descended the broken stone fragments of ruined walls and fallen pillars. They eventually made their way down to the floor below. They were in a large room littered with broken stone and mangled volumes. The books numbered in the thousands, and Whill sighed when he saw the work before them. Azzeal's staff blazed light as he called upon the sun stone set at its tip.

"Come, Zhola speaks instruction to me." said the Elf and he headed to the right, passing Roakore as he dusted himself off and coughed. Everyone followed Azzeal to a hall at the corner of the room. They followed the passage cautiously, and all but Roakore were uncomfortable in the small space. Aurora had to duck low and walk at a crouch as she took up the rear of the line.

Eventually, they came to an opening, and light from Azzeal's staff revealed a closed but partially broken stone door. Roakore pushed to the front and eyed the broken stone door.

"Back up," he instructed the group. He turned to the stone, grunted and tensed, and pushed his fists forward. The stone door boomed and exploded into pieces, and a draft sucked into the open chamber. Roakore walked forward into the darkness, and Azzeal followed, illuminating the room. Dust and cobwebs covered the book-filled shelves of this room also. The entire left wall had collapsed inward and filled half of the room with earth.

"This way," offered Azzeal as all followed his light. He led them to the right side of the room, through another tunnel—this one wider than the last. Dust-covered torches hung upon the walls; Whill and Aurora took one each. They finally came to a long stairwell. Azzeal spoke a word and touched each torch in turn, and they caught fire. Neither the flames nor the illumination from Azzeal's staff reached the bottom of the stair.

They began down the stone stairs cautiously. And though they tried to tread as softly as possible, every sound they made echoed throughout the stairwell. Azzeal took from his pouch a small, clear crystal and brought it to his lips. As he blew on it, a glow began at its core and grew until it was hard to look at. Whill shielded his eyes and watched as the Elf threw it down the stairwell. It bounced repeatedly as its glow traveled down the stair, illuminating the entire shaft. When finally it reached the bottom, it came to rest. From down at the end of the stair came a shriek and a hiss and the sound of frantic shuffling away. Something was down there, and judging by the sound of its movement and dancing shadows, it was large.

Azzeal looked back at the group and spoke to each of their minds. *This is our path; there is no other way down. We face whatever it is head on.*

Roakore laughed eagerly, and everyone looked at him to be quiet. 'Bah, what surprise we got? This be some-thin's den. 'Tis the home o' some psycho-nightmare drug- induced lunacy o' Eadon, no doubt. And I happen to make it me business o' killin' 'em," he said and shoved past Azzeal and loudly descended the stairs.

"Let's have it then!" he shouted down into the brightness of the glowing crystal. "Whatever it is dares not touch the light."

Dirk told himself that this was a moment to show his quality. He ran past them all and leapt over Roakore, his dagger and a black egg of glass shards at the ready. He traveled like a whisper down the stairs, and Roakore wondered if he might have enchanted shoes. Dirk reached the bottom of the stair and disappeared to the left. Roakore and the others followed slowly, as to hear anything from below. At first there was silence; then suddenly a hooded shadow darted across the bottom of the stair. Like the flicker of a flame's light dancing in the wind, he moved, and when the group reached the landing, there was not sight or sound of the assassin. Aurora and Roakore went left, and Azzeal and Whill followed the tunnel to the right.

They passed many rooms, and each of these they checked. Whill could not even move some of the ancient stone doors, but neither did he need to. Using their mind sight, they peered into each of the rooms but saw nothing. They could not see far due to the stone, but it was enough to see that no immediate threat lay in wait beyond the threshold.

Eventually they came upon Dirk, who sat upon the back of an incapacitated Draggard. It was moaning pitifully and bleeding from many wounds. Whill could see that its tail had been severed at the base and was now shoved down its throat. It had two blue-feathered darts in its left eye, and it had not only been hamstrung by a thin, sharp blade, but also the back of its ankles had been sliced. As Whill walked a circle around the beast, he saw yet another wound, a missing hand. This he located shortly, and he cringed when he saw where it was embedded. At first glance, he had thought it the tail stump. The beast's other hand was bent behind, pinned by a knife to its own back.

"There was another down the other tunnel, but that one died. I figure this one might have talking to do." He looked to Azzeal. "You talk Draggard?"

Azzeal nodded, still looking over Dirk's handiwork. Whill, too, was impressed. Dirk had been like a ghost; he had killed one Draggard, and somehow he had incapacitated another and taken it alive. Furthermore, Whill had not heard a sound traveling down the hall.

Roakore and Aurora came quickly to the room.

"There be a dead Draggard down the other tunnel," said Roakore, and noticing what it was that Dirk sat upon, he laughed. "Well done, laddie; you got one alive!"

Dirk ripped the tail from the beast's mouth, and it gave a gurgled cry and began to hack and retch lazily. Whatever was in the two darts that Dirk had stuck in its eyes had it heavily sedated while keeping it awake. Azzeal made a disgusted face, as if he had eaten something putrid, and bent to speak into the ear of the Draggard. What came out was a deep, guttural language made of harsh sounds, hisses, and grumbles.

"I have asked him if there are any more of his kind about, and if so, how many."

The Draggard responded in its awful language; its injured throat causing a sickening wet sound as it spoke and panted. Azzeal kicked it in the side and gestured to Roakore and yelled into the Draggard's face. On cue, Roakore scowled and bounced his great ax in his hands.

"What did it say?" asked Whill.

"That my mother tasted good," answered Azzeal with flared nostrils and a scowl. "I told him that he could answer me or face a long, excruciating death by a warrior feared by dragons."

Roakore puffed out his chest at that and got a bit taller. "Well then, let's hope he ain't for talkin'."

Aurora chuckled at that from where she stood watching their backs.

"Tell him I got a mind to chop one piece from him for every Dwarf his kind done killed. And he will live through it all."

Dirk got up from his seat and retrieved his two poison darts; he wiped them off and went to work cutting the pointed tip of the Draggard's tail off.

The Draggard eyed Roakore with a scowl. Azzeal turned from it and began to walk away. "Very well then, Roakore."

The Draggard gave a strangled cry, and finally, the terror in its eyes shone. It spoke quickly to the Elf, never taking its eyes off of the eager-looking Roakore. Azzeal listened and nodded when it had finished. Without a word, he reached down and broke the Draggard's neck. Roakore gave a disappointed groan.

"Some of you may be aware that Draggard can sleep indefinitely in a hibernation state. He says that he is one of a group of nearly fifty Draggard that have made this their den. The others are below. Three were guarding the entrance, and the third ran to wake the others." His ears perked up, and everyone listened. "And there they are."

Through the tunnels began to echo the sound of many clawed feet. The sound came from both directions. "We should let them come to us; we can make a stand at the stairs where the small space will make their greater numbers of no concern," Aurora suggested.

Azzeal shook his head. "No, they are not that stupid. They will lay in wait in the next chamber. Both of these halls double back and open to the same room. It is there they will attack; it is there we must go."

Dirk, who was no fan of straight-on combat, suggested otherwise. "We cannot simply walk into their trap; we have no advantage and are outnumbered."

"Bah! We be outnumbered, but we ain't out armed. Let me at 'em!"

Aurora looked to Roakore with a grin and more than a hint of admiration. "What do you suggest, Whill?" she asked. She looked to Whill as if he were her leader, grim faced and at attention. Whill jerked his head to her question and pondered for a moment. She hoped he would give her a task in which she could outdo Dirk's impressive performance. She had begun to dislike the sneaky man. Besides the fact that she had no respect for someone that hid within the shadows and stabbed his victims in the back, she did not like the way he watched her without watching her. The barbarian woman had done enough hunting to know the look of something that was quietly alert to her presence, and though it seemed Dirk was alert to everything around him, he focused on her more than even Whill, his supposed hero. The entire ride to the city, she could feel his eyes buried in her back as they rode atop the dragon.

Finally Whill shrugged his shoulders. "Roakore is the master of underground war tactics."

"And he would say to charge in screaming," piped in Aurora with a wink to the Dwarf king. Roakore raised an eyebrow at her and scowled. *He will take some work to warm up to,* she thought, *a lot of work.*

"There will likely be booby traps and the like; it is safer if I have a silent look around first," said Azzeal.

Roakore chuckled.

"We should send word to Zhola and Avriel that there are likely other guards about," said Aurora.

"I already have," Azzeal responded and tapped his temple with a long finger. He led the way farther down the hall. After many more turns, they came to a doorway. With his mind sight, Whill saw that beyond was a large chamber.

"Await my return," Azzeal bade the others and shapeshifted into his vine form. Before anyone could protest, the vines disappeared into the chamber.

Dirk watched the tunnel behind them and hid his nervousness at being bottled up as they were with no clear back door. It was simply not the way he operated.

Tense minutes passed as the group waited just beyond the entrance. Whill attempted to follow the Elf with mind sight, but it was blurred by the stone before him. Finally Azzeal returned and took his Elf form once again.

"The chamber is long, with many overhanging archways that span the curved ceiling's entirety. There are many traps set and groups of Draggard ready to ambush. Follow my lead, allow me to spring the traps, and take care of whatever I pass over."

"It be 'bout bloody time me ax gets some use! I haven't killed a Draggard since yesterday!" yelled Roakore. Azzeal scowled at him but could not keep a straight face while looking upon the eager Dwarf. Roakore was so genuinely excited that he bounced on his toes in anticipation. Azzeal pointed at himself. "I will shield." He pointed at Whill. "You will stay in the center of the group and heal any wounds. You, assassin—"

"It's Blackthorn, Elf," said Dirk.

Azzeal nodded curtly, and his forest-green eyes flashed. "And it is Azzeal, Blackthorn. You come up front with me; your stealth will be needed. Roakore, prepare your stones and watch our backs. Aurora you take up the rear and trust your back to us."

Aurora nodded, Roakore set his stone birds a whirling, and Dirk reached into his bag of tricks and unsheathed a dagger. Whill made a deeper connection with the energy within his blade—energy taken from his fallen foes. It was a practice shunned by the Elves of the Sun, but he was not an Elf.

Azzeal led them around the corner into the chamber and lifted a hand. A globe of shimmering energy surrounded them and then disappeared, and though unseen, they knew it remained. With the glowing staff showing the way, they began across the chamber. They walked ahead cautiously and needed not wait long for the attack. Half-a-dozen spears came rushing at them from the darkness ahead. The weapons were deflected by the invisible shield, and sparks flashed on contact.

A dozen Draggard came charging and screaming at them across the grand hall. Dirk threw a small object far ahead, and it erupted with a flash of light. Smoke poured out of the projectile and wafted up to the ceiling and curled down the arches. The group waited just outside the thick smoke. Out of it came charging the disoriented Draggard. The first to come through screaming got a black dart in the throat. Dirk hit two more in the mouth as they came charging recklessly. There was a loud explosion, and gore flew everywhere as the first Draggard's head exploded, followed by the other two. Three more came rushing through the smoke, and Dirk engaged one with his dagger and sword. Whill was amazed at the assassin's fluidity and grace. Every strike was lethal; every move was calculated. The three Draggard fell dead as Dirk twirled back, and on cue, Azzeal came in with his spinning staff and engaged the next wave.

Six of the beasts roared through the smoke with spears leading. The spinning staff connected sickeningly with skulls and limbs and backs alike. Whatever spells the Elf poured forth through the staff were deadly. Bones were crushed like dry eggshells against the thin wooden staff, spears snapped, heads cracked, and all that remained was a broken pile of dying monsters.

Roakore sent his stone bird into the smoke and laughed wickedly when he heard a telltale thud. Suddenly from the sides the walls opened, and from behind them, Draggard poured.

"Hah, now that's more like it!" roared Roakore, and he jumped to meet them. He slapped a spear thrust aside with his ax, got in close, and kicked the Draggard in the chest so hard that there was a loud crack, and the beast went flailing backward into its kin, knocking three of them to the ground. Behind him, on the other side of Whill, Aurora smashed one with her shield and hacked another nearly in two.

Whill moved to Roakore's side, and together, they eagerly met the Draggard attack. The sword of his father pulsed in his hands, and a grin found his face. Here, he knew peace; here, he knew pleasure. In battle, his mind found rest and his animal side took over. Forgotten was his pain, and embraced was the madness. In battle, he was free to be himself, free to release his pent-up rage. In battle, sanity was not needed. Whill screamed at his attackers and soon had them on their toes while

Roakore hacked at their legs. Whill took advantage of the distraction and slashed and stabbed. Those that did not fall to Whill met Roakore's ax.

Azzeal slammed his staff onto the stone, and a great wind whipped past the companions and sent the cloud of smoke blowing down the hall. The group charged after it and cut down the surprised Draggard that were on the other side of the smoke. Again the walls they had passed opened, and hordes of Draggard came rushing.

Aurora growled and discarded her massive sword and shield. She took on the beasts barefisted. Whill watched on in awe as the seven-foot barbarian woman pounded on the Draggard as though they were drunkards. A spear and tail came at her fast, but she was the quicker. She caught the spear shaft in her armpit, and as she jerked to the side, snapping it, she sidestepped the tail. Another spear came at her, and she twirled, dodging it, and came around whipping the spearhead. It took a Draggard in the neck, and the beast gurgled to the floor. A strong kick broke the knee of the spear wielder; she stomped on its head as it screamed in agony. Aurora went into a crouch and sprang to meet a charging Draggard. They came together and locked hands and eyes. The Draggard hissed and dug its claws deep into the top of her hands. In response, she growled and crushed his hands with hers. She gave a twist, and the Draggard took a knee with a howl. A spear came at her back, and she spun away as the spear impaled the prone Draggard. She punched another in the forehead and caught his tail as it came around to counter. With a twist and a jerk, she yanked the beast's tail and, spinning, sent it flying into an arch protruding from the wall. With a crack, its back snapped.

Shortly the attack was over, and none more remained before them.

"Ah, did we kill 'em all already?" Roakore protested and caught his stone bird.

Everyone waited and listened, but if there were any remaining Draggard about, they were not in a fighting mood at the moment. Once again Azzeal guided them down the hall. Soon they came to the end and entered into a large room. It had once contained many volumes, but Whill guessed by the blackened floors that they had been burned long ago. Azzeal quickly went to the far wall and began inspecting the stone with his hands. He set an ear to the wall and listened. He crept along the wall in this manner until he stopped and stepped back. He pushed hard on one of the many stones, and it slowly moved inward. There were many clicks and a groan of metal and shrieking protest. Dust exploded from the floor as a large section of wall moved inward. Azzeal grinned at the others and walked through the hidden doorway.

What Whill saw took his breath as Azzeal's light glowed brightly, illuminating a large room.

"Arshralock!" said Azzeal, and dozens of crystals upon the ceiling blazed to life in a rainbow of colors.

Upon the walls were glass-encased volumes of books and scrolls. At the center of the room were many small tables made of stone and wood that had been entwined together somehow. The room was pristine, as if it was untouched by time. It felt as though they were in a living city. As if Eadon and his legions had not driven away or killed every living thing in Drindellia.

Azzeal looked to everyone. "Brown book, red dragon," he said, and then he went to a glass case and carefully opened it. The others did the same. Each began the tedious task of searching for the book.

Whill sifted through his a section of ancient Elven books and scrolls. He could not fathom the knowledge that may be leant by these writings. He saw many intriguing titles, some written plainly and others magnificent with beautiful artwork on their binding.

The Sorrow of the Gods caught Whill's eye, along with a thick tome titled, *What Animals Think*. There were many books, manuals, and even journals. *The life of Alzzuar*, spelled in Elvish, *Ta Zhen Dor Alzzuar*. Whill let his hand linger over one scroll in particular; the title was written on an attached feather, *The Laws of Magic*. There were thirty-three volumes in that collection.

What knowledge could be gained by the reading of all of these works? Whill's mind raced frantically. "These works must be saved!" he breathed to himself and looked to Azzeal. "These books, the scrolls, the value of this collection must be immeasurable."

Azzeal nodded. "Indeed, this is a great find. Much of this knowledge is kept in the minds of my people, but there are also powerful secrets hidden within these tomes."

"Bah," said Roakore. "Can't read none of it anyhow! Just lookin' for a brown book with a stinkin red dra—"

Whill looked to Roakore as the Dwarf's voice trailed off. Roakore looked as if he had seen a ghost. His mouth hung wide open, and his eyes bulged.

"It…it…it can't be! What devilry is this? Be there an Elvish word for Ky'Dren?" asked Roakore in a strangled tone.

Azzeal looked to what had upset the Dwarf so. "Ah, yes. *The Life of Ky'Dren*," he said nonchalantly.

Roakore looked at him dumbfound. "'Ah, yes'? 'Ah, yes' what? How in the hells can there be a book o' Ky'Dren here?"

"Read the telling, good Dwarf. It may tell you what you need to know," Azzeal said and then went back to his searching.

"Who wrote it, and how did they know o' Ky'Dren?"

"The author of that book was Ky'Dren. The title reads *The Life of Ky'Dren*," Azzeal answered.

Roakore opened it and saw that it was written in Elvish. "It be written in your people's ridiculous swirl writing. How can it be by Ky'Dren?"

Azzeal sighed. "I suppose that Ky'Dren could speak and write Elvish words. Can't you? What kind of king knows not his allies' tongue?"

The last part Azzeal said in Dwarvish, with even a Ro'Sar Mountain accent to boot. Roakore was speech-less and just looked at the book in wonder.

"I found it!" yelled Aurora. "Here it is, brown book, red dragon."

CHAPTER THIRTY
The Ancient One

Everyone stopped in the search and crowded around the book, which was handed off to Whill. He opened it gingerly and skimmed over the Elvish writing.

"Alright then, back to the surface; let's see what Zhola can make of it," Whill said.

Azzeal brought with him a few volumes stowed away in one of his larger pouches. Roakore clung to the book of Ky'dren as if it were the greatest treasure in the world. They made their way out of the library without incident and found the two dragons and Silverwind nearby. Whill presented the book to Zhola expectantly. Zhola eyed the book with one giant orb, and a puff of smoke escaped his nostrils.

'The book, good, open it and begin to read. I will find what I need in the words."

Whill looked to Avriel who shrugged, which looked quite odd from a dragon. He sat down and got comfortable and began to read the Elven words.

"A dragon of blue she was, with eyes like glimmering ice. Her beauty was matched only in dreams, and her wrath was a force of nature."

Whill read on for more than six hours. Every time he stopped for a drink or a bit of his rations, he looked to Zhola expectantly, but the dragon only listened. He said nothing and moved rarely. Others of the group slept, including Roakore, who snored away.

The sun was nearly set when Whill reached the middle of the book. He was tired of reading, and his joints were stiff. Zhola saw this, and Whill jumped, started, when the dragon finally said, "We leave now. I have learned enough from the story thus far to continue to our location. I assumed so before but had to be sure. Mount up."

Roakore grumbled and swore. He was always grumpy when abruptly awoken. He mounted Silverwind, and the others mounted the dragons. Azzeal changed into his bird form, and soon they were leaving the city behind them and traveling back the way they had come. They flew on into the night and finally returned to the cave from whence they had come.

"Find your rest. At first light we make for the mountain of Algarath," said Zhola.

"Mountains, eh?" Roakore turned to Azzeal. "You got mountains here?"

"Yes," nodded Azzeal. "Drindellia has many mountains."

"And be there treasure within?"

"We mine them, yes; we use the stones and crystals in our workings of nature."

"YOU mine them! Elves mining mountains!"

Azzeal ignored the Dwarf's temper and began to eat from his pouch of leaves and nuts and berries. Between chewing, he answered lazily, "Who else is to mine the stones or have any use for them? There are no humans here, and what Dwarves there ever were are long gone."

Roakore perked up at that and looked to his revered book of Ky'Dren. His eyes flashed with wonder "Bein' that there was Dwarves here once, you be sayin'?"

"Indeed," answered Azzeal.

"Well, whatever hap..." Roakore stopped as he noticed everyone listening in. He scooted closer to Azzeal and in a lowered voice continued, "What ever happened to them?"

Azzeal eyed the book that Roakore held stuffed under an arm. "Best you hear the telling from one who was there."

Roakore's eyes went wide, and he slowly regarded the book that had somehow appeared in his lap, held in both hands. Tears gathered and threatened to burst like summer rain clouds in the Dwarf king's eyes. He sniffled and quickly coughed to mask it. Azzeal only smiled and ate his mix.

Morning came and they took to the air and flew north. After less than three hours, they could see far off on the horizon what, at first, Roakore thought to be a thunderhead. When he realized that it was a mountain, his jaw dropped.

Dirk sat between Zhola's flexing shoulders and saw too that mountain. His excitement grew tenfold as he knew the moment would soon come. Soon Whill would be led to the sword, and it would be within Dirk's reach. How he was going to steal the sword he did not know, nor did he have a plan of escape. He knew that he could not take the sword until he was near the portal they had come from, which meant that he would have to steal the sword directly from Whill once Whill had found it. The timing would have to be perfect if it was to be successful. Dirk fingered the gem that Eadon had given him. The Dark Elf had said that with it Dirk would be able to speak to him. Dirk did not doubt that with it Eadon was able to track his exact location. Dirk dared not use the gem yet, lest he be exposed. He would have to hold out until the time was right.

They flew toward Algarath Mountain under a canopy of dark gray clouds. There was a light fog, and its mist gathered on the dragons and riders, leaving the scales of the dragons glistening like jewels.

Whill looked to his wide-eyed friend gliding along to his right. Roakore stared at the mountain; it was the biggest that Whill had ever seen, twice again the size of the largest mountain in Agora. Algarath Mountain was nearly five miles wide at its base. Its snowcapped body gave way to a peak that was lost above the clouds. There, where the clouds consumed the mountains, lightning flashed behind the thick cover. To Whill, it looked as though a battle raged upon the mountain. Deep and booming thunder rolled across the sky and echoed for miles in every direction. The mountain had no brothers; it stood alone in its majesty.

Along the sides of the mountain grew green trees and vegetation. In contrast to the dull gray sky and blackened world around it, the mountain stood out as a defiant vestige of Drindellia's life force. At its base, where the mountain green clashed with the dark forest, was a ring of what at first looked like piles of jagged stone and shale, but upon closer inspection, Whill realized that they were piles and piles of bones, Draggard bones. Tens of thousands must have fallen trying to break through whatever power separated the mountain from the tainted earth.

Zhola steered them toward the mountain base. The mountain loomed above them, making even the dragon Zhola feel small and insignificant. Roakore had sung to the glory of the Dwarven gods since first seeing the mountain; now he sang all the louder.

They glided down toward the large mouth of a cave built near the base of the miles-wide mountain. Zhola did not land but flew straight into it. He growled low in his throat, and his body began to glow with inner fire, illuminating the way. Further down, the large cave curved and opened to a massive shaft in which a natural waterfall flowed. They flew swiftly down with the water-fall for a long time and finally leveled out and splashed into an underground lake.

Zhola landed upon the stone shore of the mile-wide chamber in which the lake sat. The chamber hummed with power, and the very air within was thick and heavy, and the humidity within left everything wet and glisten-ing. Deep green flower-covered vines and multicolored moss covered every inch of the cavern, even creeping up the walls and across the stone ceiling. The flowers within the cavern glowed with a rich silver inner light that left the onlookers in awe.

At the center of the lake, upon an island of glowing moss-covered stone, was the source of the great hum-ming power. A figure glowed so radiantly that it could not easily be seen within the light. Whill could make out the thin, naked figure of what looked like an Elven woman. Her legs were encased in stone up to the knees, and her humming energy pulsed through the stone island and the lake in ripples of cascading light. Her arms were out-stretched, each one growing into a thick, knotted root that grew thicker and snaked its way far across the glow-ing lake. The two roots met with others, and each of these found their way eventually to the walls of the cav-ern. Her glowing white hair danced in blue flames atop her head; energy crackled and hummed, and small arks of electricity licked at the stone-and-vine roof.

Zhola bent down to his knees and bowed his head. "It is the lady Kellallea."

Whill's eyes widened with amazement and sudden fear. This was the Elf of legend, Kellallea, the keeper of the ancient knowledge of the Elves, the taker of all power after the great Elven wars of old; it was she who had granted the Elves with the power of Orna Catorna once more.

Whill dropped to a knee and bowed as did the others—Dirk even removed his hood. There was a great pulsing of the light within the cavern, and for a moment, all were blind. When he could see once more, Whill saw the ghostly silver figure of Kellallea walking toward them across the water. Her body remained rooted to the island, and what now strode toward them, Whill assumed, was some sort of spiritual projection.

He dropped his head once more, averting the gaze of the pulsating spirit Elf and tried not to tremble like a scared puppy. She walked up to him and stopped. Whill dared look up at the radiating, naked form of the ancient Elf, and tears welled in his eyes. For her gaze was one of blissful peace and unyielding love. There was a terrifying intensity in her eyes, which shone with blinding light and pierced Whill's very soul. The power possessed by Kellallea was greater than Whill had ever witnessed, even within the deep, dark eyes of Eadon.

'Lady Kellallea, I…" Azzeal's voice cracked and failed him, and he was left weeping at her feet.

The spirit Elf smiled upon the prone Elf and put a hand lightly upon his head and stroked his green hair. She took his face in her hand and lifted his chin he smiled upon her as a child would its mother. She then looked to Whill, who could not meet her eyes directly.

"Whill of Agora, he foretold to defeat the Dark Elf Eadon, I have waited long for your arrival."

Whill bowed lower still. "Kellallea."

"Stand," she bade them all, and they complied.

Her gaze swept over them all in turn and lingered upon Aurora and Dirk. The two averted their gazes, their guilt laid bare before the ancient Elf. She looked to Avriel and strode to the white dragon.

"Daughter of Verelas."

Avriel wept dragon tears and bowed her head to Kellallea's touch. The spirit Elf stroked Avriel's shimmering white scales.

"Would that I could undo this dark curse upon you, but I have not the strength to spare."

"What is this place?" Whill dared ask. "What is happening here?"

In an instant, Kellellea was before him once again. She stretched an arm to indicate the cavern. "This is where the rivers of Drindellia's life force converge. I have held the sickness of the land at bay for the time being, but my power wanes. Soon I will be overcome, as is stone against water, and the last of what was Drindellia will die with me."

"We had feared you lost to us, my lady," said Azzeal. "The Elves of the Sun shall rejoice, for the lady Kellallea fights for Drindellia still."

Kellallea nodded. "Long Eadon fought against me and was successful to an extent. I was forced to abandon my form and take refuge here within Algarath. I have melded with Keye, and I am now the guardian of Drindellia's life force, what is left of it."

"Are you also the guardian of the sword?" asked Whill.

Kellallea looked to him with her bright, burning eyes; he held his gaze against the sight.

"I am," she answered and looked to her body, which remained rooted to the island.

"With the sword I could help you, and together, we could heal the land. When I have defeated Eadon, life will thrive once again throughout Drindellia," Whill promised.

"There is much you do not know, child. You cannot kill Eadon."

"But it has been foretold in the prophe—"

"The prophecy is a lie," Kellallea interrupted, her voice booming and echoing throughout the chamber.

Whill was speechless. Avriel gave a surprised growl, and Roakore blurted out, "Ye lie!"

"The prophecy a lie?" asked Whill, confused. "How can it be?"

"I have been connected to Drindellia for thousands of years. My roots reach to the heart of Keye and into the rivers of energy below. I have learned the truth of Adimorda and the prophecy."

"What is this truth?" Whill asked, though he dreaded the answer.

"It is true that Adimorda looked to the future and saw the rise of a great and powerful Dark Elf, and that he set in motion the creation of a weapon of great power. But what you have been told, indeed, what the order of Adimorda believed to be a weapon to defeat Eadon, has all this time been of his own creation."

Whill was speechless; he did not understand.

"The truth is this," said Kellallea. "Eadon *is* Adimorda."

Whill shook his head in denial. "No, that cannot be. How can they be one and the same? Adimorda saw the rise of Eadon and made the sword to defeat him."

"No!" boomed Kellallea's voice like thunder through the chamber. "Adimorda lied. The prophecy is a lie created to ensure the creation of a sword of power—a sword that he intends to use."

Whill shook his head the whole time, not wanting to believe it. The ancient Elf saw that he did not understand.

"To understand, we must go back to the beginning. Adimorda was one of the most powerful Elves of his time; he was a master of many schools of knowledge and, indeed, the most proficient seer that ever lived. His goal was always more power, and like so many others, he was corrupted by it. He sought the ancient texts and scrolls, always hungry for more knowledge. What he sought the most was an ancient tome said to be written by the gods themselves. It was not long before he found it, and what he learned within that book drove him mad with power lust. Eadon discovered an ancient legend, one which told of a way to attain the power of a god."

Whill listened intently as his dread steadily grew.

"It is difficult, but it is possible for Eadon to attain such power. He has already one of the swords in his possession; he needs only be given the other. To gain the power of the gods, it is said that one must possess the greatest power ever given and the greatest power taken. Eadon's own blade contains the greatest power taken, for he has laid waste to his own homeland to attain it. And by creating the prophecy, he guaranteed the creation of the greatest power ever given. Together, the sword of power taken and the sword of power given will make Eadon like a god. He needs only to be given the sword by you to fulfill his plan." She looked to Whill grimly.

Whill was speechless. She went on, telling her unbelievable tale of manipulation. "Adimorda looked to the future and saw his own rise to power as Eadon. He foretold of you, Whill of Agora, and created the blade so that no Elf could wield it, not even him. For the laws of the two blades of power dictate that the sword of power given must be given. In this way, it was meant to prevent one from attaining them both. But Eadon will be given the power within the sword if you try to kill him, for Adromida is indeed Eadon's sword, and one cannot be killed by their own blade. This is why he has kept you alive; it is why he has tortured you so. He intends for you to want nothing more than to kill him. And you have played right into his game perfectly."

Whill's mind raced as he tried to make sense of what he was hearing. The prophecy was a lie? That would mean that he was a pawn in Eadon's game and nothing more. Whill was not a savior of legend; he was not the hero of the people. Whill was the final piece in Eadon's long-awaited plan. Eadon wanted an apprentice that he could mold, one that would give him the power of Adromida willingly. It seemed that when Whill had refused to join Eadon, the Dark Elf had tried to make Whill hate him enough to try and kill him. Eadon could not take the sword from Whill—he had to be given it— and attempting to strike down the Dark Elf with his own blade would pass along the energy to him.

"But how do I defeat him, if I cannot use the sword against him?" Whill asked Kellallea.

"You are not listening, child," the ancient Elf said with a flash of her eyes. The light of the cavern rippled and pulsed brightly. "You cannot defeat him; you are a lie. I cannot allow you to take the sword of Adimorda. You have no hope of being able to control the power within the sword. It would consume you and lead to your ruin.

I am sorry, child, but your quest ends here. Long have I stood guard against the encroaching plague that Eadon has spread against this land. Long have I fought to keep the last spark of life lit. But I am tired, I am weary, and I cannot hold out against the Black Death much longer. You must pass the power of Adimorda over to me, so that I might heal the land once more."

Whill met and held the Elf's gaze. One part of him wanted nothing more than to be done with this entire business of the sword, to hand the power over to Kellallea and be done with it. He was relieved to hear that he had a way out. Another part of him did not believe the ancient Elf's story; he believed it was possibly a trick of the enemy.

"Very well then," he said to the sound of many gasps, including Roakore's and Aurora's.

"Where is the blade?" he said evenly, holding the Elf's painful stare.

"Will you give the power back to Drindellia?"

Whill did not answer. He looked to Avriel. *Do you believe her tale? How do we know that she is indeed Kellallea?*

The white dragon took a step forward and eyed the spirit Elf with a fiery orb. Roakore shifted uncomfortably and he held his great ax at the ready. Aurora, too, stood ready for battle, her shield half raised and sword cocked slightly. Dirk simply stood as he always did. He did not have a battle stance, or better, every stance was a battle stance to Dirk. But within his sleeves, he had ready a dart and a dagger. Azzeal had stood and looked to Kellallea in confusion.

"Call to the blade, Whill. If you are meant to have it, it shall come to you," Avriel said aloud.

"I cannot allow you to leave with the blade," Kellallea warned him calmly.

"Neither do you have the strength to stop me." He looked beyond her spirit form to her body, which remained in its perpetual state of constant effort. "You cannot let go, or you will lose control of the encroaching plague."

"Would you have it so? Would you see the last of Drindellia die before your eyes?" she screamed, and the entire cavern glowed so bright as to make everything appear white.

"No," he answered. "I would see Drindellia thrive once again. I would see Eadon fall and freedom rise. And I would see it done by my hand."

With that, he cupped his hands around his mouth and bellowed, "Adromida, sword of Adimorda, it is I, Whill of Agora. I summon thee."

CHAPTER THIRTY-ONE
The Sword of Power Given

The cavern rumbled, and the waters boiled. Whill watched in awe as a curved, thin hilt came out of a churning whirlpool of multicolored light near the shore. He walked toward the disturbance and reached out toward the sword hilt more than twenty feet away.

The sword shot out of the water, and Whill caught it by the sheath. He stared down at it in utter astonishment and delight. He was mesmerized by the blue swirling orb set within the hilt, which held more stars than a million clear nighttime skies. It danced in sparkling beauty and beckoned Whill to lose himself to its sheer power.

He reached for the glowing hilt upon which danced pulsing blue energy along every thin strip of glossy black leather. Kellallea's phantom hand caught Whill's and prevented him from touching the hilt.

"Will you help me? Give to me the power to restore Drindellia to its former glory. Together, we can defeat Eadon, and finally, we may know peace," she pleaded.

Whill looked from her to the blade; it called to him, beckoning to be used. He tried to pull his hand away, but it was held fast by an iron grip. Roakore stepped forward and scowled at the spirit form of Kellallea.

"You will want to be letting the man go now," he said threateningly.

The Elf ignored him but let go of Whill and smiled as an afterthought. "This weapon is beyond you, child. I could guide you in your use of it. With it, you would help to heal this plagued land, and together, we could rid your homeland of Eadon. I warn you—if you do not heed my words, you will be destroyed. You have not the skill to control the power within that blade."

Whill shook his head in denial. "You are mistaken. I must defeat Eadon. The prophecy foretold of this; the blade and its power were meant for me."

"The prophecy is a lie!" she bellowed, and the mountain shook with her wrath.

Whill attached the sheath to his belt, careful not to touch the hilt. He nodded to the others, and they mounted. Without a word, they left the ancient Elf to her silent battle against the encroaching darkness.

Her bellowing proclamation followed them out of the mountain. "The prophecy is a lie!"

They flew back toward the cave they had come to Drindellia through, and Kellallea's words echoed in his head the entire time.

Do you believe her? He asked Avriel as he rode upon her back.

She did not answer for a time but then hummed a sigh of resignation. *I do not know. She has been long without contact with others. Her mind does not work as others do, and she is of Keye now. I do believe that with Adimorda you could heal the land, and I pray that it comes to pass.*

What if she is right? Whill asked. *What if the prophecy is a lie and Eadon is Adimorda? I will be playing right into his hands.*

Again, her answer came after many strong beats of her powerful wings. Whill stared blankly at her left wing as it passed over the sun repeatedly. In that light, her wing was translucent, but it did not seem thin and weak. It was thick and strong and radiated the light as if from within.

If she is right, and if you aid in Eadon becoming a god, then the world is doomed. She finally answered.

Whill pondered the grave situation and came to no conclusions. This was but another problem in the nightmare that had become his life as of late. He finally had the blade of legend, and he had the girl—well sort of—and it seemed that Roakore would follow him gladly into the mouth of a dragon, laughing all the while. But now he was left with his old friend, nagging doubt. He could not shake the feeling of imminent doom.

What if he killed himself the first time he made contact with the sword? What if it somehow took him over? Was the blade sentient, aware? Would he become a mad dictator as had Eadon? The big problem Whill had with Kellallea's tale was that it made sense. Adimorda very well could have seen himself in the future as an all-powerful conqueror, and he could have created the sword not to defeat Eadon, who he would become, but to strengthen him. Whill had to find out whether or not anyone knew it to be true.

Precisely, said Avriel in his mind.

He was not startled by her, for he had known she was there. He had been letting her linger in his mind and observe his thoughts, as she had him. He had been startled when they had first shared each other's thoughts openly. There were many thoughts to listen to, but soon Whill realized that just like his mind, hers, too, was possessed of many different thoughts. But seeing her thoughts from his perspective allowed him to see how those many thoughts were simply a vortex of interwoven thought strings webbing out and within, and at the center of the thoughts was a blinding spec of awareness. Avriel had called it the watcher, the true self, the soul; it had a multitude of names in all cultures.

Dirk knew that the time had come, but he had not had a chance to privately attempt to contact Eadon.

He looked around at the others, annoyed. He had to redeem himself to Eadon somehow. He had failed in his original mission of killing Abram, and Eadon had needed to do that himself.

He had believed the luminescent Elf's words. The tale was one of masterful deceit and unparalleled genius. Dirk had almost laughed when he had heard the Elf say that Eadon was Adimorda—it was brilliant. He respected Eadon for his cunning, and he feared the Elf. He soon realized that nothing could be gotten over on the Elf. He was an ancient relic of a lost civilization, the destroyer of Drindellia. Eadon was a force of nature, and against him, all would be as leaves in a hurricane.

Dirk set his resolve and attempted to clear him mind. He snuffed out his annoying flicker of guilt, thought only of Krentz, and pulled his hood over his head as if from the wind. Within the cloak he bore the gem to his lips and whispered, "Whill has the blade. He has not used it, and we fly to the dragon island."

He calculated the reverse of the effect they had encountered of the sun shifting in the sky and added, "We arrive with the rising of the sun."

He fought the paranoia that possibly one of the dragons or the Elf had heard him and threw it from his mind. When there was no response, he pocketed the gem and upon clearing his mind once more, he came back to the wind. The first thing he saw was the face of the white Elf-dragon, Avriel. Her nostrils flared, her teeth were shown, and her huge, slanted eyes burned through his resolve, and all was revealed to her.

She let out a roar and attacked, flying over Zhola and snapping at the assassin. Dirk was forced to fall over Zhola's back and catch hold of the dragon's massive hind leg. He caught hold of a leg he could not wrap his arms across and was scraped upon the face by the scales.

Zhola let out a roar and angled away from Avriel. "What is the meaning of this attack?" he demanded with a booming voice.

"The assassin is a spy! He has given us to the enemy!" Avriel yelled back as she came in once again to strike.

Zhola roared and curved his head down toward his leg to devour Dirk. The assassin reacted fast, and from its sheath, he took Krone, his greatest of possessions. The dagger was the secret to his success; it was by it that he had attained so many powerful trinkets from those more powerful than himself. Krone had been a gift from Krentz, made by her people to inflict a spell of controlling the mind. With it, Dirk could force all but the most strong-minded to do his bidding. He plunged the dagger in between the dragon's scales with all his strength, and Zhola let out a howl of rage.

"Stop dragon!" Dirk bellowed. "You will attack me not and avoid the white dragon."

Dirk knew how the blade bit; Zhola would feel an engulfing, hot pain and be compelled to comply to be released of it. It worked, and Zhola's head reeled back. He roared in protest but was losing the fight for control of his mind and body.

Dirk quickly tethered himself to the dagger with his elven rope, and calling upon his enchanted boots, he leapt from the leg and grabbed the nearest spike. He pulled himself onto Zhola's back, and his instincts scream a warning. No sooner had he snapped his head back and arched his body than Aurora's huge sword swept over his chin. Dirk went with the motion, rather than against, and did a backflip over the dragon's back and grabbed hold of a passing spike near the tail.

Before the barbarian attacked, Dirk leapt from his spot and bellowed, "Up, dragon!"

Zhola suddenly veered straight up with pounding wings, and Aurora was thrown from his back and fell fast, barely grabbing the end of Zhola's tail. Zhola fought the effects of the dagger and suddenly began to shudder and convulse. The beating of the wings turned into flailing, and the snapping dragon spewed fire as it began to fall like a comet. Aurora held on strong as she found herself looking down upon the falling dragon and the rushing ground.

Dirk held on to a spike between Zhola's shoulders and chanted the Dark Elf spell causing the dagger to use more of its power. Zhola snapped at the air but could not reach the assassin; the dagger hit him hard with pain and persuasion. He leveled out once more, and Dirk found his balance.

In came Avriel from the left, slamming into the bigger dragon in an attempt to dislodge Dirk. Whill's eyes met Dirk's, and there was a festering rage there that made even Dirk's skin crawl.

"Fly lower!" Dirk commanded Zhola, and the dragon complied.

Aurora was stubbornly climbing along Zhola's spear-length spikes, steadily coming closer to Dirk. He threw four consecutive darts at her, and she was forced to duck back. The darts were deflected by her sword, and Dirk threw one more. This dart hit Aurora's sword and exploded with a flash. The explosion could not have killed anyone, but it was loud and bright and packed enough punch to throw a man across a room. Aurora was blasted from Zhola's back and tumbled through the air. As Dirk had expected, Whill and the white dragon shot quickly to save her, as did Azzeal.

"Now, Zhola, all speed! Get me to that cave before them."

"Catch her!" Whill hollored as Avriel banked hard left and went into a spiraling descent that sped them toward Aurora. She had turned in her fall and looked over her shoulder at them, terrified. She screamed something incoherent and began to flail. Avriel swooped down and carefully caught Aurora in her claws and pulled up in time to avoid becoming a pile of bones upon the blackened land.

Silverwind gave a cry and came in with her talons aimed at Dirk's head. He leapt to the right and swung underneath Zhola and around to the other side. The Silverhawk flew past, and Dirk noticed she was missing a rider. He swung around and landed once again upon the dragon's back, and he was ready for the Dwarf. Roakore's ax came across with a whoosh as the wind howled against the Dwarf's curses. Dirk avoided the blow and stabbed forward with his short sword. Roakore came across again with the heavy ax, with surprising speed, and blocked the sword.

Dirk danced away gracefully upon the red scales and weaved between the spikes. Roakore followed, hopping his hand from one spike to the other swiftly. Dirk threw a dart, and Roakore deflected it holding his ax in one hand. Again Dirk leapt from the dragon's back and, this time, came around behind Roakore. He kicked the Dwarf hard, but it was a glancing blow that Roakore rolled with.

Dirk then engaged Roakore head on, his short sword and dagger singing in the gale in blurring motion. Roakore could not keep up with such speed and was put on his toes, barely avoiding the blows. He had Dirk right where he wanted him. Roakore laughed as he hopped back from an attack and his stone bird slammed into

Dirk's shoulder. Dirk was hit with such force that he was thrown from Zhola's back along with his line and dagger.

"Yeh didn't see that one comin', did ye, sneaky pants? Bwahaha!" Roakore sang after the falling assassin.

From Avriel's back, Whill and Aurora watched as Dirk fell from Zhola and disappeared into the dark and twisted forest below.

Leave him to the dark forest, came Azzeal's voice in their minds. They flew on and followed Zhola, Azzeal, and Silverwind toward the cave.

Roakore turned his attention to Zhola. He believed the dragon to have been in league with the dirty assassin—he hadn't attempted to kill the man, and Roakore had seen how Zhola had tried to shake Aurora. He clawed his way to the middle of the dragon's shoulders and lifted his ax in a great strike.

The ax sunk deep into Zhola's muscled left shoulder, and he gave out a groan of pain.

"Die, ye gods-damned fire demon!" Roakore bellowed as he retracted the blade and struck again.

Zhola banked hard left due to the blow, and Roakore held on for dear life. Zhola had only been flying fifty feet from the ground, and he now descended and landed quickly. Roakore wasted no time and climbed Zhola's neck. With one hand, he held fast a spike as he braced his feet on others. He raised his great ax with a roar and was flung through the air with a snap of Zhola's neck.

Roakore tumbled many times and slid to a halt. He was on his feet in a flash. Zhola reigned down flame in Roakore's direction and furiously stomped toward him. Roakore could only run straight at the dragon and keep under the wall of fire.

In came the stone bird to slam into Zhola's head, cracking scales. Roakore slammed his ax into Zhola's ankle hard enough to make it sink deep. The dragon defensively dropped his entire weight down on Roakore's head.

"Stop it!" Whill screamed at them both and leapt from Avriel as she landed. He rushed before Zhola and looked in horror at the ground under his belly.

"Get off him!" he yelled.

Black smoke rolled out of Zhola's nostrils, and he bent to regard Whill. "I was attacked. He is mine to kill."

"Get off of him," Whill growled.

Zhola got dangerously close to Whill and snarled, "I have done my part; I am done with you all. Go to your fate, Whill of Agora; I hunt the assassin."

He turned from them and took to the sky, revealing a hole in the ground. Whill rushed to the edge and peered inside. There, nearly six feet down in a circular incent in the ground, was a dazed Dwarf.

"Come quickly, Roakore; we must go."

He lent a hand and pulled the Dwarf form the hole. "The dragon was under the control of Dirk, you know; he was not our enemy."

"Bah," said Roakore as he dusted himself off. "He is a dragon, and they be mine enemies." He looked to Avriel, who had heard him, and blushed. He straightened defiantly. "You ain't no dragon, Avriel; you be an Elf. It ain't your fault what was done to you."

Soon they arrived at the cave. Aurora and Whill dismounted as did Roakore. Azzeal changed from bird to Elf form. Whill said the word, and the portal blazed to life. It hummed deeply and awaited its passengers. Everyone braced for whatever might come out from the other side. The dragons did not burst forth, nor did Eadon and his legions. They watched and waited for many minutes, but still nothing came.

"Dirk somehow spoke to Eadon. He knows where we went, and he very well may be waiting," Whill told the others.

"Bah, let 'em come. We got the Elf blade now, so let 'em come," Roakore piped in as he danced on the balls of his feet.

"I will go first," said Aurora, eager to prove herself further still. "If anything lurks beyond the portal, I will report it."

"Bah! I ain't havin' no woman goin' into danger afore I be! Step aside, lass."

Roakore stormed toward the portal and walked right through. Aurora cursed the Dwarf king and said to Whill, "Can't you keep him on a leash?" She then rushed after the fearless Dwarf.

Azzeal, Whill, Silverwind, and Avriel waited for a long while. Finally Roakore hopped through the portal with a grin. "The way be quiet."

Through the portal they went, and indeed, the chamber beyond was quiet. They made their way back up to the surface without incident. But there at the mouth of the cave awaited an army. They all came to a grinding halt at the mouth of the cave. There, upon the scorched earth beyond the volcano's mouth, stood Eadon, and next to him stood his Dragon-Hawk. He wore his cloak of Silverhawk feathers, and in his right hand, he held Nodae, his blade, the sword of power taken.

Upon Whill's belt, the blade Adromida jolted, and the light within the diamond at the hilt danced and pulsed. It hummed steadily as it came to such a close proximity to its opposite. Eadon outstretched his left hand and bade Whill. "Resistance is futile, Whill. Fulfill your destiny, and take up the blade Adromida."

Behind him stood twenty armored Draquon; each one carried a trident. Beyond them waited the dragons of Drakkar.

"We should retreat back through the portal," said Aurora with trepidation in her voice. "This foe is beyond us."

"No," said Whill confidently, and he walked forward toward Eadon.

"Whill!" growled Avriel. "You are not ready for this."

Whill stopped and turned to face her with watery eyes. "Will I ever be?" To the others he warned, "Be ready to fly."

CHAPTER THIRTY-TWO

Convergence

With a hand upon the sheath of Adimorda, Whill planted his feet and faced Eadon. A grin spread across the Dark Elf's face, and his eyes glowed with fiery light.

Whill dared not strike Eadon, lest the story of Kellallea be true; neither did he think that he had the skill to beat Eadon, no matter the great power within Adimorda. He needed to buy them time to escape. He did not let his fear and doubt show upon his face.

'I have found the blade. It is over; concede defeat and I will spare your life."

Eadon's laughter shook the ground beneath them, and his smile of victory only widened. Whill could hear the hum of power emanating from Nodae. To his army, Eadon commanded, "Kill them all!"

Hundreds of dragons took to the sky, and many others charged across the ground. The Draquon gave ear-piercing cries of bloodlust and charged as well. Eadon remained where he was, the wind of his charging army blowing his long, white hair forward.

The sun began to rise beyond the volcano as Whill faced the oncoming army. "Azzeal! Shield them, and see them away safely."

Whill then reached for Adromida as the charging horde closed to within a few hundred yards. Dragons and Draquon alike swooped down upon them from on high. Whill's hand closed around the hilt of the ancient sword of legend. In that moment, Whill accepted his destiny and gave into the great, slumbering power of the blade.

Power coursed through his body and threatened to consume him with its blinding force. He fought to command control over the sword's power, and it yielded to him at once. He opened his eyes and watched as the charging army advanced, moving impossibly slow. Time blurred, and Whill found himself floating five feet from the ground, holding the sword high above his head with both hands. From him shone bright blue light, which radiated outward in electrified tendrils and pure energy. The lightning melded with Azzeal's conjured energy shield and strengthened it tenfold.

Whill screamed against the torrent of pulsing power and plunged Adimorda into the volcano's surface. There was a deafening boom and an explosion of power, which was quickly swallowed by the glowing wound upon the ground. Whill pumped incredible amounts of energy down into the huge well of lava below.

The ground began to quake as time returned to normal, and the advancing army slowed as one before the great power. The ground shook so violently that everything with wings fled to the sky. The volcano exploded with such force that Whill's companions were shot into the sky at breakneck speeds. Azzeal's shield wavered but held against the ocean of lava that surrounded them.

Dragons and Draquon alike were disintegrated in midair, and the rest were blown far and wide as the volcano spewed forth its molten destruction. Whill stood within his energy shield scowling at Eadon, who did the same. The Dark Elf advanced so quickly that Whill had no time to react. Eadon slammed into Whill's shield with so much force that Whill was thrown back into the mouth of the cavern.

Eadon was upon him in an instant. Whill parried Eadon's blows; he fought only defensively, not daring to strike the Dark Elf. Whill formulated a plan quickly in his mind. If he could get Eadon through the portal, there might be a chance of escape. The cavern was quickly falling apart all around them as the volcano violently continued to spew its contents. Whill attempted to stall Eadon.

'What do you promise in return if I give you the power of Adromida?" he screamed over the thunderous commotion of the exploding volcano. Eadon let up on his attack and regarded Whill with a wide smile.

"You shall be my second; you will have all that you ever wished. You will be king of all of Agora, answerable only to me. I will return Avriel to her true form, and your friends will be left in peace," Eadon answered.

Whill reached up with his hand and mentally pulled the ceiling down upon the head of the Dark Elf. Wasting no time, he turned and ran faster than he ever had. Through the cavern and down the stairs he flew. Behind him, there was a great explosion and the scream of Eadon.

"There is nowhere to run, boy! Swear fealty to me or you shall know suffering beyond imagination." Eadon's voice shook the very stone and followed Whill down the stairs and into the portal chamber. Whill quickly spoke the name, and the portal came to life. He turned to see Eadon actually flying toward him down the stairs. With a scream, the Dark Elf flung a fireball at Whill, which closed the distance between them too quickly for Whill to dodge. He poured more energy into his shield as the fireball exploded against it. Whill was blasted through the portal and continued through the cave on the other side and was blown clear over the ledge.

Whill screamed as he fell hundreds of feet to the blackened surface of Drindellia below. He instinctively shot his hands out toward the ground as it rushed up to crush him, and to his utter amazement, he stopped dead in his fall, mere feet from the ground. He floated there for a moment, marveling at what he had just done, when suddenly the cliff above him exploded in a rain of fire and fell toward him.

Whill tapped deeper into the seemingly endless well of power within the blade and shot himself forward through the air. He flew out over the plagued land and stole a glance behind him. Eadon was flying through the air toward him and gaining. Whill poured more power into his flight and ascended into the sky, shooting straight up. Eadon followed, laughing manically all the while.

They flew through the gray cloud cover and shot up into the clear sky. Drindellia's sun had not yet set, and the brightness of it was at first blinding compared to the dreary world below the clouds. A blast of lightning hit Whill's circular energy shield and smashed through it. Whill was jolted by the hit, and his entire body screamed in pain. His concentration did not waver, however, and he quickly healed himself of the wound and shot faster into the darkening sky.

Whill flew so high that the sky began to darken and stars twinkled to life above him. Eadon came on faster than before, bearing down on Whill with his sword leading. Whill changed direction and flew across the sky. He looked down upon the world in amazement as he saw the curve of it. Looking behind him, he knew that he could not keep the distance between himself and Eadon. The Dark Elf had the same amount of power within his blade, if not more, and he surely had more experience flying.

Whill changed course and began to descend once again. Eadon kept pace with him easily and even began to catch up.

"There is nowhere to run, nowhere to fly! Face your fate, boy!" Eadon screamed over the howling wind.

Zhola was distracted from his tracking of Dirk by two streaks of light, which shot through the gray clouds above him. He raised his head to regard the strange sight and knew it to be Whill and Eadon. They blew through the clouds with such speed as to bring with them a funnel of swirling cloud. Thunder rang out as the chasing form shot lightning at the fleeing one. Zhola knew then that Whill had tapped into the power of the blade and he was in dire trouble.

Whill was hit yet again by lightning, and this time his concentration wavered and he lost control of his flight. He managed to level out enough to not plow straight into the ground, but he still came in too fast. The world below him blurred by as he braced for impact. He hit the ground like a meteor, sending dirt and trees and stone alike flying hundreds of feet into the air. His shield saved him from the impact, but he was jarred so hard that he lost consciousness for a moment.

Eadon landed gracefully where Whill had hit and purposefully walked the few hundred yards toward him. Whill got to his feet and tapped into the blade once more to strengthen his shield. Eadon let out a scream of rage, and from his hand shot a twisted and writhing beam of dark energy three feet wide. The dark spell slammed into Whill's shield and pierced it easily. It hit Whill in the chest, and he was helpless to defend himself. His first instinct was to strike back at Eadon, but he would not.

Do it! His mind screamed, and he almost complied. He realized quickly that his mind was being invaded. He fought the intrusion and tried again to bring up his shield—anything to stop the horrible pain that wracked his body and mind.

You cannot win this fight Whill of Agora, came Eadon's voice in his mind. It resonated in his head in a deafening chorus of pain. Whill summoned more power from the blade, but it was useless against Eadon's mental attack. No matter the energy at his disposal, Whill could not hope to counter Eadon's attacks. He began to give in to the Dark Elf. He had to make it stop, the gruesome visions, the blinding pain.

"Stop! I will give you the power of Adimorda. Please make it stop!" he pleaded.

"Enough of your tricks, boy!" screamed Eadon. "Give me the power now!"

The pain intensified, and Whill felt as though he were on fire. His head felt as though it would explode with the pressure of the mental attack. He wanted only silence, peace, death, anything to make it stop. He had failed miserably. He had no hope of defeating the Dark Elf, and he gave in to defeat. He raised his free hand to Eadon's extended hand. He would give Eadon the power, and he would know peace.

Whill's shaking hand had almost met Eadon's when suddenly the Dark Elf was engulfed by the huge jaws of the red dragon Zhola. Instantly the pain subsided, and the mental attack stopped as Zhola shook his head violently and threw the Dark Elf to the ground. He bathed Eadon in fire and stomped one giant, clawed foot into the ground, burying Eadon.

"Go now!" he roared at Whill, and Whill wasted no time in heeding the dragon's words. He leapt from the ground and took flight once again, speeding toward the portal cave. Behind him, Whill heard a painful cry from Zhola and then a loud explosion. He did not look back—he did not have to—he knew that Zhola had been destroyed.

Whill flew into the cave as quickly as possible and brought his sword to bear as he shot through it. With the blade of Adimorda, he cut through the side of the portal and released a huge amount of energy into the strike. The portal exploded in a shower of light and sparks and closed, trapping Eadon in Drindellia.

Whill was shot forward by the blast and was slammed into the opposite wall of the cavern. His shield prevented any injury; without it, Whill knew he would have been crushed.

The volcano still shook violently, and the cavern was quickly falling apart. Huge slabs of stone rained down all around him, and lava had begun to pour down the stairs. There was no way he was going to walk out of the volcano. As everything fell apart around him, Whill desperately summoned a massive amount of power from the blade, and when it was too much to bear, he released the energy up toward the ceiling.

The blast ripped through the stone, sending it exploding out of the surface. Lava quickly rushed in from all directions to fill the massive hole Whill had created in the volcano. He strengthened his shield against the lava and shot out of the hole into the night sky. Once out, Whill looked down in terror and awe at the destruction he had caused. The volcano had erupted violently, and lava poured forth upon the surrounding island and into the ocean. Steam and ash and rolling black smoke filled the sky and had shot as high as the clouds.

Whill flew fast, moving toward Agora and away from the destruction. He soon came upon his friends and cried with joy to see that they had all survived the blast that he had caused. Roakore looked at him wide-eyed as he flew past. Avriel gave out a loud roar and touched his mind with hers. When they reached the shores of Isladon and landed, Roakore dismounted and ran to Whill in a fit of laughter.

"Ye can fly now? If I hadn't seen it with me own eyes, I would never be believin' it." He hugged his friend and squeezed him hard, patting him on the back.

"What of Eadon?" asked Azzeal hopefully.

"I led him through the portal and on to Drindelia. I would have been killed had it not been for Zhola. He came at the last moment and distracted Eadon long enough for me to escape back through the portal and destroy it."

"Good, then Eadon be trapped far away," said Roakore jubilantly.

"Yes," Whill concurred. "For the time being anyway."

"You did well, Whill. I had feared…But you are returned to us now," said Avriel. She bent to him, and Whill hugged her thick neck, and tears welled and fell from his eyes. The rush of the battle had worn off, and Whill felt terrible. As soon as he had sheathed the sword, he had begun to shake uncontrollably.

"There is no time to rest," warned Azzeal. "We must make for the safety of Elladrindellia with all haste. We know not what means Eadon has to travel back here from Drindellia."

"Let us go first to me mountain. There we will find rest and food, and the ale will pour endlessly. You could help me to translate the book o' Ky'dren," said Roakore enthusiastically. "And don't be forgettin' about Tarren."

Whill nodded. "I have not forgotten about the lad, and your offer sounds wonderful. But I must travel to the Elves. There is much I must learn and not enough time to learn it. Besides, I do not think that it would go over well, bringing Avriel to Ro'Sar in her current form."

Roakore hummed his agreement as he looked to the white dragon. "Indeed, that would not be goin over to well."He gave a long sigh. "Very well, I will return home and let me people know what has happened. And then me and Tarren will meet you in Elladrindellia."

Whill nodded. "The city of Cerushia is our destination."

"Cerushia it is then," said Roakore. "We will be along before the month is out." He slammed his fist to his chest and bowed slightly, and Whill returned the gesture. He then extended his hand, and Whill took it.

"May the gods see you to your mountain, King Roakore."

"Aye, and yours to the Elf lands, King Whill," Roakore said with a smile. He pulled Whill in for a small hug. He held him at arm's length and smiled. "I be glad you be returned to us lad,."

"Thanks for everything, Roakore. Thanks for coming for me. I will look for you in the sky."

Roakore mounted Silverwind, and the two flew off to the northeast, back to Ro'Sar. Whill watched them sail high into the clouds and disappear. After some time, he turned to Aurora.

"What are your plans? Do you wish still to remain with us?"

Aurora stood and nodded. "I do, that is…" She looked to Azzeal and Avriel hesitantly. "That is, if the

Elves would have me in their lands. I know not their rules on foreigners."

"We would have you, fair warrior of the north," said Azzeal, and Aurora's face was one of delight. She breathed in through her nose and straightened, smiling.

"Then I would aid you further in your quest. For your enemy is mine, and your victory as such."

"Very well then, let us be off." said Whill.

Dirk shifted in and out of consciousness. He had fallen nearly fifty feet and had broken his legs. His shoulder had been broken by the Dwarf's stone bird, and his arm was useless. How he had averted the attention of the dragon, he did not know. For as Zhola had circled overhead, Dirk had accepted his fate. But now, suddenly, he was alone. Though he knew that he would surely die here, he would rather it was by his own hand than the jaws of a dragon.

He propped himself up on his good arm until he was in a sitting position. He looked around at the darkened and twisted forest. How long would it take for some nightmare of the twisted forest to find him and eat him?

He took a dart from its small sheath and stabbed himself in the arm. His eyes rolled back as the strong pain-numbing liquid went to work. He sat there for a long while before reaching for a dagger. He thought of Krentz, and tears found his eyes. It was true it seemed.

He would die because he had tried to free his love. Regret that he could not help her after all filled his heart, and he sobbed. He did not care that he would die; he cared only that she would be left in that dark place.

Perhaps Eadon would go good on his word since Dirk had told him of Whill's location; perhaps not. He would never know.

He said aloud, "I love you, Krentz." Then he took a steadying breath and lifted the dagger to plunge it into his heart. He thrust the dagger, but it was suddenly stopped by an iron grip.

"Are you done feeling sorry for yourself?" asked Eadon. "I am afraid I still have many uses for you, my assassin. Perhaps you can kill yourself another time."

Dirk let out a tired sigh as Eadon began to heal his injuries. "Son of a bitch."

"I will take that as a thank you," said Eadon.

Dirk just scowled at the hated Dark Elf.

Whill and his friends followed the southern coast of Uthen-Arden, stopping only at night for a few hours to sleep and hunt. Once the group was well past the city of Del-Oradon, they breathed a little easier. Aurora rode with Whill atop of Avriel and thanked the barbarian gods for her good fortune. She had left her homeland of Volnoss in an attempt to save her people from the coming war, and it seemed she had found the one who could help her. The sneaky assassin was now out of the picture and along with him, the knowledge of what she had done.

She remembered how the Elf-dragon had heard Dirk's thoughts. Therefore, she attempted to only think in her native tongue and hoped that would help in keeping her secret from Avriel. She had gained the trust of the group, had proved herself an able ally. She would strike a treaty with Whill, the rightful king of Uthen-Arden, and she would lead her people in victory against the Draggard and the Dark Elves. She needed only to solidify her friendship with Whill and, indeed, Roakore as well. Then she would return to her homeland and challenge the chief of the Timber Wolf clan.

After many days of travel, they came to the borders of Elladrindellia and flew on to the city of Cerushia. Whill had never seen the Elf land, not even on foot. Below him, the land looked much like any other. It had forests and lakes and rivers running through it. Prairies and meadows abounded, along with villages and towns and sprawling cities. It was all these things, but so much more.

There was more green and more gold, more light and more moon. The trees were giants, and the flowers sprang from a dream. There were vines thick as tree trunks and ferns as tall as a horse. Waterfalls abounded for a stretch of land for most of a day, and Avriel made Whill and Aurora nearly sick, flying up and down them. In her defense, she said that she had only been following Azzeal, and he flew as a dancer in the sky.

They met no resistance as they flew into the heart of the city. Avriel flew them to the same assembly in which Zerain had been granted his strengthened sword. The council of elders was there, and the vine-covered meeting place was full of Elves. Avriel landed near the stair to the elevated speaking podium.

Whill dismounted and silently walked up the stairs and stopped at the vine podium. He looked out over the crowd of hundreds of whispering Elves. He took up the sword of Adimorda and raised it to the sky.

"I am Whill of Agora! I have found the sword Adromida!"

The End

Dear Reader,

Thank you for purchasing this book. I hope you have enjoyed the adventures of Whill of Agora. I hope that interest in the series allows me to continue the story for a long time to come. If you like the books and wish to follow Whill's future adventures, please tell everyone you know on Facebook and Twitter and so on. Its fans like you that make all of this possible.

I would love to hear what you thought of the story, so please feel free to join in the conversation at www.whillofagora.com.

If you would like, feel free to leave a review of books one and two on Amazon.

I am a self-published author and do not have the luxury of a team of promoters at my disposal. You are my team, and I appreciate your efforts and support.

Thanks again, friends, for following Whill this far. I hope to go on many more adventures with you in the future.

I have recently published two children's books that I think you will find enjoyable. The Sock Gnome Chronicles follow the adventures and exploits of Billy Coatbutton. Billy is a sock gnome living within Sockefeller Castle; book one, _Billy Coatbutton and the Wheel of Destiny_, follows Billy as he attempts his first test of mastery to see if he will become a treasure hunter like his father

Adults and children alike will enjoy this satirical romp into the lives of sock gnomes, while at the same time answering the age-old question, where *do* those missing socks go?

Thank you once again for your support,

With humble appreciation,
Michael James Ploof

Made in the USA
Lexington, KY
14 October 2013